ISBN 978-0-483-51761-5
PIBN 10510903

FORBIDDEN GROUND

BY

GILBERT WATSON

NEW YORK
JOHN LANE COMPANY
MCMX

CHAPTER I

A GIRL and a man stood facing each other on a lonely mountain path. Around them, red in the setting sun, rose the frontier hills of Albania. Something savage about the scene which the mellow light failed to soften, something primitive and, as it were, the expression of unrestrained nature, struck a kindred note with the two figures standing on the desolate track. They, too, were of the mountains—a hill-man and a hill-woman wearing the semi-barbarous costume of their race.

There was that in their attitudes and faces that told of a crisis, for the meeting was big with import in the life of each.

The girl was a splendid specimen of dawning womanhood.

It was undoubtedly her eyes that, more than all else, compelled admiration. Neither her face nor her figure had greater claim to loveliness than had those of many another girl of her race—a race justly renowned for the good looks of its women—but the tragic beauty of her eyes was all her own.

There was something arresting in her companion, no less than in her. His tall, gaunt frame, so emaciated as to suggest some wasting illness, either of mind or body, was not without indications of strength, for his shoulders were broad, his hands big and knotted. His face, cast in a large rough mould, somewhat coarse as to feature, hinted at violent passions. The eyes, close together and deeply sunken, glittered from under heavy overhanging eyebrows, glittered with a savage and sombre concentration that was ominous, disquieting. The mouth—partly concealed by a ragged moustache— was unpleasantly indicative of sensuality. The whole effect of the man, as he stood there, less intent upon

1 · 1

the girl before him than upon his own dark and brooding thoughts, was one that would have awed, and possibly even alarmed, a spectator; for in eyes, expression, attitude, there was a suggestion of imminent violence, of emotions so overwrought as to be upon the verge of an outbreak.

The girl appeared to be waiting for him to speak, and yet her expression told of one more intent upon some all-engrossing dream of her own than of one merely expectant. The light in her eyes glowed pensive, tender, with an undercurrent of girlish seriousness. Something indescribable in them spoke of the momentous and illuminating knowledge that comes only with the lifting of life's curtain; but in her case the freshness and the innocence of girlhood—hers still by right of years— though forfeited, had not taken flight, but lingered, loath to leave, transferring their allegiance gladly from the maiden to the woman.

For the moment she did not see this man upon whom she looked and whom she had come to meet—some wonderful vision, born in the inmost and most sacred chamber of a woman's heart, held her enrapt.

The wind, precursor of the night, struck chill at her, but she was unconscious of it. Dreaming she stood; herself as fair as any dream; a young presence strangely sweet, strangely full of budding life among this great chaos of dead and barren rocks.

The man was the first to rouse himself.

"Zetitzka," he said.

"Yes, Stephanos?"

There is everything in the enunciation of a name. Hers was shot forth abruptly, harshly, with effort. It betrayed neither ardour nor satiety, though in the swift glance that accompanied it lurked fear. His name was spoken timidly, interrogatively, with gentle acquiescence, though with an unconscious and entire absence of that soul to soul equality that is the foundation of abiding love. In her eyes—recalled suddenly from inward vision—this submissive attitude was still more observant; it was as if the sunshine of her nature were overcast by the shadow of his, as a smiling landscape is darkened by the sombre passage of a cloud.

He hesitated, shifted his footing restlessly like one ill at ease, clasping and unclasping the coarse folds of his capot with nervous, bony fingers. As she stood waiting he cast another glance at her, full of conflicting emotions; then, as though unable to face her clear and unsuspecting gaze, his eyes drooped moodily to the ground.

" I know not how to tell you," he muttered.

" I have something to tell you, too," she whispered.

He clenched his fists.

" I must," he vociferated angrily, labouring under suppressed excitement, his deep-set eyes suddenly blazing with a wild and irrational intensity. " I tell you I must. Listen—do not speak. Last night I had a dream. God spoke to me. He knows all. Do you hear? He knows all!"

Her brows contracted. That his exaggerated manner (exaggerated beyond even the Southern impetuosity that was his birthright as well as hers) caused her uneasiness and even pain was evident; still, with a tact born of experience, she remained silent.

" He is angry. I tell you He knows all—our meetings —our sin—and we who thought our secret safe! Fools! We forgot *Him*."

She would have laid a calming hand on his arm, but he shrank from her.

" If He has seen us, Stephanos, He understands. The priest says that He reads our hearts—that He will forgive us when——" She hesitated, then raising her head proudly: " You need not fear. I am not afraid."

" But I do fear—not only that, but—if you had seen! Had heard! And the sin—the deadly sin! I was mad. I thought it Love!" He gesticulated with savage irony. " I loved nothing—*nothing*, but my own passions, God forgive me!"

The blank consternation in her face caused him to burst forth again.

" It was the devil. He tempted me—ay, with *you!* These eyes of yours! I was as one drunken! I——" he muttered incoherently; then, with sombre conviction, " You never loved me either, Zetitzka."

For the first time her nature seemed to catch fire, to flame responsive. A passionate denial leapt to her lips,

but she crushed it back. Unaware of her self-control, he
continued:

"I knew. I felt it. Many a time I have felt you
shrink. That is not love. Love casts out fear. Our
past is black with sin. You tempted me, and I fell. I
was brutal to you. I don't deny it. I don't blame you.
It was the devil; you could not help being a woman.
Women are made to tempt men's souls with—— My God,
don't look at me like that!" His voice rose in harsh remonstrance, then sank again into sombre reminiscence:
"If I had power over you, you had power over me, too—
devilish, damnable power, consuming as the flames of hell.
I stand at the turning of the ways. This night is my soul
demanded of me. Eternal life or everlasting damnation.
My flesh is weak, diseased. You are the poison in it. But
I *will* conquer! I will wash in blood—the blood of Christ!
I *will*, I tell you, I will!"

A frenzied earnestness rang in his utterances. One could
see that he was in the grip of a terrible fear, spurred on
his selfish and merciless way by the memory of a terrible
danger.

Confronting him, motionless, his companion listened.
Accustomed though she was to his black moods, his fits
of morose and fanatical apprehension, she had never seen
him thus violent. As a rule, these morbid searchings alter-
nated with, or followed immediately after, some bout of
merely animal passion, but this time no physical pander-
ing to his senses preceded the outburst. He had come to
this meeting charged with some incontrollable emotion that
shook his whole being as a guilt-laden soul is shaken by
conscience at the hour of death.

She stood bewildered, pained beyond expression,
wounded in her tenderest and most sacred feelings. Then,
his worn and distraught appearance appealing to her
womanly pity, she found only excuses for him in her heart.

"Never mind, dear," she said gently. "Do not make
yourself unhappy. When one is ill one exaggerates. God
knows that I did not mean to tempt you. I was ignorant.
You took me unprepared. And later—now—how could
I refuse you anything? All that I am is yours. I do not
know myself. I seem to have no pride left." She pressed
her hands to her eyes, thinking painfully, then went on:

"I know you love me in spite of these wild words. God knows it, too. He wishes to bless our love, for—for He has sent——" She hesitated. A shy, tremulous light shone in her eyes, and the quick colour dyed her face.

But the girlish confidence that might have changed all, was cut from her lips by his irresponsible violence.

"I shall go mad," he vociferated wildly, clasping his head with his hands. "Will you not understand? We must part. I came here to tell you."

She stared at him uncomprehending. He continued:

"This must stop. God forbids it. We were blind; but now my eyes are opened. I have a soul to save. There is but one way. All my life it has called me; but, though I knew it would win at the last, I kept putting it off. Then you came—you, with your eyes, your proud ways that bent to my will, your body that would seduce a saint; and I forgot all except the devouring hunger for you. What did you see in me, Zetitzka? Why did you think you loved me? I was no wooer. I am rugged like these rocks—savage and lonely like an eagle with a dead mate. It was the devil's plot. I was tinder, you the spark. Which shall God blame because the furnace roared?"

He broke off, his words muttering low; then abruptly raising his head, continued:

"Don't think I try to excuse myself. I am the worst of sinners, but—but——" He stammered in desperate eagerness. "I may yet escape damnation. I must never see you again. I must work out my salvation with stripes and bitter tears. No need to speak. All is arranged. I would have told you before—but I feared—the lust of the flesh was upon me—— Come, don't stand there like a stone! After all, you are young—you will forget—it might be worse. Come, say good-bye, Zetitzka; I go now."

"You—go—now?"

He gave a sullen gesture of assent. There was a long pause.

The gulf of silence, widening momentarily, threatened to become the memorable margin of a life-long separation. The girl felt this, and became afraid. With a terrible sinking of the heart she realised her impotence, her helpless inadequacy. The blow had found her so unprepared. Many things suggested themselves to her, as her thoughts surged this way and that; things she might say, useless things, angry things, piteous things; but a dawning sense of the supreme importance of the moment saved her from uttering them. Something horribly vital was in the balance; a word might make all the difference, might fix their relation for ever.

In this girl's mind unforeseen catastrophe was giving birth to courage—the moral courage that stares ugly and naked facts full in the face. For the first time she emerged from timidities, indecisions, from the shadow of another, and became a personality. Her one instinctive desire, groping and pathetically inexperienced, yet resolute in its brave sincerity, was to get at the truth, to find out where she stood with this man, so that she might cope with the evil that had overwhelmed her.

All at once, as she stared into the blackness, a glimmer rewarded her; she met it courageously, though it spelt despair.

" I see," she said slowly, " you have grown tired of me."

His hot denial, sincere—for even at the very moment of her accusation he was invaded by longing that needed all his strength to crush—carried no conviction to her. She silenced him with a gesture.

" It must be so, or——" She broke off; then, as though conscious of some bitter irony that eluded his knowledge, " And you tell me this to-night ? "

He looked at her in sombre surprise, but she was gazing past him with an expression that he could not fathom. For a moment his dull, self-centred brain wondered if there were depths in this young girl which he had not sounded; if there were aught in her indeed beyond physical perfection, the lure that had ensnared his soul. As he wondered, a look of unmistakable horror stamped itself upon her every feature.

" No! " she cried, wheeling upon him passionately, " I will *not* tell you. You are not worthy of it. But you cannot, you shall not go! You must be a devil even to think of it! I will tell everyone. I will force you to stay. Do you hear ? *Force* you! To desert me now—now——" Something rose in her throat, but she gulped it down. " Holy Jesus! No, that would be too infamous! "

The fierce rush of emotions shook her. In her bitter

resentment, with head held high and eyes that flamed, she filled him with consternation. He stared speechless, though there was nothing in his sullen lowering brows that told of yielding.

A pause, then a swift change came over her.

"Stephanos," she said brokenly, "forgive me! I—I don't know what I was saying. I didn't mean a word of it. Don't be angry. I was mad. But see, I am calm now. I smile." She smiled up at him through her tears. "I have been wicked. It has all been my fault. But, oh, don't punish me like this! I can't bear it. I'll do anything you like—anything. Only—don't leave me. I shall be alone—*Stephanos!* The shame—I can't bear it. Oh, Stephanos, for the love of the sweet Virgin, don't leave me!"

She clung to him. She sought to kiss his rough hand with her trembling, tear-salt lips. None could have listened unmoved. Few could have denied aught to one so young, so pathetically appealing. But this man hardened his heart.

There was something final about his attitude, as, disengaging himself, he stood aloof. As Zetitzka gazed at him, hope fled, but pride came to her aid. She drew herself up.

"What am I to say to my parents?" she asked.

He raised his head, but avoided her eyes.

"No need to say anything."

"They will have to know—soon." She whispered the words more to herself than to him. The marvel was that her secret remained undiscovered.

But he only shrugged his shoulders. No words could more callously have conveyed his indifference to all that did not concern his soul's salvation. She looked up at him with a quick, penetrating glance, as though indeed she were seeing him for the first time, seeing him as he really was. She had taken the first fateful step. At present, conscious only of the bewilderment, the incredulity of this sudden immense disillusionment, the shattering of dreams how secretly, how tenderly cherished! the rawness of a wound newly inflicted, and the paralysing dread of a future full of loneliness and horror, she knew not whither this was to lead her—but she was soon to find out. This one man had been the entire sex to her. She looked at him and wondered: "Are all men like this?"

"There is more than that," she said at last, forcing herself to speak. "They believe that—that we are to be married."

He started as though stung, for marriage had now no place in his thoughts. His pale face flushed.

"Who told—how did they know?"

"I told them."

He stared at her, speechless, fear contending with anger.

"They saw us together. They questioned me. You do not know them—I tried—but they would have the truth."

"The truth?"

"Yes, I thought so. God help me! I—I was proud of it! You said once—that night—otherwise do you think that I would—would ever have——"

She buried her face in her hands. He waited, his eyes fixed moodily on the ground.

The sun had withdrawn his rays. The afterglow, rosy and luminous as a tropical shell, suffused the scene. No sound from the world of nature, save the bleating of distant goats, came to the ear. The hour was one of infinite peace.

Stephanos was the first to move. Taking a small leathern wallet from an inner pocket he looked at it, hesitated, then proffered it to his companion. She did not see it.

"Take this," he said, in a voice of one awkwardly trying to make amends.

She raised her head, but no look of comprehension came into her face.

"'Tis a thousand drachmae. 'Tis little, but——"

"Money!" she cried. He quailed before her eyes, then with visible confusion, not unmixed with the coarser nature's astonishment, he returned the wallet to his pocket.

"I meant for the best," he muttered, eyeing her askance. "I have sold the house. I shall have no need of money where I am going. Zetitzka——" he stretched out a hand, but as he noted the pale and unnatural rigidity of her expression it fell limply to his side. "Let me do something for you, as—as a friend. Your parents are poor— nay, I mean no offence—I am no Arnaut, I have known what it is to be rich. This would bring them comforts. Well, if you will not—but I thought——"

He broke off, plucked nervously at the hem of his cloak, then spoke again:—

" Do you blame me? You would not if you had heard what I did last night. Do you not see? The devil brought us together. God is snatching us apart. It is His will. He calls me. I must obey."

His tone had become the exalted utterance of the fanatic, but neither by word nor look did the girl beside him show that she heard.

" Good-bye," he muttered with increased awkwardness. Then, as she still continued silent:—

" It will soon be night. Let me see you start on your homeward way."

She shook her head.

He watched her for a moment without speaking, then suddenly, with an upward gesture of the hands as though calling upon God to witness, he turned abruptly and strode away.

CHAPTER II

A YEAR passed. Again the valleys sought to nurse their
scanty greenery through the long droughts of summer;
again, sinking to the mountain summits, the sun deluged
the world in fire; and, again, two figures might have been
seen on the path which led towards the Albanian frontier.

Both were women, one young, the other old—Zetitzka
and her mother. Before them, but still remote, the hills
that immediately overlook the plains of Thessaly were
faintly visible. The elder woman carried a bundle, the
younger a baby. The former was at no pains to conceal
her fatigue. As she stumbled onwards she kept up a
grumbling monologue; anathematising the stones, the growing darkness, and the necessity that had forced her to un-
dertake so arduous a journey.

But Zetitzka uttered no complaint. Her figure, dark
against the golden background, swayed as she sought to
avoid the larger stones that formed a growing danger as
the light ebbed slowly into the west. As far as could be
seen, both women wore the dress of Albanians of the better
class: the coarse shoes, the legs swathed in innumerable
bandages, and the ample red cloak that, concealing all
minor deficiencies, forms so complete a disguise to young
and old.

The face of Zetitzka was visible, flushed now to the colour
of clear sunset; for the dying rose that steeped all things
mantled her cheeks and brow.

She had changed in the year that had elapsed; had lost
some of her youthfulness, had grown thinner, paler, but
retained all the old interest-compelling quality which was
to her as a distinctive atmosphere; the essence of her
personality. The regard of her eyes was deeper than of
yore; more sternly reticent. Their beauty was still incon-
testable, but they were now possessed by a hard light, as
of fires eternally smouldering, kept alive by the memory

10

of some abiding wrong—a wrong too great for expression, too bitter for tears.

The mouth betrayed change too. Nature had framed it for smiles and girlish laughter, but life had taught it to shut tight lips upon pain.

There was something hideous and cruel in this thwarting of kindly impulses, this moral starvation that had turned a gladsome young spirit into a brooding soul. Yet even as a tree, blackened by lightning, treasures unwittingly within its heart that which will one day welcome the spring, so also in Zetitzka's face something survived that was destined to defy fate.

They walked—Zetitzka in front, her mother behind—slowly yet steadily, as befitted travellers who have come from far. The old woman hobbled slightly, but Zetitzka, in spite of her fatigue, moved with the easy, graceful carriage of a hill-woman, pausing occasionally to shift the bundle she was carrying from one arm to the other. Whenever she did so, she would gaze at the little sleeper. At such moments her face softened; a shadowy light, infinitely pathetic and tender, shone in her dark eyes, but only for a moment, for as she resumed the road, the old expression, hard and grievous to see, took its place.

From behind her came always the long-drawn querulous monologue of her mother, a dreary depressing sound that seemed to Zetitzka, accustomed though she was to interminable complaints, to be one with the encroaching gloom, with the sad light dying slowly in the west, and with the unknown perils of this journey upon which she had embarked.

And thus they fared forward, mother and daughter, two small and insignificant figures, slowly moving, in that great waste of rock-strewn hills.

All at once Zetitzka came to a standstill.

"We have come far enough," she said in a low voice, "Nik Leka told me that we must wait on the hillside till we saw a light."

The old woman sank on to a stone. In the dusk she had the air of a shapeless sack flung to the ground.

"Holy Virgin!" she mumbled. "How my legs do ache! We must have walked for ten hours at least. How dark it is! Your father will be having his supper now. And I alone can do his rice as he likes it. Thank God, I shall be home to-morrow! Are you sure Nik Leka said that? How do you know this is the place? What is that? There? Over there? Holy Saints!''

She pointed her skinny finger at something that appeared to threaten vaguely with extended arms.

'' That is the tree he told me about,'' explained Zetitzka in a low voice. '' The village is below us. Nik Leka said there was a blood-feud, and that they have barricaded the houses and we might get shot. He is to be in the Khan to-night, and promised to get the Khanje to show a light when it was safe for us to come.''

The wind blew lightly, wailing over the vast expanse, stirring the thin mountain-grass and snatching at the garments of the two women. Overhead, a few small clouds still retained the flush of the departed sun. Above the dark outline of hills that shut them in, now black as night, the pale green of the heavens was lit by one star. The sound of running water murmured softly, a melancholy plaint as of far-off singing in the darkness. The whole scene was deeply impregnated with the indescribable sadness that comes with night—a sadness born of mystery, of loneliness, and the death of all bright things.

The old woman groaned again.

'' You are tired? '' murmured Zetitzka; '' it was good of you to come so far with me. But I wish——''

The sentence remained unfinished. Her voice had all the hopelessness of one who knows her wishes to be in vain.

'' Tired! '' snapped the querulous voice in the dusk, '' I am dead. These stones have cut my shoes. I don't know what your father will say. I had hard work to persuade him to let me come with you. 'Tis nothing but work, work, work, what with your illness and his being crippled; and now that you are going to be away——''

She broke off with a self-pitying ejaculation; then, after a moment's pause, continued:—

'' And your baby! Why did you bring him? I will have to carry him back to-morrow—I, alone. But you never think of me. No, I am no one. Lord, how my feet ache! ''

Zetitzka looked downwards at the small body held so close to her heart.

"You need not grudge me this last day," she said with effort—then, with a sudden catch in her voice, "I—I may not see him for a long time—perhaps, never again."

"Nonsense! If all goes well you will be back in less than a week. But 'tis a pity your father could not have done it for you. It would have been more natural. 'Tis your bad fortune, Zetitzka, no male relatives. Holy Virgin, these stones are hard! But, as I said only last night, if my brother had lived—he was a proper man—but they killed him at last, peace be to his soul—though of all men he disliked peace the most. Fight! He was always fighting. He stabbed four men, as you have heard often. Why doesn't that pedlar show a light? Do you think he has forgotten? Ay, ay, no male relatives. That is what troubles your father. He has a fine spirit, Zetitzka, in spite of his legs. I thought he would have burst a blood-vessel when I told him of your misfortune. But he never saw it for himself. Not he. Men are stupid, but you cannot deceive a woman, above all, a mother."

She clucked throatily.

"I never wished to deceive you," muttered Zetitzka.

"You did," shrilled the old woman. "You pretended he was going to marry you. Marriage! Yah! And what a husband! A wretch who worked his wicked will on you, then ran away to a monastery. Coward!"

She expectorated angrily. Zetitzka did not answer. She was staring stonily into the gloom. This talk was but one of many, endured patiently, as day after day she had gone about her household tasks with all the bitterness and pathos of the grief she could not express, even to herself, locked within her heart.

"But we will have him yet," burst forth the voice by her side in savage exultation. "He did not think that Nik Leka would see him and bring the news over the frontier to us. No, he did not calculate on that. He, only a niggardly trader, so they say! Stabbing is too good for him. I would tear his heart out and give it to the dogs. By the Saints, your father was right! 'She must revenge herself,' said he, and I tell you, Zetitzka, I thought he would have broken his crutch upon the floor. ' Or by the Almighty God, I will curse her child.' "

" *Mother!* "

The girlish voice rang out sharply, with a high keen note of pain. The old woman uttered a complacent croak.

" Ah, that touches you, does it? So much the better. I cannot see your face, but it ought to be red with shame. To bring disgrace upon us—Arnauts as we are! You that we thought so young, so innocent! Your father is right, he——"

" Oh, say no more! " cried the girl, goaded to utterance. " You have said it all so often. I have done wrong. My God, yes! Do you think I don't suffer? But what is the good of speech? I have promised. I will keep my word."

" That may be," muttered the old woman, somewhat abashed. " But how was I to know? You did not tell me till you were forced to do so. You have always been a secret one, Zetitzka. Besides, when a girl loves——"

" *Loves!* "

The word blazed out. The old woman's jaw fell. Apprehensively she stared upwards at the dark and rigid figure by her side. A pause, then the words came:—

" I tell you I hate him! Hate him! Hate him! " She dashed her hand across her eyes, as though with that fierce gesture she could slay all womanly weakness. Her young voice rang hard:—" When he deserted me, I—I— oh, I can't talk about it! " With a passionate motion of the hands she relapsed into silence.

" I knew that," croaked her mother complacently. " When I put your baby to your breast for the first time, I knew it then. You remember, Zetitzka? You snatched yourself from the child and devoured him with eyes that said as plain as words: ' Is he like? ' And then you gave a great sigh of content and fell back in the bed, for there was no more likeness to that—that scoundrel, than between a yataghan and a broom-handle. You remember? "

There came a muffled assent.

" Ay, ay, well, I went straight to your father and said: ' Marco, do not trouble yourself. She will do it.' "

Zetitzka shuddered, though the night air was warm. A

terrible depression invaded her. The foundations of her
being seemed to have been demolished. Her pride was
in the dust; her heart atrophied; an apparent callousness
possessed her, the petrifaction of every gentle, tender, or
lively feeling. Her own self-contempt was so immense that
what others might think had become almost a matter of
indifference. They could never judge her as unmerci-
fully as she judged herself. Daily, nay hourly, she was
arraigned before the judgment seat of her own finer feelings, found guilty, and given over to the torture of re-
morseful thoughts. Even her mother's nagging left her
unmoved. She had ceased to care. Suffering had at least
done that for her. She hugged her pain close, taking a
cruel and unnatural pleasure in the gnawing ache that
was her companion by day and by night.

Two things only had power to rouse her: thoughts of
her child, and of the man who had ruined her. The
former awoke passionate, primitive, and complex emotions. The mother in her was strong, fierce, jealous—a
tigress defending her cub. For her child's sake she bitterly resented the contemptuous pity, or open condemnation
of her associates. She repaid scorn with scorn. Instinctively she sought to hide the little one from all un-'
loving eyes. When alone with it she would pour out upon
its tiny and unconscious person torrents of dammed-up
tenderness, devouring it with kisses, smiling and weeping
over it alternately, seeking with all the thwarted affection of a heart by nature warm and passionate to make up
to it with a boundless idolatry for the contumely of a
hostile world.

For the man she felt only hatred. Her love—if love
it had ever been—was dead. It had sprung rather from
imagination than from the heart—the devotion for a
Stephanos who had never existed. His influence over
her had been compounded of a mysterious fascination, a
physical and almost mesmeric force that had paralysed
her will, blinded her vision, and overruled her sense of
right and wrong. For the time her mental balance had
been upset. This man's dark and masterful personality
had dominated her trusting, innocent, and wholly unsophisticated soul—the soul of a woman in which lurked
the seeds of all love and hate, all self-sacrifice and revenge.

She **had** been in love with love; not with Stephanos. Wooed more by the whisper of innocent hopes than by any words of his, she had attributed these new and overwhelming emotions to love, translating his culpable weakness into strength, his merely animal passion into a noble and lifelong devotion.

Now, she knew. The shock of her awakening had been terrible. The selfishness of his desertion stood out in all its repellant nakedness. The injustice of it was what inflamed her most, for her sense of justice, though primitive, was unerring. For her child's sake, as well as her own, she now hated him with a fierce and undying hatred that longed to see him dead at her feet.

The outraged pride of her parents had fanned this instinctive passion. By every cruel means within their power, they had driven home to her poor wounded heart the conviction that the death of her betrayer was the one and only way to redeem the family honour, remove the stigma from her child, and re-establish her good name.

And she listened day after day, passing insensibly through the many stages that lie between the dumb apathy of suffering and the dumb apathy of acquiescence; till there had grown up within her the unalterable conviction that such an act of personal vengeance was inevitable, her duty before God and man, towards her parents, her child and herself.

Nor was such a conclusion unnatural when her birth and upbringing are taken into consideration.

Zetitzka came of a wild Albanian stock—Arnaut mountaineers, accustomed to treat assassination as a justifiable means of removing an adversary, or of wiping out a stain upon the honour of the assassin. Had she been told that to stab a man in the back was a dastardly deed, she would have stared with incredulity. Despite the laws that forbade Christians to carry arms in Albania, had not her ancestors stalked proudly through the streets bristling with weapons? Had they not murdered their enemies how and where they pleased? Did not the feeble Government wink at assassination, the very *gendarmes* cringing to the man who could boast of a foe removed by yataghan or pistol? One of her earliest recollections was the return of her notorious uncle after a week passed in the prosecution of a blood-feud. A decapitated head had dangled from his sash. He had been welcomed with admiring congratulations. Even so—her parents had told her times without number—would she be received when, her mission accomplished, she returned to her native village.

She was roused from sombre meditations by the voice of her mother.

" The light. Zetitzka, the light! "

Zetitzka strained her eyes in the direction of the hamlet. There, sure enough, in the pit of blackness, was a tiny point of light. Clasping her baby to her breast, and followed by the old woman, she began to descend the hill.

CHAPTER III

SUPPER in the Kahn was over. The men had squatted round an immense fire of logs piled in the middle of the mud floor; they had cut up the roasted sheep with their yataghans, torn it to pieces with their fingers, crammed savoury morsels alternately into their mouths and into their saddlebags as a contribution towards the next day's provisions. *Raki* and *patoulis* (cakes of maize cooked in wood ashes) had been passed around. The women of the party had herded in the background and shared with the dogs the remains of the feast. Occasionally, one of the men had tossed a bone to Zetitzka's mother. The aged crone had grabbed it eagerly, and, holding it in her skinny hands, had sucked at it with toothless chaps. Sometimes the bone had been snatched from her by a dog, causing her to utter shrill cries of anger, to the loud amusement of the men.

Zetitzka had been unable to eat more than a few mouthfuls. The food stuck in her throat. Shrinkingly self-conscious, she had tried to conceal herself behind her mother, but the fierce light of the fire, seeming to point her out, made all efforts at concealment vain. Her face attracted the unwelcome admiration of the men, and her child the equally unwelcome comments of the women. All seemed to know her story, and the want of reticence of her mother added greatly to her discomfiture.

Two people only took compassion on her—Nik Leka, the pedlar, and the wife of the Khanje. The former was a little wizened old man, lame from a gunshot wound, and blind in one eye from the cut of a yataghan. His fearlessness was talked of even in this land of fearless men. It was related of him, that being set upon by bandits he had killed two in fair fight and had driven the third before him, bound, at the point of his yataghan to the nearest village. Though taciturn, he had yet the gift of song, and was much in request at social gatherings. For the

18

rest, he was wild, powerful, dirty, extremely hairy, unkempt, a shrewd wit, though bluff to the point of brutality, and, like a sound but malformed nut, sweet at the core.

Taking in the state of things with one flash of his solitary eye, he drew attention upon himself with a coarse jest that set everyone laughing.

"What has come to him?" chuckled the village headman, his red face flaming in the brandished light of the fire. "'Tis as good as a play."

"He will be passing his hat round next," mumbled the blacksmith, gnawing at a bone.

"Ay, round thee," grunted Nik Leka.

And the laugh was universal, for the close-fistedness of the smith was common property.

The wife of the Khanje, who had been occupied in turning the rough spit upon which the sheep had been impaled, beckoned to Zetitzka. She was a fine woman with bare legs, of comely proportions, and long almond-shaped eyes full of melancholy. With the delicacy of perception, characteristic of her race, she divined the wishes of her guest, supplied her with warm goat's milk for the child, and even gave the two women permission to sleep in an adjoining room, where they would obtain privacy.

Within the room set at Zetitzka's disposal the darkness was combated by the red light of the log fire upon which the sheep had been roasted. This came to her in slender shafts between the rough beams that composed the wall. The smoke had filtered in through the same interstices, and, unable to find an exit, hung in dense clouds, stinging the eyes and impeding the breath.

Laying her child upon her cloak, Zetitzka stretched herself upon the mud floor. A more cheerless and uncomfortable bedchamber it would be hard to imagine, but Zetitzka, thankful to escape from the many eyes, was oblivious to her surroundings.

Many noises came to her as she lay open-eyed in the darkness. The voices of two men quarrelling rose high above the clamour. One of them she recognised as that of Shouma—a Mahommedan pervert. He had been semidrunk when she quitted the living-room. She remembered seeing him kneeling with raised hands, praying in a loud voice with intense and passionate earnestness, swinging backwards and forwards, wringing his big dirty hands in a frenzy of religious excitement, falling forward to kiss the mud floor, then rising unconcernedly to drink yet another glass of *raki*. The other was Bektsé Tchotche, an Arnaut mountaineer; she knew him by his loud ringing voice, for he came sometimes to talk to her bedridden father.

Nik Leka began to sing, accompanying himself on the *guzle* or Albanian mandoline. The weird vibrations of its one string sounded uncanny in the night, blending with the rain which had begun to fall, and now beat a tattoo with dull thuds upon the roof. The pedlar sang of war and victories over the Karatag. Deep grunts of approval escaped at intervals from the throats of his auditors. A peculiar melancholy, suggestive of death and also of subdued ferocity wailed in the sounds. The barbaric music moved Zetitzka deeply, stirred something in her breast, something primitive and fierce which claimed kindred with the dark mountains and the proud and lawless race from which she had sprung. While she listened she forgot the smoke, forgot the hardness of the floor, forgot even her baby slumbering by her side; one memory alone obsessed her—that of the man who had betrayed her. Her wrongs unredressed, always smouldering, now blazed into a white heat of recollection. Without speaking, she lay with clenched fists, watching the red rays and the filmy smoke-clouds.

She was aroused by the sudden entrance of her mother. "Think, think, Zetitzka!" she stammered in her excitement, "I am to have plenty of money in two years. I will buy that shawl, and a blue embroidered handkerchief for my head, like the one we saw last week. Well, why don't you speak?"

"Who told you?"

"The entrails of the sheep. Nik Leka told my fortune by them. He said they never lie. The Khanje's wife is to have two more children. Oh, and another thing— some enemy of ours is to die suddenly. You see! You see! I told you! They never lie. I thought of you at once. It will all come out right. By the Virgin, I *am* glad!"

A ray of red light rested on her. Innumerable and

tiny lines of shadow crossed and recrossed her face, and in these meshes shone two bright malevolent eyes that seemed to gleam with savage joy. Still excited, she moved to and fro like some restless spirit. The darkness in the room appeared to move with her shadowy figure, the floor to sway with it, while outside the wind moaned and raved fitfully.

"Won't you lie down?" pleaded Zetitzka. But her mother paid no attention, and sometimes from one part of the room and sometimes from another came mumbling and breathless ejaculations about the shawl and the blue handkerchief. Little by little, however, she calmed down, and at last in droning accents Zetitzka heard the words:

"O Lord, our Father—Lord——"

"Don't pray!" cried the girl in a tense whisper, raising herself upon her elbow.

"Eh? What's the matter? Go to sleep."

"Don't pray!" she persisted. "I can't bear it."

"It may bring good luck."

"No, no, never! It is horrible. How can you! God would be angry. It would bring a curse."

"Well, how odd you are! I never can understand you. At all events we can talk. We both start at dawn, eh?"

"Yes."

For a moment neither spoke. Then the old woman groaned.

"Oh, Zetitzka, I won't be able to sleep; the floor hurts my bones. Oh, that devil of a pedlar, is he going to make that noise all night! I wish I had my hands on his windpipe."

The twang of the *guzle* throbbed like a passionate heartbeat. Somewhere in the near vicinity a dog barked. Bark! bark! bark! it seemed as if it would never stop. The noise woke the baby. It began to cry.

"Sh-h, my precious," cooed Zetitzka; then as the pitiful wail continued, she took the little one in her arms and cradled it upon her breast.

The company were evidently dispersing. Zetitzka could hear the gruff voice of the Khanje raised in feigned cordiality, then a little later the same voice in a surly undertone cursing his wife. The sound of subdued sobbing came through the logs. In the silence and darkness these audible tears did Zetitzka good, for they spoke to her of another's sorrows.

" Have you the knife? "

Zetitzka started. The voice of her mother was as the croaking of some ill-omened bird of prey. Rudely recalled to the tragedy that overshadowed her own life, she shuddered.

" Have you the knife? " the voice repeated impatiently.

Zetitzka muttered an affirmative.

" Well, why don't you answer at once? All I want to say is, take care of it, for 'tis beautifully inlaid, and the handle is real silver. It belonged to your uncle, as you know; and so did the clothes. They are very handsome. Zetitzka, don't go to sleep. Tell me, what did that pedlar say about the monastery? "

Zetitzka roused herself with an effort.

" What did he say? He said it was on a rock. "

" Holy saints, that is foolish! There can be no water there! Well, there are many rocks; I hope you will find the right one. "

There came no answer. Zetitzka's eyes were watching the faint red rays tracing monstrous patterns upon the wall.

" I say I hope you find the right one. "

" I hope so. "

Her mother made a clucking of her toothless gums in the darkness. " Ck—ck—that is so like you, when you know nothing about it. You always were obstinate. Zetitzka, are you listening? "

" Yes. "

" What if they find you out? "

The suggestion was full of vague terror. For the first time Zetitzka considered the danger apart from her revenge.

" What would they do to me? " she whispered, straining wide her eyes towards the huddled figure by her side.

" I don't know. They could hardly kill you—and yet —if they found out you were a woman—but of course you will look something like a boy in these clothes. 'Tis a good thing you have been ill and are thin. Now, I wonder what it is like up there—on that rock. All men, eh? "

The monotonous voice broke into a little contemptuous

screech of laughter. "A pretty state of affairs! I would like to see your poor father without me to look after him. All men, and perhaps some of them are young? What waste! If only they had not been monks——" She blew her nose, then added thoughtfully: "We must find you a husband soon."

"No! no!"

"But, 'tis yes, yes." The shrill mimicking tones rose, then sank, as the old woman continued in a swift, fierce whisper: "If we can find a man to take you now—ay, you know what I mean! Now, don't be a fool!" The skinny fingers clutched the soft round arm and shook it angrily. "See then—no more nonsense! Holy Virgin, we have had too much already! Haven't I listened to these women to-night, their jeers, their titters—and I—I smiled—God forgive me!—when I was itching to tear their hearts out. And all for you, you and that child! Now we will have no more mistakes. This is your one chance of being looked upon as an honest woman—your last— you understand? Answer me!"

"Y-es."

The word was stifled, for Zetitzka's face was buried in her hands. The old woman relaxed her grip. She edged nearer, hitching herself along the floor. Zetitzka could hear the voice mumbling in her ear.

"Do it quickly. Run no risks. A woman is never so strong as a man. I have heard your uncle say that a good place is just below the shoulder-blade—there!"

Zetitzka gasped as she felt the sudden finger-thrust. A darkness spread before her eyes, compared with which the darkness in the room was as sunshine. This planning of cold-blooded murder was altogether foreign to her nature. To kill him, yes, while her blood ran high and the memory of his baseness boiled in her veins—but to sit still and scheme and gloat in anticipation—no!

The voice beside her continued:

"I tell you, you must, or never show your face again. Your father has sworn it. Not but what I feel for you— I see the danger to a girl——"

"'Tis not that——"

"What is it, then? Pooh, you can't answer! As I said before, such things are for men—but what man?—

Zetitzka——'' She paused as though struck by a sudden idea, then added meaningly: '' Did you notice Bektsé Tchotche to-night? ''

'' Yes.''

'' A brave fellow, eh? He admires you.''　.

The memory of the bold eyes of the mountaineer caused her a shudder of repulsion. He had stared at her with insolent familiarity, appraising her. Her mother's voice continued, scheming, confidential:

'' I always suspected he liked you, and to-night he said you were a fine girl. He has a good house. Shall I— shall I ask him to do it for you? If we are lucky enough to get him to consent, he might marry you.''

Zetitzka jerked herself to a sitting attitude.

'' Mother! '' she said desperately.

'' Eh? What? ''

'' If you do—if you do—as God sees me, I will never speak to you again! ''

'' Ch-a! '' grunted the old woman angrily. '' There you are—always impossible. Well, do it yourself. I wash my hands of you! '' She continued to mumble indignantly.

The light waned, for the logs in the adjoining room had fallen to ashes. The music came to an abrupt termination. Only the dog kept up an incessant clamour.

Zetitzka bent over her baby. The pure innocence of the little one was like a tonic to her. If all the world were only thus! She longed to kiss it passionately, but refrained: its sleep was so light. With her ear held close she could hear its soft breath coming and going. The faint sound was like tiny hands about her heart.

'' Mother,'' she whispered after a long pause.

'' Well, what is it? I was nearly asleep.''

'' You will be good to baby when I am away? ''

'' Of course.''

'' There are so many little things—you won't forget? Make his milk warm. See that he——''

'' Ah, you are not too proud to ask a favour! And after your rudeness! Some folk would call him an illegitimate brat—ay, and see him starve first, 'tis true.''

Zetitzka compressed her lips.

'' I am sure you will do all for the best,'' she said, quietly, though with effort. '' You are kinder than you appear. You love him—I know, I *know* you do! Who could help it! No one, not even the devil, would be so cruel as to make him suffer for—for——"

She broke off, for she could no longer control her voice. Only once did they speak again.

"You will be there by to-morrow afternoon?" asked the mother.

"Yes," replied the daughter.

Then naught but the snores of the old woman broke the silence. But sleep did not come to Zetitzka. Her brain, abnormally active, revolved in her hot and throbbing head with the torturing persistency of a machine. Goaded by it, as by some devilish and inhuman motor-power, she was forced to think, and think, and think. Bitter and hopeless thoughts gave her no peace, no rest. It was in the silence and blackness of such hours, when all the world seemed dead, that she suffered most. No personal fear oppressed her, no self-doubt arose. Only in her aching and desolate heart there lurked anguish as of physical pain. From time to time as she lay there with wide eyes and clenched fists, she shuddered and moved restlessly, setting her teeth upon a groan, striving desperately but vainly to break away from the relentless and galling memories that were a burning fire feeding upon her very life.

CHAPTER IV

THE parting between mother and daughter was of the briefest. But little opportunity for further confidences occurred—others were present, and the risk of loitering in the village street while the blood-feud lasted drove them into the open.

"When you change your clothes," whispered the old woman at the moment of farewell, "wrap those you are wearing in a bundle and leave it where you will be sure to find it again. That dress cost good money. Now, Zetitzka, enough; stop kissing your baby. Attend! Be careful of your uncle's suit. Don't stain it. Now, I go; give me the child."

But Zetitzka, absorbed, deaf, in a mute agony of grief, pressed the little face to hers.

"Give me the child, I say. Wait, I had almost forgotten—have you any money? No? Here, take these."

She gave a handful of coins to her daughter—a hybrid collection comprising piastres, a couple of medijidies, old Austrian zwanzigers, and a variety of metal discs, curious and concave in shape, all of which pass muster in Albania.

Zetitzka slipped them into the pocket of her cloak with indifference. She was still devouring her child with hungry eyes, when, with an exclamation of impatience the old woman snatched him from her arms, and began to hobble up the hill they had descended the previous evening.

In a moment Zetitzka's feelings changed into wild sorrow. This vengeful journey seemed suddenly to yawn before her as a gulf separating her from her child. She might never return. Terror of the unknown seized her, not for her own sake, but for her little one's. Rebellion against Fate boiled up in her heart. She longed to run after the retreating figure, to overtake it, to expostulate, to implore, to defy. But the irrevocable, with a restraining force final as death, chained her to the spot.

A figure of stone she stood in the beating sunshine,

straining her eyes to see the last of the little bundle in her mother's arms. But all at once the familiar form climbing the hill blurred unexpectedly, and Zetitzka became conscious of hot and stinging tears trickling down her cheeks.

Then, with swift revulsion of feeling, she again recalled Stephanos. Fiercely she dashed her tears aside. This, too, she owed to him! Great God, how he had made her suffer, this man! Anger, bitterness, and feelings goaded past endurance seethed within her.

"Stay," cried a hoarse voice.

Zetitzka looked up. Hobbling along the path that led to the village came Nik Leka. An immense pack bound upon his back gave him the appearance of a tortoise. Beneath it his little legs moved with extraordinary rapidity. When he joined her, his arms slipped out of the shoulder-straps; then, having deposited the bundle upon the ground, he peered into her face.

"Crying!" He pointed a coarse and accusing forefinger at her; then, wagging his dirty fez, "Oh, these women, these women!"

Zetitzka looked at him darkly.

"That is not all." He continued to glare at her fiercely from beneath his shaggy eyebrows. "Where are you going?

"I know," he went on roughly, as she remained silent. "No need to tell me lies. She," he jerked his head towards the hill, "she told me last night. I did not believe her. I tell lies myself, all in the way of business. But now—Sacred Name, she has left you, the old one?"

"I go alone," she answered.

He breathed like one furious, yet Zetitzka felt instinctively that it was not at her his mute rage was directed.

"Madness," he blurted out at length. "Madness, I tell you. These parents of yours—I shall give your father a bit of my mind. What are they thinking of—to send you there. Bah, *you* do not know!"

"I know."

"The danger?"

"Yes."

"But—they allow no woman there! I have never been myself, but I know. They are wild men—fanatics—

capable of—does one know? You will be all alone—you,
a girl—do you understand that?"

"Yes."

He gaped at her incredulously, then snapped his thick
fingers.

"No, you do not understand. I tell you it makes me
afraid—me, Nik Leka. While you——"

His quick, bright eye searched her face with a puzzled
frown. Her absence of fear seemed to strike him in the
light of a personal grievance.

As they stood thus, a sudden fusillade rang out—a
dropping fire from the scattered houses—and "ping"
above their heads sang a stray bullet. The pedlar glared
in the direction of the village.

"Curse them all!" he muttered; then, with an explanatory shrug, "'Tis so bad for trade." He gnawed
his moustache for a moment, then burst out with fresh
rancour: "You do not think to bring that ne'er-do-well
back?"

She shook her head.

"To—to tell him of the child, eh?"

"No."

"No? What then?"

She did not explain. He muttered something into his
grizzled beard, of which she caught only the words
"monk" and "devil." Then asked:

"To see him, I suppose?"

"Yes."

He raised his hands to heaven. He appeared to be
mentally requesting that silent witness to have patience.
Then, eyeing her resentfully:—

"All that way? And in the face of so great a danger?
Yes, danger, for I know what is in your parcel. And you
think to pass for a man? To deceive them? And you
think he is worth that risk? *He!*" Clearing his throat,
he spat his contempt noisily after the manner of the base-
born. Then with a shrug, "But, after all, that is what
it is to be a woman! And which of us is worth it?
Which, I ask you? Name of thunder, if you women could
only see us as we are. But there—that would be the end
of the world. Women? I know them, I, Nik Leka. Oh
yes, I've had them in love with me."

He raised his fez, whether out of respect to memories, or because the morning was warm, could not be determined. " 'Tis true," he insisted, puzzled at her preoccupation.

" I must go now," she said in a lifeless voice.

" Wait," he cried, and began to fumble in his pack. The object of his search was apparently buried deep. At length he clicked loudly with his tongue. " There! " he exclaimed.

Zetitzka gazed with sombre indifference at the gaudy little housewife held out for her inspection.

" For you," he muttered, as though ashamed. His manner of giving had all the awkwardness of his class. " You had better take it," he continued gruffly, " before I repent."

She thanked him; unused to kindness she was touched in spite of herself. He essayed to make light of the gift, though it was obvious that its bright cover, embroidered with beads, filled him personally with the liveliest admiration.

" Why did you give it to me? " Zetitzka asked, the housewife still in her hand.

" Why? " He raised his eyebrows, scratched his grizzled head, then triumphantly, " For an advertisement."

He laughed aloud with cynical satisfaction. " I give them to everyone," he chuckled, then paused, an anxious gleam in his one eye, but she did not detect the falsehood. " To everyone," he repeated emphatically. " One thinks of oneself. It pays. Some day you will marry and have a house. You will need buttons, and needles, and knitting pins. It will then be your turn to think of me."

When she left him a moment later, he stood staring after her. She walked with bent head, absorbed in thought. But not even this meditative attitude could detract from the free, swinging movements, the unconscious pride of race in carriage and lilt.

His own lameness occurred to the pedlar as he gazed, and he gave vent to a short growl; but, to do the little man justice, all personal considerations were driven from his mind by sympathy and admiration for this girl, lonely and unprotected, yet resolute in the face of a grave danger.

The sun rose, turning the waiting world into something

bright and beautiful.   Pearl-grey mists that had lurked all
night in the deeper folds of the hills wavered, broke, and
fled.   The exquisite freshness and clarity of the summer
morning steeped all things—the nearer hills and the more
distant mountains—in an atmosphere of exhilaration.   A
bird sprang upwards from behind a rock, and mounting on
palpitating wings, poured forth its soul in song.   Between
the stones, in the rare spaces of greenery, tiny flowers
expanded dewy petals to the sun.   The distance beckoned
alluringly, like hopes too dear ever to be realised.   A
white cloud sailed overhead—a drifting brightness in the
dreams of morning.

But Zetitzka was deaf to the lark—blind to the sunshine—unresponsive to the glad voices that called to her
from the newly-awakened world.   Her eyes were fixed
upon the stones at her feet; mechanically they showed
her where to walk, what to avoid, like servants discharg-
ing a duty of which they themselves were barely conscious.   Her red cloak focussed the fierce sunlight and
glowed out against the dun hills like an avenging flame.

Towards afternoon she reached Kalabaka.   The heat was
great.   Not a breath of air counteracted the fierce rays of
the sun.   The aloes, skirting the track, reared their spear-
like points into the deep and burnished blue of the sky,
their pale green foliage powdered thickly with white dust.
The little village lay before her sweltering in sunlight.
She looked at it with a curious lack of interest.   The
streets were deserted; only under the tattered awning that
protected a *café* hard by the railway station, several men
were to be seen drinking.   They eyed her with curiosity
as she approached, and one nudged a neighbour to draw
attention to her face.

Faint from exhaustion and want of food, she seated herself at one of the little wooden tables.   The eyes of the
men, all turned in her direction, made her uncomfortable.
In a low, hurried voice she ordered coffee and bread.
When the refreshments came, she could not eat, but the
thick Turkish coffee revived her.   The waiter examined
the coin she proffered, bit it, rung it on the table, then
regretfully and as one acting under compulsion shook his
head.   She gave him another.   When he brought the
change, she inquired:

" How far is it to Hagios Barlaam? "

" Barlaam? " he repeated, in surprise.

" Yes. How far is it? "

" Oh—a good hour."

" Which way must one go? "

" Which way? " He stared at her. " Why, *there* it is! "

He pointed over her shoulder. Turning, she followed his finger. The great buttress towers of Meteora upreared themselves in the background. The one indicated by the waiter was the second loftiest pinnacle. Perched upon its crest Zetitzka could see grey buildings, reduced by distance to a tiny huddle of roofs. Her eyes dilated as she gazed. She had to put a strong curb on her feelings to suppress her intense yet painful interest in the place.

" That is Barlaam," continued the waiter in the pleased tone with which some people impart information. " Meteora is further to the left. Hagios Stephanos is the one you see up there, on the right. Hagios Triada is back, right back there; one cannot see it from here."

The name Stephanos set every nerve ajar. It was as though a rough finger had touched an open sore.

" You cannot be going there? " said the waiter with conviction, brushing imaginary crumbs from the table. " They do not allow women to visit Barlaam."

He had to repeat his remark twice, for she sat as one in a dream, her eyes fixed on the remote pinnacle upon which lived the man she had come to seek.

She did not reply.

"You are without doubt a stranger? " hazarded the waiter, with unspoken admiration in his eyes.

" Yes."

" That is seen. The saints reward you." He pocketed the small coin which she pushed to him across the table. Then, " You do not eat your bread? "

" No." She rose to her feet. " Do I follow that road? "

" To Barlaam, you mean? "

" Yes."

" That is the way. You cannot mistake the path. You will find it rough. Would you like a mule? I can get you one in ten minutes."

" No, I will walk. Good-day.''

She passed quickly along the village street. Before she gained the open she had to run the gauntlet of the women congregated around the village fountain, but heedless of comment she continued to climb.

The path, ascending steeply, coiled upwards, now traversing the bed of a torrent sucked dry by the thirsty summer, and again, mounting in steps fashioned roughly out of boulders. Nearer and nearer came the cliffs. They frowned down upon her, oppressing her. In some shadowy way they even entered into her thoughts. Broken memories, dark forebodings hastened to her, the roots of which lay deep in the soil of sex.

All day she had been moving as in a dream, barely conscious of her surroundings—save when the waiter had pointed out the heights of Barlaam. But now she awoke with a start, recalled to actuality by the glitter of sunlight reflected from a window far overhead. It seemed to be an eye watching her. In a flash everything became real: the rocks, the path, the cliffs, all became endowed with abnormal importance, as though they had been waiting for centuries to witness something terrible, vaguely connected with her fate. With a shudder she realised herself intensely, every nerve strung up, every faculty alert.

With a swift glance on all sides she sought the shelter of two adjacent rocks that formed a small open-air chamber.

The place she had chosen lay on the left of the path that coiled upwards to the monasteries. The rocks that formed it were great boulders that had toppled down from the high cliffs long ages ago, and now lay piled up, arrested for ever amid the chaos of lesser stones, the companions of their fall.

More than once Zetitzka anxiously scrutinised the path and the sea of rocks weltering in sunlight. No one was in sight. All was still, inanimate, given over to hot, quivering air that ebbed and flowed in the midst of a profound silence, with the transparency and something of the fluidity of water.

Slightly reassured, but still full of misgivings, Zetitzka began to undress. In all her movements haste was discernible, haste that thwarted itelf, for her hands shook. At length, clad only in scanty under-garments, she stood trembling with apprehension among the grey, sun-baked rocks. For just one fleeting moment she listened and gazed, and held her breath, her eyes full of the tragic import of her task; then, opening the bundle that contained her uncle's clothes, she made haste to put them on.

The costume was simple and workmanlike—its fabric white homespun. The white skull-cap sat loosely upon her head. The white jacket, its tight sleeves reaching to the wrist, was ornamented with black braid, as were the trousers. The latter, baggy behind, but close fitting to the leg, were many sizes too large. A touch of bright colour was imparted by a scarlet sash. Over this Zetitzka adjusted the belt of soft leather, with pouch in front and tassels of black silk, in which her uncle had carried his long, beautifully-worked pistols and yataghan, or Turkish dagger. Her own leathern belt, ornamented with pins, and her necklet of antique coins, she thrust into the pocket of her woollen dress.

Standing erect in her new costume, her hand fell naturally upon the hilt of the yataghan. Acting on impulse, she drew it from its sheath. Its blade, catching the light, became a cruel suggestion of violent death. She touched it with the point of her forefinger, absently, for her eyes, brooding and preoccupied, saw only the face of the man she once had loved. Her recollections were steeped in a dumb, passive misery. Sick at heart, she looked back across a gulf of pain to gleams of hope and moments of happiness. Then she had been young and trusting; then life had seemed a promise of joy. Now she felt old and infinitely weary; her heart was stone—the future was dark. And the man? She had been his victim, and now he was to be hers. The grim justice of his sentence appealed to the primitive instincts of her upbringing. She thought of him on one of these shimmering heights. Was he thinking of her, and of the death that so surely awaited him? He had once said: "This night is my soul demanded of me." How true this was now! Before another sun could rise he would be dead. Death! She had seen it many times. Familiarity had robbed it of horror. Even violent death had never shocked her. It was natural for a man to die standing. Less than ever now did she think of it as a fate to be pitied. It meant peace and freedom from suffering.

3

She almost envied him. And this gift was hers to bestow.
It depended only upon this—this little bit of steel she held
in her hands. One thrust—— But at the thought an involuntary shudder ran through her. Vaguely disquieted,
she returned the weapon hastily to its sheath.

She was about to leave her hiding-place when an idea
struck her. Raising her arms, she drew out the pins that
upheld her hair. Like a cloud it fell about her shoulders,
reaching below her waist. Its colour was blue-black, shining with a changeful glow, bright with somewhat of the
brightness of metal, yet soft as floating gossamer. From a
child Zetitzka had heard its praises. Even her mother had
taken a proprietary pleasure in combing it. But now it
seemed to her nothing but an obstacle. Taking a pair of
scissors from her bundle, she attacked it without mercy.
In a few minutes it lay at her feet.

Concealing her severed hair and cast-off clothing behind
a rock, she moved from the shadow of the cliff. As she
did so she gave a gasp, for there, on the path within a
dozen yards, stood a monk.

CHAPTER V

THE figure that struck consternation into Zetitzka's heart was dressed in the sombre garb of a Greek priest—the long, double-breasted black cassock, the rude sandals, and the tall black hat terminating in a curious rim at the top.

A young man, apparently, for both face and figure were youthful: an attractive face, for the vivacity natural to his years was sobered by a thoughtful simplicity, stamped doubtless by monastic life.

Zetitzka paused irresolute.

A monk! Had he seen her? Did he suspect? But the young man was gazing at her with nothing but curiosity in his eyes.

" God speed you, my brother! "

His voice rang out cheerfully, its clear boyish tones strangely at variance with his attire. Zetitzka returned his salutation inaudibly. He approached her where she stood in the beating sunshine of the path. From under downcast lashes she noticed with relief that his expression was friendly.

" Do you come from Kalabaka? "

" No," she answered shortly.

" Ah! methought not. Never wittingly have I set eyes on you before. Methinks I know by sight all the folk in Kalabaka. Ay, a stranger—and your cassock—nay, tunic I would say—and your little cap, and your brave trousers! Nay, turn not away: no call to feel shame; they are wondrous handsome. Oh, la, la! " He was fingering with naïve and childlike familiarity the black braiding of her jacket. " This pleaseth me right well. I have naught so brave as this. By Saint Jerome! 'tis cunningly fashioned, fine as any vestment. But—whither go you? "

Zetitzka looked up at him swiftly. He was a new experience to her. His quaint biblical phraseology sounded strange within her ears—strange, too, coming from one so essentially boyish. But his unusual friendliness and lack

35

of reserve awoke her suspicions. No countryman of hers
would behave thus. He was a monk—perhaps one of the
same brotherhood to which Stephanos belonged; it behoved her therefore to be on her guard. Her mind, attuned
to dark thoughts, felt hostile to all strangers. Still, as she
looked at him, his expression and the guileless simplicity in
his eyes went far to disarm her. After all, why not tell
him? He seemed friendly; he might prove of use.

"To Hagios Barlaam," she said gravely.

His good, honest, young countenance lit up in pleased
surprise.

"But——" He stammered in his eagerness. "*I* hail
from Hagios Barlaam! 'Tis wondrous strange, to meet
you here. Past all question my good saint has arranged
this. You pleased me the moment I saw you. You see, we
meet few strangers."

As though conscious of her bewilderment, his last words
partook of the nature of an apology. At his invitation she
joined him, and side by side they proceeded towards the
monastery. The conversation was one-sided. The boy
talked freely, exhilarated by this chance encounter, by the
sun, the air, the exercise; unaffectedly glad, it would seem,
to have met someone of his own age to whom he could chatter without the restrictions imposed by monastic life.
Zetitzka was silent, rarely opening her lips save in reply,
turning a deaf ear to his rapid and disjointed talk, save
where it immediately concerned herself.

At length came the inevitable question which the girl had
foreseen and feared.

"Why do you go to Barlaam?"

It found her unprepared. Scorning to prevaricate, she
remained silent.

"A pilgrim?" suggested her young companion, with
deep interest.

She shook her head. He seemed disappointed: pilgrims
evidently forming one of the diversions of his monotonous
life. Then, suddenly, he uttered a pleased ejaculation.

"I have it!" he cried, bending forward to look more
closely at her; "I see it in your face."

She was painfully conscious of confusion. He continued
cheerfully.

"The reason you come here. 'Tis sorrow."

Zetitzka was thankful that the stony nature of the path gave her an excuse for averting her eyes. But her new companion, walking briskly at her side, seemed to require no answer.

"You are young to have a sorrow." He spoke musingly, and almost, as it seemed to her, with a respectful admiration. Then: "But you will assuredly find comfort in Barlaam. Wait only till you have talked with our Abbot. He will do you good."

Struck by the melancholy incredulity in her face, he continued with heat:

"It is true. By Saint Barlaam, he is a saint! Wise, devout, good—never was such an Abbot! If only I could—— What! You have never heard tell of him! *Kyrie Eleison!*"

As if to put her at her ease, he continued with patronage, yet not without a touch of visible anxiety:

"You will become one of us; yes?"

As she looked at him with brooding eyes, wherein the least observant might have read her mental distress, he came nearer, saying confidentially:

"Look you, the brethren are well on in years—of high repute and sanctity assuredly, worthy of reverence indeed, but aged. I like them all—or nearly all. And as for our Abbot—but there, I cannot speak of my feelings for him. But between ourselves, old folk are—well, they do not remember what it is to be young. You see, they cannot do things: they want to walk, when we want to run—that is the difference."

He laughed gaily, as though the mere act of unbosoming himself afforded relief, kicked a stone lustily from the path; then, the question suddenly occurring to him:

"What is your name?"

"Call me Angelos," she said, after a moment's thought.

"Your real name?" he questioned.

"No."

"Well, it matters not. I suppose I ought not to wish to know, but——" She saw him shrug his shoulders; then he continued in a graver voice: "The Abbot says that our past belongs to God, and that when one joins the monastery one begins a new life. That must be the reason you have changed your name. Oh, many come to us in sorrow;

some abide always, and some, coming but for a space, depart comforted. I wonder which you will do? As for me, I am Brother Petros, and have never been aught else," he sighed discontentedly. " More than anything in the world would I love to have a real sorrow and two names. But what good?—I am known unto all here."

" Do not wish it! " she cried impulsively.

He seemed already to have forgotten his grievance, for he had sprung to a boulder, his black robe snapping in the light breeze, his shadow, long and thin, flung forward along the track. The incongruity of his monkish garb with his agile boyish movements struck Zetitzka afresh.

" You will tell me all about the world? " he questioned eagerly when she joined him. " I have seen marvellous little, but I joy in hearing of it. Do you know it well? It must be a wondrous big place; but woefully wicked, so they say. Have a heed to that stone. Brother Nicodemus broke his leg once, but the Holy Virgin healed it in a week. Dimitri—he is our muleteer—says it was only strained; but I ask of you, would the Blessed Mother appear in a midnight vision for a mere strain? Do I go too fast? The Venerable Father calls me a goat. I love climbing, and precipices. And you? No? Ah, that is because you have not been standing in a stall since midnight——"

" Since midnight! " she echoed, roused into astonishment.

" Past question. Did you not know that it was the festival of Saint Panteleemon? The good saint would in no wise be pleased did we not stand for at least two hours longer than usual. Well, you have been journeying: doubtless that unsettles one's thoughts. Yea, it was a long service, though 'tis sinful to say so. My stall is between Brothers Nicodemus and Gerasimos. They are both very old—sixty, I believe. I find their places for them; but Brother Nicodemus is always grumbling that he cannot hear the reader, and Brother Gerasimos is for ever falling . as eep."

There was a spontaneity about his chatter that was distinctly engaging. Unexpectedness, indeed, was his dominant characteristic. The attire, quaint and outlandish, suggested only age and monastic austerity; yet here it was allied to youth and something that irresistibly called to mind the old pagan joy of living. He was full of simple and unconscious gaiety, skipping, as it were, on the hills of life. This gaiety appeared to be his cardinal quality. One felt that it was immensely natural, born of no infection, no echo in remembered word or gesture of the light-heartedness of others; but young life bubbling up in him, as obedient to natural laws as a brook dancing to the sea or sap rising to greet the spring.

Borne along as she was by the flood of his conversation, Zetitzka never for one moment lost sight of the grim task that awaited her. It formed a dark background to all she saw and heard. Even this boy seemed connected with it—an illusion doubtless due to his calling. And yet he—she reflected, as her eyes rested darkly on his ingenuous young face—had never known sorrow. And at the reflection a great envy rose up within her.

They rounded a barrier of cliff and came within full sight of the pillar-like rocks of Meteora. With an involuntary exclamation, Zetitzka came to an abrupt standstill.

At that hour something almost unnatural haunted the mighty obelisks as with an atmosphere, bequeathing to them an air of abnormality. Silent and grim, they towered from the gloom of the gorge. It was as though some Titan had fashioned obelisk after obelisk with an axe, shaping their perpendicular flanks with mighty blows, trimming here a cliff, there a precipice, carving each on its every side into awful inaccessibility, till each loomed out lonely, primeval, eternal, the roost of the sunbeams, the playground of the storms.

In some places the cliffs shone with a bright metallic lustre, as though of beaten gold; in others they receded sunless and chill into fearsome depths, mysterious with the gloom of caverns. Seen through the obscurity the rocks assumed strange and fantastic shapes. Monstrous figures might be imagined looming mistily on the sight, vanishing at length in ghostly perspective. All were dead, long, long dead. Around their knees surged grey rocks, an endless and chaotic multitude, faintly visible, tumultuous and vast as a sea of upturned faces. On all sides, save the narrow entrance to the gorge, the cliffs, towering grimly upwards, hemmed them in. The wan sunlight gilding the topmost crags served but to emphasise the gloom below, for no message from its fugitive glory fell into the ravine. There night had already encamped.

The dominant sentiment of the scene was a deep and all-pervading sense of desolation, and even of abandonment. It penetrated to the bones and begot a shudder. This feeling was heightened by the silence, for the utter absence of all sound was a thing to marvel at. The very wind, that breathed so freely in the open, seemed here to be holding its breath as though fearful of disturbing the unnatural serenity that brooded over all.

Zetitzka's heart swelled. All around seemed darkly antagonistic both to her and to her mission. The cliffs, raising themselves out of the obscurity as though cognisant of her approach, appeared to be dreadful faces threatening her. They filled her with a poignant sense of her terrible and helpless isolation. For a moment the woman in her was oppressed, shrank, longed pathetically for support. In desperation, with a heart well-nigh bursting, she raised her eyes skywards. There, in the wan rift of evening, now paling rapidly as day leaned towards night, a solitary eagle wheeled and soared. Her lonely heart leapt towards it with passionate envy. But the weakness passed. The old fierce pain probed her anew. She was an outcast until this act of retribution could be accomplished. Weakness and vacillation were not for her. She had discarded her sex with her woman's clothes. She must seek a man's sterner nature in her breast. Was she not an Arnaut? The fearlessness of her race reasserted itself. The mute, undying rancour that had accumulated day by day, and week by week, surged up in her afresh. With a courage worthy of her ancestors she matched the blackness in her heart with the blackness of this sinister gorge, and saw herself the stronger. Let it threaten—let it try to bar her way—she would go on, on to the bitter end!

A sound beside her recalled the young monk. He was watching her with a look of gratified pride.

" Beautiful, is it not? " he exclaimed. " You will come to love it when you know it as well as I. Look! " He pointed towards the heights that barred the grey distance. " There is Hagios Triada—a small monastery, and insignificant compared with ours—you can see some of the others from Kalabaka, but not so well as from here.

Hagios Stephanos lies farther off—I have a friend there whom I go to see sometimes. Hagios Meteoron is in that direction. That one there is deserted and in ruins now—there are many like that. And Hagios Barlaam ''—his voice rang with conscious pride—'' is up there. Ah! you may well stare, my brother, 'tis the most important, ay, and the most beautiful. To my mind, it, of all the monasteries, earns best the name of Meteora—' in mid-air,' or, as one should say, ' above the world.' ''

Her eyes followed his finger in amazement.

Before them, where the path lost itself in blue glooms, rose an immense wall of cliff. The lad was pointing to its summit. Zetitzka strained her eyes. Far overhead, faintly illuminated by the dying sunlight, she made out what seemed to be grey buildings, so one with the living rock, both in colour and formation, that it was little wonder she had judged them at first to be but a continuation of it. Irregular in construction, crumbling and weather-worn, not only were they balanced on the sheer verge, but in some places even projected over the abyss.

'' Holy Jesus! '' she murmured.

Astonishing as was its site, it was its deep personal significance, rather than its position, that forced the sacred name from her lips. For weeks it had never been absent from her mind. She had pictured it fearfully in wakeful hours—recognised it with a start of horror in vivid dreams—in fact, ever since Nik Leka had brought her word that Stephanos had taken refuge within its walls. Within its precincts she had enacted again and again in morbid imagination the tragedy in which fate had decreed that she should play a part. And here it was! Like all places pictured beforehand, she found the reality trenchantly at variance with her expectations—more gloomy, more strange —if possible, more sinister. The boy at her side laughed merrily.

'' But, yes.'' He nodded his head relishingly. '' No wonder you admire it. All the world marvels—everyone —even rich noblemen from distant lands oversea, whom Dimitri brings sometimes on his mules. And its fine position is the least part. Oh, the least part! I assure you, little brother, it is holy, but so holy! There is not another monastery like it in the whole world. Do you know what

it is called—for it likewise has two names? It is called—
' The Paradise of the Mother of God.' "

His voice sank, hushed and solemn. That he counted
upon her being deeply impressed was obvious. Zetitzka,
engrossed with her own anxieties, merely nodded.

" You doubtless marvel why? " he continued. Then
with simple and devout earnestness, " I will tell you—I
know all about it. It is so called because the Holy Mother
has appeared to blessed monks in Barlaam no less than five
times. Not lately, alas, but before I came here. She is
the only woman who ever visits the monastery—and ours is
the only monastery she ever visits. *Polycala!* "

Zetitzka kept silent. An alien feeling crept over her.
This youth belonged to a different world. She was in no
frame of mind to take interest in miraculous manifesta-
tions. To her the monastery was only the abode of
Stephanos—the scene of a gruesome and imminent tragedy.
All at once, as she stumbled onwards, her ears were assailed
by a harsh metallic noise. It seemed to fall from the
heights, mysteriously alarming in the dusk, awakening innumerable echoes. Fearfully Zetitzka gazed into her companion's face. His smile reassured her.

" That is Brother Elias beating the semantron. 'Tis the
hour for supper, praise be to the Saints! My stomach is
like a pilgrim's wallet—it begs even for broken meats.
Ah, there goes Hagios Triada, and hearken, Meteoron likewise! "

From distant summits other semantra were calling.
Monastery after monastery was lifting up its voice, sending forth its summons across the benighted gorges, relapsing
again into silence. The effect of these wild voices crying
to each other in the dusk was ghostly beyond expression.

Her young companion leading the way with precaution,
for in the dusk the boulders and deeps ruts were all but
invisible, they reached the base of the cliff.

Guided by his gesture, Zetitzka made out a series of
rude ladders, absolutely perpendicular, the top of the one
being lashed to the bottom of the other, the whole forming
a staircase frail and perilous in the extreme. Raising her
eyes she tried to follow them in their ascent, but they
dwindled and blurred far overhead against the immense
face of the cliff.

" Is there no other way? " she asked in a low voice.

" There is the rope and net which we let down from the tower of the windlass, but no one will be there at this time of night. Why—" he peered closely at her—" you are as white as a missal! By the bones of Saint Peter, I am an infidel beast! May I do penance if I did not forget that you had never been up before! Come, my brother, courage! See, I go first. Follow me close, and, above all, do not look down. 'Tis not so difficult as it looks. Come! "

But Zetitzka did not immediately respond. Albeit a hill-woman and accustomed from her childhood to clamber among rocks, this perpendicular ascent to dangers unknown presented a peril that could not be exaggerated.

Encouraging her by voice and gesture, the young monk led the way.

They began the ascent—two tiny figures, one above the other, mere specks on the great blackness of the rock. The only sound to be heard was the creaking of the ladders, as the clumsy lengths oscillated to their movements. Far overhead Barlaam, hooded in night, seemed to watch them in a silence that was sinister.

All at once the boy spoke again:—

" Beware of this rung," he said warningly, " 'tis rotten."

They continued to ascend.

At the top of the third length her guide paused.

" Sit here, and rest," he said in a low voice, indicating a ledge barely two feet in width. With a sickening sense of fear which she fought hard to overcome, Zetitzka obeyed. Her back was now against the cliff, but her feet dangled in space. Her companion, standing unconcernedly on the sheer brink, continued to speak:—

" We have almost arrived. Take heart. Only one more ladder."

" Where? " she questioned in an unsteady voice. As she spoke she strained her eyes into the gloom. No other ladder, however, was visible. The ledge seemed to melt into space.

" Quite near. I will show you. It hangs from the top and separate from the others. You see, that is because we draw it up to the monastery every night. 'Tis supposed to be a precaution—useful perhaps, long ago. Now, take heed; we have to creep along this ledge till we reach the ladder. Are you ready?''

" Go on! '' she cried testily. Her voice betrayed extreme nervous tension. She heard his sandals shuffle in the dusk—then silence. Suddenly realising the terrible precariousness of her position, she felt physically incapable of following. Again she looked around. Neither parapet nor railing protected the ledge. Above her, the cliff towered; below, it fell sheer. In front yawned a void, a vast, mysterious profundity full of night and terror, from which came puffs of cold air. A moment of dizziness, a single careless movement, and she would be precipitated into it. And as if to add to her alarm, a sudden rush of air swept upwards out of the darkness. With a stifled cry she saw a huge bird—its size exaggerated by the gloom—perch itself within a yard of where she sat. Panic seized her. " Holy Mary! '' she gasped. Then, as the monstrous shadow edged nearer:—" Petros! '' she screamed. " Petros! ''

In less than a minute he was again by her side. Seating himself on the ledge he put his arm about her. He felt so strong, such a present help in danger that he comforted her inexpressibly.

" Gently! '' he soothed, patting her the while. " Gently, my brother. Look you, this will never do. And you, who have climbed so famously! Why, it was in my mind to tell the brethren how brave you were. 'Twas our eagle that frightened you, I suppose; the good-for-nothing! We feed him in the monastery—at least I do—and he grows presumptuous when he sees me. You feel better, yes? Shall we try again?''

Comforted and encouraged, more by his presence than his words, she followed him. Mounting the last rungs, they neared a tiny platform projecting from the cliff and sustained by rude beams driven into the face of the rock. A trap-door set in the flooring opened immediately above their heads. To gain access to the monastery they were obliged to creep through this, a feat rendered difficult owing to the continual oscillation of the ladder. With the aid of her companion, however, Zetitzka overcame this last obstacle, and stood at length on the dark threshold of Barlaam, the gloomy heights of which had never before been trodden by foot of woman.

CHAPTER VI

IT was night. Seated upon a low divan within his tiny living-room the Abbot was engaged with his supper.

The cell of Sofronos Constantinon, Hegoumenos of Barlaam, differed in no respect from those of his subordinates. Small, bare, cheerless, its furniture consisted solely of the divan—by day a couch, by night a bed—and a diminutive Oriental table. No wash-stand, looking-glass, or other evidence of modern comfort, was to be seen. An old cupboard, dark with age and built into the wall, sufficed for the concealment of his spare clothing and for the few personal articles which he possessed. The window, resembling in size the port-hole of a ship, and in barred security that of a prison, pierced the wall at a considerable distance above the top of the cupboard. It was, therefore, impossible for the occupant to view the outer world without standing either upon the divan or the table. As the dormitory looked towards the north, no sunshine found its way through this narrow aperture. Its panes of inferior glass spoke of the dust and raindrops of centuries; the niggard light, struggling inwards, falsified the brightness of morning, the glory of evening, turning existence into a neutral-tinted monotony, colourless as the life of the occupant.

One touch of unexpected brightness alone arrested the attention—a handful of poppies arranged in a glass upon the table. Their warm tones leaped to the eyes. There was something strangely out of place, almost sensuous, in this blaze of unusual colour. It was as if forbidden dreams had blossomed suddenly into scarlet flowers.

The worn face of the Hegoumenos had an air of distinction, for, unlike the majority of those over whom he had been elected to rule, Sofronos Constantinon came of gentle forbears. There was that too in his appearance that accounted for the respectful, almost solicitous, affection that all within the monastery bore him. His countenance was

45

indicative of his mind; in it one read of a sincere and upright nature, narrow, perhaps, as was but natural when one considered the monastic groove in which his life had passed, but beautiful in its simplicity, unspoiled by contact with the world. Goodness beamed from his eyes, self-restraint showed visible in the lines of his mouth. His long white beard, descending to his chest, gave him a venerable, indeed a patriarchal air that accorded well with the flowing lines of his fur-trimmed robe.

This old man belonged to a world that is past, a world that gave birth to hermits, and saints, and ascetics. Seventy-three years of age, he had lived a life of renunciation. He alone among the abbots of Meteora had attained the distinction of "The Great Habit," the highest monastic grade, entailing almost complete withdrawal from things earthly, and a life entirely devoted to religious exercises. His black scapula, however—in shape not unlike the *epitrachelion,* or Eastern priest's stole, worked with cross, lance, skull and crossbones, the only outward and visible sign of his ecclesiastical rank—was donned but rarely, being reserved for the celebration of the Holy Communion and festivals of great religious importance.

A tallow candle, placed in a brass candlestick, stood upon a bracket fastened to the opposite wall. The shadow of Hegoumenos loomed huge and distorted behind him upon the whitewashed space between the cupboard and the window. It appeared to threaten with vague and ominous gestures. Other shadows lurked in the corners. Seen in the flickering light, the austere little room seemed a fitting environment to the aged priest.

Upon the table stood a tray with the remains of supper —not the savoury diet of vegetables served in the refectory, but Eucharistic cakes—of fine flour and stamped with the words in Greek, "Jesus Christ conquers," a delicacy reserved for his especial use. The wine also differed from that supplied to the monks, being of superior quality.

The Hegoumenos of Barlaam invariably partook of his meals alone. They were brought to his cell by a lay-brother. His day and night were as rigidly mapped out as were those of his subordinates, but, unlike them, he was condemned by his rank to pass his leisure hours in solitude. He could indeed visit the brethren where and

when he pleased—having access to their cells as one
privileged to intrude upon retirement—he could pause in
his solitary wanderings about the monastic precincts to
address a remark or even crack a time-honoured jest, but
for all that he was a being apart, and all recognised that,
although with them, he was not of them. This enforced
loneliness imparted a touch of pathos. It became visible
at times in the expression of his eyes; a look as if he had
missed something, as if, in the rarefied atmosphere of his
spiritual life, he were dimly conscious of a want that
haunted him with vague yearnings, vague regrets.

From time to time the old priest broke the cakes with
listless fingers, and, raising the cup, touched the contents
with abstemious lips. His supper finished, he pushed the
table from him and rose to his feet. Fumbling in the
pocket of his cloak he produced a horn snuff-box, from
which he helped himself to a generous pinch. As he did
so, his eyes glistened. It was his one vice, and he pan-
dered to it with the utmost self-complacency. Brushing
the dust from his white beard and moving softly, he went
out into the corridor. The barn-like gallery was plunged
in obscurity. The faint light from behind him fell upon
a bundle of sheepskins suspended from a nail, and on the
open, windowless space that, looking upon the courtyard,
gave light in the daytime to the corridor. Framed by
the latter, the leaves of a fig-tree could dimly be distinguished forming mysterious arabesques against the blackness beyond. The silence was broken only by the subdued
sound of snores proceeding from the adjacent cells. It
being ten o'clock, the majority of the brethren had retired
to snatch a little sleep before the semantron summoned
them to private meditations at half-past eleven.

The old man inhaled the night air. Its purity refreshed
him after the vitiated atmosphere of his cell. He was
about to re-enter his little room when footsteps in the
courtyard attracted his attention.

" Who is there? " he called.

" It is I, venerable father," came the voice of Petros.
" Have I permission to speak? "

" Assuredly, my son."

The boy stood below in the blackness of the court, the
Abbot above him in the gallery.

"I would have come to you before," continued Petros, "but I feared to disturb you. I have to confess that I overstayed my time to-night."

"Then you have lost your supper?"

Under cover of the darkness Petros beamed.

"Nay, venerable father; Sotiri kept back a platter for me."

"That is well; but, my son, rules are for our guidance. Try not to transgress again."

"That will I—but there was a reason——"

He related his meeting with Zetitzka. The old man, bending over the rail, listened eagerly.

"He is then here?" The Abbot broke in upon the narration.

"Yes, he waiteth to have speech of you. I left him but now, in the outer court."

"Bring him to me at once."

Petros lingered.

"My father——"

"Speak."

"He is a likely enough lad, and he has known sorrow. I found that out, I alone! It would be gladsome to have him here always. Now, if so be that you keep him, I fear that the work may be too hard—he puzzles me somewhat—silent and fearless, but sad, and assuredly no head for precipices. But I—you know me!—now if in your goodness you could devise somewhat, right joyfully would I——"

There came a soft chuckle from the gallery.

"And so you fear that I may prove a hard taskmaster?"

"Nay, venerable father! I meant not that; I would have said——"

"There, my son, no need to speak. I know. Now, go and sleep—even Samson slept on occasions, I believe." He chuckled again. "But first conduct the youth here, for it is dark to-night."

"You asked to see me?" said the Abbot kindly, when Zetitzka, guided by Petros, stood before him. As he spoke, he peered downward from the gallery at the figure clad in white that looked so remarkable in the dusk of the court.

"Yes."

" Say ' venerable father,' " prompted the youthful voice at her elbow.

The aged priest caught the whisper and smiled. " Come with me," said he, addressing Zetitzka. " We can talk better in my cell. Over the bridge, there, on your left. Come."

She joined him in silence, with a beating heart. Once within the little room, the Abbot adjusted his spectacles and turned with unaffected interest to scrutinise the stranger. His eyes fell upon the picturesque costume, strangely barbaric in the wavering candle-light—the oval face, unaccountably pale—the mouth, with its lips set firm in a line of determination—and, finally, upon the eyes, large, black, and unnaturally bright. The latter struck and held his gaze. Their hard and feverish glitter spoke of a soul troubled to its depths, and conveyed, moreover, the impression of a wild animal confronted with danger.

The Abbot cleared his throat, and took an immense pinch of snuff.

" Now, my son," said he, combing his long white beard with his fingers, " what have you to say to me ? "

Zetitzka remained silent. Her fingers underneath her jacket clasped and unclasped the silver handle of her yataghan with a nervous contraction of the muscles. Her eyes strayed restlessly from the divan to the door, and from the door to the black cupboard on the wall.

" Well ? " said the Abbot, after a long pause.

Zetitzka gnawed at her under lip.

Faintly across the benighted court stole the sound of singing. It came from the refectory. It seemed to Zetitzka as if the quavering notes were depriving her of all power of thought.

" Far be it from me to force you to speak," went on the mild voice. He paused a moment, then continued:—" I see your heart is troubled. It has for long been my great privilege, with the good God's assistance—" he crossed himself reverently—" to comfort them that mourn. All in distress have a claim on me. All here are my dear children. Now you, my son, are young—a boy ! Look on me as an earthly father. Try to tell me what troubles you."

4

He spoke in so kind a manner, putting the question with the diffidence of one who fears to intrude upon the sorrows of another, that Zetitzka was moved in spite of the blackness that weighed her down. Her reception was proving far different from that which she had anticipated. It was as if a helping hand were outstretched to her in the groping blackness of her night. For the first time since she had parted from her child, a wavering softness came into her eyes. It was gone, however, on the instant. At the memory of the man who had betrayed her —at the certainty that he was there, within fifty yards, living in an odour of sanctity, every gentle thought fled precipitately, and again her hand closed tight upon her yataghan.

Looking straight at her would-be confessor in defensive though mute defiance, she shook her head.

To her surprise a twinkle came into the old man's eyes.

"Well," said he, "as you cannot tell me, needs must I guess."

She waited, breathless.

"You have come across the frontier?"

"Y—es."

"Albanian?"

Again a muttered affirmative. The Abbot rubbed his hands.

"I knew it. Behold, none can wittingly deceive me! Now," a complacent smile lighted his face, "how think you I guessed that?"

She shook her head.

"From your raiment. Yea, verily. Sooth it is that I have seen clothes like these before, though not so fine." He touched the fringe of her scarlet sash with *naïve* admiration, unconscious of her sudden shrinking. "We have a dear brother who came to us from Albania, perchance a year agone. I mind me of the date, for it befell during the fast of the Holy Mother of God. He likewise—" the Abbot checked himself, then inquired with grave interest—"Is he known unto you?"

An indescribable alertness had come into her face.

"I think—I mean——" she stammered in confusion.

"Maybe not—maybe not," commented the old man, visibly disappointed. "Albania is doubtless a big place, for all it looks so small on the map. One cannot be expected to know everyone. But, as I was minded to say, he likewise came to me in sore need of consolation; and, being young—but not so young as you, he—but you will see for yourself, for the most part we are all grey-beards here. Now," he laid a hand on her shoulder, " I must not forget divers but necessary questions. Nay, fear not, these you can answer in a little moment. Tell me, do you belong to the true Church? "

She looked at him.

" The Orthodox Greek Church," he explained.

" I am a Christian."

" *Polycala*, praise be to God! There are many Mabom-medans in your country. But, of course, you would not have come here if you had not been of the true faith. You are very young—I marvel much——"

He broke off, for he saw that she was not listening to him, but to the distant singing.

So accustomed was the Abbot to deference, that this young stranger's frank inattention at first surprised, then awoke in him a faint sense of humour. He watched her in silence, puzzled, yet attracted. She stirred some deep but undeveloped instinct within him, something protective and paternal. The white costume, the scarlet sash, the embroideries, all looked out of place in this grey cell. The young face too, proud and strikingly handsome, yet brooding and ill at ease, was as alien to the monastery as the costume. Never before had the Abbot's curiosity been so excited. The flickering candle-light, that touched this unexpected visitor here and there with wavering gold, lent an air of unreality. For very little, the aged priest would have believed this to be an apparition. But, as he looked wonderingly at her, a something pathetically human, pathetically appealing to sympathy in her fixed and strained expression, put all superstitious fears to flig t.

" What is your name? " he asked kindly.

A swift look of distress clouded her face.

" Nay," continued the old man, " be comforted. It mat-ters not. I see well that I must first gain your confi-dence. What is that you say? Angelos? Well, that will do—'tis a good name, of lucky omen, for verily you have come amongst us as 'twere an angel, unawares." He smiled upon her, pleased with the allusion; then with a suppressed eagerness in his voice:—"Now, I know not if so be that you desire to enter the monastery? Nay, you are too young."

The proposition took Zetitzka aback. *She!*—a woman!—to enter a monastery? To become a monk! Impossible. And yet, this old man seemed in earnest. She was a boy—a boy—she must remember that. And after all, if she appeared to consent? It would gain time. It was only for one night. Thank God for that!

The Abbot marked her rising colour. Leaning forward with his hands on his knees, his eyebrows arched interrogatively.

"Y—es," she stammered. "I—I think—I might wish it."

The Abbot ladled out snuff to conceal his gratification. A new inmate for Barlaam was as fresh blood to his veins.

"Well, Angelos,'" said he, taking her reluctant hand and stroking it between his wrinkled palms. "Well, there is time sufficient for that. Verily it is a serious step, and not to be rashly undertaken. Seek advice in prayer, my son. And do naught you may repent of later; for sooth it is we all magnify our little earthly troubles. Abide here for a space, and see if so be you feel worthy. You will find our life full of blessed peace. Yet needs must you labour with your hands, for you will be a postulant or lay brother till such time as God sees fit to make you a monk. But all can be seasonably settled on the morrow. Now, I can spare you no more time—yet, hearken." He stayed her with a gesture. "I give cell No. 15 unto you; it is nigh opposite the bridge, and not to be mistaken. I will send you raiment suitable for a lay brother. Good-night, my son, and may the Sweet Saviour have you in His keeping."

He raised his thin hand in a gesture of benediction and of dismissal. She waited a moment, half expecting him to speak again, but as he remained silent, she slipped noiselessly from the room.

CHAPTER VII

CLOSING the door of her cell, Zetitzka felt anxiously for a key or bolt, but found neither. A faint light from the lofty barred window revealed her new abode as a facsimile of that of the Abbot. As she moved stealthily forward, a low and monotonous sound came to her ears, resolving itself, as she held her breath, into an incomprehensible mumbling proceeding from the adjoining cell. A heavy smell floated on the unventilated atmosphere, mysteriously suggestive of unsavoury monkish belongings. It seemed to Zetitzka—her nerves in a state of tension—as if that stale and oppressive odour were a something lurking there, some spirit of a former occupant, austere, antagonistic, peculiarly distinctive of Barlaam, of the monastery that had frowned down upon her from the heights, and now encircled her like a trap with a grim and ominous silence.

A fierce impatience possessed her. To her mind, unnaturally excited under an appearance of calm, all cross-examination was futile, a mere waste of time. The necessity for disguising her feelings had taxed her self-control almost beyond its power of endurance. More than once she had been on the point of betraying herself.

Now, in this cell, she could breathe freely, was at liberty to mature her plans. Her surroundings made but little effect upon her save as a dark and unfamiliar background to a terrible necessity. The latter stood out as a fierce white light, absorbing her, claiming her every thought, penetrating to the inmost recesses of her being. To find Stephanos, to kill him, and to fly!

But her brain, numb with suffering and the stress of long-continued emotions unnaturally repressed, was unable to respond at once to this effort of her will. As she sat there in the darkness, her head between her hands, she was distressingly conscious of a mental vacuity, and of a physical weakness that caused her brain to burn.

Yet no doubt of herself darkened her mind. She could do it. Let her but once confront him and the smouldering memory of her wrongs would flame high, would steel her heart and nerve her hand. But where was he? In this black and fearful abode of monks she must seek him now, at once!

Slowly she rose to her feet. As she stood there, a desperate woman, wide-eyed, alert, the sound of heavy footsteps came from the corridor. This noise breaking upon the intense stillness forced the other monastic inmates to her mind; made her realise also, that if she were to act at all, she must act at once. Moving forward, she opened the door of her cell. Peering into the obscurity of the passage, she wondered with a breathless and fixed intensity which of these many diminutive rooms was that occupied by the man who had deserted her. Having nothing to guide her, she moved forward aimlessly, but with anxious caution. Under her feet the old woodwork creaked, causing her more than once to stand still in sudden apprehension; but nothing seemed alive in this dead and isolated world, nothing but the night wind moaning sadly to itself among the fig leaves.

Zetitzka had formed no conception of the interior of a monastery. To her anxious straining eyes it seemed full of sinister passages, of mysterious openings, of dark and unexpected flights of stairs, leading she knew not whither. Chill and earthy draughts breathed upon her; and from overhead, among a night of rafters, came thin screeching noises that caused her skin to roughen. Mechanically, moving as one impelled by a dream, she wandered on, noiseless, groping with arms outstretched, looking, in her white costume, by the faint light that stole inwards from the courtyard, as ghostly as did the monastery itself.

Suddenly, as she paused irresolute, a dark figure crossed the court, and passed within a few yards of where she stood. Taking her courage in both hands, Zetitzka called to it. The figure paused, then approached her.

"Who are you?" cried an unfamiliar voice. Its Greek was the Greek of the islands, but Zetitzka understood without difficulty.

Her explanation appeared to arouse the new-comer's astonishment, for he uttered an ejaculation.

"You came to-night! No one told me. So, you are to be a postulant? Well, you will be under me. I am Sotiri, the eldest of the lay brethren. You will sleep with us. Come, I will show you."

In a low voice Zetitzka mentioned that the Abbot had already apportioned her a cell. The information apparently roused his disapprobation, for his manner changed abruptly.

"Why are you wandering about here?" he demanded.

Zetitzka hesitated. "I was looking for—for——"

"For whom?"

"For one of the monks. He is called—or used to be called—Stephanos."

"Brother Stephanos? Do you know him?" His voice betrayed unexpected interest.

"I used to know him."

"So you are a friend of his? That makes a difference. *He* is a saint."

Zetitzka choked back a cry of amazement. The wind wandered in from the night, and moaned faintly along the deserted passages. The sound was one of desolation and infinite melancholy.

"Which is his cell?" Her whisper barely stirred the silence.

"His cell? No. 18. But you cannot go there. 'Tis forbidden. Besides, he is not there now."

"Not there?"

"No. He prays in the Catholicon. There!" He pointed towards a shadowy building that, detaching itself from its neighbours, upreared its dome into the night.

Zetitzka caught her breath. To know Stephanos so close filled her with unexpected and overpowering emotions. Pressing her hands to her bosom under cover of the darkness, she stood speechless. Her companion yawned loudly.

"Well, I cannot stand here wasting time. I must get my charcoal. The semantron will sound soon—and I who could sleep for a week! You will find him there; but it is not seemly to disturb him in his devotions. It were better you went to bed."

The last words were flung over his shoulder as he receded.

Zetitzka entered the Catholicon. She moved noiselessly, having left her shoes in the porch. The peculiar construction of the venerable building, the mystic shadows, the chill gloom, barely dispelled by the flicker of a solitary candle burning before an icon, the musty smell of wicks, incense, and draperies, affected her not at all. Her every thought concentrated itself with a breathless and wide-eyed intensity upon a man kneeling before the lighted picture. His back was turned towards her, his head bent, the tonsure in the form of a cross being faintly visible.

It was he—Stephanos! Zetitzka came to an abrupt standstill. Something leapt to her throat, but the imperative and terrible resolution that swayed her sternly demanded self-control. Thus far everything had conspired to assist her. The monks were asleep, the courtyard and passages deserted. The man she sought was here, alone, given over to her vengeance. She had only to steal upon him, strike one blow, then fly. Before the deed could be discovered she would be far away, safe from pursuit. She tried to realise all that this would mean—the blackness of dishonour lifted from her life, the undying anguish of self-reproach alleviated, her child no longer branded with shame, but the son of a worthy mother, of one who, though weak, had found strength in suffering to avenge her wrongs. As these dawned upon her, a wave of emotion flooded her entire body, tingled through every nerve, and filled her heart with courage.

Fierce thoughts, too, came to her aid, mingled with shame and resentment. This was the man who had wrecked her life, who had abandoned her! Through her distracted brain passed memories—his words, his kisses, his physical being searing itself again upon hers in an intense and shuddering agony of recollection. They passed like bloody phantoms through the echoing halls of memory, crying to her, inflaming her to revenge. As she stood motionless, she listened to these inaudible voices till her breath came short and her eyes darted flame.

All was still. The only sound was the gnawing of mice behind the ancient woodwork. From time to time Stephanos bent his body, pressed his forehead against the marble pavement; then, recovering his former position, crossed himself devoutly.

Slowly Zetitzka's hand stole to the hilt of her yataghan. Across her face passed horror, fascination, repulsion. Into her woman's body the soul of her race rushed—a torrent of hot blood. She was conscious of it boiling around her heart, seething through every swollen artery and vein, impelling her to immediate action.

Swiftly she glided forward on silent, naked feet, a dim and avenging whiteness amid the shadows. Behind the kneeling figure she paused, drew a deep shuddering breath, and jerked her hand on high. But ere the blade could strike, her eyes encountered the face of the Virgin confronting her immediately above the monk's head. The trembling flame, fanned by chill draughts, not only caused it to shine pre-eminently forth, but imparted to it a mysterious animation.

Within the eyes that held hers with a strange and awful fixity Zetitzka's superstitious brain read warning and condemnation. Petros had spoken of a miraculous icon —Our Lady of Pity—potent to save those who trusted in her. Suddenly it flashed into the girl's mind that she was protecting her worshipper now.

Awe swept down upon her. Her hand fell to her side, nerveless. A look of consternation came into her face— the look of one who recognises and recoils from a terrible danger.

All at once the sanctity of the spot spoke to her. It resembled the voice of God raised suddenly, unexpectedly in the silence. She shrank back appalled.

The mental shock that arrested action left every limb paralysed. For a moment she stood as though changed to stone, then, turning, fled swiftly.

CHAPTER VIII

THE monks of Barlaam drifted out of the Catholicon. The hands of the cheap modern clock in the refectory pointed to eight.

Seen in the keen sunlight of the August morning, the brethren were a strange community. They were mediæval men in purely mediæval surroundings. They not only suggested, but were, the past. The world far beneath them had progressed, but they stood still, stranded on their pinnacle home as effectually as castaways on a desert island.

By twos and threes they sauntered along the cloisters, their sombre habits and long grey beards according well with the old-world architecture.

Last of all came the Abbot, walking alone in dignified isolation. The old man appeared weary and as though the strain of the long service had sapped his strength. Where the cloisters led to the courtyard he paused to speak to Petros.

" See Angelos when he wakes," he said, nodding his tall hat in the direction of the dormitories. " Show him all things needful."

" Yes, venerable father."

" We know naught of him," mused the Abbot—" his folk, I mean. I hope he has not come here without their consent. But vex him not with questions. We will find out later, if God wills. Here all are welcome. I am a sure judge of character. He hath a good face."

Petros assented deferentially, adding with the freedom of one privileged on account of his youth: " But, venerable father, fain would I know his history."

The old man smiled, then shook his head.

" He comes from the world, therefore his heart is full of unrest. Naught but the life in Christ can give peace." He allowed his eyes to rest affectionately upon the sunlit cloisters, then continued : " This youth, I see it well, is as one wounded in battle.   foe hath smitten him sore. The world is full of such—God forgive them! ''

In the boy's face indignation contended with the restraining knowledge of his superior's presence.

'' Speak, my son.''

'' Would that I could meet the foe you speak of. By the saints! '' His fists clenched—his face glowed. '' I would do penance for a month, ay, and gladly, could I but smite him.''

'' Gently—gently, my son! '' The Abbot's voice was grave, but the benevolent eyes twinkled. '' Violence correcting violence. So is it not laid down in the Scriptures. Now I go, but see to it that the lad gets a good breakfast. Stay! As you and he are comrades, he can eat with you to-day, and to-morrow I will decide definitely.''

As the old man spoke, he supported himself, one thin hand upon a pillar.

'' You are weary, venerable father? '' cried the boy with impulsive sympathy.

'' Weary? Nay, I am exceedingly strong. It may be that the sun dazzled my eyes—yet is my sight wondrous.''

Very leisurely he polished his horn-rimmed spectacles. Then, clasping his fur-edged cassock around him, began to descend the steps. Petros was at once accosted by two of the brethren. They approached him with unusual haste, to the swish of trailed sandals.

'' What said the venerable father? '' inquired Nicodemus.

'' Yes, yes; what said he? '' echoed Gerasimos.

Petros satisfied their curiosity.

'' Ah,'' mumbled Nicodemus, biting long and dirty nails, '' I hope he will appear soon. What manner of man is he? What? Not yet twenty? Blessed fathers, Barlaam is becoming a school! ''

'' Yet there may be the makings of a good monk in him,'' suggested Gerasimos hopefully. '' And, brother, 'tis from lads like this that Barlaam must needs recruit. Of a surety, Brother Petros and he will be singing here when we are naught but—but a mouthful of worms.''

Nicodemus spat hastily.

'' I remember well,'' he droned after a pause, coiling as he spoke a wisp of his long grey hair and poking it beneath the rim of his grotesque hat, '' I remember well when I joined the monastery all were of proper age. One was ninety-two. His name was—let me think—nay, it hath escaped me."

"He was so old that he died," wheezed Gerasimos simply. "What a blessed year was that—five funerals!"

"So he did—so he did. But—would I could remember his name."

Gerasimos yawned loudly.

"There used to be a Brother Josephus, too," continued Nicodemus. "You remember him? At Hagios Triada."

"He that had a wart on his nose? I remember him well. He owed me two pesetas when he died. Alack, never did I recover them!"

The bleared eyes of Nicodemus lighted with fierce disapproval.

"And where is the love of holy poverty that should inflame your sinful soul, Brother Gerasimos? Two pesetas! Of such are the kingdom of hell. Two pesetas! Get thee behind me."

Gerasimos crossed himself in visible anxiety.

Petros, seeking good-naturedly to turn the conversation to safer channels, found in the deceased Josephus a valuable ally.

"He had a mother," snuffled Nicodemus, then chuckled in obvious reminiscence. "Only think, brother "—he laid a dirty hand on Petros's arm—" she—she wanted to mount the ladders! But that was long before your time."

"So she did, so she did," tittered Gerasimos, his eyes disappearing in wrinkles.

"He was her only son," continued Nicodemus. "She said she could not live without him. My mother was more reasonable."

"That we well believe," murmered Gerasimos, with conviction.

Nicodemus shot a suspicious glance at his friend, but the simple and almost meaningless smile upon the plebeian face reassured him. After a dignified pause, he continned:

"Brother Josephus was not permitted to descend. It was judged a temptation. So he used to shout down to her from the tower of the windlass, and she used to scream up to him from the path—with difficulty, you understand, she being feeble and he deaf. She came once a year for six or seven years. Ay, every single summer as regular as leaves on our fig-tree—and all for half an hour's talk. Then, one winter—in the month of January it befell, for I remember our wood ran short—Brother Josephus died. They were constrained to tell her when she came. I was at Hagios Triada that day. They shouted the news down to her. It took a long time to make her understand." He wrinkled his forehead, then added: " There was something else odd about him, too, if I could only remember."

Leaving the friends still deep in gossip, Petros made his way toward the tower of the windlass. As he passed the door of No. 15 he paused to listen, but all was quiet.

The little old monastery basked and baked in the strong sun. The veil of quivering light and heat tempered its mediæval severity and imparted to it an air of drowsy unconcern. The sombre and blood-stained pages in its history—pages of ruthless persecution and fierce retaliation—were forgotten. The cruelty that, linked to love and self-sacrifice, still slept in its fanatical heart was disguised; and, drugged with draughts of sunlight, Barlaam gave itself up to the warm and slumbrous influence of the summer morning.

But beneath this appearance of inertia there lurked always a suggestion of barbarism, conveyed it may be by a certain old-world grimness of aspect.

The merciless light accentuated its antiquity and rendered its silence more impressive. Everything about it spoke of age. Even its shadows seemed old. Not a crumbling stone, not a worm-eaten rafter, but took the imagination back —back to the dark ages, to wild and lawless times, to an inconceivably remote past rendered dim and mysterious by the living present. This distinctive atmosphere had all the disquieting fascination, the haunting uneasy attraction that characterises the unknown. To come under its spell was to grow mentally restless, to give way to vague fears, to become apprehensive of one knew not what.

It was not wholly without animation. At times a black-robed brother would cross the open sunlit space, or descend one of the small, irregular flights of stairs, moving slowly and with feeble steps, and would disappear into some dark entrance; at times the silence would be broken by the murmur of distant voices, or by the faint sound of sandals dragged listlessly over warm flagstones.

The thin air told of extreme altitude. Nothing of the incomparable view could be seen, the courtyard being hedged about by monastic buildings, but in the pure atmosphere and fierce white light every detail stood out trenchant and clear.

There were the cloisters, with the semantron suspended between two of the squat grey pillars—the corridor, out of which opened the cells of the brethren—the Byzantine church with its circular dome, stained and moss-clad, old as Christianity itself—the black and labyrinthine passages —the one gnarled fig-tree, with leaves green and lustrous against the rotting woodwork of the refectory—the granite of the aged walls sun-steeped and weather-worn—all huddled on a tiny space, lifted high above the world.

Time seemed to have forgotten it. Death stole its inmates one by one, but the little monastery lived on, silent as are the very aged, brooding continually on the past.

Petros looked at his surroundings with unconscious approval. The little court, with its air of stagnation and decay, held for him nothing but sunshine and happiness. As he ran down the steps his youth and activity were very apparent. In his head the refrain of a Greek chant droned persistently. He had taken part in it nightly, oftener indeed than he could remember, reiterating it drowsily as he stood beside his grey-bearded companions. It expressed thankfulness—only a few words set to the old and almost forgotten chorus-music of the Greeks, but never before had it seemed to him so significant—a personal message—voicing his profound though unspoken convictions.

Where another youth would have whistled a popular melody, Petros sang church music. This he did from no promptings of piety, but simply because he felt happy.

As he drank in the freshness and beauty of the morning, the sensation of weariness and want of sleep which had oppressed him in the Catholicon dropped from him, giving place to a desire for exercise, and a healthy longing for breakfast. And all the time, in the background of his mind, he was pleasantly conscious of something unusual in the air, connected, when he allowed his thoughts to dwell upon it, with the arrival of a new inmate,

Having lowered the ladder—his daily duty as the youngest of the brethren—Petros again sought the dormitories, and, unable any longer to restrain his impatience, knocked eagerly at the door of Zetitzka's cell. It opened slowly, almost reluctantly, he thought, and the girl stood before him.

She made a striking picture, framed in the dark and narrow doorway. Her Arnaut costume, with all its bravery of white homespun and black braid, had been exchanged for a skull-cap, a tunic of coarse grey cloth reaching to the knees, cloth gaiters, and leather shoes—the sombre and illfitting dress of a lay brother. The boy looked at her critically, with undisguised curiosity, interesting himself in every detail, from her little feet, too small for the clumsy shoes, to the set of her head upon a neck unusually statuesque.

"Bravo!" He smiled encouragingly. "You look one of us already. But—that tunic does not become you so bravely as the raiment you wore last night. No matter. 'Tis a worthier garb, well pleasing to God and the blessed saints." Then, with quick sympathy as he noticed her pallor and the dark lines under her eyes, "You slept well, I trust?"

Forced to reply, Zetitzka murmured something which he took to be an affirmative, yet she gave him food for wonder, for, even as she spoke, her large wild eyes were gazing over his shoulder with a singularly furtive expression.

"Be of good cheer," he nodded reassuringly. "No call to look alarmed. None wicked dare come here. Ay, these are our cloisters; it was too dark to see them last night. Truly "—he turned upon her impulsively, his face breaking into an irrepressible smile—" right glad am I that you are here. Come, let us go to breakfast."

But Zetitzka did not move. Scarce heeding his words, she continued to gaze around her. This, then, was the monastery! *This* was Barlaam! She had seen nothing like this. In spite of the sunshine that fell like a river of flame, the place to Zetitzka's mind was fearsome—inimical. Its air of affected indifference was sinister, suspicious. It put her on her guard. At any moment something might happen. Somewhere in that unfamiliar maze of passages lurked Stephanos. At any moment one of these mysterious little doors might open, and he might come out. Faint with hunger and weary with want of sleep, she was nevertheless strung up for any emergency, prepared to confront him, to denounce him, and, if it came to fighting, to sell her life as dearly as possible.

But all was still, peaceful, somnolent. The heat quivered faintly. The quiet was unbroken, save by a subdued murmur that, stealing from the shadowy dormitories, told of the prayers that rarely ceased in this aërial sanctuary dedicated to God.

With the feelings of a trapped animal, Zetitzka cast her eyes on high. The dome of blue was flawless; above a ruined wall that fretted the east, the merciless sun was pouring his fire upon a world that had already begun to pant and groan with heat.

Her arrival on the preceding night flashed to her mind —the great cliffs, the perilous ladders. Was she, then, so cut off from the world? Was it possible that, could she see over these grey and ruinous walls, she would again be rendered dizzy by the appalling depth, would see the fields, the valley, and the river that she had crossed yesterday, all far, far below, tiny as a child's toy?

She was recalled from uneasy speculation by her companion. He was staring at her with the utmost friendliness, with an expression that betokened that he considered her in the light of a welcome addition to his personal property. This smiling and proprietary attitude chafed her. Despite his youth and evident good-nature, she felt hostile to him. He was a monk. His tall black hat and sombre cassock filled her with vague repulsion. They were the disguise of Stephanos.

"Well," he cried cheerily, "what is it? I cannot believe you slept soundly. You look as if you had seen an evil vision. Nay, be not in any wise afraid. Here all are friendly. Ay, of a truth, the brethren are right anxious to see you. Come, let us go to breakfast."

"I do not want breakfast," she said in a low voice.

He cried out in the extremity of his amazement. "Not want breakfast! What folly is this? And you who ate like a sparrow last night! Little marvel you look ill. Nay, come you must, for I am wholly purposed to take you."

Zetitzka hesitated. Again she cast an anxious glance

round the court, and again she was half reassured, half rendered suspicious by the sunlit stagnation. Not only all passion, but all life, seemed dead—all except this boy so strangely full of vitality at her side.

" Will—will all the monks be there? " she hazarded, with unaccustomed timidity.

" Where? " he demanded.

" In the place you eat—where you took me last night."

" The refectory, you would say. Assuredly, *we* monks " —he expanded his chest—" all breakfast together, except, of course, the Abbot, and lately brother Stephanos. He fasts till the evening meal—a sainted man. But think not you are to eat with us always. Nay, you are only a lay brother. It is a privilege granted you to-day by the kindness of the venerable father. He did it for my sake: he saw I liked you. Let us go. Brother Nicodemus is sometimes wrothful if one is late. He helps the dishes, and it is wise to please him. You will sit near me. I will show you everything. Ah! you will come? Good! "

Like every event that had happened to her since she had entered the monastery, that meal was an unforgettable experience to Zetitzka. The low vaulted hall of unfaced stone, blackened with oil-smoke, stained with damp, festooned with cobwebs, appeared more real than on the previous night. Then she had been in a bewildered dream, scarce cognisant of her surroundings, but now she was wide awake, silently observant, on her guard, shrinkingly sensitive to every influence of environment.

The very solidity of the refectory struck a chill—it was her idea of a prison. Its little door, so low that the monks had to stoop to enter, seemed as if constructed in order to show the thickness of the walls. The lofty windows, mere slits in the masonry, let in but little light—a circumstance, however, which caused her a vague sensation of relief.

With an extreme nervousness which she fought hard to conquer, Zetitzka seated herself beside Petros at a bench that stood before a long wooden table. The boy continued talking in encouraging tones, pointing out anything which he thought might interest her—the arm-chair at the end of the table, to be presently occupied by Brother Nicodemus; the knotted rope suspended from a nail on the wall, which

5

was used in the penance called the " *canon* "; and, lastly, his own name carved in the dining-table and surrounded with an ornamental border.

He was still expatiating on this work of art when the brethren streamed in. Each in turn genuflected before an icon on the wall, then took his place. No sooner were all seated and grace droned by Nicodemus, than two lay brethren brought in steaming dishes of vegetables which exhaled a pungent odour.

To be forced to run the gauntlet of so many masculine eyes was a terrible ordeal to Zetitzka. Scarcely daring to raise her head, she concentrated her attention upon her plate. Every moment she felt as if her secret must be discovered, and she herself denounced before the community. But the moment passed and nothing happened.

Gaining courage, she ventured a look at her companions. All wore the tall black hats of their order; all, with the exception of Petros, were aged men; all betrayed an almost feverish gluttony, saying no word but " *kalo! kalo!* " between every gulp of food or wine. The scene, the costumes, the dim light, and the knowledge that all this was taking place upon the summit of an isolated rock, struck her with an undying newness of consternation. It made her feel so far away, so helpless. The extreme incongruity of her presence there—a woman among all these men—came upon her suddenly. She could have laughed aloud in utter nervousness.

Unknown to herself, the age of the place and the outlandish appearance of the brethren oppressed her. She could not banish it from her mind that, did they but know her sex, did they but know her intentions, not one among these peaceable old men, whose entire minds were so obviously bent upon the business of eating, but would spring up in horror. What would happen to her then she dared not imagine.

Nor did the conversation, when the edge was taken from their appetites, set her more at her ease. It referred to things about which she knew nothing. Once the name of Stephanos was mentioned, but it was only a remark referring to the ownership of an object left by accident in the Catholicon. The conversation passed to other matters, but Zetitzka felt as though everyone present must have noticed her discomposure.

Several of the brethren began to take an interest in the new lay brother, displaying much naïve curiosity. Zetitzka was made to feel that her coming was an event in their lives, that all she could tell them was public property—their right, as it were; news from the great world to that isolated height to which so little news ascended.

Their questions, being of a personal and searching character, would have embarrassed her, had it not been for her young companion. As though aware of her reluctance to being cross-examined, he came to the rescue, replying to some of the questions, parrying others, and all with good-humour and a flow of high spirits that would have infected any company save that of the old men among whom he lived.

Even they, at times, showed faint signs of amusement —the involuntary twinkle of a bleared eye, the sudden expansion of a munching mouth. Their treatment of this boy astonished Zetitzka. They seemed to look upon him as one of themselves, yet with a thinly-disguised complacency, an almost paternal affection of manner, suitable had he been a spoiled child. Thus, when one of their number—Nicodemus, a sour-faced old man with bad teeth—reproved him for undue levity, the others exchanged explanatory glances, nodding, as who should say: "We deplore it; but 'tis for the lad's good."

As he ate, Petros took note of his new comrade, approvingly, but with boyish reservations. The pale face beside him, and the long, dark lashes that concealed the downcast eyes, appealed to him, he knew not why. He supposed it was because the new-comer looked young. He wished this lay brother would not look so sad, so visibly ill at ease, but consoled himself by a determination to show him over the monastery after breakfast. As an antidote to sorrow, he made a point of seeing that she too had a lavish helping of vegetables, and was shocked to the point of ejaculations at her contemptible appetite. Under cover of the general conversation, he pressed her to eat in short, indignant remonstrances—evidently full of fear lest the others should notice her shortcomings and think less of her in couse-

quence. From time to time he criticised her patronisingly.
The intense blue-black gleam of her hair, visible below her
lay brother's cap, caught his attention. He never saw his
own—the monastery not possessing a looking-glass—but he
mentally compared it with the curly locks of Dimitri the
muleteer. He hoped her hands were stronger than they
looked. He thought, too, he had never seen such small
ears. Something wild and shy about her awoke his
curiosity. Even when he spoke to her, her answers—always
short, and as it were, under compulsion—would be followed
swiftly by a silent, repressed anxiety, as if her thoughts,
tied for a moment by the conversation, were put to the
panic of sudden flight by the recollection of some abiding
danger.

This, he reasoned to himself, was mere foolishness!

CHAPTER IX

THE meal over, Petros took Zetitzka to the Catholicon. The day was hot, the sun blazing in a cloudless sky. Strong shadows lay like pools of blue ink upon the glaring dust of the courtyard. The drowsy air was stirred languidly by the hum of flies.

As they entered the sacred building, a chill breath met them, contrasting forcibly with the warm, quivering atmosphere without.

" This is the *Pronoas*," explained Petros, indicating the porch. " And those," he pointed to the mural paintings, " are the damned."

Zetitzka gazed at the evidences of man's imaginative cruelty—they struck a kindred note with some inner depth of tragedy in her heart.

" Look at that poor soul." He pointed to a shrinking sinner being thrust back into the flames by the pitchfork of a particularly malignant fiend. " Poor soul, in all verity! What joy can he now have of all worldly delights! 'Tis doubtless merited; yet I confess, never do I see him, or any of these, but I long to save . . . 'For ever and ever,' Angelos. 'Tis a solemn, ay, and a fearful thought. By the Saints, right glad am I that you came to us in time! "

" And the devils," continued the grave young voice, after a pause. " What puzzles me is why are *they* happy? They are more wicked than the sinners. Why are they happy? I cannot understand. It angers me. Look at that blue one breathing red flames; ay, he with the curly tail. He enjoys it! He laughs! Why? Had I my way——" He shook his fist at the leering face, then continued:—" Brother Nicodemus repainted him lately, he was sadly weather-beaten. ' Make him sad,' said I, as I watched from below, ' make him suffer likewise.' But nay, all must be as before."

69

Slowly they wandered into the cool shadows that seemed to doze in the silence.

" That is my stall." Petros paused before the row of black seats that ran round the interior. " Behold, it faces the pulpit. I can watch the venerable father when he preaches, Brother Elias now, can only hear him, and that with difficulty. It must be irksome to sit behind a pillar. But he is oftentimes asleep. Last night again it took place, and we lit that candle by his side, and he had to do penance. Come this way."

" Where—where does Stephanos sit ? "

The question was faltered half under her breath. She was looking round uneasily. Her guide smiled upon her.

" No one *sits* here. 'Tis forbidden during service. Did you not know that ? But there is the stall of Brother Stephanos—the fourth from mine."

She looked at it darkly. In imagination she pictured the gaunt figure of the man she knew so well, standing there hour by hour, engrossed in this world of religion, while she had been suffering, brought low to the very dust in her mountain home.

" Where is he now ? " she asked.

Petros wondered at her tone. He thought he had never seen so strange a boy.   •

" I know not," he answered indifferently.

She continued, still visibly plunged in thought:—" Is he sometimes to be found alone ? "

" Alone ? I suppose—nay, I cannot tell. What strange questions you ask."

" But—in his cell ? "

" Ay, in his cell is he alone; none but the venerable father can visit him there."

" No. 18 ? "

" Assuredly. But—how came you to know that ? "

" One of the lay brethren told me."

" Sotiri ? "

" Yes."

" So, you have already had converse with him ? He is a rude fellow. But if you do your work he dare not molest you; but take my advice and keep friendly with him as long as you are a lay brother. Ay, that is the pillar I told you of, and these are the little devils—-there are ten of them, but you cannot see them all from here. Look at that carving! You will not find its equal in any of the other monasteries. Rich travellers come from far to see it. And that screen. Come nearer. Beautiful, is it not? And that icon! Most holy! There is a legend attached to it that I will relate to you some day."

His chatter fell almost unheeded upon her ears. Her feet followed him mechanically. She felt that at any moment she might wake up to find herself back in her mountain village—back with the baby for whom she yearned; yet the weight upon her heart and the knowledge of something terrible to be done oppressed her continually. Little by little her surroundings imprinted themselves upon her mind almost without her consciousness, awakening awe and superstitious fear. The dimly-lit spaces; the venerable pillars adorned with antique pictures; the walls covered with terribly realistic representations—the Last Judgment, scenes from the Apocalypse, the martyrdom of the Saints—the high reading-desk; the pulpit of worm-eaten wood, elaborately carved, and black with age; and the icon of the Virgin that had thwarted her upon the preceding night —all associated themselves—not with Petros, not with the present, but with Stephanos, with her failure, and with the imperative necessity for doing something soon.

Troubled to the very depths, she pressed her hand to her eyes. Again she became conscious of the voice of her companion.

" The venerable father is drawn to you. He told me so. That is why he has given you Sotiri's work here, yes, in the Catholicon, and a cell of your own among us monks, instead of making you sleep with the other lay brethren near the kitchens. 'Tis unusual, but come to me if they resent it."

" What work? " She roused herself with an effort.

" Oh, there is much to be done. You must sweep the floor every day. Then you must clean the icons, stalls, misereres, and desks; yes, and attend to the candles. See, there are two now that need replacing."

He pointed to the dome overhead from which a weighty brasswork corona decorated with ostrich eggs hung suspended by chains.

" Is it worth while? "

He turned upon her in swift amazement.

"*Worth while!* To replace the candles!"

"No, not that. I meant I shall be here only for——"

She broke off in confusion. In the dim light she saw his face, full of consternation, standing out against the sombre background of the Sanctuary.

"But—you mean to become one of us! You told me so yesterday."

She did not reply.

He stared at her incredulously for a minute, then, as one who ridicules a preposterous idea:—

"Bah! I am foolish even to imagine it. You would never come here just—just to go away again! That is not even common sense. But, be cheerful, you will not always have to work; some day, you will become a monk—like me." He drew himself up with youthful arrogance. "Oh, it is a beautiful life! It pleaseth me well. Our prayers do good to everyone—even as leaven in the world's loaf, so are we."

This was a distinct plagiarism from one of the Abbot's sermons, and was delivered with unconscious mimicry of voice and gesture.

"Now," he went on gravely, pointing through the doors of open carved woodwork that led to the sacristy, "in there you will find two chests—one for charcoal the other for vestments; the charcoal you will, of course, heat for the censers; it is required at almost all services; as for the vestments—but you will soon find out for yourself which are required. Come, my Angelos." He turned from her with a beckoning gesture full of friendly invitation.

Like one still in a dream she followed him across the nave with its floor of faintly-coloured marble. His lithe young figure looked strangely full of vitality in the midst of much that spoke only of decay. Everything around them was old—incredibly old—polished and mellowed and dimmed by time. From overhead, in faded frescoes, stiff pious groups of little Byzantine saints who had witnessed centuries of worship, gazed down upon them.

"These—" he halted before the central entrance—"are called the Holy Doors. Within is the *Bema* or sanctuary. You see that table? That is the Holy Table with the baldakin above it. The Eucharist is kept in that little box and

the Bread and Wine are in the *Prothesis*. This—" he
stepped forward and touched with reverent fingers a cor-
poral of fair white linen—" is the blessed *Antimins*. Remember, it contains a portion of most holy relics, and is on
no account to be touched by the laity. The larger relics
and the most precious of our treasures are in these two
cupboards. The Abbot keeps the key, but you will see them
at the great festivals—magnificent!—all gold and precious
stones!"

Bewilderment showed itself in her face, for he added
quickly:—

" I have not explained it well?"

" Yes—but—I shall never remember all that—never!"

His eyes twinkled.

" 'Tis true!" she insisted earnestly. " Anti—Anti—
There! I have forgotten already!"

" *Antimins*," he corrected gravely. " But—have you
never been in a church before?" he added, visibly shocked.

" Yes, but not quite like this."

" Where was it?"

" It was——"

" Stop!" He raised his hand impulsively. " The
venerable father forbade me to ask questions. I have disobeyed him—may I be forgiven. Now only one thing
more and then must I sleep, for verily my eyes close even
of themselves. Do you know our hours? Nay? Then
wisely take heed, for you will have to be present at some
if not all of our services. We begin at midnight, when we
recite the night offices, and the first, third, and sixth Hours.
That lasts till five o'clock, when we have an hour to ourselves. I am wont to have a cup of coffee and go to the tower
of the windlass on summer mornings. At six we come back
here and sing the Liturgy, which lasts till eight, and on
Sundays and festivals till ten. After that we breakfast.
The others jest at my appetite. Then we sleep and are
supposed to meditate, but verily I am of a mind that the
only one who meditates devoutly is the venerable father.
At three in the afternoon we sing Vespers and the ninth
Hour. At six we recite Compline. Supper is nigh sun-
down, after the which, to bed. Behold! That is all!"

He did not wait for a reply, but began to polish the
frame of an icon.

" You will be there? " she asked.

" Where? " he questioned, still polishing.

" At all these services? "

" No manner of doubt! Am not I a monk? As important as any of them? Look, the dirt of this icon is right shameful. Hearken!—" he turned to her—" now that you are custodian you must in no wise allow things to become rusty. You see," he cast a furtive glance over his shoulder, then, cautiously lowering his voice, " Brother Nicodemus hath a biting tongue; ay, and Brother Apostoli's arm is exceedingly strong considering his great age." He nodded his tall hat, pursing his lips significantly. There was a distinct suggestion of a defensive alliance in his manner. It emboldened her to say :—" And if I need help——"

His laugh rang out, instantly suppressed, however. The rollicking sound touched a strangely impossible note in the solemn half-light. It brought into the sacred building the very spirit of youth and merriment. The dark vault overhead re-echoed the sound, but faintly, as in a shocked whisper. Petros listened aghast.

" God forgive me! " he ejaculated, with lively penitence. " Never before have I laughed here. But the fault is yours."

" Mine! "

" Ay, yours. By the rood, you are enough to make a saint laugh—if ever they did laugh." He cast a dubious glance at the row of countenances that frowned from the cornice, then resumed quickly :—" But how can one require help to clean the icons? "

She could not explain. Her imagination had pictured a possible catastrophe when she would be one against many. To cover her confusion she fell to examining the hilt of her yataghan.

" What have you there—a knife? " he asked with curiosity.

She started, for she had been unconscious of her action. " Let me see it."

Reluctantly, she drew the blade from its sheath and handed it to him. He examined it with open mouth. The cold, blue glitter of the steel caught at the light, reflecting itself upwards into the boyish face shining above it with admiration. The suggestion of violence had a strange look in the hands of a monk and in the devotional character of their surroundings.

"Saint Panteleemon!" he ejaculated again and again, turning the weapon this way and that. Then running an appreciative thumb along the blade-edge. "By Saint Barlaam, this could cut anything—anything!"

After a little he handed it back to her, his eyes following it wistfully as she returned it to its sheath.

"You always carry a knife like that?" he asked with new-born respect.

That her negative disappointed him was evident, but struck with a thought he brightened. "You could an it pleased you, eh?"

"Y—es."

"And on a pilgrimage?"

She nodded doubtfully.

"I have never been on a pilgrimage—at least, not since I was an infant, and even then it was not a *real* pilgrimage, but only journeying here with my father. But with a knife like that——" He paused, looked thoughtfully at the old pulpit, then added: "You will not be permitted to keep it here."

Her start was not lost on him, for he continued: "We are peaceable folk here—that is what the Abbot said to me once when I bled Sotiri's nose. I caught him throwing stones at my eagle; right insolent he was, and would in no wise desist. But, alas! here none are permitted to carry weapons; otherwise"—he turned to her in good-natured scorn—"do you suppose for an instant I would not have as good, nay, a better knife than that—ay, and a gun likewise?"

His gesture gave the impression of a man armed to the teeth. Calming somewhat, he continued: "It were seemly you gave it to me."

Zetitzka drew back; her hand closed involuntarily on the hilt.

"Nay, nay," he cried, flushing under the clear brown of his skin. "'Tis not for myself. I swear it! It behoves me to give it to the venerable father."

She stared at him mute, hostile.

"Nay," he remonstrated warmly. "Glare not at me like that. I am your friend. The Abbot knows well I like

you. Come, my brother, be reasonable. I am indeed constrained thereto. You must see that. Come, be persuaded."

He held out his hand, but she clasped the weapon the
tighter. He seemed astonished, genuinely distressed. A
puzzled look overspread his face. He had the air of one
forced by circumstances to the discharge of a very disagreeable duty.

" I am your superior," he said with a gravity, a dignity,
which he had not led her to expect. " All here must
obey. Look you, I also have to obey superiors—ay, all
the brethren, for hitherto I have been the youngest. A
mere boy like you must learn obedience likewise." He
paused, then her continued silence sapping at his patience,
" Come," he said firmly, " give it to me at once."

" No."

He caught her by the shoulder.

" Oh, leave it with me!" she pleaded. " I must—I
will have it!"

" *Must! Will!* Nay, that is too much!"

Her face, white and determined in the dim light, was
raised to his. Desperation glittered in her eyes. Petros was
taken aback. Never in all his experience had there been
such a novice. In righteous indignation his grasp tightened.

" Saint Panteleemon!" he ejaculated, the blood mounting to his forehead. " You defy me! Good. We shall
see who is the stronger." And with that he began to
drag her towards the door. With all her force she resisted. But his grip was like a vice. Her feet slipped in-
effectually on the worn marble flags. Another moment and
they would reach the cloisters.

" Stay!" she panted. " I—I will give it."

" *Polycala!* That is well for you. Truly you are
obstinate. By the blessed right hand of Saint Ann, 'tis
in my mind that I ought to bring you before the venerable
father after all; 'twould be safer."

Taking possession of her yataghan, he concealed it beneath his cassock. They faced each other in the solemn
gloom. Both were still breathless from the scuffle. Now
that he had been successful, a feeling of compunction arose
in the boy's mind—a feeling almost of regret for the part
he had been forced to play, and a doubt as to whether moral
persuasion would not, after all, have been kinder and also

more suited to his dignity. He had the unsatisfactory instinct that he had gained nothing—beyond the mere possession of the weapon—by his display of brute force. His liking for her was very genuine. He hoped that he had not alienated her. He much feared it, for she stood before him, her dark eyes full of resentment, her breast still heaving, her nostrils slightly dilated, the quick colour suffusing the pale olive of her cheeks, erect, defiant, unconquered in spirit.

With a vague idea of making amends, Petros laid his hand affectionately on her arm. The unexpected sensation of roundness and softness imparted by the contact made him forget what he was about to say. His fingers squeezed the firm flesh wonderingly.

" How soft you are! " he ejaculated.

With a sudden instinctive movement Zetitzka jerked herself from his grasp.

For the moment she hated this plain-spoken young monk, hated him for exposing her weakness, for triumphing over her, for treating her with this insufferable air of kindly superiority. Tears gathered in her eyes, smarting, angry tears of vexation which took her by surprise. Disdaining to hide her emotion, she endeavoured to show a brave front, staring him full in the face, though his image blurred into the wavering background of the stalls. His astonishment and consternation were unfeigned.

" You are not crying? " he blurted.

" No," she muttered, then bit her under lip.

He eyed her in grave disapproval. " You do not speak the truth. There *are* tears in your eyes. To cry perchance is weak, but to lie is wrong."

She vouchsafed no reply. He continued to gaze at her. vaguely uncomfortable, stirred into some liveliness of remorse at the sight of her grief. A great desire to become reconciled caused him to say with unaccustomed gentleness, and in a tone of apology that made him wonder when he reflected later that he had been addressing a mere lay brother:

" Tell me, Angelos, was it because I hurt you? "

Her negative reassured him. It also restored her in his estimation, for, boy-like, he would have found it difficult to excuse tears caused merely by physical pain. Forgetful of his former rebuff, and with engaging impulsiveness, he threw his arm about her.

"Nay," he protested, half coaxingly, half insistently, as she tried to free herself, "I will *not* leave you alone! See, I am truly sorry I hurt your feelings, but verily I could not help it. You believe that? Nay, you must believe it, for it is true. We are friends still—good friends, are we not? I do not mind your being soft. You cannot help it. I suppose it is the way one is born. Here we are all born hard, but at Meteoron there is one poor brother who was born with only one eye, and it is not his fault. As for your knife, it is still yours; but I have to give it to the Abbot. He will keep it for you in his cupboard—he has some useful things of mine there. But he will permit you to look at it occasionally; take comfort in that."

CHAPTER X

SEVERAL days passed, apparently uneventfully, yet for Zetitzka full of experiences that haunted her ever afterwards. No words can portray with sufficient poignancy the bewildering effect of this old-world monastic life upon the unsophisticated mind of the mountain girl. Its austerities, its unchangeable routine, its long nightly services, its hours of slothful inertia, its lofty isolation—all seemed so many bars to freedom, in all lurked dangers unknown, from all she instinctively recoiled.

Her utter loneliness—when she allowed herself to think —appalled her. Her defencelessness—now that Petros had taken away her yataghan—struck another terrible note. Her very sex—for her the root of all personality—had become a sin which it was her one unslumbering preoccupation to conceal. The knowledge that she was surrounded by men, by possible foes, never left her. Hers were all the terrors, the shrinkings, the sudden, and often causeless alarms of the spy in continual danger of his life. But all apprehensions had to be dissembled under an exterior befitting a lay brother, a '' world-forgetting, by the world forgot,'' inmate of Barlaam.

And not the monks only, but in a lesser degree, more intangible, more inexplicable, the monastery also gave her moments of vague uneasiness. Unconsciously its immense age awed her. There was, to her mind, a grim, callous air about it, that was perhaps but the reflex of her guilty conscience. That she was the one and only woman who had dared to violate its sanctity in all these hundreds of years filled her with superstitious alarm. It looked forbidding, masculine. The low-browed buildings seemed to band themselves together to cut off her retreat, to take vengeance. The very sunshine seemed a mask, the silence a snare.

But more disquieting even than her surroundings, or the vicinity of the brethren, was the knowledge that the deed she had come to perform remained still to be done. This thought tortured her, gave her no peace. It became a fever in her blood, preying on her health, becoming visible in the pallor of her face and the hard, unnatural brightness of her eyes. It even stepped over the dividing line between day and night, goading her to wakefulness, or obsessing her mind in snatches of terror-haunted sleep.

And if Zetitzka at times shook herself free from this tyranny of impending necessity, it was due entirely to Petros.

Without the moral support of this new friend it was doubtful whether the lonely and suffering girl could have endured this abnormal life. It is more than probable that she would have broken down, or betrayed herself irrevocably. But Petros, by distracting her mind, enabled her to bear up against her anxieties. He made her initiation into her duties a personal matter. Like a child with a new toy, he was for ever seeking her out, as though it needed the testimony of his eyes, oft repeated, to convince him of her existence. With the importance of youth, he made solemn assignations with her—at the end of the cloisters two minutes before the semantron sounded; or in the windlass-tower five and a half minutes before coffee was served of a morning—and when Zetitzka, as invariably happened, failed to appear, he would seek her out and overwhelm her with good-natured reproaches.

In the blackness of midnight she would hear his eager young voice at her cell door, crying:—" Angelos, rouse thyself, Matins will begin directly." Or, in the drowsy noon-day, when all the monastery was asleep, he would seek to interest her with accounts of some saintly man— " high excelling, a pious example "—who had left tokens of his earthly sojourn behind him—some relic it might be, or remembrance of meditative hours, in flagstones worn by slowly pacing feet.

Her mental attitude towards this young monk during these days of suspense was singularly complex. He alone, as before mentioned, had the power to lighten the gloom in which she existed. Yet for this very reason she was perpetually on her guard against him. She did not want her mind distracted from the one sinister object that had forced her to visit the monastery. She wished to be alone to think, to brood, to scheme. Her task, difficult enough, God knows! was rendered even more difficult by him. But against her will, something within her welcomed this boy. This weakness, when alone, she unhesitatingly condemned. His calling, and even his costume, had not ceased to repel her. Vaguely and disquietingly aware of his appropriation of her, she fought against its effect. She desired to stand alone, to stamp out all womanly weakness, to assert her independence, to tie herself to no gratitude. That one side of her nature should play the traitor to these resolutions troubled her profoundly. It even forced her to treat the young monk with a degree of coldness which in reality she was far from feeling.

But Zetitzka found it impossible to adhere to these resolutions. The life on this remote pinnacle-top was of necessity public. The services, at which she, as well as the brethren, was forced to be present, brought her into continual contact with the other monastic inmates, as did the restricted spaces set aside for recreation. Only in her cell, at certain prescribed hours, could she hope to be alone; or, if chance favoured, in one of the subterranean passages.

Yet not for a moment did Zetitzka waver, or regard the deed she had set out to perform as other than inevitable. She knew her courage—a virtue that sat upon her lightly, almost unconsciously, as natural to her as breathing. Within her heart her wrongs still cried out insistently. That she had failed once must count for naught. She told herself valiantly, that she was sure to succeed next time.

But fate, that had at first played into Zetitzka's hands, now thwarted her at every turn. She saw Stephanos but during meals, in hours of service, or hastening from the dormitories. Speech with him at such times was liable to be overheard. Nor did his leisure hours promise more success, being passed in his cell, in wandering to and fro on the small open space that overhung the valley, or in prayer in the Catholicon. In none of these places did she feel that she could again intrude upon his privacy. The brethren, seeing her flitting about the monastery like a restless and unhappy spirit, commented upon the peculiarity, but as her work was always punctually performed she escaped reproof. Often would she lie in wait in the cloisters, or lurk in the deeper shadow of some arch, or steal noiselessly across the empty courtyard, listening **or**

6

furtively watching for the man who was never long absent
from her thoughts. But it was a weary and hopeless task,
at which many a time her soul sickened. The necessity of
nursing her wrath to keep it warm became repellent to her.
Her nature, though warped for the time being and primitive in its instincts, was large and broad-minded, capable
of generous emotions, passionate to love, and fierce to hate,
but neither revengeful nor underhand. Suffering alone
was responsible for her acquiescence in the line of conduct
that had been marked out for her. Her spirit turned from
this endless spying as from a meanness. It made her indignant with herself, angry with others, bitter against
fate.

Of what she would do did she meet him face to face she
had formed no definite idea. Without her yataghan she
was helpless. What could she, a woman and unarmed,
hope to effect against him, a man? Even should she get
the better of him with one swift and unexpected leap, a
single shout on his part would bring the entire community
to his aid. What mercy could she look for then? Brooding over it, hour by hour, she felt her heart swell with
the burning and impotent feelings of a caged lioness which,
deprived of her offspring, pining for freedom and thirsting for some courageous revenge, is met at every turn by
the iron bars of fate.

Her work was a consolation to the poor girl during these
interminable days. She scrubbed the worn mosaics and
dusted the black stalls—a lonely and pathetic figure labouring to silence thought in the gloom of the old sanctuary.
Yet often, in the midst of these mechanical occupations, the
sound of footsteps from the sunlit court, or the unexpected
appearance of one of the brethren—black in the radiance
of the porch—would cause her heart to leap.

The veneration in which Stephanos was held by his
associates amazed Zetitzka. Knowing but too well the
ignoble side of his character, she would stare incredulously
when she saw him saluted with every mark of respect, or
when his piety was commented on with reverence. Not
only did all within the monastery judge him holy, but it
was even whispered that he held converse with the saints.
But his absorption into the more austere life of the community—a life that smacked more of a mediæval past

than of the somewhat lax and semi-Oriental devotion of the present—neither deceived nor impressed Zetitzka. Bitter experience prevented her doing justice to the monks' asceticism. She was in no state of mind to appreciate it. She even made the mistake of denying its sincerity. In it she saw only lip-service and hypocrisy. There could be no true religion, she argued, in a heart such as his. It was but one and that an artificial side of his nature. Of the other she felt only an overpowering and instinctive abhorrence. That it still existed she felt convinced, led to this decision by her woman's intuition, though it would have puzzled any but an expert reader of character to see in this sainted monk the man who had turned her innocent life into an endless and unavailing regret.

" He saves his immortal soul." The whispered remark had reached her as she stood one morning outside the refectory. Two of the brethren were watching Stephanos as, like a shadow, he passed slowly across the sunshine of the court. The murmur of approbation had awakened in her a hot rebellion against the Providence that had meted out suffering to the innocent and immunity to the guilty. *His* soul, indeed! What was his soul to her! The selfishness and the cruelty of it goaded her afresh— and not these alone, but the burning injustice, the terrible power that is given to one human being to make or mar the life and happiness of another. Oh, if only she had known! If only her good saint had warned her. But no, the cup of experience had been held relentlessly to her lips; blindly she had drunk of it, and the taste of its bitterness would be with her always, all the weary and shameful days of her life.

And yet—so inextricably are the threads of tragedy and comedy interwoven in life's fabric—even in these days of anxiety there occurred incidents of an almost humorous cast. Of such was her first meeting with Brother Gerasimos.

Several mornings after her arrival she was crossing the court, having performed her duties in the Catholicon, when she caught sight of him seated in a corner of the cloisters. The dejection of his attitude gave her courage to draw near. Self-centred though she was, she could not but notice tears in his bleared little eyes. He started at the sound of her footsteps. His side-long, guilty look struck her as singular, an impression that deepened as she observed that he fell to telling his beads with an obviously feigned abstraction. Zetitzka wavered. But her instinctive dread of him as an inmate of Barlaam was forgotten at the sight of his grief.

" Are you unhappy? " she asked.

" No," he said ungraciously.

With indifference—for suffering had rendered her callous to rebuffs—Zetitzka turned away. Slowly she walked to the end of the cloisters. She stood there, showing the old monk her straight back, the length of her olive-tinted neck, and the clustering blackness of her hair.

" Come back! " snuffled a tearful voice behind her.

She was unconscious of inspection as she again approached. A moment she stood before him in silence. Brother Gerasimos appeared to be weighing something in his mind, for, still keeping his eyes on her, he bit absent-mindedly at his thumb-nail.

" If I tell you "—he said slowly—" you will not speak of it to the brethren—and by no means to Brother Nicodemus? "

Her promise visibly relieved him, yet still he seemed unable to make up his mind. At length, with an indescribable air of secrecy, he produced a fragment of a newspaper from beneath his cassock, tried in vain to read it, then wiped his red-rimmed eyes with the back of a grimy hand. So forlorn and helpless was he that, greatly to her surprise, Zetitzka was moved to compassion.

" Is it there? " she questioned kindly.

The old man blinked up into the brooding, young face, which nevertheless bent above him with a light of pity in the eyes.

" Yea, verily," he snuffled weakly; " but—but the print is bad."

Falling in with his humour, she took the paper from him and glanced at the part indicated by his forefinger. The fragment was crushed and stained almost to illegibility. It exhaled also a musty smell of groceries.

" Among the deaths? " she asked in a low voice.

He shook his head.

" Where, then? "

" Among—among the marriages."

Little by little she learned that his only niece had married, and that he had not been told of the event.

" After all," hazárded Zetitzka, gently, lured into forgetfulness of self by the sincerity of the old man's grief, " an invitation——"

" It is not that," he interrupted, gesticulating eagerly, almost angrily. " It is that I am forgotten—as if I were already dead. That is what hurts."

The silence that followed was broken by the sound of distant singing. They both listened, gazing into the empty sunlit court.

" Would you have gone to this wedding? " inquired Zetitzka, looking at his bowed figure with wonder. He gazed downwards at his naked toes, twitching in his wooden sandals.

" No," he muttered; then, in shrill and querulous indignation, " *Kyrie Eleison!* That makes no difference—none! "

" Perhaps "—Zetitzka hesitated—" perhaps the letter was lost."

His mouth opened. His eyes told of swift thought.

" Could that happen? "

She nodded.

" Then—then "—he stammered in his eagerness—" you think she has not really forgotten me? "

Her answer worked an unexpected transformation. Smiles appeared at once. He was so much of an old child, both in his sorrow and in his joy, that the mothering instinct which lurks in every woman's heart came to the fore.

" See! "—Zetitzka pointed—" there is a button off your cassock."

Brother Gerasimos fumbled at the place with helpless fingers, but his expression showed a shameless indifference to buttons.

" And see, there is a stain."

" You waste your time," he remonstrated with bland philosophy. " Scratching availeth not, neither on the raiment nor on the body."

It was perhaps characteristic of his great age that he observed neither her preoccupation nor her sadness. The

exuberance and restlessness of youth would have been unwelcome to him, so effectually had the years stranded him
on the sluggish side of life. But this lay brother, so gentle
and subdued, so appreciative a listener, and so com-
mendably sparing of speech, was indeed a God-send.
Under her influence Gerasimos warmed into unusual friendliness. He surprised himself. He beamed; he offered her
snuff; he even cracked one or two little unfamiliar jests—
jests, be it understood, as old as Barlaam, and almost as
severely monastic, but which to his simple soul were the
very acme of humour, for as they bubbled from his lips
he cackled and grew glad.

When they parted he patted her arm. There was genuine, though somewhat rusty affection in the act.

"We must talk often," he announced with relish. "I
like boys. The others"—he shrugged his shoulders—
"they—they——" He hesitated, cast a comical glance
at her out of the corner of his bleared eyes, then laughed.
His old man's chuckle struck a note of alliance so confi-
dent as to be irresistible. Nodding his head, he took a
pinch of snuff with wheezy satisfaction; then, confidentially: "After all, Angelos, we must be charitable—not
judge. You take snuff? No? Ah, to be sure, when I
was your age—not yesterday; but, as I was saying——
What was I saying?"

She guided him back.

"Was I? Well, perhaps you are right, though there
were other things, too, in my mind—multitudes of them.
By Saint Pondromos, I know not whether it be the snuff
or the talk, but I feel better already! I love talking. I
el you, I could talk about nothing for a week. *Poly-
tala!*"

CHAPTER XI

ZETITZKA was in her cell. She had returned to it quickly after the celebration of Vespers and the ninth Hour, thankful to regain its privacy. The afternoon, like all these long interminable summer afternoons, had proved intensely hot, and more than ever had the stifling and incense-laden atmosphere of the Catholicon oppressed her. A faint buzz of voices came from the court, stirring the heated air languidly, as warm water might be paddled by a listless hand.

Her head ached, a protest from a nature born and bred among hills and free uncontaminated winds against late hours and absence of ventilation. But Zetitzka was unconscious of physical pain. Her protracted mental anxiety engrossed her to the exclusion of all other sensation. Moving softly, she stole to and fro in the little bare room, setting things in order and rearranging the rug upon the divan. But her actions were involuntary, for her thoughts, as ever, were occupied in seeking some solution to the old insolvable problem. She was so weary of it all. How would it end? This strange unnatural life seemed to have claimed her body and soul. It was in reality less than a week since she had come, but it already seemed years. Her past, her mother, her child, all appeared worlds away, lost in some abyss of memory. Nothing was real but this fearsome monastery, these old monks, these long, unfamiliar services, and the haunting necessity for doing something soon.

She stood looking upwards at the window. Its tiny panes, obscured by dirt and cobwebs, dimly revealed the unclouded blue that mocked her so far beyond. She had the wish to open it, but it was far above her reach; and, moreover, it did not look as if it had ever been opened since first the monastery was built. The wan light rested softly upon her face, her melancholy dreaming eyes, and her shapely and upright figure.

Rousing herself, she crossed the cell and poured a little

water into a basin. So engrossed was she in thought that the sound of the door opening caused her to start violently. It was not Stephanos, as she, brooding upon the monk, had for the moment feared, but Sotiri; a sight sufficiently unwelcome, however, for he alone of all the monastic inmates was hostile to her, bearing her a grudge, partly because she had been allotted his work, but more especially because she had been given a cell of her own near the brethren.

In tones that betrayed resentment, he upbraided her coarsely, taunting her with being the Abbot's favourite. Then, his mood altering, he abruptly commanded her to follow him to the Catholicon. It appeared that some trivial portion of her daily task had for the first time been left undone.

But Zetitzka retorted with spirit, accusing him of breaking the rule that forbade any inmate to enter another's cell without the consent of the Hegoumenos. Alarm lent indignation to her voice.

Sotiri scowled upon her. He looked a forbidding object as he stood blocking the narrow doorway—unkempt, dirty, stupid, and intensely bigoted, a specimen of all the worst qualities bred by the Greek monastical system. Zetitzka gazed at him with open dislike.

" Will you obey? " he said menacingly.

" No," she flashed.

At the reply a malevolent grin overspread his face.

" Then I will chastise you—now."

Zetitzka looked around anxiously, but her eyes rested on nothing that could assist her. All at once her face brightened. Through the open door, over Sotiri's shoulder, she could see the old cloisters shimmering in heat, and within their shadow a black figure—Petros. But, on the point of calling him, she hesitated. Would it be wise? She recalled her doubts, her resolutions. This young monk had already obtained too much influence over her actions. She must at all costs keep her independence. Were she to appeal to him it would be a tacit acknowledgment of his right to protect her. Her destiny must be shaped by none save herself.

As these thoughts flashed across her in swift intuitive reasoning, she recognised their wisdom. Her courage came to her aid. In silence, with head erect, she faced her foe.

The lay brother cast a furtive glance along the deserted gallery, then, apparently unaware of the dark figure in the cloisters, he stepped across the threshold.

" Stand back! " cried Zetitzka sharply.

Her voice, unconsciously raised, reached Petros. As she saw him leap to his feet, a feeling of glad relief came to her. Before Sotiri could do more than grasp her arm, he was confounded by the sound of his name.

" Sotiri," panted the young monk, " how dare you! Release him at once! "

Abashed, Sotiri obeyed.

" He is idle and disobedient," he muttered, eyeing Zetitzka with ill-concealed rancour. " He feigned to know Brother Stephanos. It was a lie. He merits chastisement."

Petros listened to him with ill-concealed impatience.

" And is that reason sufficient for breaking the rules— ay, and employing unseemly violence ? Come hither! "

Reluctantly Sotiri neared him.

" Begone! " The lad pointed sternly along the gallery. " Verily the Abbot shall know of this. And look you, Sotiri "—he stopped him with a gesture—" beware how you offend again, for if so be that you touch this lad otherwise than kindly, by Saint Barlaam, I will e'en chastise you myself! "

Into the ringing tones, sonorous with newly acquired manhood, had come a sudden heat of indignation. The incident had called forth qualities other than Zetitzka had expected. She could not but admire him; for the humorous incongruity of a monk reproving violence and threatening it almost in the same breath eluded her, as it did Petros himself. When the lay brother had shambled out of sight, the boy turned to her, his expression changing to one of much goodwill.

" Now, tell me, Angelos, wherefore did he molest you ? "

But freed from danger, Zetitzka had no wish to accuse; and, moreover, she was restrained by an instinctive reluctance to be beholden to him. Something whispered to her that, of little importance though this episode seemed, it had yet brought to pass that against which she had fought. A feeling of helplessness, almost of impotence, oppressed her. Within her freedom-loving soul something rebelled.

"What were you doing?" he questioned with boyish curiosity, peering into her cell.

"I was about to wash," she said reluctantly.

His irrepressible chuckle caused her to redden; but, unaware of her embarrassment, he broke out:

"Now, verily do I perceive the reason of his wrath. Bethink you, Angelos, every drop of water has to be pumped up here from the gorge—ay, by Sotiri himself, with much heat and labour, and in the summer season it all but dries up. In sooth he was vexed." He chuckled again; then, sobering, added quickly: "But the fellow has no right to enter your cell; even I, a brother, may by no means do that. And what said he about Brother Stephanos? Was he then formerly known unto you?"

Still embarrassed, Zetitzka looked up at him furtively. She had hoped that he had forgotten the accusation. How far could she trust him? Had he asked the question before, she would not have answered him; but now his championship of her seemed to have put them on a different footing. As she felt this, she grew alarmed. More and more was she being irresistibly drawn into closer connection with this young monk.

"Tell me," he prompted good-naturedly.

"Yes. That is—that is, I did know him once. But he has forgotten me—at least, I think he has, and I don't wish to remind him."

Petros nodded. That he would have liked to have questioned further was evident, but to her relief he let the matter drop.

CHAPTER XII

In time Zetitzka came to know all the brethren—Nicodemus and Apostili, dark, gloomy men, with fierce eyes, whom she instinctively felt were to be feared—Philemon, a gentle kindly soul, whose affections, in default of human outlet, had flowed to the green world of plants, and grasses and herbs, and whose dearest treasures were a few weakly bulbs nursed with infinite solicitude in pieces of broken crockery; Johannes, silent, white-haired, a mystic and a seer; Elias, the Martha of the monastery, much taken up with the little things of this life; and yet others, for Barlaam possessed in all twelve monks, though there were cells for nearly double that number.

Had it not been for the anxiety that weighed her down, Zetitzka might have taken pleasure in the conversation of the more gentle-mannered among them; but, as matters were, she sought to avoid them all.

Service over, and Petros successfully eluded, she would hasten to her cell, or seek some spot that seemed to promise seclusion. The subterranean passages lent themselves best to concealment. Carved out of the solid rock upon which the monastery was built, they led through gloom, save where, at rare intervals, an opening gave sight of the sunlit world below. More than any other part of the monastery did these passages speak of desolation. They were eloquent with voiceless memories, for as Zetitzka groped her way along them, she came upon little cells hollowed here and there, that even to her preoccupied mind told of hermit occupants long since crumbled into dust.

Here it was that one afternoon she had sought shelter. Seated on the ground where sunlight flooded the passage, her arms encircling her knees, she remained for long motionless. The air, warm as a caress, quivered up to her from the depths. Around her the rocks burned the touch, but, immersed in dreams, she suffered no inconvenience from the heat. Peace and profound silence inundated the

monastery. To one unaccustomed to the voicelessness of
the heights, this absolute cessation from all sound came as
a sort of shock—a hungering of the ears that would not be
satisfied. Thrust upwards into the light, drugged by day-
long draughts of fire, the little monastery dozed and
dreamed under the unchanging blue of the sky. Seen, as
it were a picture through a dark framework of rock, the
distance trembled faintly.

Sitting thus, Zetitzka forgot for awhile the weight that
oppressed her. Outwards, into the kindly sunlight, her
thoughts escaped as birds through the door of a cage. Her
heart fled to the hills—the high hills! She could see them
far off, veiled in lights that quivered, and in shadows that
veered. They spoke to her of home. With semi-closed
eyes she watched a cloud trail its draperies over the naked
shoulders of the mountains—then a point of incomprehensible brightness that held attention like a gleaming eye
—and, finally, some huge upland form, that, heaving itself
above its neighbours, stared backward into Albania.

Albania! Her native land! Never before had it been so
dear! Never before had all that it meant to her come so
close to her heart! Her desires outstripping sight, she
sought to pierce beyond the blue barriers to the little village that nestled in some remoter hollow of the hills. Longings and apprehensions connected with her child beset
her; and, as she gazed, her heart dumbly yearning within
her eyes, the far hills swam in tears.

Still she sat motionless, with locked fingers. Many
thoughts came to her, memories of her childhood, all seeming inconceivably happy and remote. With a wistful sadness she recalled her girlish dreams of love and of a possible lover, vague, timid, beautiful. How they had misled
her! A shrinking delicacy of mind had robbed her of
the knowledge that might have aided. Her ignorance had
been her undoing. Following the instincts of her heart,
she had not wished to pry into life. Love was a holy
mystery. It would come in its own good time.

Zetitzka looked back upon the Zetitzka of the past as
upon a person with whom she had nothing in common,
whose motives appeared now almost incomprehensible, yet
for whose weakness she was doomed to pay the utmost
penalty.

What had induced her to imagine herself in love with Stephanos? She asked herself this in amazement, in profound self-contempt.

As she sat semi-dreaming, Zetitzka brooded over it all darkly, with pained perplexity. She could not understand. Life was then cruel, and love a horror, an insult? It all hurt. Were all men like this? Was there no God to avenge? Did women always suffer? Once she had been so happy, so unsuspecting! Why had this man not left her alone? Why? Why?

Suddenly a faint sound came reverberating along the passage. Always more or less consciously on the alert, Zetitzka started to her feet, and, as the sounds continued to draw near, glided swiftly into one of the rude caves hollowed out of the inner wall of the passage. The movement was instinctive, promoted more by a state of mind that shunned companionship, than by fear of whoever it might be. From her place of concealment, she commanded the tunnel, and, owing to the darkness, could see without being seen.

Barely had she taken cover than a monk came into sight, walking slowly with bowed head. As he paused in the shaft of light, she recognised Stephanos. His back was towards her, but in the intense stillness she heard the thick click of his wooden rosary beads.

As ever, when forced to encounter this man, she was seized with indignation and loathing. But after her first inward gasp, she stood stock-still, watching him with wide fascinated eyes.

He remained almost without movement, his black figure in its sombre draperies sharply delineated against the strong light that streamed through the rock-hewn doorway. In the heart of the immense cliff, subterranean though lifted high above the earth, the silence was of the grave.

The moments seemed years to Zetitzka. An insufferable sense of oppression overpowered her. She stood transfixed, tormented by emotions almost beyond control. But as he continued to stand there, and as her agitation increased, a swift and terrible suggestion came to her. It was less a thought than one of those sudden mysterious promptings of subconscious mind occupying itself with the

solution of an old dilemma. It whispered: "If he goes
to the verge, one push will do it."

Zetitzka's heart stood still, then began to hammer in
her breast. Her blood, suspended for a breathless second,
rushed upwards—she felt it inundating her brain, singing
loudly in her ears. Would he go? Dear Saints! For
patience! for strength! Cold sweat broke out upon her as
she lurked in the blackness; her eyes, her attention, her
every sentient possibility—all riveted themselves upon the
man with a concentration so painful in its intensity that
her very existence seemed to hang upon his moving that
one little yard. And all the while her mind was scheming, planning—she would dart out, avoiding that stone,
that hole, four swift steps would suffice, then—O God! One
push!

He moved. Zetitzka's fingers twisted themselves in the
folds of her tunic.

For a moment it seemed as if he intended to follow the
passage; then, as though acting under some sudden impulse,
he slowly approached the brink.

She could now see him standing on the unprotected
verge, black against the dazzle beyond. A fierce exultation leapt to her heart. At last he was in her power. Now
was the time—now!

Not daring to breathe, Zetitzka crept forward. Stealthily
she neared him. He did not move. Her eyes were fixed
on his back. Her wild and lawless blood inflamed her to
the deed. This was the opportunity for which she had
watched, and waited, and schemed. One push, but one,
and she would rid herself of this man for ever. The
silence grew sinister; all nature seemed to hold its breath.

Within a yard of her victim she stopped, and, concentrating all her courage, all her resolution, nerved herself
for the fatal thrust.

God! What was that? An inhuman voice rang in the
darkness—staying her hand, freezing her blood—the iron
voice of the semantron, screaming its metallic warning to
the man upon the precipice brink.

Stephanos, turning abruptly, met her face to face.

"What do you want?" he ejaculated in surprise.

His deep and painfully familiar voice struck a chill to
her heart. It forced her to think of him as an imminent

danger, yet as one who had mysteriously receded beyond reach of her vengeance. An immense discouragement fell upon her.

Instinctively she had backed into the shadow, influenced not by fear, but by aversion. Still the monk held her with gloomy questioning eyes.

" Why don't you answer? " he demanded sternly; then, as she remained tongue-tied, " You are the new lay brother? "

Her reluctant affirmative barely reached him; indeed, it is doubtful if he heard, for, averting his head, he muttered incoherently into his beard.

Unconsciously relieved by his strange preoccupation, Zetitzka looked at him steadily with a concentrated hostility, noting little things about him, each with a shock of uneasy aversion, so clearly and so poignantly did each recall the past. Her eyes wandered from his heavy overhanging eyebrows to a curious red birth-mark upon his left temple. She remembered the latter well, and how it became a vivid crimson when he grew excited. He had aged much. His hair, beneath his tall black hat, attracted her notice. She had thought of it as short and black, and behold, it was long and grey! New and deep lines had graven themselves across his face. His cassock hung loosely upon his gaunt frame. Only in his hollow eyes, now fixed apparently upon space, there lurked the fires of a feverish vitality.

It was the first time they had spoken together since that ill-omened day of parting, and the tumultuous and torturing thoughts to which it gave rise flooded her heart and flamed in her eyes like signals of distress. To be so near him—to hear his voice—to recollect all—to feel again the anguish of the old incurable wound—and to know that he had escaped her—each and every one of these seemed to be a hand thrusting her relentlessly into some depth of unplumbed despair.

" Why did you seek me? "

As he asked the question he raised his head. Zetitzka found, to her surprise and relief, that she could listen to him with a certain detachment—that his old domination over her was gone. But, as she continued to look at him, it flashed to her mind that he was the father of her child. This enforced relationship, this inexorable connection between the being she loved and the being she hated filled her with an almost incredulous consternation. As she shrank from it a solitary consolation leapt to her heart. She recalled their parting. He did not then know the tie that was destined to bind them together. He was doubtless still in ignorance. That secret, at all events, was her own. She hugged the assurance to her breast. If it depended upon her, he should never know—never, never.

" Why did you seek me? " he questioned again.

The words were inoffensive, but the hard frown of his eyes imparted to them a weight of intolerable suspicion. That she should be thus insolently interrogated, and by him, left her speechless.

"Answer at once," he commanded, in sudden anger.

An instinct told Zetitzka that were she to speak, as speak she must, he would instantly recognise her. All fear of the inevitable exposure, however, vanished, swept out of sight by the violence of her passions. But before she could give vent to the volume of living anger that blazed in her heart, there came a swift change. Incredible though it may seem, he had forgotten her! She noticed with dumb amazement that his attention had shifted to the wall immediately behind her back. Into his weary hollow eyes had come the expression that had so often filled her with uneasiness—the hunted look of one who flees in vain from the terrors of an offended conscience.

Half turning, Zetitzka followed with awe his fascinated gaze. Upon the dark face of the rock some long-forgotten hermit had scrawled a cross, a rude thing, but two streaks of white paint still shining dimly in the obscurity.

Wholly oblivious of her, in silence, Stephanos raised trembling fingers to his breast and forehead. Then, as she stood in the deep shadow, mutely observant, he moved slowly away into the inner darkness of the passage, his head sunk to his chest, lost to everything save his own tormented thoughts.

CHAPTER XIII

It was the custom of Dimitri the muleteer to visit the Meteora monasteries just so often as business led his steps in their direction. Sometimes he escorted travellers thither—strangers of diverse nationalities who paid him in good Greek notes; at others, he conveyed merchandise to the monks, oil in barrels, bags of flour from the little mill on the Peneios, or vegetables from the village gardens. Once in a great while he acquired distinction by officiating as postman.

One bright morning Dimitri set out for Hagios Barlaam. His gay swagger was even more pronounced than usual, for, in addition to a load strapped upon the back of Nikola, his mule, was he not the bearer of a parcel addressed to the Hegoumenos?

It had not been without difficulty that he had rescued the latter from the grip of the postal authorities at Kalabaka. The curiosity of the fat postmaster had come perilously near to breaking the string, the sealing-wax, and the eighth commandment! Not he alone, but likewise the chemist, the innkeeper, and even the one ornamental *gendarme,* had in turns endeavoured to deduct the contents from the feel of the brown paper—but Dimitri had carried it off with a laugh.

" Find out what is in it, and tell us when you return," cried the chemist after him.

" Do not forget the two pesetas tax," shouted the postmaster.

The little group watched him indolently as he swung up the village street, his white fustinella snapping in the breeze, and Nikola two paces in front picking her way daintily over the stones.

" A popular fellow," mused the innkeeper; " he would make a bar pay."

" M—m," doubted the postmaster, a half-smoked but unlighted cigarette between his lips. " M—m—that is—

look you, if he did not drink all the profits. Yes, a good
fellow, but to my mind too leave-alone—too—— Blessed
Saint Nicholas! You have seen—all of you. He did not
even seem to care what was in that parcel! ''

The *gendarme* wagged his cocked hat.

'' You *would* choose a bachelor,'' he said; then added
sententiously, '' Bachelors are too happy.''

'' True,'' sighed the chemist, thoughtfully twirling his
wedding-ring. '' But,'' he added hopefully, '' he is young.
He may still marry.''

'' 'Twill not be the fault of the girls if he remain single,''
said the innkeeper; '' any one of them would jump at
him.''

'' I—am not so sure of that,'' objected the *gendarme*,
who was father of two.

'' *Jump*,'' repeated the innkeeper, emphasising his statement so unexpectedly with his pipe-stem on the table that
the *gendarme* involuntarily obeyed. '' But he! 'Tis a
smile to one and a jest with another, and away he goes
singing with his mule. Bah! ''—he snapped his fingers—
'' he has never been really in love in his life. Now—at
his age, I——'' He broke off with modest and far-away
smiles.

'' Muleteers are like that,'' assented the postmaster. '' I
have in my time employed three. All were unaccountable.
It comes from being so much with brute beasts. To see
him on a rock! You would say: ' a mule!' Thank
Heaven! ''—he gazed complacently upon his ample stomach
—'' I am no mule! ''

'' Yet he is a good son,'' mused the chemist. '' I have
known him all his life; and never once, since his father
died, has he grudged his mother medicine.''

'' Maybe he wants to poison her! '' tittered the *gendarme*,
who was a bit of a wag.

'' Poison her! '' The chemist snorted indignantly.
'' Would I sell him anything to poison her! No, indeed,
'tis his excellent heart; he always pays me ready money.
I wish ''—here he transfixed the *gendarme* with a meaning
eye—'' I wish all sons followed his example.''

But the *gendarme* was gazing abstractedly at his boots.

Meanwhile Dimitri was climbing the rocky path that
led to the monasteries. The day was sultry. The mule-

teer was constrained to unbutton his shirt and push back
the little round cap that sat so jauntily upon his head.
In his picturesque dress—manly, athletic, good-looking—
he formed an attractive addition to the landscape. As he
climbed he smoked a cigarette and hummed a ditty between closed lips.

His progress was not rapid—Nikola saw to that.

Already the pinnacles of Meteora shimmered through a
haze of heat. The shadows of man and mule shouldered
before them, black on the white dust of the track.

" Ai—i—eah! " cried Dimitri, wiping the sweat from
his face.

Nikola had stopped—her sides heaving.

" Come, old lady," remonstrated her master. " You
slept all day yesterday. You eat too much. You become
fat. Come! We must be there before eight o'clock. The
flies pester you, eh? Well, then, what has the good God
given you a tail for? Another effort—ah, gently! you
will loosen the straps."

Neither master nor mule gave the scenery a thought.
Why should they? Had they not known it all their lives?
Others—travellers for the most part—exclaimed loudly and
asked many foolish questions, with sudden halts trying alike
to Nikola's mouth and Dimitri's patience—but to them
it was part of their lives. When the great pinnacles
flashed at dawn, it was time to take the road; when the
crests grew death-like and grey, it was time to go home.
That was all. Yet each had their preferences. Nikola
preferred a certain secluded part of the ravine midway
between Barlaam and Triada. There dwarf oaks grew, and
a trough filled miraculously with ever running water was
to be enjoyed. She remembered this spot even before it
came into sight, and invariably quickened her step. If she
could put enough road between herself and her master she
drank deep—a forbidden pleasure; if not, she snatched at
the leaves as she walked and munched them greedily.

Dimitri, for his part, preferred the monasteries. The
monks amused him hugely. Their *mastica,* too, was an
excellent drink—trust them for that! It was pleasant to
loaf in the sunlight of the courts, smoke innumerable cigar-
ettes, and banter the brethren; pleasant, too, to stand on
the precipice brink with the village of Kalabaka a sheer

thousand feet below, and admire the microscopic proportions of his own cottage.

When—having anchored Nikola to a stone in the gorge—
Dimitri reached the top of the ladders, he found Brothers
Nicodemus and Gerasimos in the tower of the windlass.
This was a favourite haunt of the brethren. One or more
might often be seen gazing listlessly outwards and downwards. The little shell of a hut was as aerial an outlook
as the car of a drifting balloon. From it the eyes ranged
over the chaos of cliffs intersected by ravines to the far
plains of Thessaly. The brethren took a contemplative
pleasure in gazing into the distance. It fed the Oriental
quietism that saturated their lives. Under its soporific influence they rarely spoke. Occasionally one black-
robed figure, leaning over the rail, motionless, would be
heard to mutter—another would reply—then back would
they sink into inanition, and the silence would close in as
though it had never been broken.

"*Calamera sas,*" cried Dimitri in cheery greeting.

"*Ora calee,*" responded Nicodemus drowsily, while
Gerasimos blinked at the new-comer like a venerable owl
disturbed in its slumbers.

"I have brought you some flour," announced the muleteer. "I put it in the net. You had better pull it up."

The brethren looked at the windlass, which, with its
four great arms, occupied the centre of the ramshackle hut.
Gerasimos yawned.

"If we send for Sotiri—or Brother Petros," he suggested
faintly.

Dimitri laughed. Echoes repeated the jovial sound.

"Out of the way!" he cried, flinging off his little embroidered jacket. With creaks and groans the windlass
began to revolve.

"I admire strength," said Gerasimos.

"Prayer is better," reproved Nicodemus. "I was
strong once; to look at me you would have said—' an ox! ' "

Gerasimos opened his mouth with amazement.

"I was puffed up with pride of my thews and sinews,"
continued Nicodemus solemnly, " recking not in my folly
that all flesh is as grass, but God opened my eyes, and—here
I am."

"Past all doubt," agreed Gerasimos, nodding his tall

hat; then to the muleteer, who was lustily working the windlass—" What sing you, Dimitri? "

" The song of the road."

" But—methought I heard mention of arms! "

" Ay, two soft arms at the journey's end—so runs it."

" A man of sin," groaned Nicodemus, highly scandalised. -

" But," objected Gerasimos, a puzzled look on his simple face, " what did they at the journey's end? I fail to comprehend——"

" Better so," interrupted Nicodemus sourly.

Upwards—out of the beating sunshine into the cool shadow of the hut—swung the bag of flour. The monks seized it as it oscillated over space, and with one jerk drew it inwards. It fell on the rude flooring, and a cloud of white dust drifted through the doorway. The two old men —their duty done—returned to the bench. Their sombre attire, bent shoulders, and white beards contrasted forcibly with the gay dress and gallant carriage of their companion.

" Anything new? " questioned Dimitri, then with a laugh —" I am a fool—nothing ever happens here."

The brethren exchanged meaning glances.

" We have news," announced Nicodemus, swelling with importance.

" Yes, indeed," corroborated Gerasimos, rubbing his hands.

" I also have news," cried the muleteer, not to be outdone.

" What? " questioned Nicodemus. " A betrothal in Kalabaka, belike? Bah! We have heard of it already. Nay? What then? "

" Perhaps a death? " suggested Gerasimos pleasantly.

" They have broken their windlass rope at Meteoron," announced the muleteer. " Ay, as they were drawing up the net."

" Holy Virgin! " exclaimed the monks with one voice.

" Anyone killed? " piped Gerasimos.

" Worse," sighed Dimitri, inwardly delighted at the sensation he was creating.

" How worse? "

" A cask of wine smashed. I saw the spot myself—the

good wine all red on the rocks. Had it been a monk——"
He snapped his fingers with gay unconcern.

"Impious fellow!" frowned Nicodemus. "Have you
no veneration?"

"For *you?* None. Nay, scowl not at me—I have been
to Volo. I have heard——"

"What have you heard?" snapped Nicodemus.

"Nothing that I well recall. Some talk maybe in the
market; perhaps a lie. They say that the monks here——"

"All holy men!"

"Humph! But useless; are to be done away with, and
that convicts are to be put in their place. By the Virgin!—" his eyes roved speculatively over the ravines—
"They will be clever devils if they manage to escape from
Barlaam."

If there be one thing in the world at which the monks
of Meteora writhe, it is this very rumour. In a tense,
indignant whisper Brother Nicodemus explained to Dimitri
that as a malignant liar he was damned past all hope of
redemption. Gerasimos, equally moved, strove to insert
saints edgeways.

"Gently, gently, brothers," interposed the muleteer.
"Did I say it of myself. I would be sorry—look you,
my business would be gone. Convicts are not brought
up upon oil, I take it. Ay, and more. I would miss the
Abbot—and you twain know well if I care for Brother
Petros!"

"You are no fit companion for him," growled Nicodemus.

Dimitri shrugged his broad shoulders.

"I do him no harm; nay, I do him good—a jest is
worth a dozen pistevos. Have I not known him since a
child—Peste! I remember well the first time I saw him!
I gave him a ride on one of my mules; it did one good to
hear him laugh. Poor little rat!"

"Keep your pity!" Nicodemus turned a scornful
shoulder. "The lad is happy; he has chosen the better
part. And as for friends—he lacks none—all love him
here."

"Ay, do they," corroborated Gerasimos warmly.

"And Brother Stephanos?" grinned Dimitri. "He
loves him, I warrant!"

"Speak not of him. You are not worthy to clean his sandals. Brother Petros holds him in seemly veneration, as do all in the monastery."

The muleteer spat sceptically. For awhile no one spoke. Gerasimos, his head tilted backwards, drifted into the easy slumber of old age, while Nicodemus clicked his beads and stared with unseeing eyes into the sunlight. From the inner court came faint sounds of life—a far-off voice calling, then silence, broken only by the creaking of old woodwork in the heat. Far below one could see a herd of goats, a small and slowly-moving object in the glaring dust of the track.

"Where is the lad?" said Dimitri abruptly.

"Within," mumbled Nicodemus. "I saw him but now with——" he turned swiftly to his friend—"Brother—Brother Gerasimos, I say!"

"Hai! hai!" cried Gerasimos, scrambling to his feet. "Is it time for Matins? What is this? Dimitri still here! Blessed Pondromos! I dreamed I was in the Catholicon."

"We have forgotten to tell him our news!"

"So we have! Tell him, brother."

"We have a new inmate," announced Nicodemus, complacently stroking his beard.

"He came three days agone," piped Gerasimos, unable to keep silence. "He is young and well favoured—younger even than Brother Petros. And it is his pious wish to join our blessed community. God be praised! *Polycala!*"

"Ay, and he and Brother Petros are much together. You see, your pity is wasted; if the lad were not happy he would not laugh."

"I will seek him," cried Dimitri, and he swung away into the shadow.

CHAPTER XIV

SEATED in a rocky niche that edged the precipice, Zetitzka was deep in thought. So near was she to the void that from a little distance she appeared to be over-hanging the abyss. Her entire background, viewed from the monastery, consisted of immense space, the depth of shimmering valley, and the faint quivering substance of far-off hills. Her attitude told of dejection; the drooping head, the listless pendent hands, the general air of lassitude and *abandon* all testified to the immense depression of her spirits.

Sunlight enveloped her. It poured its liquid fire upon her head, unprotected save for the small lay brother's cap, emphasised the blue lights in her hair, touched the soft contour of one olive-tinted cheek.

She had almost abandoned hope. That Stephanos should escape her twice was a calamity that had upset all her calculations. Not that, had other things been equal, her perseverance would have been thus easily vanquished, but her second failure had implanted superstitious fears within a mind ever prone to credit the supernatural. It had come to her suddenly that there must be forces fighting for the monk against which, with all her courage, she was powerless. What these forces were, she knew not, but she surmised them to be connected with the monastery that had given him shelter, and with the miraculous icon that had watched over his safety in the Catholicon.

For the first time since she had undertaken the grim task, doubts oppressed her. The events of the preceding day had plunged her into a black despondency from which it seemed that nothing could arouse her. She felt bewildered—helpless. She knew not where to turn. If the present were full of danger, the future was simply unthinkable. As long as Stephanos lived she dare not go home. As little dare she continue to remain in this monastery.

Roused suddenly by the sound of footsteps in that place where all sound seemed a desecration, Zetitzka raised her head.

Dimitri had halted in surprise. The lad before him was undoubtedly the new inmate of whom the monks had spoken, but the reality was so far removed from his expectations that it set him wondering.

"Umph!" he grunted to himself, as he again moved forward, "there is one at all events who has made a mistake."

It had been in his mind merely to inquire the whereabouts of Petros, but something unusual and interest-compelling in the face before him made him forget the question.

He hailed her with a friendly smile.

"You are new here, eh?" he asked genially, seating himself by her side. Zetitzka, but half-aroused from sombre thoughts, murmured an apathetic affirmative.

"You wonder who I am?" he went on easily, with the entire lack of self-consciousness that invariably put others at their ease. "Well, that is soon told; I am the muleteer in these parts. You will see me often, for I come up to the monasteries nearly every day—not always to Barlaam, of course, though I like this one best. Now you, my friend," he eyed her with frank curiosity, "whence come you?"

Zetitzka moved uneasily. In her mountain village the sexes were somewhat rigorously kept apart. To be addressed as a comrade by this very masculine individual made her feel shy and awkward. If she had acted upon instinct she would have run away.

"Well," he said smilingly, "have you forgotten?"

Reflecting that this man was no monk, and probably had little to do with the monastery, she named the village in which her parents lived. The muleteer smacked his leg.

"I know it," he cried. "I thought you must be Albanian by your accent. Yes. I have been there. Oh! many years ago, and only once, for it is out of my beat. The Khan overlooks a little torrent that makes a devil of a noise in spring."

He continued to talk pleasantly. Zetitzka found herself listening to him with a troubled interest, occasionally raising her long-fringed lashes to steal a look at him, noting his open countenance, his easy gestures, his gay, careless manner. She could not but like him, and wondered what he would do if he knew she were a girl, and whether, with all his kindliness, he would help her.

All at once he broke off, yawned, and began to mop his forehead on which the damp curls were plastered stickily.

" 'Tis too hot here," he objected; " if we go over there? "

She followed him reluctantly into the shade, for within her heart she longed to be alone. With deft fingers her companion rolled and lighted a cigarette.

" I know someone from your village," he said between puffs, " Nik Leka, the lame pedlar."

Zetitzka listened uneasily. Already she repented of her frankness.

The muleteer chuckled in reminiscence.

" He bet me a knife once that I would not jump across the rocks above the waterfall. You know the place I mean—a mile above Kastrati? No? Well, never mind, I have the knife still. You know him? "

" Yes."

" A droll fellow; a bear, one might say, but a bear with a kind heart—when not doing business. He travels farther than I—no regular beat. A fine life; a man is his own master, no mules, only his own legs to consider. Though one of his must take a lot of consideration, for it is always crying halt! " He chuckled again, then, looking thoughtfully at her, added, " I wonder now that you never thought of peddling? "

She did not reply.

" You are too young to come here." In his blue eyes there was unaffected and somewhat wondering interest. A moment he paused, then asked abruptly: " Why did you come? "

Again she knew not what to say. Dimitri smiled.

" Well—never mind," he said lightly, pitching a stone into space. "Perhaps I can tell. Oh, no cause for fear. You can trust me—though I dare swear you have told it all ere this to the monks in confession. No? "

Despite her efforts at self-control she could not help flushing.

" I am like that myself," continued the muleteer, with fellow feeling, " though it never went so far as to cause me to enter a monastery."

" But——" she faltered. " I do not understand——"

" Not understand? Peste! Why play the simpleton? Look you——" He would have laid his hand on her shoulder, but instinctively she avoided him. " Look you," he continued, unheeding her movement, "there are two good things that can be made bad things—money and women. Money has never come my way—' one does not find pesetas in the hoof of a mule,' as the saying is, but a man does not live to be thirty without knowing something about women. Now you—from the first moment I saw you I knew what was the matter—I said to myself ' Dimitri, there is a woman in this case.' "

She would have contradicted him, but self-consciousness tied her tongue.

" Aha! " he exclaimed triumphantly, twirling his little moustache. " I am right. Oh, how could it be otherwise! For, between ourselves, in spite of these grave-clothes—" he plucked gaily at the hem of her dingy tunic —" you are not exactly ill-looking. Nay, turn not away! " He surveyed her flushing face with a twinkle. " But, my friend, you have made a mistake—yes, the great mistake of taking a woman too—too seriously. Oh, think not that I wish to malign them! By the Saints, no! My diffi-culty is I love them all. But I do not make your mistake —no; kiss and forget, that is what I say, for if a man does more he is sorry for it—afterwards."

" You are wrong," she cried, roused at last into con-tradiction.

He raised his eyebrows. She continued vehemently:

" You are wrong. It is men who are not worth it. They do all the harm. They do not care how much they make women suffer."

Dimitri's bronzed face expressed bewilderment. His eyes wandered in unfeigned astonishment from the gesticulating hands to the flushed cheeks that betrayed the emotions she could not repress.

" So! " he muttered, " you think that, do you? "

But Zetitzka, her burst over, took refuge in silence.

They both sat awhile without speaking; Dimitri thinking with unusual seriousness, Zetitzka, with averted head, striving to master her agitation. Around them brooded the great peace of the monastery—warm, sunlit, silent, steeping all things in slumber like some ancient spell.

" My friend," began the muleteer, " you have surprised me. After all, 'tis none of my business. That reminds me—I have a parcel—where shall I find the Abbot? "

She directed him in a low voice, her eyes downcast.

" Good." He rose to his feet. " I will seek him and Brother Petros too. This place makes one sleepy. Now—you—you bear me no ill-will, eh? "

She shook her head.

" That is well. Shall we say a glass of *mastica?* I could drink up the Peneios to-day—if it flowed *mastica!* You will get it in the refectory. Ah, you have found it out already? I might have known it! Not so fast—a full glass, do not forget."

He called the last words after her as she crossed the sunlit space, then watched until she entered the little low-browed door. When she was no longer to be seen he scratched his head. His face told that he had by no means recovered from his astonishment.

CHAPTER XV

STEPHANOS was on his knees engaged in flagellation. Seen by the imperfect light of a small wick floating in oil, his naked back was crossed and recrossed by dark lines. In front of him, upon the wall of his cell, hung a crucifix, a work of early Byzantine art.

So engrossed was the monk in his occupation that for some time he was unaware that the Abbot had entered the cell and was gazing down at him.

Shrinking pity, tinged curiously with an awestruck and even reverential admiration, filled the spectator's mind. Tales and legends of holy men, hermits, martyrs, and even saints, who had thus mortified the body to the everlasting glory of the soul passed before him, with no precision of detail, but only as creating a halo of veneration within which he saw this act of Stephanos.

The Abbot had suspected this. Once before he had heard the muffled sound of blows, and on more than one occasion had he seen the monk wince when chafed by his cassock. But the aged priest had little of the grim mediæval spirit that took delight in self-torture. His was a more enlightened belief, a gentler and more humane religion, strange considering his surroundings. This want of appreciation, however, he unhesitatingly condemned, judging it to be weakness and backsliding, and succeeded so well in creating an artificial mental atmosphere, that he venerated Stephanos as one in whose presence the monastery was indeed blest, a man of God, an example to all, even a future worker of miracles, a saint.

Pausing in his self-inflicted punishment, Stephanos looked up at his superior. He presented a miserable spectacle; his eyes bloodshot; his chest, covered with black hair, glistening with perspiration; his coarse and naked feet protruding from beneath the folds of his cassock.

"My son," said the Abbot in a voice that mingled unaffected humility with his office and authority, "is there need for this?"

" Ay," groaned the monk wearily, " only thus can I drive out the devil."

The old man seated himself upon the low divan. " Tell me," he said.

For some time he waited; but, as Stephanos seemed unable to obey, he began :—

" You, my son, so worthy——"

" *Worthy!* " interrupted the monk with sudden and intense bitterness. " If you but knew!——"

" Tell me," repeated the Abbot.

Stephanos pushed his long and matted hair from before his eyes. Still on his knees, he began to crawl slowly and painfully to the old man's side. There was something pitiable and even bestial in his appearance. The Abbot, bending to bless him, suddenly drew back.

" Blood! Holy Mother! You are all wet with it! "

" Would I could lash out every drop! It might wash away my sins."

" Human blood will not do that, my son."

The head of Stephanos drooped to his chest, then jerked upwards. When he closed his eyes he saw the flames that never went out.

The cell was very quiet. Everything within it looked shadowy, unreal. The calm face of the Christ, lit by the tiny wick, shone transfigured.

" Yes? " encouraged the Abbot.

" Dreams," whispered the monk.

" We all have dreams."

" But mine are evil spirits; they—they tempt me."

" But—you resist? " There was anxiety in the question.

" No. I fall—in thought—not once, often. They bring back my sin. Do you understand? I do it again. I—I *wallow* in it! "

His voice expressed remorse and self-loathing. The old priest looked at him with infinite sympathy.

" I know," he murmured, half below his breath.

" You do *not* know! " cried Stephanos with sudden passion. Then, with an apologetic gesture as he caught a glance of mingled surprise and disapproval on the Abbot's face :—" Forgive me, venerable father, but you—you have lived here always—all your life. You have fought the flesh—but have you fought things—things you remember— things you have done—that—that——" he broke off; then, after a pause, during which he stared fixedly on the floor, he continued with bitterness: " I have sinned even by coming here. I thought to escape—but I see now that one cannot do that, not till one rots in the grave."

The old man looked at him and marvelled.

" If his soul have need of this, how much greater need has mine," was his thought. With veneration, even as one seeking spiritual good touches the feet of a saint, he laid a hand on the monk's naked shoulder. Stephanos shrank back.

" Do not touch me! " he said wildly. " If you knew you would spit at me. I am a lie. I am a reproach to the monastery. Nay, you don't know me—none of them knows me; not one! I will tell you what I am—a monk with the heart of a profligate. Well," he gazed at the Abbot with a sombre and defiant stare, " you despise me now."

" Despise you? I? God forbid! I but respect you the more."

Stephanos betrayed the heat of sudden irritation.

" You do not understand," he protested, gesticulating with his naked arms. " You make of me a whited sepulchre. But the fault is mine—ay, and the guilt. I can bear it no longer. Listen. I will tell all."

" Alack! " thought the Abbot, " he is distraught. Vigils and fasts have worn out the feeble body." Aloud he said: " Come, my son, sit here."——

By any other of the brethren the invitation would have been esteemed an honour, but Stephanos muttered a refusal. The Abbot, however, reaching out a hand, raised the peni- tent and sate him by his side on the divan.

" Take time, Brother Stephanos," he said in a studiously matter-of-fact voice; then, having snuffed and blowing the brown grains from his fingers, " perhaps, to-morrow——"

" No," pleaded the monk, with a return of his irrational excitement, " to-morrow may be too late. *Now*."

There was a silence.

All at once Stephanos began to speak.

" I have deceived you. That is part of my sin. You thought me holy. I allowed you to think so. I am the worst of sinners."

A gentle incredulity shone in the old priest's eyes.

Stephanos continued: " You never asked why I came here."

" Did I not? Yet I remember well we spake thereof. You fled from the world."

" I fled "—he paused with bowed head, and hands knotted together—" I fled from a *woman*."

He uttered the last word with extraordinary rancour. So full of animosity was his tone, so unpleasantly did it jar on the Abbot's humour, that the old man was conscious of a sudden warning of sympathy. Accounting this a weakness, he pressed the monk's hands between his own with additional kindness.

" Do not tremble, my son. Be comforted. Your conscience is clear. I know all."

" You do not know all. I tell you I deceived you. I kept it from you even in the confessional."

The Abbot withdrew his hands. Stephanos did not move. The flickering candle-light shone upon the old man's face, revealing its agitation.

" This sin you speak of—you did not conceal it when you took the Lesser Habit? "

The monk bowed his head in assent.

The Abbot gazed with incredulity at the culprit. He recalled how he had given absolution to this man upon his entry into Barlaam. For a moment he was lost in bewilderment, for never before had such an offence come under his notice. To his simple and truthful mind it appeared impossible. Then, in a wave, came grief and a sense of bitter personal disappointment. Rising, he crossed the cell, and fell on his knees before the crucifix. There ensued a few minutes of tense silence, then the Abbot pressed his lips to the relic, crossed himself devoutly, regained his feet, and looked down at Stephanos.

" Tell me," he said, " tell me all."

The monk quailed at his tone. But even as his conscience shrank, there came to him strength born of his wild and disordered imagination. Raising his head, he stared his superior full in the face. His eyes betrayed no fear, though darkened by sombre shadows.

For a full minute he sat silent, collecting his thoughts. Then in short and broken sentences, that gave his listener the impression of violent agitation imperfectly restrained, he burst forth:

"I lived alone in a hut on the outskirts of an Albanian village. I was partly Greek—I had books—I killed no one—that was enough for them—they despised me. My God! The very children threw stones. May Satan——"

The Abbot silenced him with a gesture, and asked, "Why did you continue to live there?"

"One place is as another. I was a trader once, and have seen cities, but God told me to forsake my calling and to worship Him apart. I was in Albania when His Voice reached me, so I stayed."

He fingered the lash absently, muttered incoherently, then tossed his dishevelled head.

"Continue," said the Abbot.

With an effort Stephanos obeyed.

"I tilled the ground. I had saved money, and one requires little to eat."

"True," assented the Abbot.

"God was with me," continued the monk in an awe-inspired voice. "We walked together, and I was happy until—until *she* came."

Terribly agitated, he broke off, wiped the sweat from his face, then continued: "I noticed her first on the hillside. Her walk—her proud free air fascinated me. She was with another girl. I avoided them; but—I trembled. The next time she was alone. She spoke to me—she asked the time of day. The words were naught; it was her look—full of pity, and—and like an angel from Heaven. It moved me so that I answered her gently—I, who hated her race. She came to me in dreams, evil dreams. I was wretched. I prayed and fasted without avail. Struggle as I might, I was chained to her by every thought. Ay, asleep or awake I heard her voice calling me, tempting me. I hear it still."

There was a profound silence. The Abbot's grave and troubled eyes never wavered from the penitent.

8

"We met again," continued the monk, "not once, but often and in secret—for I persuaded her to keep our meetings from her people until—well, until they could no longer be concealed. When with her I forgot all, even my soul. I set myself to win her. But when alone I fought, I prayed, I cried aloud to God, and beat myself. But what good! To see her was again to forget all—all but her. And each time I met her I sank deeper. Venerable father, I tell you, it was a devouring furnace. I was on fire. I thirsted for her as for a drop of water in hell. Her eyes! her voice! My God!"

With a gasp he again broke off. The breath of uncontrollable passion filled the quiet cell. The monk sat with his hands knotted together at arm's length. His eyes haunted and unseeing, stared fixedly at the floor.

Abruptly he resumed: "One night a storm raged in the mountains. She was returning from a fair, and came to my house for shelter. 'Twas the first time she had been there. I could not bid her begone. We stood side by side listening to the thunder and the rain. Every time it lightened I saw her face. Once in sudden fright she clutched my arm. The devil tempted me. I resisted— God! how I resisted! but—I fell."

He covered his face with his hands. The Abbot sat quite still and looked at him. Into the old man's eyes— grave, yet innocent as a child's—crept a bewildered expression, that slowly gave place to comprehension and horror. Calm and untroubled as was his life, this aged priest had yet moments when the sorrows and sins of others racked him as though they were his own. The story struck him as with a physical blow. It filled him with feelings of repulsion for the brutal passions it portrayed. Nor did it lose by the circumstances under which it was narrated (though the Abbot thought not of them)—the profound silence of the monastery and the semi-naked fanatic confessing in the gloom.

While they sat silent, the door opened softly—so softly that, immersed as they both were in thought, neither noticed it.

"Tell me more about her," said the Abbot, forcing himself to speak calmly. "Did she love you?"

Stephanos shuddered. "She said so; but I do not think she understood. I—I had some power over her."

"Poor girl!"

The monk bit savagely at his finger-nails.

"And—did you deceive her? Did you promise her marriage?"

Stephanos glanced furtively into the old man's stern, truth-compelling eyes.

"Answer, my son."

"There was some talk of it," muttered the monk, abashed; adding suddenly, "She tempted me."

"No," cried the Abbot sternly, "your own evil passions tempted you. With all my heart I pity her."

Stephanos raised his head, visibly taken aback.

"But——" he began.

"Not a word. She was alone, defenceless, your guest, and you—you—— It was brutal! You behaved like a devil—and then like a coward! However great your subsequent sin, this alone——" He broke off, deeply agitated, then asked: "Have you seen or heard of her since?"

"No."

"There—there was no child?" A flush crept into the Abbot's pale face. At the answer he drew a breath of relief.

"Thank God, at least, for that!"

A moment's silence, then the old man spoke again: "I will try to find her."

Stephanos started, fear shone in his eyes.

"She may—she is sure to be unhappy. It is plain to me that she loved you. Something may perhaps be done for her—some sisterhood, perhaps. God will direct us—— What is that?"

The door had again creaked—this time more audibly than before. The faint sound, grating on the intense silence, had a mysteriously uncanny effect. It conveyed the impression that the little door was being softly and stealthily pushed open by a cautious hand. Both men listened. Stephanos raised his head.

"What is it?" he asked in a low voice, looking at his superior.

"The door," murmured the Abbot. "Methought—nay, I feel sure it opened."

" Perhaps the wind? "

" There is no wind to-night."

The voice of the Abbot betrayed superstition. As he spoke he made the sign of the cross, his eyes turned with lively apprehension towards the space, now a foot in width, that gave sight of the blackness of the corridor. Again both men listened, holding their breath; but the silence was now profound—unbroken. The monastery lay plunged in the utter quiet of the summer's night.

" It is strongly borne in upon me that we must pray for this poor girl," said the Abbot softly.

" For *her!* " cried Stephanos, taken aback.

" Assuredly."

" But—she is a *woman!* "

" Women suffer for our sins."

" They *are* our sins! " Stephanos jerked himself erect, his deep-set eyes blazed, the veins on his neck stood out like whipcord. " They are our sins," he vociferated; " we come here to escape them. The devil made them to lure man to destruction. A woman brought sin upon earth. A woman tempted Saint Anthony. A woman——"

" A woman gave Jesus Christ to the world," interrupted the Abbot, gazing with dim eyes at the crucifix.

Stephanos followed the old man's gaze. His head, affected by long fasts, felt strangely light and weak. He felt emotional, almost hysterical, on the verge of angry tears. Shudders from overstrung nerves ran through him. Everything became infected with this physical weakness to the point of hallucination. The Abbot's shadow on the whitewashed wall menaced darkly—the light from the Holy Image sent a ray of intolerable brightness into his brain. He felt it going in and in as though it were a gimlet. The pain he suffered amounted to torture.

The silence lasted so long that Stephanos grew uneasy.

" You say nothing, venerable father? " he muttered.

" Why did you desert her? " demanded the Abbot. Painful constraint was audible in his voice. It was the tone of one who strives to hold all personal prejudice in leash till he has thoroughly sifted the truth. Stephanos felt and resented the change. It seemed to his disordered brain as though there were a conspiracy against him.

And yet, despite his fanatical contempt of human criticism, he was vaguely conscious of a desire to stand well in the opinion of this one man.

"It was God's wish," he cried, half eagerly, half defiantly. "Since a boy I had longings for the religious life. I was not as other boys. God and the devil were always fighting for me. I would sin, then repent, then sin again. But somehow—somehow I felt that one day God would conquer—would—how can I tell you?—would take me to Himself."

He stared fixedly at his hands still grasping the lash, touched a smear of blood with the point of his forefinger, traced a cross absently, then continued: "O venerable father, don't you understand? This woman was of the devil—she *was* the devil. He came to me, in her likeness: he tempted me, and I fell. Then God sent a Holy vision to fight for me—to call me. Was I wrong to obey? No! And once here what could I do but keep silent till God bade me speak? At first, I confess, conscience seemed to reproach me. To take the vows and keep back aught— yes, that seemed deadly sin. But I was in God's hands: He brought me. We still talked together face to face, as you and I do now. With prayer and tears, here, in this cell, I besought guidance. And God spoke in the night. He said: 'Stephanos, crucify the flesh. But no word of confession to man.' I obeyed. If He told me to fling myself over the precipice, I would do it. Think you I care for *your* penances?" He sat erect; his voice rang with a fierce splendour of scorn. "No:—God is my judge. I wait for Him!"

The Abbot listened in silence. His benevolent face expressed consternation and amazement. So accustomed was he to put himself in the place of the sinner that his mind, by mere force of habit, sought the old familiar groove. In vain. For once his divine gift of sympathy was at fault. His view of life was a peaceful sunset; this man's was an eclipse. The confession had, however, one redeeming quality—sincerity. The Abbot felt that at last he was in possession of the whole truth. He tried to think of this as an extenuating circumstance. Again he failed. Being without precedent in his experience, it took him aback.

The Greek monastic system, he knew well, did not look too closely into the bygone sins of those who entered its ranks. It salved its conscience by becoming responsible for their souls from the moment of their joining the community. Had Stephanos but confessed all at the time of his admission into Barlaam, nothing could have been advanced against him. But his offence lay in that, by making an incomplete confession, he had obtained absolution under false pretences.

Two things struck the old man as he stood there plunged in painful thought. The first was that the wretched being before him had no idea of the gravity of his offence, the second that it was his duty, as Abbot of Barlaam, to report it at once to his ecclesiastical superior, the Bishop of Trikala. The latter arose from a suspicion in his mind that this sin demanded a punishment other than the light penalties it was his custom to inflict. His whole nature—tender-hearted to a fault—shrank from such an extreme course; but from the moment that it revealed itself as a duty, he did not hesitate. Yet deep wells of pity were stirred within him. Poignant disillusionment in Brother Stephanos—his pride, the shining light of the monastery—gave place to a sorrow that had in it much of the Christ-like quality of suffering for others.

The unhinged note, the wild and blasphemous pretensions, the boastings, the scorn, all struck the Abbot with unfeigned anxiety. Never before had he met a monk so charged with violent passions, so forgetful of the deference due to his superior. For the first time it occurred to him that Brother Stephanos was not altogether responsible for his actions.

His austerities, too—the Abbot looked with troubled and infinite compassion at the crouching figure upon whose swollen and naked back the blood was scarcely dry—pleaded powerfully in his behalf. Whatsoever his offences, he had punished himself with no sparing hand.

But it was with a soul, not with a material body, that the aged priest felt that he had to do. Stephanos represented to him one of the little community for whose spiritual welfare he judged himself responsible. His prayers for the world—for the millions of men and women unknown to him—were the natural outpourings of a love that embraced all God's creatures, tender, yet necessarily impersonal; but his prayers for his own children were the very voice of his heart, hopeful, yet full of fear—petitions sent daily to the Great White Throne inscribed in the blood and tears of the intercessor. For them he fasted and did penance, for them he denied himself all comforts, watching while others slept, praying while others kept silence. He lost sight of his own soul in his anxiety to save theirs. He had one ardent desire, never omitted from his prayers, to meet God at the last, face to face, and to be able to say: "Lord, here are the little ones entrusted to me—Thine—every one."

But now it was brought home to him with a conviction that gained momentarily in strength, that the case of Brother Stephanos had escaped beyond his personal control, that he must submit it to a higher judge. Yes, whatever it might cost him in grief and shame, he must write, stating all things clearly, asking for instructions. It would take two, or even three weeks, before he could receive a reply. Not only was Trikala distant, but the Abbot had a suspicion that the bishop was at that moment travelling round his diocese. Meanwhile it might be necessary to inflict some form of penance, and even to isolate this erring brother from the other inmates of the monastery. These, however, were matters requiring thought, in silent and devout meditation.

In the low, measured voice of one who weighs his words carefully, the Abbot spoke, touching on the heinousness of the sin both as regarding its commission and its subsequent concealment, seeking to bring its seriousness home to the sinner.

For the former, said the aged priest, looking down at the monk with grave eyes, naught but the humble and contrite heart would atone; but regarding the latter, more complicated in that it partook of an offence against the monastic order, he would inform the culprit of his decision later.

Stephanos listened unmoved—callously, thought the Abbot, with pain—and was still doubled upon himself in an attitude of unreasoning stupor when his superior quitted the cell.

CHAPTER XVI

THE sun had set in one of those stupendous conflagrations that metamorphose the west into a furnace and all nature into a hushed spectator. From its lofty natural tower—like some Simon Stylites on his pedestal—Hagios Barlaam watched the dying light.

Picturesque at all seasons, the little old monastery drew romance to itself in the highest degree as dusk crept upwards from the ravines. The giant crag that supported it towered from the profound and sombre gorges into the last delicate rose-flush of day. At that hour the venerable buildings, coldly grey at other seasons, became almost beautiful, suffused with transient colour that imparted a warm and fugitive glow to their weather-beaten walls.

But, though lifted above the light mists and fast-encroaching gloom to a twilight of its own that was tender, luminous, and all too brief, Barlaam seemed to die with the dying day: it masked itself in shadow, grew slowly grey and wan, blurred gradually into one nebulous but coherent whole, and, while still retaining the faint outlines of human structure, became as far as possible one with the cliff and with the night.

It was in this hour of dusk that Barlaam most impressed the imagination. When the gloom of imminent night enveloped it, it loomed upon the sight but as a fantastic shadow-monastery, less apparently real than the rocks at one's feet, less visibly substantial than the clouds overhead. It became ominous, fabulously sinister. It passed into an atmosphere of legend. Its loneliness and isolation awoke awe. Mystery haunted it about. One gazed upwards from the path at ghostly rampart and dim beetling crag, and wondered what manner of men dared to inhabit a place so desolate, or to call it by the familiar name of home.

But its inmates had no such imaginative fancies. Familiarity had robbed their wild surroundings of wonder.

120

In an indifferent way it is to be supposed that they were proud of their monastery, for they smiled when a rare traveller expressed admiration, but shrugged apathetic shoulders if questioned as to its age. Their ignorance and lack of curiosity were alike remarkable. They did not see the use of talking about it. It was there: nothing more was to be said.

If forced by some persistent visitor, they would reluctantly admit its precarious situation to have disadvantages —the ladders did not suit old bones, to be obliged to work a windlass whenever it was necessary to bring anything into the monastery was without doubt a drawback—but time and custom had minimised these inconveniences; and true it was, if transferred elsewhere—an event that rarely happened—the brethren became homesick; they missed the height, the silence.

But if atmospheric effects and imaginative phases escaped them, such fancy as they possessed found abundant vent in superstition. One and all, from the Abbot to Sotiri, shared a credulity almost beyond belief. Their ignorance fanned it, their meditative life fostered it. It became not only a part of their religion, but of their very personalities, the subsoil from which sprang many of their thoughts and actions, binding them to the present, linking them with the past, pointing upwards to the future. Thus, they would take pleasure in referring to this spot or that, to this object or that, in reverent but appreciative tones; cross themselves, or genuflect, as they drifted aimlessly through the courtyard, or paused a moment in the shadow of the cloisters; cherishing in their simple minds the memory of some legend, or miracle, handed down by word of mouth from the past—how remote a past none among them knew or cared.

But, for all that, it may well be that, unknown to them, the material aspect of the monastery possessed a certain influence over their minds; that Barlaam, glad at sunrise, drowsy at noon, haunted at dusk, or sinister at nightfall, stirred even their thin blood to unconscious reciprocation. Certain it is that one among them, Petros was not indifferent.

Beside Zetitzka on the precipice brink, the boy had fallen into a reverie that accorded well with the pensive scene unrolled before him. His duties for the day over, he had captured his new comrade as she was on the point of retreating to her cell, and had persuaded her to accompany him, explaining that upon this vantage-ground of all places was to be found the coolness that came only with dusk and the night wind.

The girl had allowed herself to be persuaded, not without difficulty.

They seated themselves upon the verge, within a few yards of the spot where Zetitzka had met Dimitri on the preceding day. Together they gazed at the mountains of Albania, black against the tender sky—at the valley, far beneath them, self-withdrawn into some enchanted atmosphere midway between the repose of night and the constraint of day—at the river that reflected the afterglow —at the village of Kalabaka, dim in the underworld, with one light like a drowsy eye twinkling faintly through mist-wreaths and trails of windless smoke—and, lastly, across the shadowy ravine at the solemn and uplifted mass of Meteoron.

No one else was in the outer court, only the boy and girl, alone, with all the wonderful world at their feet.

The little space of level ground seemed all the more dangerous to Zetitzka, seen thus in the gloaming. No attempt had been made to smooth the inequalities of the plot. Rocks at the unprotected edge assumed fantastic shapes, holes lurked, shadows cheated the eye. A stumble, and one would be precipitated into the blackness of the abyss. Yet Petros would often stand poised on the extreme verge and point out to her where the swallows nested, or where his eagle was wont to perch; or he would leap from rock to perilous rock where a missed footing meant death, and all with an assurance born of long familiarity, as though to hang over a precipice with a thousand-foot drop were as simple as to cross the courtyard.

They conversed in low voices, with long hushed pauses.

The little that Zetitzka could be induced to say never failed to interest her companion. Her ideas had for his unsophicated mind the charm of novelty and unexpectedness. They seemed also to carry weight, to be the outcome of experience far beyond her years. Again and again while she was speaking he had the feeling that he was listening to someone double his age; so that it needed the testimony of his eyes—turned abruptly to the brooding but singularly attractive face at his side—to convince him that it was only the new lay brother. Unknown to himself, it was the feminine point of view that took him aback, tantalised him, allured him.

And yet another thing. The views of this Angelos appeared to be all turned to a minor key, which to Petros was incomprehensible, seeing that the world was so fresh and full of interest. They forced him reluctantly to think of sad things and—as his experience of " sad things " was limited—of the death of Brother Jerome, an aged member of the community who had died but a year agone. Over the grave in the populous little cemetery among the rocks the brethren had droned a lugubrious air that wailed of dust unto dust. The words, as well as the dirge, and indeed everything connected with this his second remembered funeral, had impressed the boy profoundly, affected him with a sense of awe, of pity tinged with distant hope, a feeling too of being one of the guests at a mysterious marriage feast—so firm was his faith—and yet of the personal remoteness of such a calamity, so full did he himself feel on that bright May morning of life and the joy of all created things.

That the new-comer's outlook should remind him of this melancholy experience was remarkable. Petros, somewhat at a loss, attributed this fact to the secret sorrow which marked this boy, as it were, with a halo of romance, a distinctive atmosphere that dignified even such menial occupations as the sweeping of floors and the dusting of stalls. In his heart, Petros felt slightly awed. There was at times a grim and tragic intensity about his new companion, noticeable even in her very sparingness of speech, that could not but impress the boy, himself so prone to gay and spontaneous volubility. Her attitude was certainly disquietingly suggestive. It seemed to open hitherto unsuspected doors to possible experience; vaguely alarming, it is true, yet mysteriously alluring, if only on account of its incomprehensibility. No doubt the world was an evil place. It had cruelly blighted this young stranger; for, guided by some instinct for which he would have been at a loss to account, Petros felt convinced that

Angelos had not been ever thus—was not, indeed, thus
by nature—but was suffering from temporary depression attendant on the blow of which the Abbot had
spoken. Warm-hearted and intensely sympathetic, the lad
had at once set himself to counteract this baleful influence. Steeped in the monastic atmosphere of piety, and
radiating a faith as simple as it was sincere, he had sought
to apply the balm of religion to this troubled soul, but he
had found his new companion strangely irresponsive,
strangely apathetic. She did not disbelieve, she did not
argue, but she looked at him with melancholy, inscrutable
eyes that made him feel she was far beyond his reach.

Not that Petros despaired; his nature was too optimistic
for that; but for the moment he ceased to wrestle, consoling himself with hopes centred upon the efficacy of
personal prayer. When with her he not unfrequently tried
other tactics, seeking to banter her out of her preoccupation, contrasting her with other boys he had known—light-
hearted, strong-limbed, thoughtless lads from Kalabaka
and Kastrati, who on half-holidays took pleasure in visit-
ing the monastery. His tone when touching on the difference would be grave and dignified, as befitted a monk
admonishing a presumptuously-sorrowful lay brother.

" Look at your hands," he cried on this occasion, pointing in the dusk to where they were clasped about her
knees. Zetitzka, startled, put them quickly behind her,
for, essentially feminine, they constituted a danger.

" Well," bantered the boy, " have you ever seen a man's
hands like that? "

" Nay, be not vexed! " he continued quickly, as she
remained silent: " By Saint Barlaam, I like you in spite
of them! " He nodded cheerfully, as one who triumphs
over obstacles; then, with engaging impulsiveness:
" Hearken, Angelos, I will tell you somewhat of importance. 'Tis a secret, but I can trust you. A week agone
I besought the Holy Virgin to send me something young.
I had in my mind a dog or a cat to keep me company in
my leisure hours—Dimitri comes so rarely. Alack! I
prayed with little faith; for, between ourselves, I had besought the boon many times, and I was discouraged. Truly
was I answered, not according to my deserts, but out of

her divine compassion. Mark! a dog or a cat, prayed I
—and she sent *you!* "

He laughed in triumph. But Zetitzka made no comment.

" The venerable father was right, as always," Petros
continued earnestly. " Prayer is always answered, even
mine, as Brother Nicodemus says, the least deserving."

As though the reflection had suggested some familiar
orison, she heard his beads click in the hot dusk.

The big stars palpitated out, one by one. A planet,
serene and untroubled, kept bright vigil above the black
line of roofs. The night around them had no audible
voices, for the murmur of the river Peneios far below,
and the singing of the nightingales in the village orchards,
grew faint and died long ere they could reach the heights.

The brethren had all eaten and gone to their cells. The
old monastic buildings shrouded themselves in night, drawing the darkness like a cowl over their little bleared window-
eyes.

For awhile the conversation circled about the monastery,
with occasional flights into a profaner world. Petros took
pleasure in making Zetitzka his confidant. He chatted
freely of many things—of his friendship with Dimitri; of
fasts and ceremonies; of a manuscript he had lately un-
earthed from the dust of the library, full of breathless
entertainment concerning cannibals and missionaries; of
his fondness for certain rich—and, alas! rare—kinds of
food; of the annual visit of the bishop, chiefly memorable,
it appeared, for a feast wherein all took part—ay, even
the lay brethren; whereupon Zetitzka was smacked on the
shoulder and bidden to be of good cheer. Everything in
this dying monastic world was fresh, and young, and full
of interest for him.

His exuberance and love of " make believe " vitalised
even the saints—the grim, mediæval saints who stared
wide-eyed and wooden from the entablatures, or frowned
out of stiff little Byzantine frames with backgrounds of
tarnished gold. Zetitzka was initiated into their charac-
teristics, and learned, somewhat to her amazement, that
Saint Pondromos still interested himself in the healing of
toothache, colds, and similar ailments; that Saint Pan-

teleemon was a sure ally against oppression, connected, it came out, with Brother Nicodemus; that the very name of Saint Barlaam—if pronounced in time and with sufficient faith—was sufficient to rout a multitude of devils.

Every topic upon which the boy touched was so saturated with the monastic atmosphere that Zetitzka, listening, half bewildered, half indifferent, could with difficulty convince herself of its reality. It all seemed a part of the night that hemmed her round, of the abysmal blackness that yawned at her feet, and that cut her off so hopelessly from the familiar world below.

He had his visions, too, this young monk, of all the fine things he was certain of doing " one day." Zetitzka wondered dully at his enthusiasm. By Saint Barlaam, he would leave the world better than he found it! He would evangelise the heathen! He was all fire and zeal, all for doing brave things with life, complacently oblivious of the fact that life proposed to do things with him. That fine quality in him demanded fine responses from existence. Limitations he cheerfully ignored rather than scorned. It seemed to his youthful and generous mind as easy for the future Petros—an ecclesiastical dignitary, mark you, of no mean lustre!—to erect and endow fifty monasteries, as for the present Petros to eat his supper.

From his enthusiastic though hazy descriptions, Zetitzka caught sight of a renovated Barlaam, with every cell occupied, with even richer vestments, cheerful in its air of perennial religious festival, and Petros himself, its much beloved Abbot, in a cassock trimmed entirely with new fur.

He had wasted but little time upon thought, having been mostly taken up with sensations. For him, the present was tinglingly alive, the one thing important. The future, though alluring, was but a golden dream. His days had been so ordered for him by that mediæval monastic system of which he was the product, that he had formed no scheme of life, or of the universe, beyond what he had gathered from ancient manuscripts, from the sayings of the Abbot, or from fragments of misleading knowledge picked up from the brethren. And yet there fell from him at times a suggestion that was no mere echo—an independent thought that searched and probed, a hint of another Petros of whom this boy was but the raw material. At such moments of insight an older and less self-absorbed person would have foreseen the man that was to be—a stronger, maturer personality, mellowed by experience, with a deliberate conclusive outlook on life; for in this young monk there lay dormant potentialities of feeling and of action of which neither he nor others were as yet aware.

But these glimpses were fleeting, for at the next moment he would be heard chuckling over some boyish escapade, or seeking to enlist Zetitzka's sympathies on account of some trivial offence which had brought swift penance in its train.

" S-sst! " he cried suddenly, pointing a fearful finger on high. " See that bat? Brother Nicodemus says they are evil spirits. He prays to be guarded from them—so do I! "

He muttered apprehensively as the little rodent zigzagged overhead. But Zetitzka barely heard the monkish Latin of his prayer. Her thoughts were centred upon herself. More than ever in the mysterious starlight did all that had happened to her since she left her home seem a dream from which she still hoped to awaken. This boy also, whose companionship circumstances had thrust upon her, seemed at this quiet hour as visionary as did her surroundings: his simple confidences came to her like an echo from a world with which she had nothing in common. His so-called troubles were to her mind too childish to arouse sympathy. To sleep in church! To break an icon! She could have laughed in the bitterness of her heart.

She felt tired, both physically and mentally. The tension of the last few days, combined with loss of sleep, had told upon her, and now she felt glad just to sit still and do nothing—thankful, too, for the kindly night that hid her from men's eyes. More especially at such times did the recollection of her child come to her. Her recent past had been so bound up with its tiny helpless existence, her every thought both by day and night so consecrated to its well-being, that, separated from it, she felt lost. Its absence created a void that nothing could fill. A sense of physical incompleteness oppressed her. Her strong young arms felt empty. She missed, and yearned for, the small head nestling against her breast. It was

as though something vital had been wrenched out of
her body. Starting from uneasy sleep, she would often
listen eagerly for the little breath that she was so accustomed to hear coming and going beside her. Then suddenly she would realise that she was alone—in Barlaam—
and motionless, wide-eyed, she would lie sick with longing
in the blackness of the night.

But now, soothed for the moment by the welcome
obscurity, her fears temporarily lulled by the deserted
aspect of the courts and the comforting presence of this
boy who had constituted himself her companion, Zetitzka
allowed herself to drift. Her mind did not sanction this
quiescent attitude: it was persuaded into it in spite of
itself. She knew it would not last long. The emotions
she had undergone had been so poignant, so swift in transition, so heaped one upon another, that they had predisposed
her to welcome any moment that promised rest and peace.
She was faintly aware of this change in her mood, but
had neither the energy nor the ability to trace it to its
source. She was too tired, too filled with the feelings of
one who has been worsted in an unequal fight. Something had proved stronger than she. Was it the monastery?

With an effort, Zetitzka remembered how Barlaam had
scowled down upon her in the dusk of her arrival, before
she began to scale those fearful ladders; she also recollected
how she had matched her resolution against its stern veto
and had arrogantly fancied herself the stronger.

What had happened? Although she had retained her
footing in these forbidden precincts, although none of the
inmates had discovered her secret, yet, after all, she was
no whit more advanced in her projects than she had been
upon the day of her entry. More! The monastery had
bent her to its service; it had crushed her pride, it had
thwarted her persistently. By surrounding the man, who
was to have been her victim, with a guard, not merely
of religious services and fellow-monks, but of superstition,
mediæval as its own mysterious past, Hagios Barlaam had
robbed her of her prey. There was grim irony in its attitude. It seemed to wait, to tolerate her desecrating
presence but for the furtherance of its own sinister
schemes, meditating doubtless some dark act of vengeance

upon herself which eluded her knowledge, but which filled her with vague apprehension.

As these thoughts passed through her mind, Zetitzka cast a nervous glance over her shoulder. There it was!—dark, fearsome, crouching in the dusk against the background of benighted hills. It appeared to be watching her. It also had a wrong to redress, an insult to avenge.

The sound of approaching footsteps broke upon the silence. Looking towards the inner court, Zetitzka and Petros could see a figure emerge from the cloisters.

" 'Tis Brother Stephanos," commented the boy, in a low voice.

It was as though a hand of ice had been laid upon the girl's heart. In a flash her lethargy dropped from her.

The monk neared them, dim in the obscurity.

" He does not see us," whispered Petros again. " Shall I speak to him? "

" No! no! " implored Zetitzka. She could with difficulty control her voice, for she felt herself trembling.

The experience of the night before rushed to her mind: it had haunted her all day—the harrowing confession overheard in the blackness of the corridor. Unable to sleep, goaded by relentless thoughts, she had been impelled to seek Stephanos, had been unable indeed to keep away, with no clear idea of what she, a woman and unarmed, could effect, hoping against hope that fate might in some unexpected way prove her ally. But the discovery that the Abbot was already with the monk had banished hope from her heart.

To a mind brooding upon previous failures, and more than half persuaded to attribute them to some supernatural agency, the coincidence came as a final shock—a final proof. There was no longer room for doubt. Fate had decided against her, and she had stood there, with no suspicion that she was playing the part of eavesdropper, but overwhelmed with an immense dejection, chained also to the spot by the sound of the deep, familiar voice speaking of her, of her child, of the wrong its owner had done her—had stood there motionless, till the imminent fear of discovery had enforced flight.

And now she looked at the dim figure, watched over by some mysterious Providence—looked at him with feel-

9

ings too tumultuous for words. His presence there, alone, on the precipice brink, taunted her. It mocked her with the unattainable, as though it jeered: " See! I am here. Death is at my feet, but you are powerless to punish me."

Again the bitter injustice of it ate like vitriol into her heart. There came a mist before her eyes. She had to put a strong curb upon herself to hide her feelings from her companion.

The quiet night kept watch. These tormented human souls were part of it, raised high above the sleeping world, one with the clouds and the stars.

Yet the strangest, the most singular phase of the situation, eluded Zetitzka, even as it remained unknown to Stephanos. The man and woman who had branded each other's lives, who brooded upon each other's memory continually, who were to each other as tinder is to flame, were stranded together upon this remote pinnacle-top, so near, yet never coming into contact.

CHAPTER XVII

SLOWLY Stephanos turned and retraced his steps. Zetitzka drew a long breath.

" Verily," murmured a voice at her side, " verily, a good man ! "

She turned sharply towards her companion.

" *Good!* " she cried. The bitter and scornful emphasis caused the boy to stare at her in astonishment.

"'But assuredly," he insisted, " such holiness bringeth honour to the monastery. Already do they talk of him at Hagios Triada and Meteoron. 'Tis even prophesied he may become a saint, ay, and work miracles ! " He paused to give this expectation full effect, then with a burst:—
" O Angelos, right joyful would it be for this dear Barlaam to possess a real saint, abounding in love and miracles. Bethink you, pilgrimages and pilgrimages would come here, and much glory to God and our monastery would accrue."

But she did not reply.

" You like him not ? " said Petros brusquely.

She stared at him in sudden alarm.

He continued:—" I saw you look at him to-day, as he passed you in the Catholicon. You have bad thoughts, my friend; naught but prayer and fasting will purge them away. But ill becomes it for me to admonish. I do not like him myself."

" Ah ! " she cried, letting out her breath in a gush of satisfaction.

" Nay," he continued dolefully. " Be not glad. It is because my heart is vile."

" No."

" But, yes, otherwise I would by no means have these thoughts. The venerable father says I ought to conquer them. But there "—he shrugged his shoulders with outstretched hands—" the evil one is stronger than I."

131

" Why do you dislike him? " she questioned sombrely.

He thought awhile, then embarked upon a tale of how a harmless anecdote, culled by Brother Gerasimos from the *Neon Asty,* had been robbed of all humour by Brother Stephanos.   According to Petros, the unexpected presence of the monk had fallen like a blight upon the company.

" That is so like him," commented Zetitzka with bitterness.

" I told all to the venerable father," continued the boy, " and he explained it was because the thoughts of Brother Stephanos were fixed alway on lofty and devout matters. But he himself is not thus, yet he meditates much.   It puzzles me mightily.   I wonder sometimes if the blessed saints were gloomy and hard spoken.   I doubt it, for they have kind and gracious countenances, ay, and some of them look as if they were trying to smile.   Have you taken heed of Saint Sebastian in his icon near the *Bema?*   Right charitable does he look, ay, in spite of the arrows."

Zetitzka saw his tall hat wag meditatively in the dusk, then she caught a whisper:—" Much is still hidden from me, but I will assuredly know all when I become an abbot."

They sat without speaking for several minutes.   The night breeze fanned them lightly, bringing faint scents from the sleeping valley.   All at once Petros yawned, then stretched himself.

" It is late," he said, " let us go back to our cells."

" Wait," cried Zetitzka.

He looked at her with drowsy surprise, for her tone was constrained.   But the night hid her expression from him.

Something had come unexpectedly into her heart, a feeling as if self-control were exhausted, an imperative desire born of the hour and his kindness, to confide, to seek advice, to find someone who would befriend her.

" I want—I want——"

Petros, drowsy, indulgent, waited with mild curiosity; but the dark figure beside him said no more.

" What is it? " he asked.

" Nothing."

Her tone gave the lie to the word.   It roused in the lad's mind a keen desire to know.

" Is it——? "

" No, no; it isn't." She had sprung to her feet. " Never mind. Let us go in."

He, too, got up and began reluctantly to follow her, for she had started to cross the court. He could see her flitting before him, black and misty in the starlight. Her behaviour puzzled him immensely.

Suddenly, when least he expected it, she came back hastily, stood before him, gazed into his face doubtfully, questioningly, almost wistfully, as though seeking something. Her manner was strangely agitated; her eyes very dark and lustrous. She filled him with vague uneasiness.

" Well," he said awkwardly, " what is it? "

" It is—no. I don't think I can tell you."

" If 'tis your secret——" he began somewhat scornfully, but broke off as he heard an unmistakable choke. Impulsively he laid a hand on her arm.

" Don't touch me," she cried testily; then with an involuntary catch in her voice that went straight to his heart, " O Brother Petros, forgive me! I—I can't bear it."

" Never mind," he soothed, entirely nonplussed. " Nay, think not of it any more, though I know not what you mean. Come, you are tired. We will go to bed."

" No. I must speak." She caught his arm. He felt her trembling. For a moment she paused, then all at once the words overflowed, vehemently, recklessly, goaded into utterance by distress, forced from her too by hot Southern impetuosity.

Petros, more and more bewildered, could make nothing of it. It appeared that this unaccountable lay brother wished he were dead—that he ought to go back somewhere, but dare not—that something—Saint Barlaam alone knew what!—had been all useless, worse than useless.

Amid much wild talk one thing was obvious, even to Petros. His new companion was miserable. But before his sympathetic but bemused brain could think of anything to say, there came another swift, inexplicable change. He was urgently implored to forget the whole incident. Being of a literal turn of mind, he gravely pointed out that this would be impossible.

"But you will tell no one," she entreated.

"Nay," he replied, after thought. "The Abbot would not wish me to repeat it. But tell him yourself. You have no idea how sweetly he can comfort."

In silence they walked slowly side by side to the dormitories.

Barely had Zetitzka entered her cell than she again heard his voice.

"You mean not what you said?" he whispered earnestly.

"What?" she questioned.

"About going away."

She pressed her hand to her brow. The darkness, the silence, and the whole distressful and hopeless situation weighed like lead upon her.

"I—do not know," she murmured dejectedly.

He came nearer.

"You cannot—you must not go. Nay, you have only just come."

"Hush!" she whispered, for in his eagerness he had raised his voice, "hush, you will wake them."

He continued rapidly, but in more guarded tones:—

"One does not come to a monastery to leave it at once. It is a serious step. You have scarcely seen aught of our life. Is it the food you do not like?"

"No, no."

"Then wait a month—two months, and we will talk of it again. When you have witnessed one of our great festivals you will wait to see another. The Abbot liketh you well; he would be sore grieved if you departed now. And I—what would I do? I would be right miserable."

She shook her head. He seemed conscious of her disbelief, though the darkness shrouded her from his sight, for with renewed earnestness he went on:—" 'Tis true, I would be very lonely now without you. Moreover, it would not be grateful to the Blessed Virgin. She sent you. You are a direct answer to prayer. Dear brother, stay."

Zetitzka could not but feel touched. He was so sincere, so tremendously in earnest. Instinctively her heart warmed to him. She had ceased to fight against his influence. The fact that she now relied upon him and even clung to him for support failed to alarm her. Independence seemed a doubtful good. It was much more to the point that in her loneliness, and in this prison-house of her adversity, she, at all events, possessed a friend.

CHAPTER XVIII

MORNING mists filled the ravines. White, diaphanous, clinging, they lay like a becalmed sea, above which the pinnacles of Meteora floated like islands into the faint gold of the sunrise. Every rock and stone, every leaf and twig in the submerged area glistened with moisture, dawning in chill, wet lights, blurring as the mist clouds shifted, fading mysteriously into a background of grey nothingness.

Already, even in the gorges, the heat was oppressive. The windless air hung heavy, and as if no ventilation had kept cool during the long night these bedchambers of nature, whose walls were giant cliffs, and whose ceiling was the sky.

Along the rough track that climbed and descended alternately came Petros and Zetitzka. They walked rapidly, making light of the irregularities of the path.

"What said the Abbot when you asked leave?" inquired Zetitzka.

"At first, when I mentioned Lavra, he looked grave; then, after thought, said he: 'My son, take this.' See!" —Petros proudly held up an antique metal cross suspended from a rosary—"this is hollow and containeth a small but most precious relic. I wot not precisely what—a bone or holy hair, belike. The venerable father said 'twould ward off aught evil. He gave it to me. Assuredly, 'tis high honour to be so entrusted."

For a moment he swelled with importance, then, forgetting his dignity, executed a leap over a boulder.

"We need not return till Compline. We have here store of victuals—bread and wine—ay, and *sweetmeats!*" He nodded back at her appreciatively. "The venerable father is ever thus. You do not know him yet. He would give the very cassock off his back. I bespake Sotiri to tend him well, and in no wise to forget his midday meal. I forgot it once, and was mightily penitent, but the venerable father was of opinion that he had eaten as usual! By the saints, you are accustomed to hills—one can see that!''

His eyes rested upon her with frank approval. Her movements were free and unconstrained, a gait rendered possible by the scantiness of her lay brother's costume.

Suddenly aware of critical inspection, Zetitzka reddened. There were times when the woman in her would out— when this short tunic seemed to her a bold and indelicate covering, revealing more than it concealed of her limbs.

To her relief he did not notice her confusion.

The tone of their conversation was lighter than Zetitzka had imagined possible. Had she been informed, upon her arrival in the monastery, that before a fortnight would elapse she would not only go on an expedition with this young monk, but would chat with him easily and naturally, she would have contradicted her informant with scorn. For the latter, absence from the monastery was responsible. She felt as if an immense and crushing weight had been lifted from her heart—as if only now, for the first time for many days, she were able to breathe with freedom. From the moment that Petros had proposed the outing, a secret and feverish anxiety had possessed her lest some unforeseen obstacle should prevent it taking place. Not till the ladders were descended did she believe that she had really escaped; and now that she was actually on the path, now that every onward step was carrying her farther and ever farther from Stephanos, a profound sense of emancipation filled Zetitzka's heart with inexpressible relief. For the monastery and her enforced servitude within it, she was conscious only of an instinctive aversion, a repugnance that had deepened immeasurably since her repeated failures had compelled her to realise that she must bow to the veto of Destiny. Her presence there, among these old and fanatical monks, had become a mere tempting of Providence, an act of foolhardiness that could now lead to nothing but discovery. With all her might she longed never to return.

It was but an inevitable reaction from the long days and nights of haunting anxiety, that all that was young in Zetitzka, all that clung pathetically to the gay and laughing side of existence—the side so sternly denied her by Fate—should welcome this change, should greet it with outstretched arms, should turn to it gladly, as children turn to merriment, and flowers to sunshine. Barlaam once behind her, her feet, as it were, once more on the " *terra cognita* " of the world's level, all her surroundings became changed. As to a prisoner restored to freedom after languishing in confinement, all nature spoke to her with new voices. She seemed to listen to a personal message in the lark's song, to rediscover something touchingly tender and intimate in the familiar faces of wayside flowers. The past became an evil dream, the present a welcome reality.

" See! " cried Petros suddenly. " The mist clears. There is Meteoron."

Her eyes followed his pointing finger. Up the sheer face of the cliffs the mists smoked and shredded, allowing the summit to struggle through. Petros, hands to mouth, shouted loudly. His cry came back to them, repeated many times, as the precipice snatched at the sound; then, after an interval, the ghost of a far-off greeting fell from the heights. It sounded thin and weird, like the scream of a bird, and, looking up, they saw the face and beard of an old monk, hundreds of feet above them, gazing out of a rude door or window.

" Why do they build monasteries so high? " inquired Zetitzka in a tone of wonder.

" 'Tis safer."

" From brigands? "

" Nay, from Crusaders."

He laughed at her puzzled face, and gladly embarked upon the tale of how the monasteries of Meteoron were founded long, long ago, in the dark Middle Ages, by hermits fleeing from the lances of knights who hunted them down, as men hunt wild animals, among the rocks.

Zetitzka listened with interest, her eyes travelling up the face of the stupendous cliff to where, precarious as an eagle's eyrie, monastic roofs showed grey against the blue. The story of bloodshed and adventure stirred her to excitement.

" And did the hermits kill them too? " she asked eagerly.

" They could easily roll rocks upon them from up there."

The young storyteller surveyed her wide eyes and heightened colour with mild astonishment.

"Nay," he replied; "I think not so."

"Then what did *they* do?"

"They—they prayed for them."

Her contemptuous exclamation awoke his annoyance. Informing her that she was little better than an infidel, he led the way with much dignity. Indifferent to his displeasure, Zetitzka followed, her thoughts still on the heights.

"What I want to know——" she began.

Petros, his indignation forgotten, waited till she had rejoined him. "What I want to know," she repeated, "is, how did they get up?"

"Who?"

"The hermits. How did the first one get up? There were no ladders in those days.".

Petros' eyes twinkled.

"Listen, my boy. When I was young and foolish—a mighty time ago—I asked the same question of Brother Nicodemus; whereat he made reply that, as God in His infinite wisdom had not seen fit to enlighten us on the subject, it was presumptuous of us to seek to find out. There!—let that be an answer for you likewise."

"'Tis no answer," she retorted, determined to have the last word.

As they wandered on, conversing cheerfully, even her companion shared in her sight the glad metamorphosis of nature. He was no longer a part of the monastery. She almost forgot her instinctive dislike of his monkish costume when she looked at his bright young face, that smiled responsive to the summons of the day. More than ever did she feel kindly disposed towards this young monk. Little by little he had endeared himself to her. Her debt to him was deeper far than she was aware; but even the proportion of which she was cognisant awoke her gratitude.

She imagined her feelings towards him to be similar to those she might have had for a brother. Zetitzka had never had a brother; but the thought came to her that, if she had, and were in trouble, his companionship would be as welcome as was that of this young man.

As they rambled on, their talk reflected the glad

emancipation of their minds, for to Petros also was this rare holiday an intoxication. Yet all the time it was on thin ice that this boy and girl drew near to each other. Zetitzka, by casting off the gloom that mentally isolated her, and had hitherto proved her safeguard, stepped all unawares into the zone of danger. Her movements— unconsciously betraying the shape of her supple young figure—her pleasure in the rare flowers that grew among the rocks, her voice, her expressions, her smile, all triumphantly proclaimed her sex. The gaze of Petros, resting upon her with no conscious realisation of her charm, seemed yet to touch some mysterious chord of natural affinity between the sexes that vibrated harmoniously within her bosom. Under this kindly influence much that had been repressed crept into being, blossomed, and grew glad. Nothing but the lad's immense ignorance of women saved her from discovery. And even accepting this ignorance in its entirety, it seemed at times as if he *must* see, so unmistakably did the feminine shine forth in all she thought, and said, and did.

How long would this blindness last? Each hour that added to their intimacy added to her danger, for each found her more off her guard.

Only once during that happy walk did her material surroundings force her thoughts back to Stephanos.

The comrades had paused where the path, coiling downwards and doubling upon itself, permitted a backward and last view of Barlaam. The pinnacle, upon whose precarious summit it was perched, rose like a shaft out of the blue ravine along which they had been travelling, its base still in shadow, but its crest in sunlight. It was the first time since her admission that Zetitzka had seen the monastery from a distance and, as it were, in perspective; and the marvel of its position struck and held her anew.

It seemed impossible to imagine that upon the tip of that upright and slender finger of rock she herself had lived and undergone emotions so harrowing. It filled her with incredulity, and with an overpowering sensation of personal insignificance. It appeared to her now as impossible to associate her loneliness and her despair with that airy and fantastic summit as to imagine a heart-rending drama enacted in the nest of a bird. She gazed at it in mute wonder. How tiny it seemed! How far off! How frail! Surely a child's touch could topple it over into that misty ravine? And yet—and at the thought her blood grew cold—at that very moment Stephanos and Destiny were there, awaiting her return.

And, as if further to emphasise the sinister accompaniment to the gay carol of life, as Zetitzka watched, a dark speck sailed between her and the azure dome that roofed Barlaam—an eagle wheeling ominously; and the grim note of tragedy that had darkened her life seemed for the moment to darken nature also.

A shout from her companion startled her. Petros was endeavouring to attract the attention of an old man standing, staff in hand, at some little distance from the path. The stranger presented a wild and ascetic appearance, one with the cliffs and the rocks.

"'Tis Brother Johannes, the hermit," cried Petros eagerly. "Hi! Johannes, wait! I come." Then turning to Zetitzka: "Keep ever to the path, Angelos; I will overtake you."

Obedient to instructions, Zetitzka walked forward alone.

CHAPTER XIX

THE mists had vanished. The world was bathed in sunlight and barred with shadow. To the west, delicately neutral-tinted clouds had piled themselves high above the rampart of cliffs. Not the faintest breeze stirred; the heat was on the increase.

Before Zetitzka the gorge opened itself out into a more spacious valley, green along a hidden watercourse with the foliage of dwarf oaks; permitting the eyes to travel over quivering distances to far uplands beyond. Below was to be seen the red of village roofs, while dots of whiteness on a sunburnt slope told of goats in search of pasture. Zetitzka stood and watched the scene, unconsciously influenced by its beauty. The tinkle of goatbells, thin and clear on the breathless air, pleased her. They sounded familiar. She felt at peace. She had a day of respite—" a whole long day " she again told herself with a sigh of relief; and at the thought something of the brightness of morning passed into her heart and became visible in her face.

She was roused from the dreamful state into which she had sunk by the sound of a child crying. Moving quickly round an opposing rock, she came face to face with the cause. On the outskirts of a thicket a woman was gathering firewood; a little boy assisted her, while, in a rocky cleft hard by, lay a baby, from which came the cry that had attracted her attention. The plaintive sound drew her towards it instinctively. Her expression softened to a sweet and womanly tenderness. Forgetful of all save that it was a baby and unhappy, she took it up and cradled it within her arms. Her touch acted as a charm. After a few spasmodic sounds, the crying ceased. Then she remembered its mother. The woman, a few paces off, was staring at her stupidly, in utter amazement not unmixed with alarm; even the little boy from behind his

142

mother's skirts was gaping at her with wide-eyed apprehension.

"See," Zetitzka smiled reassuringly. "She sleeps."
The woman drew near.

" 'Tis true." She whispered the words under her breath; then, her eyes passing swiftly with increasing amazement from the smooth face to the monastic garb: "What manner of man are you?"

"I—I am a lay brother," murmured Zetitzka flushing. "But I love children. How old is she?"

"Twenty-one weeks," muttered the woman mechanically, her eyes still riveted in astonishment upon her questioner.

"She is big for her age. And heavy! You need not be frightened; I am used to children."

"I am not frightened. One can see—Holy Virgin! never did I know a man to hold a baby thus!—even her own father is not always so careful. And you—where is your mother? What do you here? Do they teach you to nurse babies in your monastery?"

Zetitzka, confused, but responsive, echoed her laugh. The two women continued to converse. The opportunity of talking to one of her own sex was seized by the girl gladly. Around them capered the little boy, his fear forgotten.

Suddenly Zetitzka started. She had caught sight of Petros standing rigid with amazement on the path. "Good-bye," she said hastily, and thrust the child into its mother's arms.

"Hi! hi! Why so sudden?" exclaimed the woman after her; but turning, she too caught sight of Petros, and said no more.

The comrades walked on side by side. Zetitzka, half dreading, half anticipating the reproaches she knew to be imminent, kept her eyes fixed on the path.

"Hearken!" broke out Petros, coming to an impuisive halt. "What have you to say?"

"Nothing," she answered shortly, walking on.

"How nothing?" he cried, following her and gesticulating in his excitement. "You break one of our strictest rules—ay, verily, break it before my eyes, and —and call it ' nothing '!"

"What rule? I broke no rule."

"And how about talking to a woman! Looking her boldly in the face! Laughing with her—ay, *laughing;* I saw you myself!"

"I forgot that," she said, and looked at him curiously.

"Aha! Now you see! Oh, you are in a parlous state; my poor brother! Forgot? Ay, 'twas the devil made you forget; he has ever a woman up his sleeve. In sooth, you will have to be chastised, for it behoves me to tell all to the Abbot. Nay, be not thus alarmed, it is soon over."

"You may have to endure stripes on the bare back," he continued, not without sly relish, deepened by her sudden gasp. "Ay, or perform the *canon;* or fast, peradventure for a day; or wash the brethren's feet. I have done all in my time. Believe me, fasting is by far the most grievous. But, as the saints live, right sorry am I that this happened to-day. Alack, 'tis ever thus in life! How wise and full of knowledge is our worthy Nicodemus: 'Women,' said he once in my hearing, 'are one of the roots of trouble.'"

Petros spoke as might have Solomon, wiped the perspiration from his shining face, hitched his bundle more comfortably on his shoulder, and added: "Let us go on. 'Tis too hot here. What were you doing to the infant?"

"I was putting it to sleep."

He stopped dead—his mouth opened to its widest.

"You were putting it to sleep! *You!* Holy Pondromos!"

"Yes; the poor little thing was crying. I knew at once what it wanted. It was good the moment I took it up. You need not laugh. There is nothing amusing in that." She tossed her head. "Is that breaking another silly rule?"

"Nay," chuckled Petros, "I think not so; but we will ask the venerable father."

"He! *He* knows nothing about babies!"

"He knows about everything. Oh, smile an you like, but his wisdom is wondrous, far above that of this world! Moreover, you confound things, as ignorance does ever; it is no question of whether he be versed in the ways of infants, but whether or no a lay brother be permitted to put them to sleep."

" Them？ Only one."

" One sufficeth," said the young monk loftily.

They walked on side by side for a few minutes without speaking—Zetitzka deep in uneasy speculation—Petros, who had evidently forgotten the incident, humming a chant.

" Well," said he, suddenly catching her eye, " why look at me like that？ "

" Like what？ "

" As if—nay, 'tis unheard of—!—almost, forsooth, as if you pitied me! If you envied me now it would be seemly. I am a monk."

She did not explain, but after a moment asked:

" Do you never speak to women？ "

" God forbid! " He crossed himself hastily.

" You fear them？ "

" I do *not!* " he cried, nettled by her air of compassion.

" Then why avoid them？ "

" Because——Why ask foolish questions？ "

" What would you do if you met one here, on this path？ "

" I would not look at her."

" But if she spoke to you？ "

" If she spake. H—m. First would I make the sign of the most blessed cross—thus; then would I answer, one word belike, without looking. The venerable father says it is ever well to be courteous."

" But—if she went to Barlaam？ "

" Barlaam! " He almost shouted the name in his amazement. " You lose your wits. No woman goes there."

" But if she did？ "

" If she did？ " A boyish smile crossed his face. " Methinks I would hide—peradventure in the cloisters—and send Brother Nicodemus to hold parley with her."

He did not notice her sudden silence, but at the next turning of the path, cried eagerly: " Behold, there is Lavra! "

Before them, where the ravine gave to the valley, forming the last stand of the pinnacles of Meteora, rose a tower of rock, its summit crowned by the ruins of a monastery.

" My father and I lived there between the plague and the earthquake," whispered Petros at her elbow as they

10

gazed upwards at the abandoned dwellings, naked in the pitiless glare of the sun. "My father feared naught save the wrath of God, but they do say——" and he poured into her ears a tale of distinctly mediæval quality wherein monks and devils played an equal part. Zetitzka listened, her face puckered.

"But——" she expostulated, "you lived there after the plague, did you hear them?"

"Nay, but I was only a child and slept soundly of nights. Moreover, Brother Nicodemus says that they are in sooth fiends, feigning to be monks. He says likewise that as long as my father lived—and I tell you Angelos, a right sainted man was he—they were afeared to come."

"And now——?"

"Now you are here. For long have I wanted to go—I thirst for adventures—but no one would come with me."

"But—I too might have refused."

"But you will not! Behold, we are within its very shadow! The ladders are behind that rock; they are easy of ascent. You *will* come?"

"You—you are sure that it is only at night the devils sing?"

"Ay, and at dusk. We have all the day before us. Once Brother Apostoli heard them at nightfall and ran away with so pious a haste that he came near to breaking his neck. He was in sorry plight, for the devils had beaten him sore, and sober speech had departed from him. Dimitri said he was drunk—at times Dimitri is little better than a Turk. But—you are not frightened?"

Her negative reassured him; still chatting, he led the way to the ladders.

CHAPTER XX

THE long happy hours of that summer day drifted by, linking experiences into a golden chain that served to bind the fates of Petros and Zetitzka yet more closely together. There was that in the isolation of their surroundings that made each take conscious comfort in the other's presence. Upon closer inspection, the monastery proved depressing in the extreme. Not a building but had been shaken by the fierce spirit of the earth. The keen sunshine, pouring from a sky of unalterable blue, emphasised the sense of desolation. An air of tragedy haunted the ruins, for long ago a plague had stamped out the monastic inmates.

Hither and thither they rambled, Petros leading the way. For him the place was full of unforgettable memories.

" Here was it—" he had paused in the shadow of the refectory—" that my father and I first broke bread. By the Saints, it seems like yesterday! "

As they stood together in the porch of the Catholicon his ejaculations of regret were heartfelt. The building, so familiar to him, was ruined almost beyond recognition. The roof had fallen in. Gaps could be seen in the walls. Among the rubbish that encumbered the floor grasses and wild flowers had planted themselves, their delicate green and scattered stars of colour strangely gay amid the pervading desolation. Though much had vanished, the place was not without evidences of bygone sanctity, mysteriously appealing to the imagination. The corona lay all twisted among fallen rafters. The Holy Doors, that had aforetime concealed the *Bema*, had been flung to the ground; and, as the comrades paused in the entrance, a carrion crow, uttering a hoarse cry, flitted upwards into the sunshine.

Unaccountably subdued, ut happy in each other's com-

panionship, they wandered out to the level plot that overlooked the precipice. Here, as in Barlaam, Zetitzka was
conscious of towering height.

"This is where I played," said Petros. He spoke in
a low voice, noting details with a curious eye, his thoughts
visibly in the past. Zetitzka looked at him compassionately.
She could see the lonely little boy stranded aloft with the
melancholy self-absorbed man.

"I played at monasteries," he explained with a laugh.
"I was the Abbot and these stones were the monks. It
was a new game. My brethren were silent, and gave no
trouble; when one disobeyed I flung him over the precipice."

Nothing loath, he continued to tell of his past. The
Hegoumenos of Barlaam had offered a home within the
monastery to the widower and his little son, but the offer
had been declined. Lavra, haunted though it was by reputation, appealed more to the broken-hearted man in search
of solitude and the consolations of religion. There had
he and Petros passed many peaceful years, visited by few;
there had he prayed, and watched, and waited, and there
at the last had death found him.

Never before perhaps had a child been brought up
under circumstances more strange, amid scenery more wild
and gloomy. And yet Petros, with the adaptability of
youth and the happy temperament which was his birthright, had extracted pleasure from these early years—he
even held them in happy memory. The ladders, from the
day on which he had been allowed to climb them alone,
had proved an unfailing source of amusement; the services—which his father, with a curious religious zeal, had
conducted single-handed in the Catholicon—had filled him
with solemn and important pleasure, as though they were
a religious game. Nor, as it would seem, had his
father neglected his education. It had been a pastime for
the lonely man to instruct this fresh, young mind so full
of avidity for information; to fill it with devout thoughts,
and rigorously to exclude from it all knowledge of the
world. He had possessed the gift of making lessons interesting, for Petros did not regret these hours stolen from
the sunshine and his play. Of the lad's mother he had
spoken only at rare moments, as of an angel in heaven;

of other women, and the part they played in the scheme of created things, he had spoken not at all.

All this did Zetitzka glean by degrees. The narrative was told disjointedly, in spurts of remembered incident, interlarded here and there with appeals to old-world saints and quaint monastic phrases, sounding well-nigh risible on the lips of one so young. At times the narrator paused to fling stones into the gorge, or exclaim at the heat, or suggest a raid upon the luncheon wallet.

They broke their fast in the shadow of the refectory. Everything tasted good, even the sour, black bread and the thin red wine strongly impregnated with resin.

The meal over, the boy lay among the weeds, indolently happy, while Zetitzka seated herself by his side. Petros, producing a cigarette—a treasure begged from Dimitri—puffed away with boyish satisfaction. It did not even seem necessary to talk. A sparrow fluttered down from the eaves for a dole of crumbs, and, emboldened by the silence, a lizard like a little green flame darted from out a crack in the masonry. Above the ruined walls a skylark could be seen beating his wings against the roof of the world. The thin, faint rapture of his song just reached their ears.

The memory of that summer's day was destined to become one of the dearest possessions of this young monk —dearer than aught else in the world. Even at the time, though he took it for granted with the careless assurance of youth, it was full of peace and quiet happiness—no Nicodemus or Apostoli to look sour, no duties to perform, only this new companion to impress and patronise—a delightful experience for one till now the youngest in the community.

The air, at that height ever delicate and renewed, exhilarated their spirits like wine. The blue sky was heaven's own smile; the sunshine the very soul of gladness. It was impossible to believe that in a world so fair there could be such things as unhappiness and despair. Very beautiful, too, was the scene unrolled below them. Sun and heat had woven a veil, azure and shot with gold, in the loom of the morning. This translucent fabric, flung over the wide panorama of gorge and cliff, valley and mountain, had a certain festal air as of cloth of gold.

Zetitzka watched Petros through semi-closed eyelids, half dazzled by the strong reflected sunshine, as he lay face downwards among the luxuriant weeds. His tall black hat—always an incongruous object—had fallen off, and his thick brown hair straggled unheeded to his shoulders. The touch of femininity which the latter might have imparted was more than counterbalanced by the strong outlines of his face. A wondering and unconscious admiration tinged her thoughts. Had her mind possessed culture, it might have likened him to a Viking, or a young Greek god. The feeling that would have prompted the simile was there, although the thought was beyond her.

Many times in course of conversation was she tempted to forget his calling, lured by his manner and face to think of him only as a type of young, gay, and vigorous manhood. But his costume, his beads, and the glimpse of his tonsure, when he turned his head with one of the quick movements habitual to him, all brought her back to the truth. And each time the reality caused her a shock of almost incredulous amazement.

When he spoke of his childhood's home in Athens and told how his father had taught him to read and write, a quick gleam of comprehension came into her face. She now understood how it was that he had seemed so superior to the others—why he did not giggle at mistakes in the service, as did Brother Gerasimos, nor expectorate on the Catholicon floor, as did Brother Nicodemus.

Suddenly, in the midst of a monastic anecdote, Petros looked up to find her eyes fixed upon him. Something in their dark, inscrutable depths seemed to reflect uncomfortably upon his youth and inexperience. He stopped short and plucked testily at a weed.

"What age have you?" He put the question half defiantly, then at the answer gave a crow of triumph.

"Eighteen! Then I am the elder!" His fingers caressed the down of his incipient moustache. "Holy Pondromos! You do not look your age. There is scant promise of hair on your face."

"The saints forbid!" she ejaculated.

"That is mere foolishness and envy. A beard becometh a monk bravely. All the brethren have beards. I likewise will have one—soon. Now you—" he inspected her with unqualified commiseration—"You might as well have been born a woman!"

"You need not despise women," she muttered in a stifled voice, gazing past him to where the distant hills could be seen above the ruins. "My boy, you have much to learn. You think all women bad, and are afraid even to speak to them. That is wrong—all wrong. A woman could teach you much. She may not be as brave as a man —but—but she suffers more."

Petros gasped. An acolyte daring to lecture a monk! A novice addressing a superior as "boy"! The offensive epithet topped the situation.

A heat of indignation leapt into his face, but cooled as his glance rested upon the culprit. Unconscious of his displeasure, Zetitzka was gazing into the distance. She was seated in a pensive attitude, her cheek impressed by the knuckles of her brown hand, her eyes full of sombre thought. Seen in relief against the deep purple shadow of the refectory wall, her chin and the column of her throat glowed with the lustre of alabaster.

Petros stifled an impatient exclamation. There was something about his companion that thwarted indignation. She baffled him, awoke his curiosity, lured him to her by some personal magnetism that, while quickening his interest and even awakening his affection, made him vaguely ashamed, as of unmanly weakness. By rights he ought to put her in her place, instruct her in the respect which was his due—yet he kept silent. He wondered at himself, sought to excuse himself by calling to mind her unhappy past, of which he knew nothing, but which was visible in a subdued and wordless melancholy that, eluded for a time as her mood lightened, invariably returned like an oppressive memory that refuses to be banished.

CHAPTER XXI

ACCUSTOMED to the occasional advent of a lay-brother, Petros had looked for something illiterate, dirty, and a child of the soil, for the Greek monasteries recruit principally from the peasant class. But this boy lying beside him expressed himself with fluency, was clean in person, and disconcertingly original in thought.

As he pondered, the solution of part of the mystery came to him. Her quaint Albanian accent reminded him that this youth came of ancient race. Petros had never been to Albania, but, living so near the frontier, it had often stirred his boyish imagination. Brigands lived there! According to Brother Nicodemus, to whom the unknown invariably suggested evil, it was the terrestrial headquarters of the devil himself. Brother Stephanos had come out of Albania, and by his very reticence had added to the supernatural interest of the country. The blue barrier of hills that reared themselves on the sky-line alternately allured and repelled a mind simple and credulous as that of a child; and sometimes, when the sun sank behind the summits in a sea of blood, the boy would stand on the precipice brink and wonder with unspeakable awe if the red that stained the west were a sign that God was angry with Albania. And now this strange youth had come to them from that mysterious country—what wonder if he were different from others.

"And you are content to pass all your life like—like this?"

As Zetitzka asked the question in a tone of wondering compassion, she waved her hand towards the courtyard. The sunlit stagnation of the place exemplified well the monotony of his existence. He stared at her, still in amazement. Musingly she continued:

"I have never been in a monastery before. We never see
152

monks where I live. There are priests—but they are all married."

" Assuredly."

Her look of interrogation forced him to explain.

" All priests marry in our church, or become monks like me. Did you not know that? *Kyrie Eleison!* you are wofully ignorant, methought that was known to everyone. If their wives die, then must they at once enter a monastery. Brother Elias was married before he came to us. He spake once to us of his wife. He said that what he loved most in the monastery was the blessed silence."

" But once they have taken the vows monks cannot marry? "

" Nay, by no manner of means."

" And you, you must stay here for always and always? "

" Past all question."

" Until you die? "

He made an impatient gesture. " Saint Barlaam, you ask always foolish questions. And, moreover, all this is well known unto you! Why look at me thus? It is not seemly. Nay, I will *not* be pitied! I am by no means going to die yet! "

Zetitzka smiled involuntarily. Her rare smile was singularly winning. A glitter of white teeth, and a dimple at the corner of her mouth, like the impress of a tiny finger, came into view. Her eyes lost their habitual sadness. Her heightened beauty glowed out, revealed itself in its true colours, soft, and inexpressibly sweet. So womanly did she look that the marvel was that her secret should remain undiscovered. But Petros merely frowned upon her with comical disapproval.

Sobering suddenly, she continued to follow the trend of her thoughts:

" It seems such an idle, useless life: no work, except for the lay brethren, and for the monks only long, long prayers, instead of walking about bravely with a knife and a gun. To me it seems no life for a man. Now you "— she nodded at him—" if you met an enemy——"

" But I have no enemy."

Wonder tinged with envy looked from her eyes; then

she nodded again. "True," she said, thoughtfully; " but
—but if you had, would you kill him?"

"Saint Barlaam!" he almost shouted. "*No!*"

"Why not?" She held her head high. "It is nothing
to be ashamed of. Men are always fighting. My father
has killed a man: he tells the story often. It is rare to
find a man in our village who has not killed someone. And
as for my uncle—people speak of him still, for he killed
five enemies before he was killed himself!"

Her evident pride in these deeds of prowess made him
gasp. Petros had heard rumours of Albanian Arnauts,
and their bloody feuds, but from the lips of one so young
and gentle they came with a strange note of incongruity.
A strain of racial lawlessness was apparent at times in
the new-comer's voice and manner. It repelled Petros,
and yet mysteriously attracted him, for he felt unaccountably drawn to his companion.

"Have you killed anyone?" he asked in an awe-struck
voice.

Her expression altered swiftly.

"No," she muttered, averting her face. It became
plain even to him that she was ashamed of the confession.

"I rejoice!" he cried, clapping her on the shoulder
with a heartiness that made her wince—"I rejoice exceedingly! Think, only if you had! Why, your life would
have been an endless penance—fasting, vigils, stripes!
Holy Saint Basil! And they might even have expelled
you!" His tone expressed a fearful appreciation of the
gravity of the punishment. Then, with a burst of compassion: "You would be cast on the world, my poor
brother—and, believe me, the world is a terrible place.
Brother Nicodemus says so. He says it is as full of devils
as is Meteoron of monks. Some take the shape of money-
bags, some of forbidden dainties, and some of women who,
if you hearken unto them, change into fiends and fly off
with your soul!"

The serious manner with which he imparted this
astounding information took Zetitzka aback. Credulous
enough herself—for the folk-lore of her race related many a
grisly and supernatural legend—she might have believed
him, had not her experience of life taught her otherwise.

" Can it be possible," she thought, " for one almost a grown man to believe such tales! " An amused and almost imperceptible smile lurked within her eyes. To Petros her slightly incredulous expression was but another proof of her ignorance. He, too, smiled indulgently. Their mental attitude towards each other was curiously similar.

Then, boyishly anxious to remind her that on certain matters she would find him uncompromising, he said, with simple earnestness:

" As for what you said of my calling, it grieves me sore to hear you talk so foolishly—nay, sinfully! It is a beautiful life. We monks endure want and even affliction, counting loss as gain. We give up the whole world for the sake of the Kingdom of Heaven. That is better than killing people! What can *you* know? You, forsooth! who had not even heard of the blessed *Antimins!* And, moreover, your words contradict your deeds. Why did you come here if not to lead this holy life? " He paused triumphantly, but no reply came. Warming, he continued: " I would that I could show you, but I too am ignorant. You must ask the venerable father. As for me, I have vowed with God's help to abide in the monastery in virginity, temperance, and devotion to the last breath of my life. I tell you, Angelos, I am proud to be a monk. I have chosen a truly good and blessed work, if so be that I persevere, for good works are performed with labour and accomplished with pain."

He paused, breathless. Into his usually merry face there had come a fervent look. His words—had she but known it—were merely a quotation from the office of the " Lesser Habit," but the conviction in his voice infused the old monkish service with deathless vitality. Noting her hesitation, he added with melancholy emphasis: " I fear me, Angelos, you will never become a monk."

" And you," she questioned, " will you never regret it? Nay, be not angry! I want to know. You are young——"

" *Young!* "

" Surely to be young is better than to be old. And it is sad to shut yourself up like this before you know anything of—of life."

He looked at her, half wondering, half wistful.

"Life? I suppose you mean life down there——" He nodded dubiously towards the shimmering valley. "Does that bring happiness?"

To his astonishment, all light seemed to fade from her eyes, and, though he coaxed her to explain, she would say no more.

As far as was possible, during the long day, did the comrades avoid the interior of the monastic buildings. These mere shells, consisting of little more than roofs supported by tottering walls, were too eloquent of the sadness and evanescence of existence to appeal either to Petros or Zetitzka.

It was after all but natural that this boy and girl, both so unconscious of the significance of their relationship and of the inevitable awakening that hourly drew nearer, should be engrossed with each other. The present was all in all to them. They brought the very spirit of young life into the ruined courts. In them the intimate needs of the moment found expression. They stood for the "now," that is always present, in contradistinction to the "then," that is either unborn or has ceased to be. All around them whispered dead voices. The past cried to them insistently—wailing of vanished lives, of the inevitableness of death, of the stern facts of existence, commonplaces, perhaps, but nevertheless great poetic truths—illustrating its lesson with grass-grown court and deserted cloisters; but, with the bright and egotistic thoughtlessness of youth, they shut their ears to its warnings.

Towards evening a change was observable in the weather. The heat had increased. Not a breath of air was to be felt. From the north ominous clouds, ragged and dun, came creeping over the face of the sun. The skylark had vanished, beaten earthwards by the oppression in the air. From where they were they could see the path coiling downwards towards the village of Kastrati. Great shadows, like immense birds of prey, swept it continually with their wings. From the ruins no sound came. The silence was profound and vaguely disquieting.

Petros and Zetitzka had risen to their feet. All at once the lad started to cross the court, and the girl, unwilling to be left alone, followed him. Reaching the verge they stood side by side, without speaking; behind them, the ruins; before, and immensely below them, the valley, still in sunlight, but being devoured momently by the approaching gloom.

Both were moved by feelings of awe; Petros too by sensations of ill-defined superstition connected with demons and hostile spirits of the air.

Suddenly the boy turned to look for his companion, and experienced relief to find her by his side.

"It comes this way," he whispered. Barely had he spoken, than a mutter of thunder made itself heard. It was like the roll-call of innumerable drums, muffled, far-off. Rain began to fall, at first in huge reluctant drops, warm on the face and hands, then faster and ever faster. At the instigation of Petros they sought shelter in the porch of the Catholicon. The storm broke over them with an unrestrained fury suggestive of the tropics. The lightning blinded their eyes, alternately snatching at their surroundings, then relinquishing them to gloom. The thunder drew near and became all but continuous, exulting in its strength, bellowing in organ-like bursts that roared loud above the shouting of the cliffs. All nature became one vast orchestra whose deepest note was thunder and whose highest was the newly-arisen wind wailing among the ruins. There was something grand in the storm, something peculiarly appropriate, too, in those elementary voices raised suddenly in the silence. The gorges had found expression.

"You are not afraid?" exclaimed Petros.

By the light of a flash he had noted her look.

She was glad that a sudden crash diverted his attention. How could she have told him her thoughts?—that this storm recalled the fatal night in the mountains when she had sought shelter in the home of Stephanos. The memory nearly stifled her. She had to put a strong curb upon herself to conceal her agitation. How vividly, how poignantly it all came back—awaking anger, shame, and bitter unavailing regret.

"It grows late; needs must we be going back," he cried, bending his head to hers and speaking loudly.

"No, no," she remonstrated.

" But, yes, in an hour they will begin Compline."

" Wait till the rain stops."

She snatched at any excuse; but the rain had no intention of stopping. On the contrary, it increased in violence, falling in dense sheets, obliterating the hills, hoarsely vociferous on tile and flagstone, breeding rivulets innumerable that fled from the roofs and guttered into the abyss.

The loneliness of their surroundings made them intensely conscious of each other, almost as though they were the only living beings in the world. At an exceptionally alarming flash he drew her further back into the porch, and, once there, allowed his arm to remain about her shoulders. She made no effort to release herself. His touch imparted a sense of protection, of human companionship for which she was grateful.

While they stood thus they were startled by a muffled roar—not of thunder, but of something within the monastery—then silence, broken only by the steady thresh of the rain. They looked blankly at each other.

" Can it——" Petros checked himself, his eyes still fixed on hers in wide apprehension.

" Yes? " she whispered uneasily.

" Do you remember that story of Brother Nicodemus? "

" About the devils? "

" Yes."

" I don't believe it."

" What? "

" I don't believe it." Zetitzka spoke with what her mother termed her obstinate manner, but for all that she cast a nervous glance over her shoulder. Her disbelief shocked, yet vaguely reassured him.

" And if there were devils," she continued quickly, " you said they came only at night. It is not late enough for them yet."

He shook his tall hat ominously.

" Nay, but it is parlous dark. Peradventure they have mistaken the hour."

Bidding her await his return he ran off into the rain. In a few minutes he was again with her, a grin on his wet face.

" An adventure ! " he cried gaily, shaking the water from his tall hat. " The ladder has gone ! "

She stared at him blankly. He continued:

" The rain must needs have loosened a rock. It has fallen on the ladder; two lengths have gone."

Still she stared, within her eyes a dawning consciousness of the gravity of their situation.

" Then—then we are prisoners ? "

" Ay, past question. 'Tis a rare jest ! "

" But—we will have to stay here all night ! "

His face betrayed that he had not calculated upon that.

" You will miss Compline," she continued nervously.

" Yes, and the midnight services. The Abbot will be vexed. Ah, that sobers you ! And moreover no one will come near this place. It is haunted."

He stood before her, stroking his chin.

" It is true," he faltered. " I never thought of that. Backsliding at all seasons—God forgive me ! But—" and he regained his cheerfulness, " be not thus downcast. The good saints will protect us. One holy saint can, an he has a mind, rout a multitude of devils. Perhaps even they will reveal unto us a way. Ah, the tower of the windlass ! "

Together they hastened to the rude hut that, as in Barlaam, overhung the abyss. One glance was sufficient. The rope was rotten.

" No hope here," said Petros, chuckling.

She flashed an indignant glance at him.

" One would say you were glad ! "

" I *am* glad. Nay, be not angry. Look you, Angelos, all my life I have earnestly desired an adventure, so this pleaseth me right well. 'Tis doubtless my vile nature. Brother Apostoli says there are seasons when I merit the lowest depths of hell. He ought to know, for God hath revealed to him wondrous high matters in his prayers." He wagged his head solemnly, then asked: " And you, are you so desirous of getting back ? "

Her hasty negative made him smile.

" Then make no more ado. 'Tis but for one night. The venerable father will of a surety send to seek us when he sees that we do not return. After all, 'tis not our fault. It was a devil loosened that rock, helped thereto by the rain. And if the fiends should come, have we not the Abbot's cross? It exorciseth mightily. We have here no breviary wherewith to say matins, so God will lovingly overlook it if we sleep."

" Where? " she asked in a low voice. As she spoke she cast a fearful glance towards the monastery. The rain had ceased. Under the cope of night the ruins had assumed an even more ominous aspect.

" In my cell," he said, replying to her question. " The one wherein I was wont to sleep when a child."

She looked at him, her indignation gone, nothing but a longing for sympathy left. Something virile about him comforted her inexpressibly.

" You will not leave me," she pleaded.

The request slipped from her, almost unawares. She neither wondered at it, nor regretted it. Her sense of dependence upon this young monk had reached a new stage. It now stirred her into a troubled sweetness, essentially feminine—the instinctive pleasure which every true woman feels in being protected by a man to whom she is not indifferent.

CHAPTER XXII

IN the sunlight the dormitory of Lavra would have been melancholy—in the dusk it was depressing beyond words.

"That was my father's cell," explained Petros, indicating a little door. "He died there—and this "—he pointed to another—"was mine."

They entered the latter. Zetitzka made out the usual cubicle, stripped, however, of all furniture.

She looked round disconsolately.

"We will sleep on the ground," continued Petros, "many holy hermits slept thus, Brother Nicodemus says it breeds rheumatism and is highly acceptable to God. He never does it himself. Come, let us pray and then we will lay us down."

In the gloom she heard him repeat a pater noster, followed by a fervent petition to the effect that they might be guarded from evil spirits. She did not join in the prayer. Something in the vibrating masculine tones of his voice disquieted her for the first time.

"Now, let us sleep," said Petros with a yawn.

He stretched himself at full length upon the floor. She, however, remained standing, strangely ill at ease.

"Will you not lay yourself down? " he asked wonderingly.

But still she stood, gazing at his outstretched form under cover of the dusk. A feeling of nervousness possessed her, tying her tongue, and making her acutely self-conscious. What though he imagined her a boy—she knew him for a man. And yet, under the strange circumstances in which they were placed, she could have overlooked this, were it not for a shrinking fear of the morning and the dread of discovery. Hitherto, in her cell, with the one exception of Sotiri's intrusion, she had been alone, free to perform unobserved the details of her woman's toilet; but here no privacy would be possible.

"What is it?" came the drowsy voice at her feet.

"Let me go away," she said hurriedly, in agitated tones.

"Go *away!*"

"Yes. I will go into the corridor. It is cooler there."

"Nonsense! Have you a mind to meet your death—to speak naught of things evil? Come, are we not brothers? Let us sleep side by side in love and sweet friendliness."

The prospect embarrassed her. She bit her underlip—frowned—shrank into herself. Even his unconsciousness failed to restore her ease. A feeling of impatience at the whims of this unaccountable youth ruffled Petros, but changed to good-natured acquiescence as she muttered that if he remained she would be unable to sleep.

"As you will," he cried, springing to his feet, "I go to my father's cell."

But even as he opened the door there came a swift rush of wings. Zetitzka could not tell whence it came, but in the hot darkness something cold and invisible fanned her cheek, stirring her hair and roughening her skin with fear. She uttered an involuntary cry.

"What is it now?" demanded Petros.

"I don't know. It is—it is something in the cell! I am frightened. Stay with me."

He peered at her over his shoulder in perplexity. She looked like the intangible form of a wistful and perverse spirit.

"I can make naught of you," he grumbled. "At one moment 'tis ' Go,' and the next ' Stay.' Do you know your own mind?"

"N—o—o."

"Then how may I know it?"

"Oh, don't talk! Just come back." Then, as he hesitated, "Has it gone? Shut the door quickly, or it may come in again."

He obeyed her reluctantly. The door once closed, a sense of security caused her to breathe freely.

A last glimmer of light struggled downwards from the little window above their heads, for the storm was over and the sky was clearing fast. After a few desultory efforts, conversation languished.

From her voice, Petros could tell that she was drowsy. He, on the contrary, became every moment more wide awake. Noting that she had sunk to the ground, he stretched himself beside her, and tried vainly to woo sleep by repeating a prayer associated with his father.

Disquieting thoughts came to him as he lay open-eyed in the darkness. Accustomed only to profound silence, or to noises so muffled as to be unimportant, Petros found himself listening intently to her breathing, and to her uneasy movements as she sought relief from the hardness of the floor. Never before had he slept in the same cell with anyone, not even with his father, and he vowed with determination that he never would again. To know his companion so close that he had only to put out a hand in order to touch her, was distracting. To calm his thoughts he concentrated his mind upon the icon of the Blessed Virgin, his favourite among all the icons in the Catholicon, and now separated from him by so great a space of benighted road, but other thoughts thrust themselves forward. He could not tell what they were, for rather were they feelings than ideas, but none the less perturbing on that account. Had he been alone he would have risen and prayed aloud, but the fear of awakening his companion kept him motionless. The idea, that perhaps, after all, the devils had entered the cell, came to him in a sudden rush of terror, causing him to shut his eyes tightly in case he might see them. After repeating every prayer appropriate to the occasion which he could call to mind, he cautiously looked- around. Only darkness, broken by the faint pallor of light from the window. He listened intently. Only silence, caressed rather ,than ruffled by the gentle intaking and outgiving of Zetitzka's breath. The peaceful somnolent sounds calmed his fears, but awoke a sensation of loneliness. He had never felt it before to quite the same extent. Her propinquity, added to her state of oblivion, made this feeling unbearable. He longed for her to speak, to give him the comfort of conscious human companionship. But the soft sounds continued without intermission.

Of a sudden he could stand it no longer.

" Angelos," he whispered.

No answer. Zetitzka was far away in a land of dreams.

He put out a hand to touch her, then slowly drew it back. "Nay," he thought, "it would be right selfish to disturb him."

Standing erect, he flung out his arms, taking care, however, to make no noise, then turning slowly went out into the corridor.

The night was charged with electricity. It steeped the senses of the young monk in a soft and enervating languor. It deepened also the emotional mood that, like the vague unrest of spring when April is at hand, throbbed and tingled in his blood.

A night of forbidden dreams! The world sought to tempt him. It was robed in beauty, alluring in its mystery. The cliffs shone in the starlight, like wan faces watching him above the gloom of the gorges. A great planet glowed like a jewel on the dusky bosom of night. The distance had ceased to be the plain and the river he knew so well. It too had allied itself with the powers of darkness, and was now naught but a temptation whispering of something he felt, but could not put into words—a something which he vaguely feared was evil.

With all his might Petros sought to banish the emotions that beset him, but in an environment so favourable they flourished and grew apace. He was filled with unrest, saddened with longing. The latter troubled him the most, though for what he longed he knew not.

His ignorance added immeasurably to his trouble. It was like fighting a foe in the dark. All knowledge of life had been purposely withheld from him by his father, and later by the monks. He had been of so tender an age when first he had joined the monastery that the brethren, with a delicacy that did them credit, had taken a pleasure in keeping him in the happy ignorance of childhood. Nature had sought to enlighten him, as Nature will, but her unaided efforts, instead of explaining the mystery, but added to his bewilderment. He had carried his difficulties to the Abbot in the hour of confession, but the aged priest, to whom this young soul, white and unspotted, was a something beautiful amid the contagion of the world, had contented himself with teaching the boy to combat all incomprehensible emotions by prayer. To himself the Abbot murmured:—" Not yet, not yet, time enough to tell him when he is older. Yet, if only I could keep him ever thus! In blessed innocence. Holy Mother of God, what a victory! What a perfect pearl for thy crown!''

As he stood there in the darkness, leaning against the worn coping-stones of what had once been a parapet, it came to Petros suddenly, with the sinister exaggeration of fears born in the night, that he must be intensely wicked; not merely with the wickedness common to humanity, but of a heart given over to depravity, of a soul lost, abandoned. The hot night seemed full of devils, as though the spirit of darkness hovered overhead with invisible bat-like wings. The world upon which he looked down, as a sailor from the mast-head might gaze upon a mysterious sea, seemed the veiled form of evil, of which the stars were the eyes, cold, vigilant, malevolent. He was alone, terribly alone, warring not only with the external and invisible spectres of his imagination, but with himself, with his traitor heart that had laid siege to the peaceful citadel of his soul. Horrified at his wickedness, he fell to praying aloud, repeating instinctively the prayer set down in the penance called the *canon*:—

''Lord Jesu Christ, Son of the living God, have mercy on me!'' At every repetition he abased himself towards the ruined Catholicon.

The moon circled above the monastery, steeping everything in silver witchery. To Petros it seemed like God's own smile—a visible answer to prayer. Uplifted in spirit, but still vaguely disquieted in mind, he again sought his ce l.

He paused upon the threshold. It was as if a transformation had taken place during his absence. He had left it dark—he now beheld it bright. Moonlight streamed inwards through the little window. It formed a broad shaft of radiance that fell upon the floor and upon the sleeping form of Zetitzka. All else was vague, shadowy, obscured into unimportance. Only the sleeper stood out bathed in a wonderful white light—the one important thing in the cell. She lay in the limp abandonment of sleep—on her back—her head pillowed on one round bare arm. She looked peaceful—almost happy; for sleep by touching away a line of care, had given back to her somewhat of the untroubled expression of her girlhood. The moonlight etherealised her comeliness, brushed with silver the curves of her shapely figure. The fringe of her long lashes lay upon her cheeks, and soft through parted lips came the breath of dreamless slumber. Above all things she looked intensely feminine. No longer upon her guard, everything about her whispered of the woman.

Petros gazed in silence—holding his breath. Could this be Angelos, the lay brother! Very slowly he approached her, taking care to make no noise. Why he did so he knew not; obeying, it would seem, some instinct of which he was unaware. When he was come within a couple of yards, he stopped suddenly.

In the hot night, unfastened doubtless by some restless movement of the sleeper, the breast of her lay brother's tunic had fallen open. Upon this the eyes of the boy were riveted. Through the black rift of the dingy garment, white in the moonlight, shone the pure soft outlines of her woman's form.

Petros stood as if turned to stone. The expression in his eyes passed slowly from incredulity to horror. For awhile he stood trembling, fascinated, impotent to avert his gaze. Then, of a sudden, the girl moved, and as if set free from a spell he fled from her presence.

CHAPTER XXIII

ZETITZKA awoke and rubbed her eyes. For a moment, imagining herself at Barlaam, the fear that she had overslept beset her. But her surroundings speedily pointed out her mistake.

In the cold grey light the cell stood revealed in all its nudity. Its only redeeming quality was the glimpse it gave of the world without—the glint of pale blue sky seen through the broken window.

As she sat up the girl's eye fell upon evidences of Petros—the empty wallet in which they had carried their provisions, and the cloak of the young monk, disarranged, as though hastily flung aside when he awoke from sleep. These proofs that a man had shared her cell, had actually slept beside her all night, struck Zetitzka with sudden consternation. For the first time she realised the enormity of the situation. In the darkness it had seemed only natural that he should stay and protect her, but in the uncompromising light of day it assumed monstrous proportions.

With a sudden guilty start she remembered how she had entreated him to remain with her, and at the remembrance she became one burning blush from head to foot. Was ever anything so improper, so indelicate, done by a girl before? What had he thought of her? What did he think now? And then, with an immense insurgence of relief, she recollected that she need not feel ashamed, for in his eyes she was but a boy.

She was thankful that he had quitted the cell before she awoke, but she wondered where he had gone. Perhaps, she reflected, to the Catholicon to pray.

As her sleep-bemused mind picked up one by one the loosened threads of existence, there came again the memory of Barlaam and of Stephanos. It was as if a black cloud had driven suddenly between her and the sun.

So, this short holiday was nearly over! In a few hours at most the dull dead weight of the monastery and of her mission would press again upon every moment of her life.

But bravely fighting her depression, she reminded herself that she could still count upon a brief period of respite —that all had gone well—that her secret was still her own. With a feeling almost akin to self-congratulation, she rose to her feet.

Standing in the middle of the little cell, she carried her arms above her head, her hands seeking for the long hair that used to fall in profusion about her shoulders. It was not the first time that force of long habit had deceived her. Again the cropped tresses reminded her that the massive and shining coils that had adorned her head were now lying concealed among the rocks. Recollection brought with it regret for the uselessness of the sacrifice. Deep in her inmost being the spirit of undying coquetry awoke, whispering to her that had she not thus robbed herself of her chief beauty, she might still have been attractive. But even as the echo of this idea made itself heard, instinctive and primitive, not so much hers as that of countless dead women speaking through her, she blushed again, answering a thought that scarcely existed, with all the innocent consciousness of a child.

The silence of the place was so intense that Zetitzka caught herself listening for some faint indication of monastic life; then she smiled as she called to mind that all the inmates were dead, ages long ago, and that she and Petros were the only living souls upon the pinnacle-top.

The wind breathed gently upon her through the open window. Its purity spoke of the heights, and its freshness of the dawn. Moving softly, she folded her companion's cloak, then sought to make a scanty toilet, though the denuded cell supplied nothing that could assist her, not even a basin wherein to wash. Observing that her tunic was unfastened, she buttoned it hastily. In all her actions there was a deftness, a silent celerity, that told of one naturally neat-handed. She move noiselessly, almost stealthily, as though she feared to awaken the echoes, and at times she paused again to listen, her head slightly on one side. Before she quitted the cell she fell on her knees and prayed.

Prayer came more easily that morning. Ever since her arrival at Barlaam prayer had seemed a mockery. How could she approach a God whose name was Love, with nothing but hate in her heart? But now a gentler mood had come to her; a wish to draw near to God; a desire to live at peace with all men. Absent from Barlaam, the load of her wrongs seemed to press less heavily. With an instinctive shrinking she felt that they were only awaiting her return, but for the moment she strove to banish them from her mind, and succeeded beyond anticipation. Encouraging kindly thoughts, she included the names of Petros and the Abbot in her prayers. Then, with peace in her heart, she stepped lightly into the corridor.

The sun, barely above the ruined buildings, sparkled upon the water that lay in pools between the displaced flagstones. It winked a merry eye from the metal ball that topped the dome of the Catholicon, it danced hither and thither, flinging jewels of light over trodden weed and trembled blossom, turning the courtyard into a garden and the cloisters into a palace.

Already the heat fought with the freshness of the summer dawn. A haze, filmy as wafted gossamer, quivered along the summits of the broken walls. Far off, seen through gaps in the ruined masonry, the river and the hills seemed still to slumber, dreaming dreams that fell from the blue of the sky.

Zetitzka's nature responded joyously to the beauty and the brightness. She was young enough still to float buoyantly on the tide of hope—the tide that ebbs in later life and leaves us stranded on the shores of time. The softened feelings in her heart centred themselves on Petros. Thoughts of him stirred feelings of glad anticipation— and yet for the moment she was in no hurry to join him. It was enough to know he was there—her friend—a sure ally in case of danger. Still semi-dreaming, she took pleasure in recalling facts connected with him; things he had said; his laugh; his expression when under excitement; his sunny nature, that seemed to have drawn to itself all that made life joyous. A sigh broke from her. His memory filled her with wistful regret, with an envy that was free from all covetousness. Life to him was still a white unwritten page; to her it was already defaced by a black and shameful experience. A gulf lay between them, yet her feelings overleaped it. The law of nature that commands that opposites be drawn to opposites had unconsciously influenced both. He had instinctively felt attracted by her air of reticent experience—she by his engaging candour and simplicity. The young man and the young woman had gravitated towards each other as naturally and inevitably as youth is allured by youth, and laughter is rendered responsive by laughter.

Yet always Zetitzka felt immeasurably the elder, despite his two or three years of seniority. To her he seemed still a child, the more so on account of his airs of boyish dogmatism and fancied knowledge of the world.

As she stood in the early sunlight, with the monastery basking around her, she drew the bright morning into her blood, exquisitely alive to all the sweet communicable influences of nature. And it seemed indeed as if the beneficent and immortal spirits—called by mortal names of sun and breeze—were graciously aware of the unconscious worship in the girl's heart, for they hovered over her like a flutter of imminent wings, gilding her blue-black curls and stirring her garment's hem. It might well be, for they had seen nothing fairer than her face, fresh as the dawn and full of quiet reflected brightness as the blue overhead— a presence strangely sweet amid the ruins of Lavra.

All at once the intense solitude of the place made her conscious of loneliness. Feeling that she had but to find Petros to have this sensation dispelled, she ran towards the ruined Catholicon. He was not there. She called aloud, but her clear girlish voice was answered only by lugubrious echoes. With a growing anxiety, which she strove in vain to repress, she searched the cloisters, the refectory, and the various buildings that huddled on the small restricted summit. All were desolate, voiceless. Thoroughly alarmed now, she hastened towards the precipice that concealed the ladders. A rope made fast to a post caught her attention. It dangled in space, forming a connecting link between the monastery and the uninjured portion of the ladders full forty feet below. Zetitzka gazed at it in bewilderment. Petros had spoken of no rope! She knew for certain that it had not been there on the preceding night. Then, in a flash, the truth struck her. Petros had put it there! He had escaped by it! She was alone in Lavra!

CHAPTER XXIV

AN hour later Dimitri, preceded by Nikola, fared leisurely up the path that led past the base of Lavra. The muleteer took a fearful pleasure in tempting Providence by choosing a track whereon few villagers would travel. This he did partly to shock the neighbours, and partly—as he himself expressed it—" for fun." Be it noted, however, that he chose sunrise and not nightfall for the adventure.

He cast a glance at the ruins as he approached. But overhead nothing stirred. Desolate as of old, Lavra frowned into the summer sky.

Suddenly Dimitri halted. A look of excitement overspread his bronzed face. He had caught sight of the broken ladder. Before he had time to recover from his surprise, something lying athwart the path attracted his attention. It looked, he thought, uncommonly like a human body—a remarkable object anywhere; but here, distinctly uncanny. Dimitri was perturbed into making the sign of the cross.

The more phlegmatic Nikola plodded forward. With sudden shame at his indecision her master made haste to follow her example. When he came near, he saw to his astonishment that the body was that of Angelos, the lay brother.

Quite unconscious, Zetitzka lay at the base of the ladders. There was an inert pathetic abandonment in the apparently boyish figure clad in dingy grey, lying there to all intents lifeless, as though already a clod, one with the stones, the cliffs, and all the inanimate fabric of the revolving earth. She lay partly on her side, one arm extended, the fingers of the outstretched hand still tenaciously grasping the rotten rung—doubtless the immediate cause of the disaster. Her head, from which the lay brother's cap had fallen, was tilted back, revealing a scalp wound above the right ear. The latter had bled freely. The vivid red, scarcely dry, contrasted with the jetty blackness of her hair and the death-like pallor of her face.

Dimitri looked at her with bent brows, then gazed upwards at the monastery. Many questions suggested themselves, but no answers. The muleteer was aroused from the puzzle by the sound of Nikola sniffing curiously at the girl's face.

"Sacred name!" he ejaculated, in sudden self-condemnation. "I stand here gaping while the lad bleeds to death!" Then, with a resounding smack on the grey hindquarters, "Out of the way, old lady!"

Kneeling by her side, he ran his fingers tentatively over her limbs. Suddenly his hands fell limply to his sides. With a new interest, at once breathless and absorbed, he gazed into her face. It was upturned to his, the eyelids closed, the mouth quiet; but for its whiteness and the blood-encrusted hair, it might have been the face of one asleep. The muleteer's eyes strayed from her face to her figure. For a while he gazed at her, like a man overwhelmed by an impossible idea, yet not so much incredulous as bewildered. Mechanically he took her hand. It lay in his—limp, small, brown, hardened by work, yet not without a certain feminine delicacy. Dimitri drew a long breath, then slowly nodded comprehension.

It was characteristic of the man that he did not again touch her. When she showed signs of returning consciousness, he moved discreetly to a little distance. Languidly she opened her eyes.

"Where am I?" The mountain dialect came naturally to her lips. Dimitri was watching her intently.

"You have had a fall," he said in Greek.

Zetitzka looked at him, almost, he thought, as though she did not see him, then gazed helplessly at the ruins overhead, at the broken ladder by her side, and, far up the cliff, at the dangling rope. She tried to sit up.

"I must go," she said, and fainted.

When she again recovered consciousness she found herself lying on a cloak. A space had been cleared for her among the stones. She noted these things in the listless indifferent fashion of a person recovering from an illness.

Her head gave her great pain; she felt, also, unaccountably weak. But these physical sensations were as nothing compared with her distress of mind. Some black cloud overshadowed her. She tried to recall it, but it eluded memory. And yet it must be something horrible and imminent, such a shadow of depression darkened her spirits. Curiously enough, it was the thought of her child that started the rapid and illuminating train of ideas that swept her onwards to the moment of her accident. Never before, save once, had she felt so helpless, weak, and abandoned—the victim of a fate that beat her down with reiterated and cruel blows.

She was alone. In all this grey world of rocks and frowning cliffs, not a sound, not a movement. She lay in the shadow of Lavra. At a distance of a few yards she could see where the path wound, glaring white in the pitiless sunshine, and up and beyond to where the serrated outline of cliffs gnawed at the oppressive and sinister splendour of the sky. The heat was on the increase. The rocks that were already submerged flung it off like the breath of a furnace. It weighed on the heart and withered all impulses of strength and energy. The whole scene, with its entire absence of life, saturated in sunlight, and brooded over by profound silence, seemed unreal as a phantom landscape, or an uninhabited planet wheeling its lonely way through space in a fulgor of eternal sunshine.

Dim memories of a man, seen like a vision upon the first opening of her eyelids, came to Zetitzka as she lay sunk in stupor. Where was he? She did not care. He had gone. Yet how to account for the cloak, a coarse brown garment which she could see with her heavy, listless eyes without turning her head?

These and other questions forced themselves upon her, vaguely, indefinitely, almost as though they concerned someone else, and yet the effort to answer them was beyond her.

She made no effort to rouse herself. She knew that some time she must go—but not yet. She did not care. What worse thing could happen to her? And, moreover, when she tried to move, her right ankle gave her such pain that she was glad to lie still. She wondered with indifference if it were broken.

She wondered, too, with equal indifference what would become of her, of the Zetitzka who had made such a mess of life, whom no one wanted? Despairing thoughts chased each other through her feverish brain. She seemed to have sounded the deeps of life, to have reached the butt-end where she must crawl to die, to have tasted the ultimate sorrow that lay at the heart of the world. Her recuperative energy—hers in common with all young things—had been, as it were, suspended for the moment by this final catastrophe—the desertion of Petros and the shock of the fall. She felt as though nothing could touch her now.

A sound roused her—approaching footsteps. A man came into sight carrying a tin can, evidently full, for his care lest he should spill its contents was visible.

His eyes, meeting hers, betrayed a comical mixture of anxiety, relief, and self-reproach.

"You are better!" he cried. "I had to go far. These rocks, look you, no water. Drink this; 'twill do you good. It should be brandy; but I have not even wine to-day—nothing but oil."

He held it to her white lips, and seemed disappointed that she could sip so little. Without interest, without curiosity, Zetitzka noticed details about this man—noticed them in spite of herself, for they made but little impression upon her bruised and deadened brain. He had a strong, good-looking, sunburnt face, with something reliable in it. His picturesque costume struck a not unfamiliar note. The white of his kilted fustinella spoke to her unconsciously of the mountains; while the scarlet of his sash, wooing her eye with a sensation of brightness, essayed to lift her mentally into a region of colourful things suggestive of a world far removed from this great depressing chaos of rocks. But wearily she closed her eyes.

"You have forgotten me," he said. Then, with an evident wish to be recalled to mind: "In Barlaam, last Monday. Dimitri, yes. By the Lord! 'twas fortunate I came this way.'"

He seated himself by her side. She remembered him now. But he seemed different from the man she had spoken to in the court of Barlaam. There he had been bluff, rollicking, almost arrogant in his air of virile health and strength; but here he was subdued, unaccountably gentle. She attributed the change to her accident, and for the first time felt a slight warmth of gratitude.

Meanwhile he was tearing a coloured handkerchief into strips and talking softly—a soliloquy, independent of answers. That wound, by the saints. R-r-rrp! went the handkerchief. He would try not to hurt. R-r-rrp! What was the good of a handkerchief he never used? Could the head be raised? Oh, the least thing! Confound his fingers. Strapping a pack-saddle was more in their line. What! the ankle too? There, how was that? Why, he was prepared to wager Nikola against a brass nail that things looked better already.

Zetitzka scarcely heard him. She gave herself up to the unusual feeling of being waited on. When he had finished, she tried to thank him, but her lips trembled. Touched by his kindness, and prompted by his evident curiosity— which shone naïvely through his stout assertions that he did not want to know—she endeavoured to relate the misadventure.

" You—you came down that rope! " he cried in amazement. Her account seemed to make the feat more real, yet more impossible. At her answer his expression of blank incredulity changed to one of bewilderment. Greatly mystified, he sought relief in scratching his thick crop of hair; but the exercise brought him no nearer a solution. Doubts beset him. Not that he doubted her word: it was impossible to listen and disbelieve. But the whole insoluble mystery of her presence weighed upon him.

He looked long at her with unusual self-consciousness; for, unused to dissimulation, it needed continual effort to feign ignorance of her sex. He wondered what her age might be. She looked extraordinarily young in that monastic costume: he surmised she might be on the verge of twenty.

Then, for the first time, the impropriety of the adventure struck him. Petros and this fine-looking girl up there alone all night. Dimitri's blue eyes twinkled. And her stay in the monastery? Barlaam! Where women were looked upon as incarnations of the evil one? Again Dimitri suppressed a chuckle. But his unworthy suspicions were put to ignominious flight by the innocent candour in her face.

" You are right," he cried, as though answering a remark. " 'Tis none of my business. Name of a Saint! you carry God's truth in your eyes. And I who thought—" he spat with vehement self-contempt, then, glancing at her penitently—" Devil take me, I always think evil of others—that is because I am like that myself. But I have a heart "—he thumped that organ with unnecessary violence—" yes, a heart that is sensible; it likes you; you have courage."

Zetitzka replied faintly that it was nothing, that any boy would have done the same.

Dimitri stared. But all he said was: " Well, what is to be done now? "

What *was* to be done? The world was so wide, and yet there was nowhere to go. The only two places she knew—her home and the monastery—were closed to her. Petros had discovered her secret. She was sure of that— his sudden flight, her intuition, her guilty conscience, all pointed unmistakably to the fact. Only too well she knew his feelings about women. She could never go back to the monastery.

For the first time, in spite of her suffering, she realised how dependent she had become upon the comradeship and support of this boy. She saw now that had he not been there she would have left long ago, probably after her second failure to fulfill her promise to her parents. That she dared not go home seemed to make no difference. She tried to imagine Barlaam—the friendship of Petros changed into aversion. The prospect appalled her. It would be bad enough now even if he kept her secret. But would he? She had no reason for imagining it. He was one with the monastery in every word and action, as much as a limb is one with the body. It was not to be expected that he would keep silent. He had the start of her by several hours. The chances were that by this time he had told all. Her imagination shrank from the scene it conjured up, the whole place in a ferment, seething, furious, thirsting to avenge the sacrilege. No! A thousand times no! She could never go back to the monastery.

12

Apart from anxiety about her future, she was conscious of acute personal disappointment, as if she had irretrievably lost something dear to her. How, she asked herself, had Petros found it in his heart to desert her? She did not blame him—she only sorrowed. It brought home to her how much this bright-faced lad had become to her. She had imagined that she cared for him only as a prop, but she now discovered that what she felt lay deeper than that—and she was right, for the tie that bound her to him was the reliance which a sincere, staunch, and reticent nature reposes upon the loyalty of a friend. This discovery took her by surprise, and a great inarticulate sadness welled up in her heart, and became visible in her eyes.

The muleteer, who had been watching her intently, bent forward.

" You are in pain? " he asked, mistaking her emotion. " That ankle? It ought to be bound up. And I—who have nothing." Then, after thought—" I must take you back to Barlaam."

" No, no! "

" No? " He eyed her in much perplexity.

Her gesture left the matter in his hands.

Dimitri saw that he was expected to take charge. This forced him to think. His thinking was merely a blind groping in possibilities, with nothing stable save a woman, a mystery, and a rotten ladder—and none of these, he reflected whimsically, were celebrated for stability. Had it been any other girl, he would have taken her straight to the village; had it been an ordinary lay brother, he would have taken him at once to the monasteries. But this was neither—and yet both!

The conundrum was also rendered more difficult by her reticence. He was forced to pretend she was a boy. He fumed inwardly, jerking at his little moustache. That he, Dimitri, should in all seriousness be asked to act as guardian and knight-errant to a young woman masquerading as a lay brother was certainly a state of affairs bordering upon the fantastic.

The sight of the white face and the bandaged head, however, plunged him abruptly into a penitential mood. How could he, brute beast that he was, remain inactive when this brave woman was suffering in heroic silence?

And yet he felt conscious of unusual hesitation, totally unlike himself.

"You might come to our house," he said kindly. "My mother is there. But——"

Zetitzka waited.

"It's—it's——" His eyes were fixed on Nikola. "It's the oil I am taking to Meteoron—promised for daybreak. Besides—Barlaam, eh? You belong there, you know. They might let you stay with us one night; not more. And, another thing——"

Scratching his chin, he continued with much gravity: "There is my mother—eh? 'Tis against your vows to speak to women."

But from her answer it appeared that to speak to women was not such a sin after all.

She could barely finish the sentence. The cliffs seemed to be toppling over: the sun—that had at last reached them—to be growing dark. She felt as though she were sinking again into blackness, and only by a great effort of will could she retain her hold upon the conscious world. Dimitri's voice came to her from an immense distance.

"I am a mule. A mule, do I say. I flatter myself. The more shame to me! We will be proud, my mother and I, to welcome you. You will see—she is famous for bandages, the little mother! Curse the oil—the monks must wait. I wager you have had no breakfast? No? Ah, I thought not. Come; we will go. Nay, you must not move. Let me lift you. Have no fear; I will handle you like eggs, you will see."

In spite of her size and weight, Zetitzka felt herself caught up, borne away, all, as it seemed to her, in a dream.

In another moment she was seated upon Nikola's back —the barrels of oil having been removed and rolled into a crevice of the rocks, where, as Dimitri remarked, they would be safe from observation till his return.

"I give you much trouble," she faltered, inexpressibly ashamed of her weakness.

"*Trouble!*" He laughed with genial irony; for a moment his eyes rested on her with unusual warmth of regard; then, bending forward and speaking with simple earnestness:—" By the faith! 'tis the best stroke of work, the best——"

He became abruptly silent, betraying an exaggerated and altogether unnecessary apprehension lest the sure-footed Nikola should stumble—a gratuitous form of insult which the little mule received with the silence of contempt.

The memory of that ride came back to Zetitzka afterwards as a haunting and distressful nightmare—the jerkings of the mule; the hardness of the pack-saddle; the pain of her ankle; and the terrible faintness which she struggled to overcome; their distorted shadows, black in the glare; the grey world of rocks; the frowning cliffs; the pitiless blue of the sky; the fierce sun pouring his concentrated fire upon the empty gorge.

They moved slowly and in silence, Zetitzka holding with both hands to the saddle-peak, jolting painfully—Dimitri leading Nikola with unusual care and an occasional curse, seeking to minimise the dislocating upward jerks and sudden sharp descents; his attention not so fully occupied but that he found time to steal many a wondering glance at the pathetic figure in the grey tunic.

At the junction of the two paths Zetitzka could no longer stand the torture.

" How far? " she questioned.

Dimitri looked at her anxiously.

" Not far now. A little ten minutes; just beyond——"
He broke off with a startled oath, for, round a turning in the track that led upward to Barlaam, two old men came hurrying—the Abbot and Brother Nicodemus.

CHAPTER XXV

THE level sunlight, slanting athwart the monastic roofs, fell upon the dormitory of Barlaam. In the mellow golden illumination the old woodwork, polished by generations of dead hands, took on wonderful high-lights, vying in intensity with the lustrous note of the great fig-leaves hanging motionless from their gnarled branches. All the many little doors in the corridor were closed, save one, that of Petros.

The long heat of the summer day was well-nigh over, but the air in the drowsy court—so effectually shut in by the circle of low-roofed buildings—still hung slumbrous and heavy. No sound was audible save the murmurous buzz of flies, and at times the faint scream of far-off swallows, as they darted hither and thither in the breathless air. Yet the silence was not oppressive, but gave rather the feeling of deep and unbroken peace—of peace so profound as to partake of the spirit rather than of the body.

All at once the door of the Abbot's cell opened, and the old man appeared on the threshold. His thin silvery hair, unconfined by the customary headgear, fell to his shoulders; his white beard descended to his waist. The flowing lines of his black robe lent to his somewhat bent figure an air of dignity, and even of grace. As he stood there, so venerable and full of quiet serenity did he appear, so harmoniously one with the old-world, time-haunted, sun-steeped aspect of his surroundings, that he might well have been taken for the incarnate soul of the place.

Resting both hands upon the railing, he leant over and gazed long into the empty court below, from which the sun was gradually withdrawing his rays. His movements were leisurely, meditative; his expression that of one recalled from some calm region of the spirit, to whom the world of reality is as a passing show, "an illusion," as he himself would have phrased it. For a full minute did he stand thus, as if forgetful of the reason that had summoned him from meditation; then suddenly he raised his voice.

"Brother Nicodemus," he called.

A pause; then the refectory door opened, and the monk in question came shambling across the courtyard.

"Has Brother Petros returned?"

"Not yet, venerable father."

A look of anxious wonderment came into the Abbot's face. He stroked his beard. From the court below the monk gazed up at his superior. His plebeian, bigoted, and dirty countenance expressed virtuous disapproval, mingled with that ill-natured satisfaction with which some natures hail the trespasses of even their best friends. These feelings, however, he was careful to conceal—though voiced later to the brethren.

The Abbot spoke again: "As soon as Brother Petros returns, tell him that I would have speech with him."

Nicodemus snuffled assent, upon which the two men separated.

Within her cell Zetitzka heard the command. Stretched upon the hard bench that did duty for a bed, the physical pain she suffered was all but forgotten in the stress of mental anxiety. Ever since her fate had been decided by the arrival of the two aged monks, the poor girl had been racked by fear. The ascent to the monastery by means of rope and net, which on another occasion would have taxed her nerves, was as nothing compared with the dangers which awaited her at the top. When she found that Petros had not yet returned, she experienced relief; a temporary respite, however, for she knew well that sooner or later the young monk would come back; and then—what would happen then? She dared not allow herself to imagine, for she feared the worst.

Crawling to the door—oblivious of pain—she posted herself so that she could see without being seen.

Slowly the moments passed! To Zetitzka, crouching there, listening, waiting, they seemed interminable. Every sound within the monastery brought her heart to her mouth. Never before had the place seemed so replete with hidden menace—its very air of sunlit stagnation, of remote antiquity, was a mask behind which lurked hostility and terror. Now, indeed, Zetitzka felt the weight of an added desolation. There was no soul in this aerial prison-house to befriend her. Her thoughts fled to Dimitri. There had been something about the muleteer, particularly during their last interview, that set her at ease. He had made no protestations of friendship, yet his strength, good-humour, unspoken sympathy, all made her feel that here indeed was a man on whom a woman could rely. Her heart had sunk when he had been forced to leave her, and now with all her might she longed for him to be again by her side. His parting words still rang in her ears. "Be brave," he had whispered, as she had been drawn upwards into space. "Be brave. We will meet again soon."

A sudden sound caused her to start and stare anxiously along the corridor. Was it Petros? But, no; it was only Brother Apostoli sauntering across the courtyard. At last she heard the voice of Nicodemus addressing the young monk—mingled reproaches and interrogations, as it seemed, to neither of which did Petros appear to make reply. At the little bridge the elder brother left him, and the sound of approaching footsteps told her to be ready.

Her agitation was extreme. Only imperative necessity forced her to keep her ground. As Petros drew near, she stood up and, nerving herself to the encounter, opened wide the door of her cell. Raising his eyes, he saw her white-faced and irresolute upon the threshold. A flash of guilty knowledge leapt to the eyes of both.

It is noteworthy that, next to their eyes, their hands betrayed their feelings—his raised suddenly to ward off evil, hers pressed to her bosom to fight down timidity.

"Hear me," she whispered. The boy receded a step —his expression haunted her afterwards; it was transfixed with fear, with horror, and yet with something of the helpless fascination with which a little bird watches the advances of a snake.

"You must hear me," she said, rendered desperate. "You are going to the Abbot. He will question you. You must not betray me."

He seemed incapable of speech—unable to move **or avert** his eyes. She wondered if he had heard.

" Do you understand? " she said breathlessly, insistently; then, with a tremble in her voice, " Oh, Brother Petros, you were my friend! I can explain all. I will go away soon. I promise it by everything holy—only—don't betray me! "

Still he stared at her. Hollow-eyed, with disordered dress, his appearance told of his night in the mountains when, driven by the scourge of thought, he had stumbled he scarce knew whither.

They were interrupted by an opening door. The Abbot's voice reached them. Hastily Zetitzka receded into her cell.

CHAPTER XXVI

"So, my son, you will tell me nothing?"

The interview had lasted some time. Petros, with hands clasped behind him, stood in front of the aged priest. The Abbot's face expressed disappointment. Between his eyebrows two perpendicular wrinkles gave the impression that he was puzzled as well as grieved.

"You will tell me nothing?" he repeated in a low voice. Petros looked up uneasily. His eyes encountered those of the Abbot.

"I can tell no more," he burst out. "O venerable father, ask me not!—I beseech you!"

The Abbot nodded indulgently.

"There—there, my son," he said, for the boy was shaking. "No need to distress yourself. Take time. I do not question you now as your superior, but as one who loves you. I see well you are distracted. It grieves me sore. I have known you long—sixteen years—and never before to-day have I seen you thus."

He paused—his right hand strayed mechanically to his horn snuff-box, then, as though suddenly conscious of the action, dropped dejectedly to his side. Somewhat of the dying radiance of day strayed through the obscure panes of the little window. Everything in the cell stood clearly out, from the agony upon the suspended cross, to the handful of faded poppies flaunting their withered scarlet against the grey of the wall. This fleeting light was like the smile of the dying—brightest before death. The silence was full of sadness.

The Abbot continued seriously:

"You fled from Lavra before dawn, leaving Angelos to face the descent alone. You wandered among the mountains, all day, it would seem, without rest and without food. At length, impelled by an awakening sense of duty, you returned to Barlaam."

Petros˙ muttered an affirmative. The Abbot became graver.

"You have no excuse to offer—no reason to give?"

Petros shook his head.

The Abbot continued: "To me is your conduct very strange—so unlike the lad I know. I—I cannot understand." He gazed with unaffected anxiety into the downcast young face before him; fingered his beads absently; then, as though struck by an idea, he leaned forward.

"Did you see aught in Lavra?" he whispered in an awestruck voice. Petros started, then flushed crimson.

"Aught evil or forbidden?" suggested the Abbot fearfully.

The boy stared speechless into his superior's face. Conviction fell suddenly upon the Abbot. Was not the place of evil repute? Brother Apostoli's adventure flashed to his mind, as well as many tales spread by the peasants. And he had allowed these two boys to visit it! Much he blamed himself. Why had he doubted? Were not Holy Writings full of such tales? In the fulness of his penitence, he burst forth:

"My poor lad! Nay, no need to speak. I see—I see. My relic has availed naught; yet it is of extreme potency, and was blessed by a bishop. Alack! 'tis very plain a devil has appeared unto you, possessing your weak body, and driving you forth into the wilderness."

Petros listened with downcast head, tortured by an hysterical desire to laugh.

"But we will cast him out," continued the simple old man, eagerly. "Yea, we will cast him out. Now, God be praised that you have returned to us. That is already much."

In the silence that ensued, Petros heard the muffled click of beads. The dusk had fallen: the bowed head of the Abbot with its tonsure and long hair, became every moment less visible. Again the old man spoke.

"The anxiety you have caused us, my son, is as nothing to the wrong you have—under evil influence, I wot, but none the less certainly—inflicted upon another."

Petros raised his head quickly.

"Brother Angelos. . . . Yes, he might have been killed."

" Killed!"

" Assuredly! Did you not know? He fell from the ladders, and now, even as we speak, lies grievously wounded in his cell."

" But—but——"

" Ah, you are confounded and without speech. So is it ever with those possessed. You have acted selfishly—cruelly—as one distraught, knowing not evil from good. Thank God, Who in His goodness gives you a chance of redeeming your unworthy actions. Rejoice, my son; be of good cheer. I give Angelos into your charge. For his sake I grant you permission to enter his cell by night as well as by day. The lad is ill—feverish and in pain; be to him a good Samaritan, nursing him with love and all brotherly tenderness. So will the memory of your offence be forgotten. Now——" He passed a hand across his eyes. " I am weary, and fain would sleep. Good-night, my son. Well? Did you not hear? Saint Barlaam! what is this? "

Petros had fallen to his knees.

" Venerable father," he cried, grasping the hem of the Abbot's fur-edged cassock with both hands, " I entreat—I implore you not to make me do this thing! "

Desperately in earnest, his voice rose in supplication. The old man stared, speechless.

" I—I cannot, I may not, say more. If it were my own secret—— But my tongue is tied. It must be that I am possessed by a devil. Nay, not as you imagine. Be-think you, would I act thus—of my own free will? Great God!—no! " He made a hard, wringing motion of the hands; then, with fresh vehemence: " O venerable father, be merciful! "

The Abbot was overwhelmed. The distress of the young suppliant seemed to shake the little cell, filling it with a breath from the turbulent world of unrestrained emotion, strangely at variance with its atmosphere of ancient peace. It agitated the old man painfully, stirring in his aged body the memory of passions overcome by prayer, of youth conquered by the years. His heart went out to the boy. He seemed to see himself in this young, impulsive nature that took the little things of life so seriously—him-self, how long ago! Had he acted as his affection dictated,

he would at once have given way, but the responsibility of
his office brooked no weakness. His duty was plain.
Obedience, implicit and silent, bound all within the monastery. So stringent was this rule that it was never questioned. The Abbot's amazement was but the more complete.

Petros, however, mistook his silence for vacillation.

"Send Brother Nicodemus," he proposed eagerly.
"For him will there be no danger."

The naïveté of the request brought a smile to the Abbot's
face. He called to mind that in many ways Petros was
still a child.

"Tut, tut! my little son," he remonstrated, patting him
on the shoulder; "your looks are wild, your words are
naught but foolishness. 'Send Brother Nicodemus,' say
you—and wherefore? If it be wrong for you, it will be
wrong for him likewise. Bethink you; to tend the sick
is enjoined on us by the dear Lord Himself. Nay, I am
too lenient. But 'tis the foul fiend speaking within you.
He abhors good actions. Now, no more words, but do
even as I tell you, for holy obedience' sake."

The futility of further argument struck Petros with consternation. For the first time in his life it awoke in him
a spirit of rebellion, of impotent despair similar to that
which goads a wild animal on finding itself trapped. Respect for his superior and life-long training sealed his lips.
His eyes, however, betrayed the state of his mind.

The Abbot rose to his feet: tall and erect—no longer a
frail old man, but the soul of authority made visible. Before his steady dominant gaze the eyes of the poor boy
fell abashed; his head drooped to his chest.

"Rise, my son," said the Abbot, quietly. Petros
obeyed. The Abbot placed his hands upon the young
monk's shoulders.

"Shall I tell you somewhat?" he asked.

A muffled affirmative answered him.

"It has ever been my great hope," began the aged
priest, with unusual gravity, "that on no distant day,
when I have gone, you may be even as I am now—an
abbot. My son, I have watched you—trained you, with
God knows how much love and fear. To no one else in
the monastery could I leave the work of my life, stead-

fast in the assured hope that, with the dear Lord's assistance, all will be well—as well, nay, perchance better, than it is now. But youth is impetuous—a straw in the wind of the world.''

He paused. His eyes, resting on the downcast face, grew wistful in their anxiety—yearning to help, yet pathetically conscious of the gulf of years. He continued:

'' When you are the Abbot of Barlaam, my son, you will understand. For the present, be assured that what I command is best, and ''—he paused again to give his words full weight—'' must be obeyed. Now go. Take Brother Angelos his supper.''

Ten minutes later Zetitzka was aroused by a timid knocking. Upon her answering, someone appeared in the low doorway who, though all but unrecognisable in the dusk, she instinctively felt to be Petros.

Her heart beat very fast. An unconquerable shyness sealed her lips. The obscurity seemed powerless to hide her.

Trembling and with downcast eyes she waited nervously for what he might say or do. There followed a long and disconcerting silence. Then Zetitzka heard the clatter of a tray hastily set down. The door closed—in sudden panic as it seemed, for the sound of flying footsteps came to her, receding faint and ever fainter into the distance.

CHAPTER XXVII

" THE venerable father says he is possessed by a devil."

Nicodemus spoke in a hushed and awestruck voice, addressing Brothers Gerasimos and Philemon. The three monks were seated on the wooden bench that ran round the tower of the windlass. Before them and below, the gorges swam in sunlight; behind, the rude capstan extended its four gaunt arms. The net used for the ascent lay on the floor, while close by was to be seen the clumsy iron hook fastened to the end of the rope.

The brethren, side by side, all clad in rusty black, and slow in movement, resembled aged crows.

At the remark of Nicodemus, his friends crossed themselves with grave faces.

" Verily, he is much changed,' croaked Gerasimos, wagging a mournful head.

" He has even lost interest in bulbs," wheezed Philemon, biting black nails.

" I am sorry for the lad," said Gerasimos, " truly sorry. He cheered us. I love him. Yea, I miss his young laugh. The venerable father did wisely to command that he be treated as usual. Devils must not be crossed rashly, but with many pious precautions." He spat thoughtfully into space, rubbed his ragged moustache with the back of his hand, and continued: " I confess to ye twain that I was in high hopes to expose the foul fiend this very morning. I beguiled our dear afflicted brother into a corner and read to him a murder case out of the *Neon Asty.* ' If it be a real devil,' thought I craftily, ' it will rejoice over murder.' But, no. The lad gazed at me the while with a lack-lustre eye."

" You take too much interest in murders," reproved Nicodemus.

" They make my flesh creep," said Gerasimos simply.

Nicodemus scowled. " Flesh was made to mortify, not

to creep. But were I Abbot of Barlaam, I would inflict a grievous penance. The lad's inattention during service is a scandal. Did neither of you twain notice it?''

" Ay, did we,'' corroborated Philemon eagerly. " And so did the venerable father. I caught him looking often, in sorrow as it would seem, for he made two mistakes in the 6th Hour.''

" So he did,'' assented Gerasimos, stroking his beard. " So he did. But methought it was the fault of his eyesight, for it fails him sadly, in spite of his spectacles.''

" Spectacles! '' Nicodemus ejaculated with harsh intolerance. " I marvel much that the Abbot maketh use of such worldly things. *I* have no need of them. I take it we were born without spectacles.''

He faced the others triumphantly, with the air of one who clinches an argument.

" *Polycala!* '' ejaculated Gerasimos. " How clearly and well you expound anything that is not Scripture, Brother Nicodemus—and yet——''

" Yet, what? ''

" We were born without clothes, you remember.''

" I do not remember,'' said Nicodemus sulkily.

" The eggs were good to-day,'' remarked Philemon, after a pause, during which all three sat without moving, their eyes fixed dreamily upon the ravine. Gerasimos turned his head indolently, like an old tortoise sunning itself in the heat.

" One pistevo and one paternoster,'' said he drowsily, " that is the time to boil a good egg.''

" They say two pistevos at Meteoron,'' mused Philemon, " but that is because the Hegoumenos likes his eggs hard.''

" Did you notice Brother Stephanos at breakfast? '' struck in Nicodemus, his voice warming with devout enthusiasm. " He ate naught.''

" The more for us,'' murmured Gerasimos.

Nicodemus turned upon him.

" You pervert my meaning. You make a god of your stomach—carnal-minded, lusting ever after the flesh-pots of Egypt.''

" Nay, I never think of Egypt,'' returned Gerasimos composedly.

" Peace, my brethren.'' Philemon raised a dirty hand.

" This is not seemly. Leave it to lads like Petros and Angelos to quarrel."

" Bethink you they have quarrelled? "

" Beyond a doubt. Were they not aforetime ever together, even as David and Jonathan? And now, as I passed by the dormitories, I chanced on Brother Petros with a tray and a white face, evidently of two minds whether he should enter or no."

" And did he? " inquired both monks, with insatiable curiosity.

" He did, for I watched; but he was out of the cell before you could doff your cassock."

" I never doff mine," commented Gerasimos.

Philemon scratched himself thoughtfully. " Something ought to be done," he said, shaking his head. " If, peradventure, the Abbot be unable to exorcise the evil spirit, Brother Stephanos might prevail. For I hold it is not safe that it be allowed to roam about seeking whom it may devour."

" Surely you confuse," piped Gerasimos eagerly. " That is the work of a loose devil, not of an imprisoned one."

" It is all one—I make no distinction between fiends. The holy fathers made none, and that is good enough for me."

This, being sound doctrine, was hailed with an approving chorus of *"Polycalas!"*

CHAPTER XXVIII

PETROS, bare-headed, bare-footed, and ungirt, was seated upon the precipice brink above the ladders.

Suddenly a shadow sailed across the face of the sun. Raising his head listlessly, the boy saw his friend the eagle poise itself gracefully on extended wings, hover a moment with talons outstretched, then alight within a dozen yards. A moment of intent, keen-eyed, questioning inspection, then the bird, visibly reassured, waddled closer, its ungainly movements on the rocks contrasting ludicrously with its superb and easy mastery of the air.

Petros had won as much of its fierce, suspicious, and untamable heart as it had deigned to bestow, won it by self-effacement, patience, sympathy, quiet movement, and tit-bits begged from the monastic kitchen or saved from his own meals. He was fond of birds—Saint Francis had preached to them. They brought out certain tender and lovable qualities in the lad's nature, thereby fulfilling a duty to him which humanity had neglected. And in return for tranquil observation these shy and capricious little people of heaven and earth had ended by accepting him almost as one of themselves.

But upon this occasion, after the first indifferent glance, Petros took no notice of the eagle, but sat with his eyes resting upon the distance, lost in thought. The bird ceased to approach. For a moment it, too, gazed into the distance; then, with a sudden staccato movement, it bent its head, sharpened its beak upon its claws, and began to preen its plumage.

The face of the young man looked grey in the strong light, worn with distress of mind and want of sleep. Conscience upbraided him continually. Every moment seemed to add to his sin. He would have to tell all to the Abbot in the hour of confession; but, having been to confession upon the day preceding that of his visit to Lavra, it was

not imperative that he should again confess for three, or
even four weeks. This, however, in no wise exonerated
him in his own mind, for there was a tacit understanding
in the monastery that should a monk have aught upon his
conscience he must unbosom himself without delay.

Like one in a dream, Petros gazed around. There, basking in the keen sunlight, were the ancient walls of Barlaam. Every seam and fissure visible, they resembled aged
faces seen in the unflattering mirror of the morning.
The boy looked at them with a dull wonder. Was this
indeed Barlaam? It seemed strangely unfamiliar; the
eagle likewise, the opposing cliffs, and the gorge down
there, still in shadow. He wondered why. The feeling
of comfortable and light-hearted familiarity with his surroundings had gone, everything appeared to be alienated,
estranged.

Particularly was this the case with Barlaam. In his
imaginative and boyish way—making of it, indeed, a sort
of lonely game—Petros had often amused himself with pre-
tending that the monastery possessed a personality; that
it, like its inmates, was capable of likes and dislikes.
Its different aspects at different hours furthered this fanci-
ful idea. Unlike his fellow-monks, Petros was keenly alive
to the thought that generations of brethren, extending
like a human chain far back into the past, had lived
where he lived. This fact endowed the silent little monastery with an atmosphere of mystery and romance. It also
made the place human and endearing; for' was not his
existence but a continuation of theirs? Hitherto Barlaam
had always seemed to smile upon this young dreamer of
dreams; even on grey days, or nights of storm, its supposed mental attitude was kindly, protective, almost paternal.

But now the spirit he had so lightly evoked became a
terror. In spite of the benediction of sunlight, the monastery appeared to frown, to threaten, to denounce. *It
knew!* Not a stone but cried sacrilege. The tiled roof of
the dormitory—a shimmer of golden-red stained with
shades of various green—seemed to stand out and away
from the rest in shuddering notoriety. *She* was there!

It is impossible to trace all the thoughts that chased
each other through the young monk's mind as he sat mo-

tionless upon the precipice brink, a prey to conflicting and often entirely contradictory emotions. To essay to do so would be as bewildering a task as that of an artist who might endeavour to sketch some wild mountain scene in swirling mist.

An obstinate denial of facts held first place. Angelos *was* a boy! Petros dwelt upon their former intimacy, eagerly recalling every boyish trait, persistently ignoring all that was unmistakably feminine, till he almost persuaded himself that nothing had changed.

" Angelos, the lad he had so often scolded and patronised, the boy he had wrestled with in the Catholicon! A *woman!* It was absurd."

Then the memory of Lavra flashing into his mind, trenchant, incontrovertible, his castle of disbelief tumbled about his ears.

And yet it was impossible to dissociate this enemy, this " woman " from the boy he had made his friend. He had come to know this lay brother so well. He had only to close his eyes and he could see the familiar figure in the dingy tunic; the short, lustrous, wavy, black hair that seemed for ever rebelling against the conventional cap; the face, olive-tinted, with the indefinable expression of one who has known sorrow, and the great mournful eyes. Even her occasional bitterness was attributed to the unknown injury that caused her to appear at times hard and unbelieving, and translated in the lad's mind into an additional cause for sympathy. Yes, Petros knew and heartily liked every trait; ay, and every tone of the voice, soft and serious, with its slightly foreign accent. They were as pleasantly familiar to him as the snuffle of Brother Gerasimos, or the benevolent smile of the Abbot, things comfortably safe in this world of danger—and now he was suddenly asked to hold them in abhorrence!

Gradually a doubt grew within his mind—the first that had ever attacked him. If Angelos were a woman, were women really as evil as he had been led to believe? He gasped as this unexpectedly occurred to him, then earnestly, conscientiously, set himself to probe further. One by one he recalled and pondered over her actions, even her looks, seeking to discover wickedness, but finding only allurement and charm. Little by little he fell under the spell of these reminiscences, remembering many an incident that at the time had seemed to him unimportant, but now became momentous and endowed with unexpected fascination. Unconsciously they wooed him into a tender and pensive reverie; and, as he sat immersed in dreams, his eyes lost their anxiety and the lines of care all but vanished from his brow.

Then all at once, with a start, he recalled his wickedness and his concealment of sin. In a thrill of horror he crossed himself, then fell to praying aloud. And again, his prayer ceasing as suddenly as it had begun, his beads fell from his listless fingers, and longingly, yet fearfully—, as one fascinated against his will—he gazed towards the shimmering dormitory.

The eagle edged closer. His bright unwinking eyes fastened themselves with a fierce impatience upon this unaccountably-dilatory purveyor of monastic tit-bits. Then angrily—as a man might shrug protesting shoulders—he fluffed out his feathers.

Petros looked at his friend vacantly, yet finding in his silent presence a certain odd and companionable sympathy. His air of proud aloofness reminded him of Angelos. He knew by experience that he had only to raise an abrupt arm for the bird, apparently so confiding, to betray alarm. Vaguely he wondered if the eagle also were a fiend in disguise.

What was she doing—what thinking—as hour by hour she lay alone in her cell? What did women think about? But barely had he formulated the question than he shrank from an inquiry so depraved; and yet, at the very next moment, he scoffed at himself; for, after all, it was only Angelos, whose thoughts he knew to resemble his own in their longing for sympathy and companionship. But no —he again recoiled—it was in very deed one of the forbidden sex who had penetrated to the monastery fraudulently, deceiving all, even the venerable father, doubtless with evil intent; perhaps a fair seductress like the woman who had tempted the worthy Saint Paphnutius. How ran the legend? To get rid of her the saint burned off his right hand; the woman fell dead; he prayed, and she returned to life, and became a nun.

Again he looked towards the monastery. Not a soul was

in sight.   All was quiet.   The brethren were in their cells.
Was she also asleep?   The Abbot had given him leave to
enter her cell at all hours; but thus far, beyond thrusting
her food within her door, he had not availed himself of
the permission.   But now——?   Was it not his duty to
see that no further evil happened to the monastery?   With
a woman—one never knew.   He would fain, also, com-
pare her with his recollection of the boy he had known.
He would just peep in.   Peradventure she slept.   And if
awake, he could always run away; ay, or make the sign of
the blessed cross.

Rising to his feet, he walked slowly in the direction of
the dormitories.

CHAPTER XXIX

The impulse carried Petros as far as the little bridge that connected the court with the dormitory gallery. Upon it he paused irresolute. Had the girl's cell been a lion's den it is doubtful whether the boy would have suffered from such an entire evaporation of courage. His imagination, fed upon the supernatural, intensified his fear. Everything conspired to fan it. A sudden greyness, as a cloud trailed its shadow over the heights, became to him the frown of an all-seeing God.

At her door he paused again. Listening intently, he could hear no sound. Opening the door stealthily, he peeped in.

Zetitzka was lying on her divan. For the first time since that unexpected meeting in the corridor Petros voluntarily looked at her. Everything about her, from her little naked feet to her unconfined hair, seemed different, and as if it had acquired a new and subtle significance.

Her eyes were closed, but he could see her face nestling in the soft black cloud of her short hair. It looked white and drawn. It affected him. He had not expected it to look like this. His fear greatly diminished.

Still he peered, standing in the passage ready for immediate flight, his body bent forward, supporting himself with one hand upon the lintel, not daring to breathe. But Zetitzka did not move. The cell was shadowy and retired, full of cloistered quiet, slumbrous yet cool in the warm hush of the summer noon, infinitely peaceful. It seemed impossible to associate it with the presence of aught evil.

Petros was thinking swiftly. She was like Angelos— yet not like Angelos. He could not have told the difference. Of course, she had to conceal her real name. He wondered what it was. And her sorrow? Did devils have sorrows? To be a devil at all must be matter sufficient for sorrow! But she did not look like a devil. Ah, that was the wile of the evil one; Brother Nicodemus had often dwelt on that. With fascinated curiosity he watched her, swayed mentally this way and that. The wickedness of her! To dare to pollute Barlaam! The effrontery! To pass herself off as a boy, to deceive everyone! Yet she looked neither wicked nor bold, only pathetic and lonely, lying there with anxiety and suffering imprinted upon her white face. The more he studied her, the more she reminded him of Angelos; and the more his fears diminished. Memories rushed to his mind, of how he had been obliged to assist her on the ladders—her dependence upon him in countless ways—her bewilderment when he had explained her duties in the Catholicon. All, by ascribing to her the reassuring characteristic of helplessness, conspired to restore his courage. Other memories, too, came crowding to him: her winning sympathy and companionship; her sadness and the haunting appeal of her great wistful eyes; the touching quality of her gaiety, a sunny flicker that came and went, requiring to be coaxed into life, an unobtrusive echo of his own.

Suddenly remorse and shame caused his face to flush. She was ill—lonely—in pain—his fault! The Abbot was right, as ever; he had acted selfishly. His desertion of this companion who suffered so bravely and in silence struck him for the first time as cowardice. She had but him in the monastery, she had entreated him to befriend her, and he had fled her presence; thrust her food within her cell as if she were a wild beast; and now he was spying upon her privacy with unworthy curiosity. In swift contrition, he flung the door open to its widest.

With a start, Zetitzka opened her eyes. Petros was standing on the threshold. His figure, black against the flood of light, exhaled a faint odour of incense. She looked up at him with troubled, questioning eyes, flinging at the same time a coarse rug over her naked feet.

" Do—do you want for aught? " he stammered.

Her negative scarcely reached him. At one bound all his fears had returned. Everything about her, from her hands to her voice, proclaimed her sex—the sex that he had been taught all his life to hold in abhorrence. She was fully as embarrassed as he.

" Will you not be seated! " she faltered.

" Nay ! " he cried.

She did not speak again, and he was beyond speech; every thought seemed too alarming for words. They faced each other in a long silence that was full of constraint. The old ease, the old familiarity of intercourse had gone. They had become clouds of inexpressible feeling towards each other.

Zetitzka feigned to be interested in the pattern of her divan-cover, but in reality she was thinking with an almost painful intensity. More prominent even than the indescribable relief that came with the certainty that he had kept her secret, was the sensation of alliance connected with this young monk. This new factor in their relationship brought him alarmingly near. It bound his fate to hers. She could never again think of him with indifference. Swiftly Zetitzka was realising one of the profoundest truths of life, that the closest tie between two human beings is a bond of secrecy upon a thing which vitally and fatefully concerns both or either. This bond had brought about a sense of intimacy in one night which years might not have accomplished; for in touching the chord of a secret and mutual experience, it made each feel that they had gone deep into each other's lives, and that these lives would retain this impression for ever.

Gradually, too, new feelings, all connected with this boy, were introducing themselves into Zetitzka's mind.

Dimly she recognised how much it must have cost him, a monk, to keep her secret—how deeply he had offended against monastic laws and against his own conscience— and all for her, to save her, the enemy of his order, a woman! Inexpressibly touched, inexpressibly grateful, a wave of some new emotion surged up in her heart. This unlooked-for chivalry filled her with wonder and admiration, with a sense of confidence, of dependence, of touching and vital obligation.

But Petros, all unaware of her thoughts, stood riveted to the spot. His fingers twitched nervously upon his beads. His throat was dry. He knew he ought to flee—yet was conscious of a guilty inclination to remain. Had she cast a spell over him?—for these alarming sensations must surely be of the devil. His mind, working in its old groove, tried to think of a prayer, but could not. It tried also to feel appropriate horror and repugnance; but that also failed. He could do nothing but stand before her, his whole, shrinking, fascinated soul within his eyes.

Suddenly Zetitzka moved, and, fearful lest he should again encounter her gaze, Petros looked hastily at the door. The tray which he had brought an hour ago attracted his attention.

"Saint Barlaam!" he ejaculated. "You have eaten naught!" Then, forgetful of his resolve, and looking full at her, "You must eat, or you will become ill."

The unconscious solicitude in his voice brought about that which neither pain nor anxiety had been able to accomplish. Zetitzka's mouth trembled, and her eyes filled with tears. She felt the emotion rising, and fought hard to conquer it; but it was beyond her control. In her feeble state she could not keep back her tears, and was distressingly conscious of them trickling one by one down her cheeks. In sudden confusion she averted her head, for the young monk swam in a blurred mist, and for naught in the world would she have had him witness her distress.

But he saw it. It affected him deeply. It finished what her fascination and her mystery had begun. Not that alone, but the sight of her sorrow disarmed him of his only weapon by robbing him of the fear that had been his one safeguard. In a flash the woman, that to his mind constituted the danger, vanished, to give place to a human being, lonely, helpless, and in pain, seeking only to conceal her unhappiness. A great tenderness of compassion welled up in his heart.

"Weep not," he implored. His voice shook, and, nearing her timidly, he stretched forth a hand.

But Zetitzka did not respond. In the dead hush of the cell the sound of her grief was pathetically audible. She seemed to have forgotten him.

Petros gazed at her in consternation. He longed to comfort her, yet knew not what to say. Why was she crying? Was it because she was wicked? But, manlike, he refused to believe that aught so fair to look upon could be evil. Little by little he began to take an unconscious pleasure in looking at her. Her hand masked her eyes, for which he was grateful, but her tremulous mouth

and the long curve of her throat set his heart beating in-
explicably. Unversed in women's looks, he had no
standard of beauty whereby to measure her; but com-
parison had no place in his thoughts. He did not even
realise that she was beautiful. He forgot why he had
come; forgot his wickedness and distress of mind, forgot
his fear, and her disguise, forgot everything except that she
was there.

At length Zetitzka spoke. She did not look at him, restrained by a feeling of unconquerable shyness. Her words
awoke him as from a trance. What was she saying? That
she could never thank him enough. That as soon as she
could move she would go away.

The latter was the only thing that seemed momentous.
It struck him with consternation. Its meaning suddenly
dawned upon him, not with relief—as he had expected—
but with an unimaginable vacancy of prospect.

"But—but you cannot be moved yet!" he protested.
"In a week or a month——

"Are you in pain?" he added quickly, for her face
had contracted. Then, as the wound in her head, from
which the bandage had fallen, caught his eye: "Holy
Saint Basil! your hair is matted with blood."

Her indifference to the injury stirred him to fresh protestations.

"Saint Barlaam! yes. It must have been like this
since yesterday. How I have neglected you! But that is
over, thank God!"

Eagerly, with a temporary return of his old boyish manner, he proposed various monastic remedies—"potent and
high-excelling," as he quaintly phrased it—warmly recom-
mended an ointment made from rats' bones and blessed by a
bishop, which, he gravely affirmed, had cured Brother Nicodemus of a grievous stomach-ache "only a week agone";
and, as an alternative, that the soles of her feet should be
rubbed with the fat of a young dormouse. Zetitzka, upon
the divan, listened dubiously.

"Be of good cheer," he cried, observing her reluctance.
"I know of somewhat that will work a miracle. Wait; I
returu at once." Still talking, he ran off on silent naked
feet.

Zetitzka awaited his return with secret apprehension.

What other strange remedies would he propose? Her feeling of constraint had by no means passed away. In his presence she felt painfully tongue-tied, self-conscious, shy. Petros, too, had changed. His former light-heartedness had gone. It was as if a stranger had taken his place —one older, graver, and, like herself, ill at ease. The change depressed her, though she accepted it as inevitable. She knew well it was impossible for things to have gone on as before. Yet she could not help offering up a sigh to the memory of the old, gay, frank comradeship that could never be again.

In a few minutes he was again with her, bringing water and clean rags.

" I could not come at it," he apologised, as he set them down by her side; and thereupon explained that one of the relics in the Catholicon—a bone of St. Thomas—was famous for instilling faith into unbelievers, thereby healing them of all ills, both temporal and spiritual; but— and his face fell—it was in a case, of which the Abbot kept the key, and being the hour for meditation, the venerable father must on no account be disturbed.

With a hand which he tried in vain to steady, he set to work to cleanse the wound. The blood had encrusted round it, so that many applications of the wet rag were necessary. Zetitzka allowed him to help her with a troubled gratitude. That he, as well as Dimitri, and in much the same manner, should tend her wound, struck her as strange. Yet she accepted the coincidence—as she accepted much that occurred to her during this distressful period of her life —with the acquiescence of an almost pathetic resignation, as though indeed she were but a straw blown hither and thither by the breath of adverse destiny.

They made a strange picture in the bare little cell, these two, boy and girl, he bending over her, where she lay upon the couch, with anxious solicitude, she raising her pale face to his with pathetic trustfulness, her eyes closed, her lips compressed.

Her nearness mastered him. A subtle sweetness, like a perfume, emanated from her young and wholesome womanhood. It intoxicated him. The fear lest she should notice his agitation forced him to continue. But the effort was almost beyond his strength.

And again, as he tremblingly applied the rags, his eyes were drawn from the wound to the face, fair as a flower, and upturned to his.   And as he gazed, the reality, the inconceivable reality, bore down upon him with a disconcerting newness of shock, for it cried to him more forcibly than any human utterance: *" This is a woman! "*

CHAPTER XXX

LOVE fell like a bolt from the blue upon Petros.

All that had puzzled, tantalised, even irritated him, now stood revealed in a new light, rose-tinted, full of wonder and fascination. With bated breath he reviewed the past. He stood aghast at the memory of his former daring, was filled with sudden remorse at the recollection of his former brutality. He wondered at his past self with an immense, an incredulous, and at times an awestruck amazement. Sweet saints! how could he have acted like that? If it could all happen again!

Nor did he accept the metamorphosis without frequent protests from incredulity. There were times when it seemed impossible that Zetitzka could be anything but a boy: even in her presence, and while speaking to her, he was tempted to fall into the old familiar form of address; and then, the truth striking him, he would pause bewildered, under the influence of his old fear, his old superstitious misgivings. But as time went on these doubts became less frequent, and finally ceased.

To apprehend in its entirety the revolution that love wrought in the life of Petros, it must be remembered that this seed of passion had fallen on virgin soil. All these years his capacity for love had been steadily gathering power. It had grown with his strength, ripened with his manhood. Monastic life, instead of starving, had in reality fostered it. The society of the aged and unattractive had but made the reaction towards youth and comeliness the more inevitable. It not only entered into, but revolutionised his life. His old boyish light-heartedness and love of fun gave place to a serious outlook, exaggerated possibly by his youth, but which could never again become the thoughtless gaiety of the past. It was, at it were, a turning-point in his existence, for all unconsciously he had been waiting for love—and it had come.

205

It had come, but the crux of the situation was that he did not recognise it. His ignorance of the world of emotion, and in particular of all that concerned the sexes, was so profound that the significance of what had befallen him escaped him entirely. Love? He knew it by name, for it was daily on his lips. Was it not an attribute of the Deity—a moral force that permeated the world, linking soul to soul in a golden chain of prayer and self-sacrifice? Some vague ideas of married love, it is true, hovered through his brain, born of his father's devotion to his mother; but marriage for him was so obviously out of the question, that the mental atmosphere that made it possible did not exist.

Still, this strange and troubling malady that had so unaccountably attacked him preyed upon his thoughts night and day. It affected his appetite, his sleep, his life. It could not be explained away. In an immense and bewildering chaos of perplexities one thing alone stood clear—it emanated from Zetitzka.

But for what reason it associated itself with her puzzled him entirely. He spent long hours during the services in the Catholicon, and alone in his cell, striving fruitlessly to understand. Her memory clung to him, even in snatches of dreaming sleep. When standing in his stall between Brothers Nicodemus and Gerasimos, he could no longer give his attention to the reader, nor even to the Abbot. His eyes strayed continually to the dark recess beyond the *Bema* where Zetitzka had been wont to wait. To his imaginative mind it still retained the haunting, elusive charm of her personality. When spoken to, he would not infrequently forget even to reply.

Absent from her, and particularly during the first two days of his passion, he made certain he was possessed by a devil; but when with her, he firmly believed that something holy had happened to him—that he was inspired, that this wonderful inexplicable happiness was as divine in its origin as the tongues of fire that had descended upon the Apostles. This latter belief, gaining ground, obtained entire possession of his mind. It was doubtless due to this, as well as to his ignorance, that while his physical being responded instinctively to the summons of love, his passion remained pure, ascetic, spiritual.

And yet, in spite of the fever, the unrest, the longing, in spite even of the despair that came with thoughts of her inevitable departure, there were moments that compensated for everything. In these moments the heart of Petros swelled: he breathed ecstasy; everything, even the meanest objects, became transfigured by the knowledge of her existence; and he went about his monastic duties in the unspeakable radiance of some light of his own, invisible to other eyes.

The brethren, though dulled by age, and engrossed in their round of trivial occupations, remarked and wondered at the change. Petros did not notice them, and if he heard the scraping of sandals when the monks genuflected, or smelt the heavy clinging odour of incense, or saw the warm quivering stain of early sunlight falling athwart the gloom of the sanctuary, it was but as a background to the one woman.

After the first stings of remorse, conscience ceased to trouble him, so effectually had Zetitzka cast a spell over his soul. Overwhelmed in the wonder of the present, he rarely questioned the future. And, moreover, so beautiful was this experience in his eyes, so allied to things divine, that although he knew concealment to be wrong, he stifled his conscience by the assurance that did the Abbot but know, he, too, would be filled with rapture.

The attitude of the Abbot at this period may be judged from the following conversation:

" He is in there again," mumbled Brother Nicodemus, jerking his thumb towards Zetitzka's cell.

" Ay," commented the Abbot blandly, " he cultivates holy obedience.

" Even so, my son," he continued, as Nicodemus raised sceptical eyebrows. " It was at first sorely against his will, poor lad. But now have I good hopes. Youth is ever a tonic to youth. We be old men, and no companions for him. I remember well——" And the kindly old man, helping himself largely to snuff, told a simple tale of his own youth which went far to prove his case.

CHAPTER XXXI

THE visits of Petros to Zetitzka were more frequent than even the monks imagined. The first step taken, others came easily. The boy, drawn to her irresistibly, could not keep away. She, too, came to expect him; his visits were to her the only bright spots in the long and wearisome days. They wooed her from thought, from the anxiety that haunted her when alone; they gradually engrossed her, and became something all-sufficing.

Being excused attendance at the Catholicon, and, indeed, all monastic duties, on account of her accident, she was always in her cell to welcome him. Many a quiet uninterrupted hour they had together. At five o'clock on these bright summer mornings, the midnight services over, Zetitzka would hear the quick step of the young monk hastening along the gallery to her cell. It never disappointed her. At eight o'clock, after the Liturgy, he would again return, for a moment it might be, to inquire how she was, and to tell her that breakfast would soon be ready; but, standing in the doorway, he would often forget the moments till roused by the call of the semantron. Then, in the warm noon, during hours set apart for meditation, when the monastery was lapped in silence and slumber, they would meet again—Petros, with heavy eyelids, sleep-oppressed, but forgetful of all save her, until, solicitous for his welfare, she would beg him to seek rest in his cell.

At first Petros, keenly alive to the danger of discovery, was full of fear for her sake; but soon, rendered callous by the obvious blindness of the brethren, the peril of the situation ceased to trouble him, and he gave himself up with his whole heart to the intoxication of the moment.

The marvel of it was with him continually. She was to all appearance the Angelos whom he had known, the same face, the same voice, the same costume; and yet as different, in the mental attributes which he now imputed to her, as day is from night. To his simple, credulous mind this was nothing short of a miracle.

He awoke to her beauty. It spoke to him in many ways. He marked how it lighted the dingy cell, how it had power to make him forget her surroundings—dear saints! not her surroundings only, but the monastery, his whole life, his duty, everything! When she smiled, the world leapt into light—when she spoke he listened entranced, as to sweetest music. Sometimes in gazing at her, as she lay on her divan, all that he had been told about women would flash to his mind, causing a sudden boyish heat of indignation. By Saint Barlaam, what lies it all had been! What wicked slanders! In a burst of young and generous emotion he longed to rush out and impart the glad tidings to the brethren, and more especially to the Abbot. They, too, had been deceived; they, too, might be capable of sharing in this incomprehensible happiness!

With reverential awe his eyes would wander round her cell. Everything in it spoke of her, from the couch whereon she lay, to the basin on the rough box that did duty for a washstand. A feeling almost as though he were committing a sacrilege would come over him as he noted these trivial details, a sensation similar to that which had affected him long ago when for the first time, as a priest, he had entered the Holy Doors and penetrated to the *Bema*, or inner sanctuary. Fascinated, in the newness of his adoration, he would hang upon her every word. When she fell silent, he would hunger for her to speak again. Her faltering articulation of Greek and a way she had of pronouncing the vowels—a soft and fascinating sibilation due to her Albanian accent, a peculiarity he had scarcely noted before—now struck him as beautiful. He could listen to her for ever. Even her lay brother's tunic, ugly though it was, had become transfigured. Could he but have had his way he would have clad her in a robe of bright blue, similar to that worn by the Blessed Virgin. Still, even in that unworthy masculine garb, she looked chaste and fair —without doubt because she was a woman. More and more he held himself in contempt for his former blindness and stupidity.

Their conversation differed from the tender and egotistical babble of lovers conversant with the trend of their emo-

14

tions. Upon the part of Petros it was a groping in the dark, a following of blind impulses acutely conscious of their physical effect, but ignorant as to their purpose; the uttering of disjointed and even incoherent things, things so entirely unpremeditated that they seemed to his superstitious mind to be the voice of some mysterious power speaking with his lips—things that, when he sought to recall them afterwards, fled his memory, leaving behind only a profound self-dissatisfaction, and a mass of impressions confused, unsystematic, and contradictory as life itself.

Upon the part of Zetitzka, hovering all unconsciously on the verge of a dawning and involuntary tenderness, it consisted mainly of a frank and unfeigned interest in his life. She would question him about his work, take pleasure in being told trivial details connected with the services, refuse to see in the low moved voice of the lad, in his sudden fits of silence, in the burning intensity of his gaze, an adequate reason for personal apprehension. No suspicion of the goal towards which she was hourly drifting crossed her mind. In the midst of much that was still alien and full of fear, this boy comforted her. He alone, of all the monastic inmates, knew her secret, and was prepared to stand her friend. There were other and more personal reasons for her predilection, but Zetitzka did not realise them. More than once, however, the fear lest in being too much with her he was neglecting his duties caused her to remonstrate; but after listening to his eager denial and discovering that his visits were in accordance with the expressed wish of the Abbot, she said no more, her silence masking a sensation of vague though exquisite relief for which she was at a loss to account.

Not that Petros was Zetitzka's only visitor during these days of confinement. The Abbot, ever thoughtful of her welfare, would look in daily, and, seated beside her upon the low divan, would seek to get in touch with her inner life, coaxing her with a gentle and kindly sympathy into the giving of her confidence. Little did the aged priest realise how near he was at times to the discovery of her secret, for it went to Zetitzka's heart to deny the good old man anything, and it was only by a great effort that she remained irresponsive. Disguising his feelings, the Abbot would turn the conversation to things temporal. His ignorance of up-to-date medicine equalled that of Petros, but he was a firm believer in relics. His disappointment, when her injuries were not miraculously healed after she had been induced to kiss the bone of St. Thomas, was heart-felt. Looking down, through his great horn-rimmed spectacles, upon the obstinate little ankle so nervously exposed at his request, he marvelled immensely.

Her greatest apprehension was lest Stephanos should come to see her. That he had no valid reason for so doing—being neither of a charitable nor a sociable disposition—made no difference to her uneasiness. Many a time did her imagination torture her by picturing his sombre figure darkening her doorway—or his deep voice denouncing her to the brethren. But her fears were without foundation. The monk was too absorbed by his own thoughts, too engrossed with his austere life, to think of one so insignificant as a lay brother. Sometimes, when her door stood open, she would see him in the blaze of sunshine crossing the court—but he never came near. It was almost as though he inhabited a different world. And as day followed day, lulled into fancied security, there were moments and even hours when, to her surprise and relief, Zetitzka almost forgot him.

Certain among the brethren, however, privileged to visit the invalid, would drift in occasionally. To their simple minds this accident was a welcome and thoughtful dispensation of Providence. At first the présence of these old monks embarrassed Zetitzka, accustomed as she had been to privacy within her cell; but she was made to feel—more by their manner than by actual exhortation—that this was a sinful attitude, and that she should rejoice greatly in that her perishable body could afford interest to her elder brothers.

These old men came in time to have almost a feeling of affection for the sufferer, who lay there in seemly silence, gazing up at them with embarrassed eyes. They did their best to lighten her loneliness. Brother Philemon solemnly presented her with one of his bulbs planted in a cracked jug. True, the root in question had unaccountably defied the laws of nature for two years " come the holy festival of Saint Panteleemon," but—and here his finger wagged impressively over the moist earth and his bleared eyes lightened—one never could tell what wonderful and subterraneous miracle might not be taking place at that very moment!

"You think too much," he would say in friendly remonstrance. "Whenever I come in I behold you thinking. Nay, 'tis presumptuous! God thinks for us all. Behold this bulb? Does it think? Not so, yet Solomon in all his glory is not to be compared unto it. *Polycala!*" He scraped the object in question with the long black nail of his forefinger, then in tones of an almost incredulous admiration, "*It's all in there!*"

Brother Gerasimos, too, sought to contribute to her amusement. He would read her tit-bits of a gruesome nature from a worn copy of the *Neon-Asty*, gloating over them in snuffy awestruck tones; and as he read slowly and with difficulty, the little old monk would often pause with open mouth and eager eyes, anticipating horror and creeping flesh.

Sometimes one brother would meet another on the threshold of her cell, and plunge straightway into some time-worn theological argument. Then would Zetitzka be forgotten, and the war of words would fluctuate in a desultory manner, ruffling the ancient peace; while, through the open door, beyond their gesticulating figures, Zetitzka could see the inner court shimmering in its habitual atmosphere of drowsy sunlight.

When at last they wandered away they left in Zetitzka's mind bewildering and contradictory impressions. Their kindness and entire absence of suspicion were an undying reproach, yet she could but feel relieved that they had gone, grateful for the silence that had once seemed so oppressive, for, wooed by it, she could again give herself up to her thoughts, and listen undisturbed for the step of Petros.

CHAPTER XXXII

ONE day after Compline the heat was greater than usual, the air hung heavy even on the heights; far over the plain of Thessaly a thunderstorm growled and worried.

Zetitzka had been roused from a restless and troubled sleep by the entrance of Petros. The lad was pale; indeed, his pallor and lack of appetite had become noticeable of late, rousing comments even among the brethren. After a few commonplaces relating to monastic affairs, they fell silent. The weather affected both, though neither gave it a thought beyond remarking on the unusual heat. The magnetic tension in the atmosphere had affected the boy's blood; and the low and distant muttering, as the storm rolled sullenly westwards, struck a sympathetic note with the feverish beat of his heart.

The moment was full of breathless restraint—troubled happiness quivered in the air; things that suggested themselves for speech seemed to either too sacred, too momentous, for words. Suddenly it flashed to the mind of Petros, with all the illuminating force of an idea occurring for the first time, how ignorant he was of all that concerned the past of this being who had come to fill his life.

Stirred, it may be, by some instinct of unsatisfied curiosity and possibly of undefined envy for the years that had known her and in which he had no share, he suddenly broke through his reserve, and entreated her to tell him something —anything.

Zetitzka, listening and watching from the couch, passed a hand across her eyes. She had been expecting such a question—but not like this, not put in this tone. His eyes, his voice embarrassed her, stirred something that she had never felt before, even during her first meetings with Stephanos. Timidly she allowed her eyes to travel from his sandalled feet up the stiff folds of his cassock, to his

boyish face, strangely moved and stamped with a **great**
seriousness. His expression touched her profoundly.

Drawing a long breath, she looked upwards at the niggard light from the window, then downwards at the rough
wooden boards that composed the flooring. The cell seemed
all at once too small to contain the feelings that were
stifling her. An imperative longing for freedom seized her,
for some great uninhabited space where she could run away.
Yet, even as her mind formulated this wish, she was conscious of its insincerity—for there was fascination, as well
as danger, in this new Petros.

But this eager young questioner had to be answered.
Recognising the precariousness of her position, something
fluttered in her girl's heart, like a frightened bird in a cage.
Hastily averting her eyes, she said:—

" I will tell you. But not now. Perhaps—to-night."

Feigned indifference lent unintentional chill to the embarrassed words. Instinctively the boy drew back. Unversed in woman's ways, and with the exaggeration of
youth, he feared that he had offended—feared, too, that
he had alienated her, perhaps for ever. He longed to
speak, but dared not. And Zetitzka all the time lay there
with downcast eyes, apparently unapproachable, and lifted,
as he poignantly felt, far above his level.

How she had twined herself about his heart, this mountain girl! filling every nook and cranny with the sweetness
of her personality, intensely realised; till for him there was
nothing in the past, nothing in the future, save the luminous fact of her existence! And now it was all over!

What was that? It was but a word, yet it had power to
stop the beating of his heart. Again? Yes. She was asking why he was leaving her. *Leaving* her! Holy Mother
of God! He could have laughed aloud in the glad revulsion of his feelings. Then—she was not indifferent?
She cared? She wanted him! The cell leaped into light.
Joy deluged him with hope. With one bound he reached
her side.

" Zetitzka! " he cried.

It was the first time he had dared to pronounce her
name—her real name, confided to him in one of their recent
interviews. The word rang in the profound quiet of the
cell. In it was heard a new note of dominance—the un-

conscious strength of one who trembles, yet exults in the dawn of power. Breathlessly Zetitzka listened. Fear, apprehension, reluctance, passed swift as light across the shadow of her mind, paralysed and rendered impotent by a delicious weakness that drugged all other feelings. Slowly, and as one constrained thereto, she raised her head.

The eyes of the girl, great and timid as a stag's, neither black nor blue, grey nor violet, but all these shades blended in a soft and velvety darkness, drew his heart irresistibly as a magnet. A thrill of overpowering emotion, of whose significance he knew nothing, overwhelmed him, an undreamed-of sensation that caught him up into the zone of things vital as life and inexorable as death. He stood before her, incapable of movement, his breast rising and falling, unable to look away. Those eyes! Those eyes! They claimed his brain and his heart together. Their look seemed to him afterwards, when he was capable of coherent thought, to be something loud and stirring, like the voice of the semantron, yet silent, intense, penetrating like prayer. Nay, more, to strike him as with a physical blow. Had he but known it, these were but the birth-throes of love, young, overwhelming, incomprehensible; love that comes but once to all, bringing with it delight and sorrow, the wrench of death and the pang of life, the agony of disseverance from the old self, the birth of the heart instinct with new hopes, new fears, new desires.

Zetitzka, utterly taken aback, was unable to avert her gaze. She, too, could do nothing but stare, her flushed face upturned to his, the breath coming and going with effort between her parted lips. Their souls met and knew each other in that long, ardent, questioning look. The light within Zetitzka's eyes passed slowly from tremulous incredulity, to a warmth of dawning responsiveness, softly suffused and shining in the twilight of the cell.

Thus Destiny played artfully for this girl and boy. The sorrows of the one, the innocence of the other went for nothing. Out of the great world of many millions of human beings had they been chosen, just these two, to meet and love.

CHAPTER XXXIII

THERE are periods in the lives of each one of us that are remembered only as the shrine of an emotion. Periods in which it may be supposed that the body breathed, ate, slept; that the sun shone or the earth was veiled in rain, but, all unconscious of material things, the soul looks back and beholds only the heart's awakening, the brightness and the glamour.

For the few, these periods are the prelude to happiness, the first link in a long chain of love, the dawn of a cloud-less summer day, when the sun of the heart fills every hour with pure, deep joy, sinking slowly at life's evening with unabated fire to the dark inevitable horizon. For the many they stand alone, blinding, brief, a dream of bliss too beautiful to last, welcomed with ecstasy, savoured with rapture, believed in with passionate faith, relinquished with agony, remembered with tears.

Such a period came to Zetitzka.

Had she been a girl with no previous experience of life, she would have abandoned herself to it unconsciously, in-stinctively; erring perhaps through ignorance, drifting away on the enchanted tide.

But Zetitzka was a woman. Her eyes had been opened. Life had seared her too deeply to make forgetfulness pos-sible. Shame and remorse—her constant companions—had made it their cruel industry to keep open the wound in-flicted in the days of her innocence. Vowed to a hopeless and unachievable deed of vengeance, encompassed by dan-gers, yearning for her child, harassed by fears and doubts, oppressed by the vicinity of Stephanos, she of all women appeared triple-armed against this weakness of the heart. And yet her very preoccupation had paved the way to that heart's undoing.

This that had happened had come to her unexpectedly.

To say she was taken aback gives but a faint impression of the complete shock of her surprise.

That Petros, discovering her to be a girl, would fall in love with her was a contingency that had never dawned upon her; his youthfulness—that lagged so far behind his years; as well as his calling—that forbade all thought of marriage—making the supposition in the highest degree improbable.

Engrossed with her own anxieties, she had passed with unseeing eyes the boundary-line where indifference merged into liking, liking into affection, affection into love. To his feelings for her she had rarely given a thought. And indeed, as long as he had supposed her a boy, his treatment of her had naturally given rise to no suspicion. His behaviour, during the distressful days that followed their visit to Lavra being, to her mind, fully accounted for by the fact that his conscience was laden with the guilt of concealment. But now the scales fell from her eyes.

Her reception of the truth surprised her no less than the truth itself. It complicated still further her position in the monastery—God knows complicated enough already! It was so hopeless—so ill-advised. And yet, when it flashed upon her through the eyes of Petros, her heart tremblingly welcomed it as one welcomes a dear and unexpected guest to a desolate house.

And what wonder, poor girl? Zetitzka would have been more, or less, than woman had not a love so pure, so delicate, so virginal, and so amazingly unconscious, touched her inexpressibly. In trenchant contrast to the debasing passion of Stephanos, it raised her to the serene heights from whence it came. It surrounded her with a mute atmosphere of worship, and while thrilling her with gratitude, yet stung her with a pang of unworthiness. More— it restored her faith in humanity, and re-awakened all that was best in her.

And yet there was another and a darker side, which forced itself upon her when she was alone, in the silence of her cell. It summoned to memory her child, and the vengeance to which she was bound; it reminded her sternly that Petros was a monk, and pointed out the gulf that must for ever yawn between them.

But her heart again became voluble, silencing all hostile voices. Metaphorically, it closed its ears to warnings, and its eyes to consequences. It insisted upon its right to a little happiness. The cup of life held out to her dry and thirsty lips was too enchanting. She was so lonely. She yearned with an inexpressible craving for just this love and sympathy; not for the baser side of passion—her soul sickened at the humiliating recollection—but for the ideal and spiritual of which her nature had hitherto been starved.

And here was that for which she had been pining; here, at her feet; here, in excess, offered spontaneously, unconsciously, a gift free and unconsidered as sunshine! And even as a flower, tempest-tossed through the passage of many darkened days, instinctively expands its petals to sunlight, so did Zetitzka open her heart to love.

CHAPTER XXXIV

A FIRM step broke unexpectedly upon the silence. The old and rickety woodwork of the corridor creaked complainingly. So accustomed was it to being patted by soft and shuffling footfalls that this free masterful stride made every plank cry out.

Zetitzka, startled from some dream of thought, listened while the sound was yet far off. Expectation imparted a fugitive colour to her face and the light of hope to her eyes. But as the footsteps neared, then paused, and the sound of conversation terminating in a gay laugh reached her ears, her disappointment voiced itself in a sigh. It was only Dimitri.

She had been expecting the muleteer, for something told her that he was a man of his word. But coming, as he did, on just this wonderful day of days, she more than half-wished him away. This, while he was yet unseen. But when he stood before her the sight of his burly frame and genial open countenance so recalled the memory of his former kindness that she accused herself of ingratitude.

Impulsively she stretched out both hands, then withdrew them nervously.

Dimitri's laugh was that of a man who seeks to conceal an emotion.

" How then! Am I not worth a handshake? Ah, that is better! Well, how goes it? "

It occurred to neither that his manner of shaking hands might be more gallant than was to be looked for in a muleteer accosting a lay-brother. Dimitri's grasp was of a piece with his personality. An unaccountable feeling of safety passed from his fingers through those of Zetitzka.

" Well, how goes it? " he repeated in a big resonant voice tuned only to hills and open air. As he spoke he beamed upon her interrogatively. Then, as though already answered:—"But I need not ask. By Saint Barlaam! you look better already. They must be famous doctors, these monks."

Zetitzka found nothing to say. But at his words, and more perhaps at his tone, which had the warmth of an ill-disguised admiration, into the clear olive of her cheeks there stole a flush of colour. This delicate heightening of her complexion was like the quick flutter of a danger signal —her sex sending messages of distress along the current of her blood.

But it was at her eyes that Dimitri looked. "Where the devil," thought he, "did they learn that look!" And little wonder that he stood amazed, for they were luminous with a magical light both soft and dreamful; the eyes of a woman whose heart is whispering secrets to her, who gazes full at some incredible happiness invisible to others.

The muleteer had thought much about her since they had parted in the ravine. Her presence in Barlaam still puzzled him immensely. A rollicking appreciation of the humour of the situation still lurked in his mind—without which, indeed, he would not have been Dimitri—visible in a half-suppressed twinkle; but as he looked at her lying on the rude couch, so strangely incongruous with her surroundings, incongruous despite the lay-brother's costume, amusement was lost in amazement.

"By the saints!" he blurted suddenly. "If they knew you were a woman——"

He broke off, instantaneously aware of his indiscretion. For a moment Zetitzka stared at him aghast. Then Dimitri, watching her intently, saw the warm colour inundate even her neck. His distress was as poignant as hers.

"Forgive me," he stammered, throwing out apologetic palms. "I did not mean—at least—not so soon. What the devil, I am a mule!"

Zetitzka's confusion abated. Strange to say, in the midst of her discomposure, she experienced an unaccountable feeling of alleviation, as if the initiation of this man into her secret not only relieved her of the necessity for continual imposture, but somehow, in a vague indeterminate way, constituted him an ally.

He seated himself diffidently at the far end of the couch.

His big breezy presence, his air of exuberant vitality, and the bright colours of his picturesque costume seemed strangely out of place in this austere little cell which had witnessed only thin-blooded lives passed in mortification and prayer. Zetitzka, stealing a glance at him, was as much impressed with his incongruity in the midst of these monastic surroundings as he had been with hers.

"You wonder, doubtless, how I found out," he went on, his eyes directed to the ground. "Well, I had my suspicions, yes, from the first. Look you, as a rule a lay-brother so young is stupid. Faith! have I not seen! He says yes, and no, then yawns, and thinks of his dinner—but *you!* . . ." His arms expressed his lively appreciation of the difference. Then, sinking his voice confidentially:—"And the other day at Lavra, when you fell——"

Zetitzka caught at her breath.

"No, no! All was right. I told no one, not even my little mother. Faith of a muleteer! You need not mind —no. It was nothing—nothing!"

His tone implied that the discovery of disguised damsels was for him an every-day occurrence.

"And you thought I had deserted you; run away, eh? Not so! although I confess it had the air of it." He chuckled. "Think only how droll, those old fellows arriving just then. In two little minutes I would have had you safe in our home. They had the best of it that time; but you and I will beat them yet. Faith! I would have carried you off under their noses, just—just for the jest of it, but there is something about the Abbot—a look—a tone—a something, that makes one do his will.'"

He wagged his red fez like a man who wonders, then, producing a small wooden box, and taking therefrom tobacco and paper, began to roll himself a cigarette.

Zetitzka listened to the facile current of his talk, partly unheeding, partly grateful.

"I am glad you are better," he said genially; then, with a return of the twinkle, "So you live up here, eh?"

She assented dubiously.

He struck a flint and steel that he carried at his

belt. The thin blue smoke drifted through the cell. It hovered in filmy clouds, slowly moving, then dispersed and became invisible against the dirty grey of the walls.

Awhile he continued to talk, outwardly jovial, but inwardly racking his brains for subjects of conversation likely to put her at her ease.

But to Zetitzka his gay monologue came as an echo from an indifferent world. Her every thought was on its knees before this wonderful thing that had befallen her. In spite of his cordiality and her gratitude, she almost bore this man a grudge for coming between her and the delicious sea of dreams in which she would fain have lost herself. Motionless on the divan beside him, she sat gazing at the door, a rapt look on her face, her head slightly bent as though listening for the sound of a voice. Dimitri pursed his lips, then elevated his eyebrows.

"And now," he rubbed his palms together, "can I be of any service? Only," he added hastily, "only if you wish it. If not, in God's name let us speak of something else. As for me, I like to talk of anything—anything." He stroked his chin; then, with the air of a man who, in justice to himself, considers an explanation necessary, "Look you, when one passes all day with a silent person like Nikola, one talks for two—or becomes a mule." He shrugged his shoulders again, this time in whimsical protest against such an unpleasant metamorphosis. Then, with an unusually bashful glance at the silent girl beside him, "I say—you don't know how I—how I—by thunder!" he smacked a muscular leg. "Even if permitted, not a woman in Kalabaka would climb these ladders, or try to live up here with these monks. They would be terrified, I give you my word—I, who have heard them talk. But you—it is easily seen you are of the mountains."

Finding his eyes fixed on her, Zetitzka nodded slightly.

"Women are not welcomed up here as they merit. What will you?" His gesture apologised for defective hospitality; then, waving his whip, "You did not come for the pleasure of this? No, I believe you. Peste: 'tis bare as a licked plate. I could have given you better at my house—much."

"Yes," he continued, "my mother was disappointed.

I told her; but not all. You should have heard her scold. She wanted to see you—to nurse you. She is full of curiosity about the monks. She pities them. If a woman may not give her care, she gives her pity. She *will* give something! . . . Few people come up here," he continued, after a pause. "Pilgrims, friars, hermits, and such quaint folk. Travellers, too—last season I brought no less than five. They pay well, these animals—twenty pesetas a day. We do the round of all the monasteries— Kalabaka and back, but, you understand, nothing regular; were it not for the carrier business I would be badly off. I come up here also to see—by the way, what has happened to him?".

"Who?" asked Zetitzka in surprise.

"Brother Petros."

She felt herself trembling.

"'Tis passing strange," he grumbled, more to himself than to her. "I thought I knew the lad like—like my pocket, and yet to-day, in the cloisters——" He turned abruptly to the girl, who was striving to master her agitation. "Why would he not speak to me? Oh, he answered, but only a word, he who as a rule cannot find time for all his chatter. Can he be sickening for an illness, eh? What think you? You have a woman's wits; you see him often?"

"I—I don't know."

"Is he—is he off his food?"

"We do not eat together—now."

"No—o," he scratched his head. "No, I suppose not. And yet—he thinks you a boy—he might have—curse the monasteries! It may be some pious fit—but 'tis so unusual. Now I—were he not a monk, I would say——"

She waited anxiously.

"I would say he was in love, but "—he laughed incredulously—"that is, of course, impossible."

She could hardly control herself. How much did he know? How much did he only guess? He frightened her, so apparently outspoken; yet perhaps some dark design lurked beneath his words.

"Well!" he beamed upon her. "It appears 'tis I who talk."

Forced into speech, she could only murmur confusedly.

His eyebrows arched with unfeigned astonishment, then, eyeing her with a return of the old involuntary twinkle, "Nothing to say? Lord! what a wife you would make!"

A pain shot to Zetitzka's heart. His words harrowed her—suggested possibilities. For a wistful moment she allowed herself to picture existence as it might have been had the man who loved her been free to marry. Dimitri, his eyes averted, felt, rather than saw, her distress. It made him indignant, combative, conscious of his impotence to help. He understood also, and sympathised with her natural reluctance to take a stranger into her confidence. "If," thought he to himself, "if I can get her to tell me without telling, the rest will become my affair."

Full of this plan, he began to speak in a pleasantly discursive manner—the manner of one who talks for the pleasure of utterance, rather than for audition. He touched on Albanian inns, the price of wines, inferior fodder, and other topics well within the range of his experience. Deceived by his apparent artlessness and relieved by the change of subject, Zetitzka threw off by degrees much of her reserve and even volunteered remarks about the dear familiar land of her birth. The muleteer listened with gravity, his curiosity well under control. But when Zetitzka was lured into mentioning her journey, he made a mistake. For the life of him he could not repress a swift gleam of dawning comprehension. Zetitzka saw it, and became dumb.

"You were about to say?" suggested Dimitri pleasantly.

She shot a swift and troubled glance at him.

"Nothing," she said; then, ashamed of her ungraciousness, she continued in a low, hurried voice, "I know not why I told you all this. I mean—to you it can be nothing."

Her words, and still more her expression, struck Dimitri with self-reproach. They made him aware of his strength and her weakness. Springing from the couch, he stood before her.

"Do not think that I wish to force you to tell me," he cried. "No—God forbid! I seek to find out only because I wish to befriend you. Look you, to help, one must know, not guess. You are in trouble: I can see that much, though what it is, the devil take me if I know! Perhaps I have spoken too soon. Well, I can wait. One day you may require a man who has a strong arm. Now "—his voice changed to sudden gruffness—" I wonder much what that little she-devil of a Nikola is doing? "

Something rose in Zetitzka's throat. Her eyes again sought his face, but he was studiously inspecting the lash of his whip.

" The last time I came here," he went on, with an appreciative grin, " she dragged a boulder a quarter of a mile. I found her with her forelegs tied to her obstinate little neck—for all the world like a trussed fowl. And then—what think you? She had the impertinence to look at me, as who should say, ' You see this? 'Tis all your fault.' Just like a woman! They are all alike, bless their hearts! Ah, well! I must be going. Good-bye."

He stood before her, a broad-shouldered figure that seemed to fill the cell, flicking carelessly with his whip.

Zetitzka longed to speak. This man had said little and done less to materially assist her, yet during the short time she had known him he had inspired her with confidence. The bluff and manly directness of his proffered friendship had touched her more, perhaps, than she was aware. His very presence, and a certain breezy open-air sanity about him, lulled her fears. And now he was going away! With a sudden reaction she blamed herself for her foolish reticence. Friends were none so common in her friendless life that she should shrink from the confession that would once and for all put his sincerity to the test. For very little she would now have told him all—have besought his assistance—but he did not again question her.

" Good-bye," he said, and smiled.

She forced herself to return his smile.

" Good-bye," he said again; then, answering the look in her eyes: " It rests with you."

She hesitated. Her teeth impressed her under-lip. Again the old involuntary shrinking, that was stronger than her will, beset her.

" Yes," she murmured. Then, nervously changing the subject: " I heard you laugh as you came in."

15

Whimsical amusement at her vacillation lurked for a moment in his eyes; then, falling in with her humour: "Yes, I laughed; but only at Nicodemus. I pretend to be an infidel, just to see him spit. It always succeeds. To-day he called me a green bay-tree, and hoped to be present at the burning! He has called me so many bad names, all taken from Holy Writ, that he is somewhat at a loss now. But green bay-tree was good. Old Gerasimos now, is friendly. He told me the news."

"What news?" Zetitzka spoke with indifference.

"You may well ask, you who know their lives. If one of them sneezes, 'tis an event. Let me see! Well, for one thing, that surly one—you know him, Brother Stephanos—is going away."

Her expression arrested him. Unable to conceal her feeling, she could only stare; but her wide eyes and parted lips spoke for her.

Dimitri returned her stare. For a moment there was silence; then Zetitzka recovered herself.

"He goes away, you said?" She could not keep the note of relief from her voice.

"Yes."

"For—for always?"

"No: for perhaps a week."

A shadow darkened her face. Dimitri continued:

"They tell me 'tis a penance set him by the Abbot. Gerasimos was full of the wonder of it. Up here they think him a kind of saint, you know."

"Yes, I know." Her upper lip curled, though there was but little scorn in her nature. He paused a moment in surprise, then continued:

"'Tis said the Abbot sends him to collect rents from the farms. By the saints! 'tis a jaunt, and no penance! Lord!"—he struck at his boot—"they are droll fellows, these monks!"

A silence ensued. Zetitzka sat with unseeing eyes fixed on the opposite wall. Dimitri did not again look at her.

"When does he start?" she asked at length, in a voice so low that the muleteer was forced to strain his ears.

"To-day, I believe."

"Did"—under cover of her tunic her hands trembled—"did Brother Gerasimos say what he had done?"

"But, no. 'Tis doubtless something foolish, some trifle —eaten too much, or slept too long. What a life! I asked him, but the wily old rat said it was a secret of the confessional. That was because he did not know himself."

Before either could speak again, the sound of footsteps came from the corridor. They both listened.

"Well," said Dimitri, "I must go. I have left two bags of charcoal in the tower of the windlass. Good-bye. Be brave; but "—he looked at her—" no need to say that."

A little of the admiration that he strove to conceal became visible in his bronzed face. More: as he paused, reluctant to leave her, a wistful expression, almost timid, and strangely foreign to him, came into being. But with eyes fixed eagerly upon the door, Zetitzka sat motionless, oblivious to all save the footsteps that momentarily drew near.

CHAPTER XXXV

Dusk had fallen before Stephanos came to take leave of the Abbot. The courtyard was full of twilight that was clear and yet opaque, like deep water. The huddle of monastic buildings loomed dark against the dying rose and green of the after-glow. The sense of solemnity was augmented by the waning light. It glimmered home to the eyes in mysterious shapes, and spoke to the ears in a silence that knew of no interruption. A sense of vague expectancy brooded over the monastery. The solemnity appeared to have affected it also. No stir of life came from the deserted cloisters. All was quiet in the dark refectory. Even the little rocky platform, seen through the doorless arch that led to the outer court, was desolate, perched on the brink of fearless declivities, alone with the silence and the night.

Stephanos found the Abbot in his cell. The old man did not hear his knock, nor when Stephanos, fancying himself invited to enter, lifted the latch and stood before him, did he open his eyes.

For a while the monk, restrained by a feeling of respect, remained motionless, watching his superior. The Abbot, seated on his couch, appeared overcome by the heat. White and frail, he leant against the wall, his head tilted forward—his customary attitude in sleep, for, like many a holy father the tale of whose austerities had come down to his descendants as a blessed example, the Abbot rarely, if ever, lay prone upon his couch. When the heaviness of thwarted slumber overpowered him, he would merely close his eyes for a few minutes, scarcely losing consciousness. This relaxation occurred sometimes at meals, sometimes during meditation, but never at devotions.

" Holy vigils," he was in the habit of saying in exhortation, " purify and enlighten the soul. Blessed angels keep company with those who watch and pray."

228

In spite of the air of exhaustion noticeable in his attitude, such infinite peace, such calm abstraction, such spirit shining through matter was to be observed in the Abbot's countenance that Stephanos felt a pang of envy. It seemed to mock him with the unattainable, and thrust him back remorselessly into darkened places, unvisited by hope.

All at once the aged priest opened his eyes.

" Is all ready? " he questioned, raising his thin hand in benediction.

" Yes, venerable father."

" You have the papers and the wallet? "

" Yes."

" And somewhat to eat upon the road? "

" I shall not need it."

The Abbot looked at the gaunt figure standing before him—looked with sadness and compassion, for this journey had been arranged in order to isolate the monk until his sentence should arrive. " Poor troubled soul! " thought the old man; but aloud he only drew attention to the fact that the monk had forgotten his sandals. Stephanos excused himself. He wished, he said, to be permitted to travel barefoot. The Abbot gave his permission, remarking at the same time upon a cut on one of the monk's feet, and advising him to recommend it to Saint Barlaam.

The talk then turned upon the various farms which the monk was about to visit, his superior telling him somewhat of the tenants and the manner in which they were to be approached. He further cautioned him as to his behaviour when in the world, and of the necessity for being ever watchful to keep up the monastic reputation.

Stephanos, his eyes downcast, made no comment.

" You have one great safeguard," continued the Abbot, not without approval. " You speak little. The recluse Theonas passed thirty blessed years without speaking at all."

Stephanos muttered inaudibly into his beard.

" Journeys are serious things," continued the Abbot, shaking a wise head—" serious things, and not to be lightly undertaken. The world is so large. But our dear Lord Jesus Christ journeyed in it continually; 'tis a boon to follow in His sweet footsteps."

Pleased with the ingenuity of the argument, he took a prodigious pinch of snuff.

But Stephanos gnawed the ragged ends of his moustache. His fear of this journey was very real. In the monastery he was tortured, but safe; beyond its precincts he was exposed to mortal sin. His prayers and supplications had been of no avail: he had little faith in his powers of resisting temptation. But the night before he had been forced to scourge himself in order to overcome sinful thoughts. Zetitzka had appeared to him in a dream, tempting him, and it had needed the most violent effort of his will to tear himself from slumber. She might be somewhere in the world he was about to visit. The thought nearly overcame him. He trembled with terror, unreasoning fanatical anger, and the fear of a passion fettered but not killed.

"You have my permission to speak," said the old man, noting his agitation. But Stephanos still kept silent. It needed but little perception to divine the emotions that were rending him, for there was something ominous in his speechlessness.

"It is my will that you go," continued the Abbot with firmness. "Remember that it is part of your penance. It is my will, likewise, that upon your return to Barlaam you keep silence, save at prayer and divine service, until such time as I grant you permission to speak. I will inform the brethren, that they tempt you not to disobedience. Now "—he rose to his feet—" come, my son. I will speed you on your way."

Stephanos stood for a moment as though he had not heard, for the blood rushing to his head made him dizzy. His strength, sapped by cruel fasts and long vigils, proved unequal to the tasks imposed upon him. Only inner fires sustained him, while preying continually upon his peace of mind.

Together the two men left the dormitories, taking the key of the trap-door with them. Neither spoke. It was as though both consciously kept silent, moved thereto by the surrounding gloom, and by an inexplicable feeling of finality that cast its shadow over this farewell.

At the moment of departure Stephanos kissed the hand of his superior. The Abbot blessed him in a low moved voice, commending him to God and the company of the Blessed Saints.

Looking into the dark abyss, the monk was again attacked by a feeling of dizziness. Mastering this weakness, resolute, and with a scornful expression, he began the descent. The Abbot, leaning over the ladders, watched him as he descended from rung to rung, until the darkness hid him from sight. Still the old man stood, straining his eyes into the gorge, his lips moving mechanically.

This parting saddened him. His great hopes concerning the future of Stephanos had been cast down. In that apparent strength of will, that fierce desire for abnegation, that frenzied eloquence, he had seen the makings of a great preacher—a saint—a torch new-lit by God Himself. Now, alas! he saw nothing, and feared much. His fears—for the shadow of the anticipated instructions from Trikala was with him continually—grew in the silence and the darkness until they touched his own life. At such moments of dejection the rumour that the monasteries of Meteora would one day be given over to convicts was in the habit of coming to him, a nightmare arousing deep and unavailing regret. It came to him now.

. Acting under an imperative desire to see the beloved buildings, so threatened, he groped his way to the door of the hut. There they were. The starlight shed its lustre upon them. In dim solemnity they stood out, the arcades, the refectory, the cloisters, the dormitories, the old walls that had stood for seven centuries, the dome of the Catholicon watching over all.

The eyes of the Abbot grew dim. It was his beautiful home and he loved it. Was it indeed true, as some said, that " everything in the ancient monasteries was dying, save Christ in the tabernacle "; that the monks no longer, as in the first centuries, " co-operated with the vital energies of nature, while they praised God in song "? With a great desire to discover the truth, he searched his memory, questioning conscience tremblingly, with a fervent prayer for guidance. But, painfully aware of many personal shortcomings, the Abbot could yet find no flaw in the system. To him all seemed well and as it had been throughout the ages. Dying? Nay. The spirit of prayer was alive as it had been from the beginning, as it would be to the end. The monastery, too, was alive, doubly alive, as it seemed to him in that hour of silence and of stars. Its ancient stones, that had watched so many holy lives till they, too, partook in mystic religious communion of the love and longing, the groans and prayers that had risen night and day, now appealed to him with the pathos of the inarticulate. "Help us!" they seemed to cry. "Without thee are we lost!"

"O merciful God," prayed the Abbot inwardly, "my life for theirs, if it be Thy will."

His thoughts returned to Stephanos—his poor tormented son wandering in the darkness on the mountains. For him also he prayed, in silent renunciation, humbly relinquishing his own desires.

As he raised his eyes to the profound vault of heaven, a star fell from the zenith. The old man watched it with superstitious awe. What might it portend? To avert possible evil, he made the sign of the Cross.

Still under the influence of what he had seen, he was about to cross the courtyard when an unexpected sound brought him to a standstill.

"Who is there?" he cried.

"It is I," replied the voice of Petros.

"Blessed saints! You startled me. Why are you not in your cell?"

"I could not sleep, venerable father."

A note of dreaming happiness in the young monk's voice struck the Abbot as remarkable. Such accents surely accorded rather with one visited by angels than with one possessed by a devil. In much perplexity he peered into the young face, but his eyes were feeble, and could see nothing clearly in the obscurity.

Side by side they slowly crossed the court.

"And how is Angelos to-night?" questioned the Abbot. "It was in my mind to visit him this morning, but finding Dimitri coming out of his cell, I feared to weary him."

"He was much better this afternoon."

"That is well. Thanks are due to Saint Ann, for I took our holy relic of that most devout and blessed among women into the lad's cell last night. *Polycala!* We will burn two fine wax candles before her icon. See to it, my son."

Petros did not answer.

"He is a good lad," continued the Abbot, his thoughts still with the invalid. "Patient under tribulation, of a silent yet submissive mind; truly an example to us all."

Petros listened with attention. It gave him keen though guilty pleasure to hear praises of Zetitzka.

"And you, my son, I notice that you are much with him. I have said naught, but it hath pleased me mightily —yea, mightily. Holy obedience is ever grateful unto God. Full well I wot that it hath been a hard matter to accomplish."

"No, no!" protested Petros.

"Ay, but I fear it; yet is it not without goodly result. Behold! I see a difference in you already. 'Tis true. Now, tell me: have you found out aught about him?"

Petros came to a sudden standstill beneath the branches of the fig-tree. His conscience leapt in fear to his face.

"I wish not to pry into confidences," went on the kindly voice by his side, "yet fain would I know more about the lad. He is young—a mere boy, and strangely reticent. His mother must needs be anxious. Does he speak of her?"

"No—o."

"No? That is strange. Yet has he not forgotten her, of that I feel sure. Last night I entered his cell while he slept. His beauty amazed me. I hope he is happy. There were tears on his eyelids—and yet, he smiled. And so he has told you naught?"

"He—he has promised to tell me somewhat. I go to him now."

"Go in Christ's name, my son. Full of joy am I to find that you follow where the sweet Master leads."

"O venerable father!"

The protesting cry arrested the Abbot.

"What aileth you, my son?"

"Speak not thus kindly. Every word hurteth. I am unworthy. Yet is it something beautiful. At times I long to tell you—and at times I fear that if you knew you would never forgive."

" Christ knows, yet is He ever ready to forgive."

" Have patience, only have patience!" Petros' voice shook. Then the imminent departure of Zetitzka flashing across him with a terrible, unmitigable sense of loss, he continued passionately, recklessly:

" It will not be for long now. Only a few days. Then all will be over. My God! My God!" He wrung his hands in a burst of uncontrollable despair. " She is going away!"

" *She!* Alack! this is indeed the frenzy of madness. *She!* In the name of the dear Lord, whom do you mean?"

" I know not. Nay, God forgive me. I do know, but I may not tell. I—I—— Oh, heed me not! I know not what I say. O my father, I am miserable!"

Broken down by the violence of his emotions, he clung to the old man's arm. Anxiety filled the Abbot's heart. He attached no importance to the wild words. His every thought was taken up with the fact that Petros, his little son, his best beloved, was still tormented by the devil.

For some time he spoke to the young monk. In all he said there rang the note of hope, and of a faith that was firm as the rock upon which Barlaam was built. Whatever his personal troubles, his speech hinted not at them; all were thrust out of mind by the eager desire to comfort. But his words were unheeded. To Petros they remained mere empty sounds, scarce reaching his ears, much less penetrating his heart.

" All will assuredly come right," concluded the Abbot, in a tone of gentle and happy optimism. " Have I not prayed for it? Do not I know? Age has its privileges likewise. It can see farther. Youth is still at the bottom of the ladders, but it thinks it is at the top. When I was young I was in great fear lest God would refuse my one desire. I trembled, knowing full well my unworthiness. But He overlooked it; and behold—I am an Abbot!"

Petros, who had straightened himself, made no movement. The aged priest, still in the past, smiled contentedly to himself in the little starlight that found its way beneath the branches of the fig-tree.

" Venerable father." The boy's voice came low and agitated.

" Yes, my little son."

" I beseech you, give me your blessing."

He knelt at the Abbot's feet. The great leaves of the fig-tree embowered them as with a canopy. In the warm darkness the hand of the superior sought and found the bowed head. Comfort dwelt in the beautiful words, and should have passed like a sweet odour into the troubled soul; but despite his efforts to force himself within their influence, Petros felt only a spiritual coldness that, while vaguely terrifying, left him unmoved.

CHAPTER XXXVI

THROUGH the thin partition that separated the cell of Zetitzka from that of Apostoli came the droning voice of the latter reciting his breviary. In the hush of the night the sound was distinctly audible. Petros and Zetitzka listened uneasily.

" He will of a surety hear all we say," whispered the boy.

The girl assented.

" Another time——" she began.

" Nay, I have waited so long. Let us go to the outer court. At this hour no one will be there."

She cast a glance at her bandaged ankle.

" If "—Petros flushed—" if I may carry you? "

Her faint protest was met by a breathless rush of reasons —he was strong—he would be careful—he could go there blindfold—there was no other way. In tremulous silence she allowed him to lift her from the couch.

In spite of his boasted strength, Petros felt as if her weight were too much for him, for in the emotion of the moment his head swam and his heart drummed loudly in his ears. The weakness passed. Reverence, tenderness, and an immense pride took its place. Neither spoke. Slowly, carefully, moving like one caught away into a heaven of dreams, he carried her out into the night.

The warm contact of his encircling arms communicated itself to her in a thrill of exquisite happiness. So conscious was she of the reverence of his attitude that all fear, all shyness even, vanished. Shutting her eyes, she gave herself up to the intense realisation of the moment.

As they passed the end of the cloisters that faced the refectory, the door of the latter opened suddenly. In the lighted entrance stood a black figure. He had not seen them, for the darkness of the night hid them like a curtain, but instinctively Petros stepped behind a pillar. Zetitzka felt his arms tighten round her. The sense of being protected by the man she loved was so sweet, and so wonderful, that it made her almost indifferent to what might happen.

"Methought I heard a noise," Sotiri's voice remarked.

"Perchance it was a rat; they increase fast," answered another of the lay brethren. Then from within came a querulous voice, broken by coughing, that bade Sotiri close the door. The light disappeared, and all was again still.

Having set her down upon the log of wood that, overlooking the void, formed one of the favourite resting-places of the monks, Petros seated himself beside her. Like one drugged, he allowed himself to drift away on the transport of the moment. It was good to be there, just he and she, alone, in the kindly concealing light. The few dozen yards that separated them from the sleeping brethren might have been so many leagues, so cut off did they feel from the unimportant life of the monastery. The past and future ceased to exist. The present meant only them; they became the one thing important in this world of shadows. Their physical selves, their pulses, their breathing filled the universe.

To Petros everything dimly seen in the night appeared to be a part of this wonderful experience, to share his feelings. Were not the familiar hills his confidantes, the unchangeable stars his friends? For the world, down there, with its many inhabitants—if indeed he recalled it at all —he felt only pity. To sit there by her side, to watch the profile of her half-averted face, filled him with feelings far beyond comprehension.

Their material surroundings made more impression upon Zetitzka than upon Petros. Everything to her was still full of mystery and novelty. The sense of being uplifted on that pinnacle still took away her breath, particularly when, as now, she looked down from the sheer brink of the precipice. The air seemed to circulate more freely here; it fanned the little curls on her forehead and brought with it a pleasant sensation of coolness, grateful after the long heat of the day. But in the night this seat did not look so perilous, or it may be that her companion inspired her with courage.

The great purple spaces, star-powdered and hushed, that

extended from the immediate blackness below to the dim
line that was the Albanian frontier, enticed her. The
absence of detail was soothing; it allied itself to reverie.
And, strange to relate, as she sat there, without speaking,
her thoughts were as much with her child as with Petros,
for tenderness with unconscious art had enshrined them
together in the inmost sanctuary of her heart.

The great happiness that had come to her with the
knowledge of his love was with her continually. It ebbed
and flowed around her like the waters of a warm, sentient
sea, islanding her even from the memory of sorrow. She
feared to think of it as hers, lest it should suddenly take
wings. But she felt it intensely.

A sudden movement caused her to look at the boy beside
her. His rapt young face was gazing into hers with an
air of expectancy. His attitude reminded her that he had
brought her there that she might tell her story. With
the recollection came consternation and repugnance.
Everything conspired to fan these feelings—the youth and
innocence of her companion, her abhorrence of the past,
and an instinctive and shrinking delicacy that recoiled from
putting such a tale as hers into words. And, more than
all, dwarfing even these into insignificance, came the sudden
apprehension that were she to tell all she might lose his
love.

"I cannot tell," she faltered.

He looked at her face, so near his own, so pale and
beautiful, yet so full of distress, and his heart leapt in
sympathy.

"Nay," he cried eagerly. "Nay, it matters not at
all."

While she drew a breath of relief, he continued hastily:

"If it could only be known unto you what I feel! It
is without doubt a miracle. It is you!"

"Don't," she said brokenly. "I bring unhappiness
wherever I go!"

He contradicted hotly. As he spoke the innocence and
candour of his nature struck her again. In many ways
he, as well as the monastery, seemed above the world. She
could not have believed that a grown man could have retained to so great an extent the appealing simplicity of
childhood. There was to Zetitzka something extremely

touching in his attitude. It was as if his trust in her were akin to his trust in God. This worship—pure, yet burning as a flame upon an altar—while flattering, caused her pain. The fear lest she might fail to come up to his ideal made her anxious. For nothing would she have disappointed him. His confidence in her awoke an almost protective tenderness. Hardness and suspicion fell from her like ignoble armour for which she had no longer any use. She became all woman—all the best of woman, soft, tender, pitiful, and unselfish. Knowing by bitter experience the danger of passion, she dimly realised that she would have to exercise circumspection; not for her sake, but for his. Engrossed with the present and blinded by its radiance, she forgot the future with the demands upon an all but superhuman courage and self-sacrifice. For the moment her every thought was for him. Experience had come to her with a crown of thorns. God helping her, it should not wound him. Her duty, she felt with solemnity, lay in defending this young monk against himself; in keeping him body and soul without stain, so that, at the last, no shadow of remorse might darken his life.

But would she have the strength? Was this resolution compatible with the inherited tendencies of her nature? —with the hot and lawless blood that ran in her veins— with the fierce passions of an ancestry who laid shadowy hands upon her, binding her to them, the living to the dead, across the gulf of years? She, too, hungered for love, and all that love brings. And moreover, she was pitifully conscious of weakness, the weakness of a woman who loves so utterly that her dearest happiness consists in giving.

At present, self-denial seemed possible. But with her it was still the dawn. Seen through rose-light, the features of this enchanted land of love showed rapturously unfamiliar—the promised land of her most sacred dreams. Her past experience availed her nothing, for it was full of discords, whereas this was all harmony. Love in its most beautiful aspect was so new to her. She could not yet tell how it would influence her actions, nor how far she could depend upon herself. At present she only welcomed it with tremulous and inarticulate gratitude. She was like one who, ignorant of its effect, drains for the first time a sweet but intoxicating draught. The sweetness was with her still, the intoxication was to follow.

The breeze stole upwards from the sleeping plains in long-drawn sighs and warm, panting breaths. It, too, seemed to share their emotion. Under the magic of its touch the blood of Petros tingled, and gladdened, and remembered, as though past lives were stirring within him, and his every nerve vibrated in unconscious unison like the singing chords of a harp. These sensations, so powerful, obliterated thought. It was as though his body had suddenly and unexpectedly found a myriad tongues, clamorous and incomprehensible, and yet so united that they were but one voice crying passionately to him out of the darkness, summoning him he knew not whither.

" Zetitzka! " he cried.

His arms were outstretched. His eyes burned into hers. For a breathless moment she shared his emotion. All the woman in her yearned for him, for his arms to enfold her, for his lips to kiss her; yearned, and hungered, and thirsted, with a longing that well-nigh overcame her; yet all the time something deep down, that was her better self in arms against her heart, fought, and fought, and would not be conquered.

Instinctively, as one face to face with danger, she had drawn back. In as far as a woman could, she understood this boy. The knowledge called forth infinite pity. With a sudden prompting of tenderness that overcame all fear, she took his hand. All his blood, all his life, seemed to Petros to rush violently into that hand, leaving the rest of his body weak and helpless. Her touch was at once a consecration and a torture. His strong fingers, interlaced with hers, tightened convulsively. The pain struck some chord of primitive emotion—gave her a fierce pang of pleasure. More—it deadened the hungry ache in her breast. Even so, had circumstances been otherwise, would she have had him seize her and crush her until breath almost left her body.

To know that his sensations were shared filled Petros with ecstasy. A pure deep feeling rose from his heart. It refined and elevated his every thought. Unconsciously, it summoned to mind holy things, and solemn moments in his life, when, as now, his soul had been awed by the presence of something incomprehensible and divine.

A subdued solemnity, as it were a tender twilight of the spirit, crept over him. He feared to wake from the dream of paradise. The day had sounded a note of profound happiness; in the morning the world had been changed and renewed in the light of her eyes; and now heaven opened to the touch of her fingers.

This final miracle seemed to Petros the solution of all his troubles. To hold her hand. He could think of nothing more wonderful: nothing more precious and intimate.

The moon rose behind the dark buttress-tower of Meteoron. The atmosphere imparted to it a red golden hue. It looked near and unnaturally large. The distance crept into view, soft and ethereally bright, shrouded in veil behind veil of silver haze. Enchantment held the world sleepy-eyed. A night created for the sheltering of tenderness—when soul speaks to soul in silence that is more lucid than speech.

The wan illumination shone straight upon his face. Zetitzka marvelled at his pallor and at the look in his eyes. His hat had been discarded, his long hair fell to his shoulders. An old-world air lent asceticism to his appearance. He might have been a mediæval saint carved in alabaster and painted in sombre colours against a background set with stars.

16

THE great constellations blazed in the clear-obscure of the summer sky. Here and there a planet glowed with fiery yet tempered splendour. These innumerable eyes of heaven seemed to smile upon Zetitzka. They peopled the night with sympathy. Often before had she watched them, and was no stranger to the feelings they aroused. But now, for the first time, their beauty and mystery called aloud to the beauty and mystery within her heart. Comprehension thrilled her. They knew. Her soul mounted to them on beating wings.

But the eyes of Petros did not leave her face.

"Zetitzka," he said, "ever since that day at Lavra, I——" He broke off, then continued quickly:—"It was terrible; but all at once it was only wonderful. I tried to think it evil, but it was you. You are the answer to everything. You *are* everything. When I am near you it is heaven—when you are away, even for a moment, something cries out here——" He touched the breast of his cassock. "Zetitzka—" his voice suddenly vibrated with intense and profound conviction——"*this* is love."

The pressure of her fingers answered him. For some time he sat without speaking, and she felt he was wrapped in the wonder and solemnity of his discovery. Then he leant towards her and said: "Tell me about love, Zetitzka, I want to know. I must know."

But she could not trust herself to words.

In the moonlight, she saw a great seriousness come into his face—the rapt expression which she had noticed before when he spoke of holy things.

"The Blessed Virgin is a woman too. Before you came I prayed daily to her icon. I even thought her beautiful —but now——"

Zetitzka sat erect.

"No!" she protested, deeply moved. "No! no! no! You must not love me like that."

For long she spoke earnestly, reasoning with him, seeking—with God alone knows how painful and pathetic a conscientiousness—to lead him back to the loveless path of duty.

She had small skill in speech, this mountain girl, but she had a great heart. In faltering inadequate words she tried to keep the cruel facts before him, as if in convincing him she could convince herself also. She reminded him that he was a monk, vowed to God and a life of religion; that his calling must come first, always first; that he must not love her; that she must go away soon; that all was doubtless for the best, but he must not love her; no, he must not love her; he must not love her. And always she returned to this protest, hastily, insistently, feverishly, speaking only to silence the passionate longings of her heart.

It was a strange scene in this little monastic court, in the pale sad splendour of the moon—this boy and girl engulfed in the waters of passion—he but half-conscious of the tide that was sweeping him far from familiar landmarks, ignorant alike of its significance and its goal—she struggling to retain her footing, seeking to drag him back into the shallows; and all the time yearning for that against which she fought.

As she leant towards him, seeking for words, her face faintly visible in the surrounding gloom, but her eyes shining, she trembled and shook with a passion that equalled his own. The fear of alienating his love caused her torture. But she persevered.

And Petros listened, his chin sunk to his hand, his eyes fixed on space. She could see by his attitude that he was inwardly revolving all she had said.

"I must not love you?" he repeated at length, speaking slowly and incredulously; then, with swift scorn: "But what use to tell me that? For I *do* love you!"

He continued: "They told me that this"—in the dusk she saw him indicate the monastery—"was the only perfect life. I believed them. They said that the world was wicked, and that women were evil. Again I believed them.

Why not? They were wise, and I ignorant. To me it appeared good and safe to abide here alway—all my life. It had been my home for long: I had nowhere else to go. Ay, and not that only, but of a truth it seemed wondrous sweet to give my whole life to God. You see—then I was happy. I did not know! I did not know!"

Unable to bear the keen note of pain in his voice, Zetitzka averted her eyes. It seemed to her that even in gazing at him, dimly seen though he was in the darkness, she was spying upon his grief, upon the profound and distressful stupor of one awakening for the first time to a hopeless reality. Again he burst forth:

"But why may I not love you? Why? why? As if it were aught sinful! Sweet saints! it is as beautiful, as holy as—as prayer! Zetitzka, God is love! Why may I not love you?"

And again Zetitzka could only listen in a pained silence, stirred to the depths, acutely conscious of the gulf that separated them and of the love that drew them together.

"Ah!" he cried. "You cannot answer. But I *know!* It comes from God. It is part of His love. It is above this——" Again he indicated the monastery. "I cannot explain, but I feel it. I marvel much that no one has ever told me of it. But "—he turned to her, his face shining—"we have found it—you and I, Zetitzka—and we will keep it always."

The strain of self-control was telling upon Zetitzka. She felt at the limit of her endurance. How to tell him? How to convince? Her arguments had proved useless as handfuls of water flung in the face of a great fire. But one way remained.

"Listen!" she said, sharply. "No; do not speak. Only listen. I will tell you—will tell you all. Then—then you will not love me any more."

He stared at her, incredulous, yet awed into silence.

In the clear moonlight, lifted high above the sleeping world, surrounded by the solemn quietude of the monastery, she told him part of her story.

It was but a fragmentary record of what had befallen her; for she purposely omitted much concerning the man who had wronged her, revealing only his desertion and that he was the father of her child. Neither did she reveal the reason of her visit to the monastery.

Surely it was sufficient to tell him that she was not the pure woman he had imagined her, and that he must banish her for ever from his life.

In the pain of the recital, Zetitzka lost sight of the unusual ignorance and innocence of her auditor, forgot everything save the bitter past and that voluntarily she was signing her own death-warrant. The pathetic tale, finishing upon a note of hopeless despondency, came abruptly to a close.

Bewilderment fell upon Petros. He did not understand. He shrank from asking. His mind was in a whirl. Depths hitherto undreamt of suddenly yawned before him. They had been there all the time, but he had not even suspected their existence. His ignorance, by awakening imagination, attributed to them peculiar mystery and horror.

The sense of her actual words—which, though suggesting much, expressed for him so little—passed over his head, but he was doubly sensitive to the inflections of her voice, sharing to the utmost limit of his powers every emotion it betrayed.

Her moonlit face was an open book. In it were to be read shame, grief, and remorse—a dark record, yet lighted and made beautiful from within by the brave effort to do right. Petros heard, rather than saw, these conflicting emotions, and the indefinable something that lent dignity to her confession. The latter inspired him with reverence. That she should suffer at all awoke his indignation. So lofty was the pedestal upon which he had placed her, that suffering connected with one so perfect seemed monstrous. One thing, however, stood clear. Someone had wronged her.

As this struck home, all the innate chivalry of his nature was for the first time aroused. It cried aloud to all that was strong in him. In response, his manhood started up— eager, nay, burning to make her wrongs his own, to comfort and protect her—ay, with his life, if need be—in the face of the whole world.

Eagerly he spoke. Indignation against the man who had deceived her mingled half savagely, half incoherently, with expressions of a worship that was oblivious of even the shadow of a doubt. She was everything to him. He had known nothing else. He wanted nothing else. Could she understand one person being everything and the whole world nothing? Could she?—could she?

Leaning towards her, so close that his breath stirred her hair, he poured forth a torrent of passionate yet authoritative tenderness that swept aside all dreams of opposition. Zetitzka's heart swelled. Glad and involuntary tears filled her eyes. All that was womanly in her, all that was clinging and weak, all that longed to be loved and worshipped and taken possession of, went out to him. She exulted in this new tone of domination. Her joy drowned every dissentient voice. To silence her conscience she promised herself to keep him pure in heart. But, oh! to be happy, even for a little time! To forget everything save this joy that had come to her so unexpectedly! To let herself be borne away on the current of this love that surely was more beautiful than any other love since the world began!

His hand, his eyes, demanded an answer. The hot night seemed to demand it too, for a hush had fallen, as though it also were listening and waiting. At last it came—the confession of a heart that would not be stilled.

" Yes," she whispered—" yes, I understand."

CHAPTER XXXVIII

DAY after day passed in the little monastery above the world—passed as they were wont to pass, like other days in the uncounted years. All went on as usual—the long services, the hours for meditation, the meals in the bare refectory, the monastic tittle-tattle, the listless silence, the sun-steeped repose. But for Petros and Zetitzka all was changed.

For them everything sounded the same intensely personal note—a soft, unobtrusive, and tenderly sympathetic accompaniment to their feelings. Nature offered them her gifts with both hands—the golden gift of sun, the silver gift of stars, the diamond gift of dawns sparkling in dew and caressed by crystal airs. They accepted all with the unconsciousness of children or of lovers, accepted it as their right, their minds engrossed on higher matters. During these halcyon days they moved through monastic life in a golden haze, through which the monastery, its inmates, the wonderful view, everything, seemed far off, nebulous, unimportant, almost unreal, for was not the only reality this miraculous flower of love, that had blossomed to unexpected beauty within their hearts?

They lived for the moment, thereby discovering for themselves the secret of happiness. There were times, however, when stern facts refused to be forgotten, when it was impressed upon Petros that he was living in sin, and upon Zetitzka that she was mad to linger there in momentary danger of discovery. But these occasions were few and soon forgotten.

One morning they were together in the cloisters, when the voice of Apostoli reached them.

" Tear it from out your heart, Brother Gerasimos! "

" Nay," responded a mild voice; " I think not that it is evil."

The two monks came into view, drifting round the sunny

247

end of the Catholicon into the shadow below the arches, Apostoli frowning and denunciatory, Gerasimos expostulatory and with a comical air of a schoolboy taken to task.

" How not evil? " said the former harshly. " When it concerns a woman! "

Petros and Zetitzka listened. Gerasimos, looking up as he approached, caught Zetitzka's eye and bestowed upon her a glance replete with confidential meaning.

" Thoughts about women," continued Apostoli, with rancour, " should be banished from the mind of a worthy monk."

The face of Petros flushed; his eyes lit up; but he repressed his indignation.

" Behold! " cried Apostoli, in godly triumph, " Brother Petros is moved, and with reason. Ah! "—his gesture included Zetitzka—" ye twain are young—boys—yet is one never too young to fly from evil. Let this be a warning unto you."

He continued his tirade against the forbidden sex. His language was exaggerated, yet obscure, mystical, full of veiled threats and suggestions of mysterious malevolence that gave to his gaunt figure and forbidding countenance the air of some grim prophet of evil. Ceasing abruptly, he shuffled away, followed at a little distance by the unrepentant Gerasimos.

Zetitzka and Petros were left alone. The boy was bursting with feelings outraged beyond words. The peace of the shadowy cloisters seemed to mock at his agitation. Suddenly his eyes met hers. A magnetic and irresistible current of attraction flashed to his brain. There came a swift revulsion. He forgot his indignation: his eyes grew soft, luminous, tender; his fists unclenched; his muscles relaxed; everything but the girl before him passed into utter indifference.

Zetitzka had resumed her duties in the Catholicon. She performed them gladly, for they brought her into hourly contact with Petros. A change had come over her. Her health had benefited by the enforced rest, and more still by happiness. In some respects her long period of suffering became as though it had not been, and as though she herself had stepped back to the days of her girlhood. A subtle something, that was charm, emanated from her whole being. Love did for her what sunshine does for flowers. Even the Abbot and the brethren wondered at times to see her face shining with some incomprehensible feeling that made it as " sunshine in a shady place." And more and more did her presence become an incongruity in this old monastery, among all these white-bearded monks.

Zetitzka's nature had always possessed a faculty for growth and change. Life, inscrutable and apparently unscrupulous, had employed two men as its tools. They were moulding her into what she would ultimately become —the one by the force of suffering, the other by the power of love. Stephanos had paved the way for Petros. His treatment of her had unconsciously prepared her to welcome the pure worship of the boy with a gratitude that turned her love almost to adoration. The former had covered her with shame, the latter restored her self-respect.

The pathos of the situation lay in the fact that though she had at last found the one man in the world constituted to heal and fill her heart, whom she loved, and by whom she was beloved—yet he was denied her. Both were young, nature had formed them for each other, life had brought them together, instinct commanded them to love, everything approved of the union, everything but man, who, with his self-imposed laws, stepped in and forbade it. In a sense Petros was as dead to her as though he were already in his coffin.

Zetitzka's conception, at this precise period, of the nature of her passion, of its significance, its goal, and the moral responsibilities it entailed was nebulous and contradictory. Nor could it well be otherwise, for the mountain race from which she had sprung was as uncontrolled in its love as it was lawless in its hate. She, poor girl, the daughter of primitive forbears, had but one adviser—her heart. She lived in and by her feelings—swayed this way and that —now fancying herself capable of renunciation, now dimly and tremblingly aware of that within which would one day demand fulfilment.

But as love gained upon her, gained day by day with swift but insidious advances, silencing all voices save its own; fusing itself into her living, breathing existence, into her dreams and waking moments, into her capabilities for hope and fear; stealing her very heart from her bosom—all lofty and self-sacrificing resolutions sank from sight like castles of sand before the sweep of a resistless tide, but to be rebuilt, however, as she fell again under the influence of disinterested feelings.

More and more as time passed did Petros become inseparable from her very life; more and ever more did the sunshine of his love transform the darkened world of her loneliness into a blessed land of joy and light. His physical being—that material self that to her enchanted vision so radiantly portrayed the youth, the freshness, and the beauty of his nature—awoke in her feelings too tremulous, too tender for expression. Carried away by them she would touch the coarse stuff of his cassock, or at times even allow her fingers to pass lightly and caressingly over his hair. It was curious to note in these timid overtures the birth of a fierce and jealous emotion—the instinct of the woman asserting its claim to the man of her choice—an instinct faint and tentative as yet, but destined to become strong and imperious.

Zetitzka's feelings towards Stephanos had undergone a change. She tried to banish him from her mind, but when his memory forced itself upon her, as from time to time it did, it no longer aroused the fierce emotions that had been hers when first she came to the monastery. She still feared him, with an instinctive dread as of something repellent and hostile, and had she been informed of his death, her first sensation would undoubtedly have been one of unspeakable relief. But she herself no longer wished to kill him.

Many influences had been at work. The spiritual atmosphere of the monastery, so remote from the world, so saturated in the profound peace that brooded for ever around that isolated height, had insensibly wafted her away from all violent associations. Many of the shadows that had darkened her past—and particularly the bloodthirstiness of her race—seemed already dim and distant.

Yet Barlaam had never ceased to overawe her. Little by little, as previously narrated, Zetitzka had fallen under this spell; had persuaded herself that some supernatural power of which she was ignorant, but which she fearfully surmised to emanate from the monastery, forbade her again to attempt the life of Stephanos. This incomprehensible something that endowed the low-browed buildings with a soul and a purpose, appeared to the credulous mind of the mountain girl an insuperable barrier erected between her and her goal. At first it had filled her only with impotent anger, but now, bending to fate, she had accepted the veto.

The inmates, too, had contributed not a little to the change. The Abbot, for example, had unwittingly influenced her for good.

But the great factor, without which all others would have been as nothing, was love. It softened and changed her entire nature. Even hate lost its power to embitter when confronted with her great happiness. It became but the shadow of what it had been, prompting only a longing to fly to some place where she and her child would never see or hear of Stephanos again.

And although hate and love had changed places, yet the latter carried on the plan of action laid down by the former. Hate had brought her to the monastery—love kept her there. Day after day prudence insisted—'' You must go away. There is nothing to keep you now.'' But love whispered: '' Stay yet a little while. Petros loves you.'' And so she stayed.

But she knew that in giving way to the prompting of her heart she was living over a mine, and that every moment of stolen pleasure might prove the last.

Of Stephanos, however, no tidings came. He had disappeared as completely as though the world into which he had vanished had been a bottomless pit. Only his untenanted cell, his empty stall, and the vague suggestion of danger which, like some fluid magnetism in the air, bid her be continually on her guard, remained to testify to his existence.

That he would soon come back she knew well. A week at most was the time computed for the task which he had set out to perform. What she would do upon his return, or in what way he would influence her future actions, were questions which she was unable to answer, although they suggested themselves to her. She was no nearer the solution of the problem than when first she had entered the monastery. Stephanos still lived, her people still demanded his death, and she, poor puppet, blown by the tragic breath of fate, drifted hither and thither, and found no abiding spot whereon to alight.

Neither did any news reach her from the little Albanian village but two days' march from the frontier. It also was lost in silence, a silence that she apprehensively felt to be expectant, sinister. Had it not been for her child, this absence of news would have been a relief rather than an anxiety, for Zetitzka could picture only too well the reproaches which her procrastination must be calling forth. And, meantime, like a lull in a storm, came these few days of almost uninterrupted happiness.

Everything conspired to favour their love—the indulgence of the Abbot, the ignorance of the brethren, the services and leisure hours that threw them continually together, the restricted spaces, the glorious weather that gave to them days of continual sunshine and nights of quiet stars.

Only the monastery frowned upon them, with the sullen resentment of one forgotten.

CHAPTER XXXIX

WITHIN the court of Barlaam Dimitri paused. The sound of the reader's voice came from the Catholicon, rapid, high-pitched, nasal. Brother Apóstoli was gabbling the service. Distance softened the sound, mellowing all that was disagreeable till it became almost natural and as though born of the fine weather, as is the hum of bees. At uncertain intervals a subdued murmur, hoarse and transitory as a breaking wave, marked the responses.

The courts, the passages, the cloisters, the galleries, all were deserted, given over to sunshine and shadow. Something in the murmurous sound of prayer, and in the vacant spaces quiet with brooding sanctity, made Dimitri feel like an intruder. A subdued solemnity pervaded this pinnacle-top, so far removed from the world. It lent a distinctive atmosphere to the old grey buildings. They were so still, so mute; they appeared to listen, dumbly reverent under their low-browed roofs. They might have been praising God for His gift of seven hundred years.

Moving softly, Dimitri went to the outer court. It was here that he had first met Zetitzka. He recalled the circumstance, with all its attendant detail, and looked long at the particular part of the log upon which she had then sat. A feeling of being face to face with something big came to him. It inspired an unwonted seriousness.

As he stood there, lost in thought, his white fustinella swaying softly in the breeze, his little embroidered jacket, with its rows of bright metal buttons, setting off the breadth of his capable shoulders, his red sash attracting the light, his round cap perched jauntily upon his head, manly, picturesque, his appearance contrasted forcibly with the hushed and austere attitude of the monastery at his back, with its grey monotony of tone as of a perennial twilight, and with its immense age that seemed for ever brooding upon an inconceivably remote past. His air of health and strength, of manhood at its prime, of frank and sensuous joy of life, seemed almost an insult to this collection of decrepit buildings. It smacked of the world, of irreverence, stamping him a pagan thing almost as irresponsible and soulless as the sunshine that rioted godlessly in the silent courts.

Yet those who took him at the valuation of the monastery would have been misled, for Dimitri was no mere thoughtless embodiment of the world's frivolity. His good looks pleased less for their own sake than for some inherent quality of strength and self-reliance, revealed in the steady blue eyes and in the firm lines of the mouth. To see him one instinctively felt him to be a good fellow, a friend worth having.

Suddenly, with his eyes still fixed on the log, he made an impulsive movement of his shoulders, as if to throw off some weight. As he did so he laughed. The laugh was directed against himself. It was a mirthless protest. Yet in it rang a note of genial irony, the outcome of a resolve not to take himself too seriously, that was characteristic of the man.

The long service was over. Dimitri watched the brethren saunter along the cloisters. The Abbot crossed the inner court and passed in the direction of his cell, a venerable figure, slow moving, full of quiet dignity. The monks separated in small groups. Nicodemus and Gerasimos—as usual together, and as usual arguing—stopped awhile under the fig-tree, then disappeared into the cellars. Dimitri waited patiently, but no one else came out of the Catholicon. Neither Petros nor Zetitzka were to be seen. He would have inquired their whereabouts, but unusual self-consciousness restrained him. Little by little the courts resumed their former lifeless appearance. A great peace fell. Only from the refectory came the sound of voices rising faintly, then dying away, a mere ripple on the sea of silence.

The muleteer entered the Catholicon. He moved almost on his toes. Several candles were burning before the icons, mingling their feeble artificial light with the wan and niggard light of day that struggled inwards through windows so small, lofty, and begrimed with dust and cobwebs as to be almost useless for the purpose of illumination.

In this mystic twilight the mediæval adornments showed faintly, a sheen of marble, a glimmer of gold, receding into the formless gloom of the arches.

As Dimitri hesitated, the sound of a voice came to his ears, a mere murmur, but clearly audible in the silence. It came through the little cupboard door, to the left of the *Bema*, that led to the library. Instinctively, he moved in its direction.

The library of Barlaam was a secret chamber. To gain access to it, two doors had to be passed, the former of which was so carefully concealed within the Catholicon wall that it would have escaped the notice of anyone not conversant with the building. Lighted from above, the little vaulted chamber gave shelter to a collection comprising a couple of thousand volumes, all books of divinity, the writings of the fathers, and Venetian editions of ecclesiastical works. The majority were printed, but some were in Byzantine manuscript, copies of the Gospels in small and large quartos, beautifully written upon polished vellum and dating back to the eleventh and twelfth centuries. To the brethren they were useless, for none save Petros and the Abbot could read either Hellenic or ancient Greek, but all within the monastery reverenced them as sacred relics, and guarded them jealously—as much, it may be, on account of their incomprehensibility as their antiquity. Brother Johannes occupied the post of librarian—a sinecure, for the gentle dreaming old man did nothing to justify the appointment save count the volumes periodically. Petros, at his own request, was permitted to dust them, to the no little amusement of the brethren, who could not imagine why he took the trouble. From his father the young monk had inherited a love of books; to ponder over the crabbed characters, to feel the smooth and polished vellum, and to feast his eyes upon the ancient illuminations—these were to him constant and never-failing pleasures.

It was to this retreat that the voice led Dimitri.

Standing in the narrow and dark passage that connected the two doors above mentioned, the muleteer could see the whole interior of the library without being himself seen.

Petros and Zetitzka were together. That they had come with no intention of looking at the books was evident, for the volumes stood undisturbed upon the shelves. Seated

side by side upon a low divan that ran round three walls
of the apartment, the comrades were deep in conversation.
From his place of concealment Dimitri could see the face
of Petros. One glance served to enlighten him.

Fierce pain shot to the muleteer's heart. Something
throbbed in his temples, hammered in his ears. A feeling
comparable only with intense physical nausea attacked him.
As long as he lived, Dimitri never forgot that moment.
Later, when he heard that a young fellow in Trikala had
stabbed a successful rival, he merely nodded his head.

Zetitzka was speaking. Her words appeared to come
from an immense distance; from somewhere in the light
to where he waited in the darkness. No idea that he was
playing the part of eavesdropper crossed his mind.

If his suspicions had needed confirmation, they would
have found it in Zetitzka's voice. It betrayed love as unmistakably as the blush of a cloud betrays the dawn. Incredulity swept over the listener. *Petros!* The lad at
whose innocence and ignorance of the world he had so
often smiled! Who knew nothing of women! Who was
part and parcel of Barlaam!

Not till that moment did Dimitri realise all that
Zetitzka meant to him—all that he hoped for; more, much
more; all that he had determined to gain. It had grown
within him unperceived, yet surely and swiftly, urged into
maturity by the Southern impetuosity of his blood. He
had been so sure. That had been his mistake. He saw
that now. Relying on his own strength of purpose, he had
imagined no obstacle which could not be overcome. The
breezy optimism of his nature had blown the breath of hope
even into the labyrinths of love. Why not? He knew
himself. He had ardour sufficient for two, tenacity enough
for a dozen. He could wait. Her past was nothing to one
who was resolute to possess her future.

As he stood there in the darkness, not leaning against
the wall, but firm on his feet, his fists clenched, his eyes full
of sombre and jealous fire, a thousand broken thoughts
came and went like lurid colours in a kaleidoscope—fragments of the past, dreams of happiness scarce formulated,
schemes for the future. And shooting through them like
a tongue of flame through whirling smoke, this new sensation that was a gnawing ache and a keen pain in one. But

no fear, no ultimate doubt; for the indomitable quality of this man's blood equalled the occasion.

As he nerved himself to speak, a faint sound from the interior of the Catholicon arrested him. Having no wish that others should discover what he now knew, he retreated noiselessly.

A moment later Petros and Zetitzka were roused by the sound of a strong cheery voice.

"What, Brother Johannes, you here!" it cried. "Going to count your dirty old books? Nay, come with me into the court, and I'll tell you a good story about Meteoron. Tush, brother, I make no noise! Yes, yes, of course I respect the place. What say you? Never seen me pray? Well, you've something to live for, after all."

17

CHAPTER XL

HALF-CONCEALED behind one of the squat grey pillars of the cloisters, Dimitri waited for Petros and Zetitzka to leave the Catholicon. When at length they appeared, they paused awhile conversing on the top of the steps. The young monk was talking; his words, however, did not reach the muleteer. Zetitzka was looking into the boy's animated face: that he engrossed her to the exclusion of all else was evident. Her countenance had a new light of happiness in it that caused it to shine, singularly sweet, amid the stern monasticism of her surroundings. Dimitri set his teeth hard.

He could not bring himself to interrupt their conversation, but waited, though the moments seemed interminable. The sound of a distant voice, raised suddenly in the silence, appeared to recall the lovers to forgotten duties, for they parted—Zetitzka to her cell, Petros towards the refectory. Dimitri followed the latter.

Hearing hasty footsteps behind him, Petros looked round.

" Dimitri! " he cried, then broke off, catching sight of the muleteer's face.

Dimitri stood silent, then suddenly he laid a heavy hand upon the boy's shoulder.

" I must speak to you," he said.

At the tone of his friend's voice, Petros forgot the supper awaiting him in the refectory, forgot even his customary service to the Abbot.

" Now? " he inquired.

" Yes. Come to the tower of the windlass."

They did not speak again till they had reached the structure. It was empty. Not a sound came either from the monastery behind, or from the world below. Seen through the open end of the hut, the crags, and farther off, the plains, swam in a golden mist. The sense of being suspended over space was ever present. A touch, a gust of

258

wind, and it seemed as if the ramshackle hut must collapse into the gorge.

Both men remained standing. Neither spoke—Dimitri striving to master his agitation, Petros merely wondering. The muleteer's eyes were fixed on the distant hills, as though seeking something he could not find. Suddenly he wheeled upon his companion.

"I saw you in the library," he said.

The stern denunciation in his eyes caused the sunburnt brown of the lad's complexion to deepen suddenly under the down of his cheeks. Yet his gaze did not falter. On the contrary, he returned Dimitri's stare with a candid innocence of regard, though there was that in his face that told of a mute appeal for comprehension.

"How long has this been going on?"

For a moment Petros felt inclined to resent this cross-examination, but an earnestness, strangely compelling, in his companion's manner induced him to reply.

Dimitri looked at him searchingly. The boy seemed to feel no shame. His face was unusually grave, but his eyes held a strange inward light, while his voice told of a subdued and solemn gladness. Sorely perplexed, Dimitri continued to stare at him. Had he forgotten his vows? How far was he guilty? There was something in his expression that disarmed suspicion. It baffled the muleteer; more, it made him angry; but rather at something within himself than at this young monk, who—devil take him—eluded anger.

Suddenly the crux of the matter flashed across him.

"You love her?" he asked.

"Yes."

"She loves you?"

"Yes."

The replies carried conviction. The tone of the last affirmative amazed the muleteer, even through the pain it inflicted. It seemed not so much an answer to his question as to some inner voice in the lad's own bosom whose mouthpiece, he, Dimitri, had unconsciously become. It was the hushed, reverent, and almost incredulous recognition of a truth too wonderful, too beautiful to be true.

"You made her love you?"

The baseless charge conveyed nothing to Petros. But

full of the idea, urged by a jealous pain, Dimitri continued, passion overcoming reason.

" I see—I see now. By 'r Lady, yes. You have known it all this time—and I—like a fool—hoodwinked! "

He broke off with a gesture. Unworthy suspicions again tainted his mind. The night spent in the deserted monastery—these two, alone—the freedom of access to her cell at all hours, by order of the superior—the ignorance of the brethren that raised no obstacle to their companionship—the simplicity of the Abbot, itself almost a connivance—all were known to him, for little passed in the monastery without coming to his ears.

" If you have wronged her——" he broke out thickly.

Startled by the menace in his companion's voice, Petros stared at him in amazement. There was a troubled look in the boy's eyes that told of one striving vainly to understand; but no guilt; above all, no shrinking. Again Dimitri felt abashed. Muttering something that sounded like an apology, he held out his hand.

Petros took it frankly, then a look of grave concern overspread his face.

" I am guilty, Dimitri," he confessed, almost in a whisper.

The muleteer started, but Petros continued quickly. " Ay, guilty of the sin of concealment. Nay, shrug not your shoulders; 'tis a black sin, God forgive me. Since Lavra I have known, yet have I hid the knowledge of it from the Abbot."

It was noteworthy that for the moment he remembered only his broken vows, as though the yoke of monastic life —the yoke that subjugated all upon whom it fell, to the dead level of unquestioning obedience—had at length reasserted its sway. But at the next moment the lover leaped out.

" How could I help it? "

The cry rang with an indescribable intensity of fervour.

Dimitri drew a long breath. His heart was like lead. Anger had left him; only wonder and pity remained.

The sun was sinking behind the mountains. The austerity of the great cliffs became soft, even tender. Their crests shone with the dull lustre of beaten gold. Here and there, where the sun struck fire from a flint, it

was as if a jewel flashed, or a star had fallen; the light
of its presence trembling on the verge of profound abysses.
The distance was a sea of splendour above which the more
remote of the crags towered like sentinels, or floated like
islands.

Something of the fugitive glory fell into the little eyrie
of a hut. It, too, became transfigured. The opening—its
window and door in one—looked down upon many of the
adjacent hills. It had become a square that allured, while
it dazzled. The level beams, slanting inwards, suffused
the faces of the occupants. This world-wide peace reproached the two men. It formed a trenchant contrast to
their agitation.

"Yes, I blame myself," cried the young monk passionately. "Yet, I vow, as God seeth me, that it was for her.
Only at first, not later," he added hastily, as though eager
to correct a false impression. "Nay, later I would have
done it for myself. Brother Nicodemus would say that I
am damned. But—I care not. No; I care not!"

He repeated the last words with defiant obstinacy, his
head in the air, a touch of his old boyish impetuosity.
It was evident that he was trying to convince, talk down,
not the muleteer, but some invisible personality, his other
self, the twin possessor of his soul. His sincerity was un-
questionable. He recoiled from even the possibility of de-
ception.

"We must think of her," said Dimitri gruffly.

The face of the boy lighted.

"She cannot stay here."

There was no comment.

"She must go away—at once."

Still no reply.

"Come," said the muleteer, disguising his feelings
under rough impatience. "Saints above! what do you expect?"

"I?"

"Yes, you."

"Nothing."

Such hopeless misery became audible in the word that
Dimitri looked hastily at his companion. The lad's appearance shocked him. He recalled the Petros he had
known all these years, merry and boyishly serious by turns;

the young presence that appealed at sight to the sympathies of everyone, even to soured old men like Nicodemus and Apostoli—above all, the youth and the gaiety! The contrast was poignant. It made him indignant, as though he had been decoyed by fate into playing the part of executioner. His anger vented itself upon his companion.

"You are a monk," he blurted with unreasoning animosity; then, as his victim winced, he continued with more and more heat.

"My God, this is too much! You fall in love—*you*, a monk! You make love to her; ay, you do; no need to look at me like that, confound your innocence. What? You pretend to teach me—*me!* Dimitri! versed in the affairs of the heart! And now that you have done all this harm, you wish to keep her here—here, in Barlaam. Sacred Name! Imbecile! And the danger? To her? Bethink you, if they caught her—Apostoli, for example. Ah, that touches you near? I should think so. You had forgotten. That is what it is to be a monk. Ah! to the devil with all monks!"

He broke off with a violent gesture, his face aflame; then muttered, "There, there! No need to take it like that."

But Petros did not move. His eyes stared as though fixed on some invisible catastrophe. Dimitri's compunction increased.

"You could not tell," he continued, gruffly as ever. "Were I your age, and a monk, and ignorant, I would have done the same. As it is, I have often done worse, and now —I preach!"

His gesture signified profound self-contempt. A moment of silence then, "Brother Petros," he said softly.

Eliciting no reply, he continued:

"Bethink you. You are a monk. I have been against it from the first, God knows; but it was none of my business. You cannot marry her. Look you, she is helpless —a woman. Moreover, she loves you, and women are weak when they love. Believe me, I know; I who speak to you. Her life is not here—'tis there." He gesticulated towards the sunlight. "Let her go. Look you, she has but us to help her. I," he drew a deep breath, "I am nothing to her. She does not even see me. But you—she will listen to you. Let her go. For her sake.''

He stopped suddenly, awed into silence by the trouble his words evoked. He felt awkward, ashamed, for he recognised that he was face to face with some naked emotion—despair, it might be—stripped of all shreds of the reserve that constitutes decency.

The chin of the young monk had sunk to his chest. He was incapable of pronouncing a word, but deep in his throat he made an inarticulate noise like a man imperfectly stunned by a blow on the head. It was pitiful.

All at once he wrenched himself away, as though the scrutiny of a fellow-being had become insufferable to him and strode to the opening of the hut.

The muleteer watched with apprehension. Petros now stood stock-still, his hand clutching the rail, his slight figure an intense black against the intense brightness of the sunset. He was fighting—fighting.

The utter silence was broken only by the faint creaking of the rotting woodwork, as the heat left it at the slow and relentless approach of night.

It was his utter loneliness that moved Dimitri. He looked lost, helpless; he had no one to whom he could turn; and yet, he was only twenty-one. His visible pluck made this the more affecting. Dimitri thought of his own mother, and all that she had been to him in moments of boyish distress. Just a word, a hand passed caressingly over his hair, a motherly shoulder against which he could rest his head—just these, but these at the time had been everything. But Petros had no mother, could recall the touch of no woman's hand—save one, and now fate was demanding of him never to touch it again.

He stood on the brink of a despair as profound and inimical to life as the chasm that yawned at his feet. There was courage in his attitude. His head was uplifted as though he were looking someone—his sorrow it might be —straight in the eyes. His long shadow fell black as a pall across the decayed flooring of the hut, and loomed immense and extravagant athwart the windlass. By a fantastic trick of circumstance, strangely symbolical, this shadow appeared to be hung upon two of the mighty arms which, with the upright that supported them, took the form of a cross.

CHAPTER XLI

At length Petros turned his back on the light. Dimitri, hearing him approach, feigned interest in his whip. His practised ears noted the extreme listlessness of the boy's movements, audible in the dragging of his sandals over the worn flooring. The muleteer shrank from speech. There was a nakedness about the grief he had been forced to witness that seemed to silence comment.

It came to him that he had wofully misjudged Petros. He had thought of him only as a boy, almost a child, incapable of deep feeling. But this despair spoke for itself. It filled the witness with suppressed resentment and a longing to do something violent. It also woke respect for one who could feel so passionately, yet take punishment with head erect and no complaint upon his lips.

" I will tell her," said Petros. He spoke as if all emotion had been drained out of him. Dimitri nodded, but without looking up.

" For when had it better be? "

" To-morrow," muttered the muleteer—" to-morrow night."

As he spoke he felt, rather than saw, his companion wince.

" I can be here," he continued with constraint, " with Nikola. We can take her as far as the frontier "—he paused, and stroked his chin—" or farther, if necessary."

Petros assented. Again a casual observer would have judged him indifferent, but his unnatural calm filled Dimitri with vague alarm.

" She has told me something—not all," said the boy in a low voice. " I am loath to send her back to her parents. They treat her cruelly. She said she had only her baby."

The muleteer looked towards him quickly.

" Her child! " explained Petros.

" Her *own* child! "

264

" Yes."

" But—she is not married? "

" No."

Dimitri still stared at the shadow that now represented his companion. That this information conveyed little or nothing to the boy did not surprise him; but to him it was illuminating. It did not account for Zetitzka's presence in the monastery—though that the one had to do with the other struck him as a possibility. It was characteristic of him that the only lively emotion he felt was a grim animosity towards her betrayer. Being practical, however, the present at once claimed him.

" Why did she come here? " he questioned.

For some time there was no answer. The silence was broken only by the far-off bleating of goats driven homeward at nightfall. Somewhat surprised, Dimitri repeated the question.

" I know not," said Petros slowly.

" You don't know! "

" Nay; she never told me, and I never thought to ask."

There was such indifference to all immaterial considerations in the answer that Dimitri uttered an exclamation. As he pondered, it struck him as strange that neither he nor Petros knew much about the woman they loved.

" I did think of it once," continued Petros, " on that day after Lavra. It seemed a sacrilege then. But later "— he drew a deep breath—" I saw it was naught—less than naught. I forgot all about it."

Dimitri grunted.

" Do *you* know that too? " whispered Petros.

" What? "

" That nothing matters—nothing!—so long as she is here? "

There was no reply. Petros looked up at the big figure looming in the dusk. He seemed to see his companion in a new light. It was as though a wave of sympathy had brought them together.

" Do you love her too? " he asked reverently.

Dimitri laughed. There was pain in the sound.

Petros stared at him in wonder.

" I have no time to make love," said the muleteer. He

paused, then added bitterly: "I leave that to monks!"

He could not resist the thrust, yet felt ashamed the moment it was uttered. But, like a previous sarcasm, it passed harmlessly over the head of Petros.

"I thought all the world must love her," said the lad simply.

Dimitri chafed.

"Time presses!" he cried. "And you and I talk of ourselves."

His irritation aroused his companion. For awhile they conversed in low tones, for the mysterious shadows that had crept upwards from the ravine seemed to impart an air of secrecy to their interview. There was melancholy in the waning light. Nature seemed to grow grey and wan in sympathy with hopes destined never to be realised. It encompassed the young monk, isolating him from his companion, making him one with the slowly blurring ghost of the monastery. It ate into his heart like a corrosive acid—it and the silence, which was profound, impassive, disdainful, symbolical of laws imperious and irrevocable. For these preparations made him feel as though he were deciding the hour and manner, not so much of his own death, as the death of someone whose life was inexpressibly more precious to him.

"We must get her away without anyone seeing," concluded Dimitri. "And afterwards"—he turned abruptly to his companion—"afterwards—next day—what will you do?"

There was no reply.

"Come! you must have some plan. Devil take me, if I like to let you face it alone! They will miss her: they will question you. Come, rouse yourself! This is important—for you."

"Is it?" The boy's voice had sunk into some depth of numbed sensation. Dimitri muttered an oath.

"What will you say?" he asked impatiently.

"I will tell the venerable father."

"All?"

"All."

"Well, 'tis perhaps the best thing. It must come out—in confession, eh? But—he will be angry."

Petros kept silent.

" You don't care! "

The boy sighed wearily. " You don't understand," he cried. " Why talk of me? Anger—penance—it is all one. Can't you see? Can't you see? " His voice rose in sudden and querulous remonstrance: it was as though he reproached his companion for dragging him upwards to where suffering was forced to become articulate. " Can't you see? Nothing will matter then! "

Again a rush of impotent anger swept over Dimitri. He could have cursed the monastery.

" Brother Petros," he began, " when two dogs fight, one ought not to be muzzled."

" Fight? There can be no talk of fighting between us."

Dimitri's brows contracted. The loyalty and candour of the boy's nature reproached him with double-dealing—nay more, with falsehood. Goaded by remorse, he muttered inarticulately:

" What is it? "

The young voice came to Dimitri from the darkness. He had not noticed before how dark it had become. The slow irresistible progress of the night, blurring all details, stealing inwards from the gloomy world without, burying all things deeper and deeper as though it were a fall of impalpable black dust.

" I have deceived you," muttered the muleteer awkwardly. " I—I—— How am I to tell——? "

There was silence. Not only the motionless figure at his side seemed to be listening without movement, but everything—the hut, the shadows, the windlass—seemed to be listening too.

Dimitri continued:

" You asked me if I loved her. I said no. It—it was a lie."

A faint movement came from the darkness, whether of surprise or anger the muleteer could not tell. He continued sternly:

" I lied to you. Do you understand? I love her. Good God! can't you speak? Don't you hear? I lied to you! "

" Why? "

There came a short mirthless laugh; then: " Why does one ever lie? I was a coward. Yes," he insisted angrily, as though contradicted, " a coward. If another said that——'' His gesture was ominous. '' Yet it would be true. But you—I saw—fighting it out—the devil of a business! By the saints! a lesson to a shirker like me!''

'' Then—you love her too? ''

'' Yes.''

'' I am glad.''

Dimitri's jaw fell. He had nerved himself to the confession, prepared for anger, reproaches, above all, for jealousy. But this——!

'' Yes, I am glad,'' repeated the voice at his side, in an imperturbable monotone, which, more than anything else, more even than the sinister gloom of the surroundings, troubled the mind with suggestions of profound and hopeless desolation. '' I am glad. She is alone—unhappy. There will be no one to take care of her. I ''—his voice faltered—'' I must stay here. But you are free.''

Dimitri stood awed. Not a doubt of the intensity of this love came to him. Had it not been visible in the boy's agony as he stood on the precipice brink? Was it not audible still in the dull note of pain? Yet—to give her up—and to another——!

'' If——'' he began, but paused, mentally recoiling from what he was about to say.

'' What? '' questioned the boy.

'' If you were free—if there were no obstacle, no cursed monastery, I mean——''

Petros stared at him in dull astonishment.

'' By Saint Barlaam! I have a mind to do it! Why not? I hate the place for what it has done to you. See, then, Brother Petros, if you will run away with her, devil take me but I will aid you by every means in my power— ay, even to lying to the monks till I'm black in the face! No need to thank me. I do it for her sake.''

He had laid an appealing hand on the boy's arm. In the darkness his deep voice vibrated with intense earnestness. But Petros had no thought of thanking him. The figure the muleteer touched stood motionless and silent, as if turned to stone.

Dimitri continued: '' Child that you are, you don't know what you will miss. How should you? They have kept you in ignorance. You have rights. Do you know that? Every honest man has a right to a good woman's love.

Here they seek to rob you of it. Don't talk to me of
vows! Did you know all you were promising when you
took them? No, I bet you didn't. Bah! they made you
sign an agreement with your eyes shut. It's like selling
a spavined mule to a blind man. Cheating, that's what
they call it down there in the world. Don't talk to me
of religion! I know the good God. He is just: He would
scorn to act like that. He made men for women and
women for men. He will forgive if you stick to her, and
treat this cursed monastery like—like that!" He snapped
his fingers. "Hey, now! What is it?"

Petros had disengaged himself brusquely.

"You know not what you say!"

The muleteer uttered a contemptuous exclamation.

"It is true," continued Petros vehemently. "It is true.
You speak heedlessly, in ignorance. You do not understand. I have sinned—yet, God forgive me! I would
joyously do it again. I must bear the punishment. I am
a monk. Naught under heaven or on earth can alter that.
My place is here."

Dimitri shrugged his shoulders. Yet even in the midst
of his very genuine sorrow, he was guiltily conscious of a
selfish joy. Indignant with himself, he said sullenly:

"'Tis you who do not understand."

"I do understand. It means that you will love her, and
take care of her when I am dead—dead to her. Yes, that
will be best."

For long neither spoke. There seemed nothing further
to say. For his part, Dimitri was bewildered with the
transformation of the boy he had known into this voice
beside him. But, through amazement and indignation, his
heart went out in sympathy to the lad who, he surmised, was suffering as only those can who have staked
their all upon one throw of life's dice, and have
lost.

A faint cry reached them. Weird and remote, it wailed
disconsolately from the benighted passage. Dimitri listened, but the sound was not repeated. The monastic
silence closed in, resettling itself like the waters of a black
and stagnant pool momentarily disturbed by the plunge of
a stone.

"Someone calls," he said in a low voice.

There was no comment.

" Who can it be," he whispered uneasily, " at this hour? "

A muffled sound beside him indicated absolute indifference.

CHAPTER XLII

UPON the same evening, about the sunset hour, there strode along a lonely path a solitary figure in monastic garb. Stephanos, for it was he, was on his way to collect the rent of an outlying farm, the last of his places of call.

Around the monk a fine wild landscape extended, especially towards the west, where the hills, rugged and blue as uncut sapphires, shouldered the after-glow. Between these, but rapidly blurring in the waning light, lay ridge upon ridge, heathery, craggy, full of formless obscurity and already withdrawn into conscious isolation, anticipating the night. All was bare, barren, with the treeless nudity that saddens the traveller on Grecian uplands, due—if the peasants be credited—to the depredations of the marauding Turk. A fine, savage, natural landscape none the less, with never a sign of man's hand or a trace of his passage, save the path worn by countless generations of feet, and flung in loops, like a coil of grey rope, round buttress and hummock, rocky rise and channelled slope.

The monk walked rapidly, with bowed head. His sombre figure, now climbing, now descending, but throwing the miles behind it with long preoccupied strides, might have been mistaken for a phantom, for his naked feet were noiseless on the stones.

There was something feverish and insistent in the solitary wayfarer, in the knotted hands clutching the rosary, in the bowed head, and in the tense and nervous energy of the movements, that formed a trenchant contrast with the deep' and all-pervading peace that, "falling, as day fell too," brooded over mountain and valley. This contrast was further emphasised by his eccentricity; for his stride, though long and unwearying, was not continuous. At times he would halt abruptly, fall into profound contemplation, his eyes fixed vacantly on the stones or the misty outline of the hills, then, rousing himself with an effort, would hastily resume the road.

The darkness was rising steadily like an exhalation. Objects at a little distance melted and blurred into each other, baffling vision. Background and foreground were merged into one beneath the tent of night.

All at once a dog barked. The sound, breaking rudely upon the silence, was sufficient to arouse fear in an unarmed man, for dogs in the mountainous district of Thessaly are savage as wolves. But the monk betrayed no alarm. Swinging round a rocky spur, he became conscious of a dull red glow relieving the obscurity upon his right.

The animal came bounding along the track. Its bestial clamour never ceased. Stephanos, muttering a prayer, continued to advance. Reaching the monk, the dog checked abruptly, seized by the instinctive cowardice of animals confronted by fearlessness in man.

Before Stephanos could gain the cottage, the door opened, and a woman's voice was heard calling the animal by name. It, however, seemed unable either to leave or attack the wayfarer. Its deep growls changed to a pleading and nasal whine, a sound of almost human intelligence.

Raising his voice, Stephanos informed the woman of the object of his visit.

" My man is ill," she said apologetically. " But come in."

Stephanos refused. He preferred to wait, he said, outside. The woman disappeared. Through the open door her voice could be heard, raised slightly, as though her auditor were deaf. A man's voice answered her, then all was still. Without, in the darkness, the only sounds were the clicking of the monk's beads. The ghostly mass of farm buildings loomed out, a darkness against a darkness that was broken only by the dull glow that, issuing from the cottage door, formed a pathway of faintly-graduated light.

All at once Stephanos drew back, for the woman appeared in the doorway, holding a lighted candle. His sudden movement took the dog by surprise, for it leapt aside, the coarse hair upon its neck bristling.

Looking at the visitor with frank curiosity, the woman said:

"My husband says why not come in? He expected you to stay the night."

The monk stood before her, silent, with averted eyes. She continued: "Last year it was Brother—Brother Johannes, I think he was called; and the year before, Brother Apostoli. They both stayed over-night. It is late; there is no inn near, nor other house for the matter of that. Will you not change your mind and stay?"

"Nay, I must be gone."

"Well"—she shrugged her plump shoulders—"it is as you like, of course. You look tired, and the night is dark. I am sorry you must go. You will, at all events, eat something; we would be loath to turn a stranger supperless from our door. I have been baking, and——"

"Give me the money and let me go."

The woman stared at him in amazement. Her first impulse was to take offence; but something, for which she could not account, tied her tongue. In silence, that was not without dignity, she paid him and watched while he concealed the money beneath his cassock. Mumbling something that might have been a valediction, he turned abruptly and strode away. Still she watched, the receipt he had given her held absent-mindedly in her hand, her lighted face eloquent with the feelings she longed to express.

A few minutes later, Stephanos, rounding a corner with his usual precipitation, came into collision with another wayfarer. The latter, all but invisible in the darkness, was on his hands and knees, for his head came in contact with the pit of the monk's stomach.

"A hundred thousand devils!" vociferated an angry voice. "Who are you, and what do you mean? Cannot you take heed where you walk? May an honest pedlar not look for an accursed key without being assaulted?"

Want of breath prevented Stephanos from replying. The stranger gave vent to a short laugh.

"I seem to have knocked the wind out of you, at any rate. That will balance our account. Well, are you dumb as well as clumsy? Eh? Give me a match."

Stephanos handed him flint and steel. The unknown

18

took it ungraciously. Stephanos, looking silently down on the blackness that represented the stranger, made out a blurred mass, without detail, faintly distinguishable from the track. For some time the pedlar was heard groping in a bundle, swearing to himself the while; then a candle flickered into light. It made a little circle of kindly luminosity in the midst of this wide surrounding blackness. The two men showed plain, the one erect, the other still on his knees. The key found, the unknown rose to his feet and held the lighted candle close to the monk's face.

"Stephanos!" he ejaculated in surprise.

"Brother Stephanos," corrected the monk.

"Ay, to be sure. You know me?"

"I know you, Nik Leka."

The pedlar laughed, then suddenly sobered. Blowing out the light, he asked:

"Where are you going? What! To Barlaam? You cannot reach it to-night. Better turn back with me. I sleep at the farm you have just passed. No? Well, you know your own business best, and perhaps 'tis better to part before I tell you what I think of you."

Since recognising Stephanos, he had slid naturally into the dialect of the mountains.

The monk made no reply. Irritated by his silence, the pedlar broke forth again.

"'Tis not complimentary. Oh, be sure of that! Why didn't you marry the girl instead of running away—you coward?"

Still the sombre figure did not reply.

"She was too good for you," accused the gruff voice, as though airing an ancient grievance. "I know her, an angel, young, pretty. What did she see in you? Blessed saints! in *you!* But women are too good for men. They will have it made up to them in heaven, poor dears." Then, with a swift rush of anger: "By God, monk or no monk, you deserve to be flogged!"

Stephanos trembled, not from fear, but from the violence of his effort at self-control. His thin hands clenched upon his rosary. The touch of the worn beads steadied him. He drew a long breath.

"You do not understand," he muttered.

"Understand? Faugh! I understand enough. If she had asked me to kill you, I would have done it with pleasure. God in heaven! she even touched the heart of an old crab-apple like me—*me!* Nik Leka!"

He threw out his arms, then, recalling his pack, began to buckle it on to his shoulders.

"But she did not want you killed," he growled, tugging at a strap. "Women are soft. They pardon too easily. Ah, she has courage! A fine girl! Few women would have made the journey alone—and all for a man who had deserted her."

He spat angrily, and turned to resume the road.

"What journey?" inquired the monk.

"To Barlaam, of course."

"*She!*—she went to Barlaam!"

"Assuredly. What have you done with her?"

"What do you mean?"

"Bah! why seek to deceive me? You know well what I mean. She went to Barlaam to see you; two—no, three weeks ago. I saw her at the frontier Khan myself. She has not returned; that I know. She had a disguise. She might have hoodwinked the monks—but not you, for you knew. What have you done with her? Out with it! Where is she?"

Stephanos stood dumb.

Nik Leka came a step nearer. The two men were now so close as to appear one. The pedlar's solitary eye glared upwards to where the face of the monk made a visible pallor under his tall hat.

"If," said he thickly, "if you have done that angel any further harm, ay, even so much as injured her little finger, by God, I will kill you as I would a mad dog."

The deadly earnestness in his voice struck a grim note. This was deepened by the darkness and loneliness of the scene. There ensued a pause in which the silence was deep. Then the voice of Stephanos, so strangled as to be scarce recognisable, gasped:—

"Barlaam! She—Zetitzka, in Barlaam! Holy Virgin! 'tis not possible. No." Then, with ungovernable violence, and seizing the pedlar by the shoulder:—"Old man, you are deceiving me! You say this to tempt me. Are you the devil! She did not come to Barlaam. She dare not. She dare not! You made up this lie. Confess. I adjure you by the love of the Crucified, for the sake of your immortal soul.''

All self-restraint had gone. Nik Leka could not see his wild haunted eyes, nor the sweat beading his pale face, but he heard the frenzied insistence in his voice, and felt, and resented, the vice-like grip of his hand.

Roughly he shook himself free.

'' I told you the truth,'' he said gruffly. '' She did go to Barlaam. 'Twas I who told her you were there. She has not come back. I tell you she had a disguise; her mother spoke of it in my hearing. She carried it in a bundle under her arm. I warned her of the danger, but she would not take advice. Women are like that.'' He scratched his head, then, with a despairing gesture— '' Sacred Name! this is brain-splitting! Look you, she must be somewhere, that brave girl. But where? If one only knew that she was safe!'' He turned to the black figure beside him. '' Come; think! It is your duty to help her, yours of all men. Holy Saints! the very least you can do. You must have seen her. Did no one arrive at Barlaam lately, within the last ten days? She would pass for a boy. You *must* know! Think! Think!''

An exclamation of enlightenment broke from the monk. So fierce and full of horror was it that Nik Leka stared apprehensively. On the quiet night there poured forth a stream of curses, wild ejaculations, hysterical threats— incoherent, unrestrained, the ravings of insanity.

Nik Leka's first impulse was one of self-defence. Instinctively his hand sought the hilt of his yataghan. But his alarm was causeless, for the monk had forgotten him.

Foreseeing vaguely the danger to the community if this madman were allowed to go free, and forgetful of his own age and the pack upon his back, he attempted to seize him. But Stephanos tore himself from his grasp and in silence, rendered the more impressive by his outburst, fled into the night.

CHAPTER XLIII

ALONG the benighted road Stephanos rushed wildly, like the madman he had become. But one thought possessed him—to reach Barlaam and denounce the sacrilege to the brethren. Horror, fear, and indignation lent wings to his feet and a spurious strength to his wasted body. Under their influence his impaired vitality blazed into fresh life; like a fire that leaps into flame before it expires.

On, on, through the darkness, his long cassock impeding his movements, loose stones spinning from beneath his feet. The starless night blinded him, but the fierce flame within, fanned by the memory of the pedlar's words, hounded him on.

At length the inevitable took place. Missing the track at a point where the presence of a great rock cast it into still deeper shadow, the monk plunged headlong among a chaos of stones, recovered himself, staggered, and finally fell heavily to the ground.

For long he lay without movement, partially stunned. Blood welled from a cut in his head and fell drop by drop upon the ground. His breath came in gasping sobs, and his overdriven heart bumped and checked.

At length consciousness returned. With an effort he sat up. The darkness was impenetrable. No vestige of the path was to be seen; and in his fall he had lost all sense of direction. Giddiness and nausea seized him; but passed, as he pressed his brow against the cool surface of a rock. It behoved him to be careful—to nurse his strength. It was not his, but God's, lent to him for a purpose. He must make haste. Barlaam was far away. It would take all night to reach it. The pedlar's words, the discovery he had made, and his first impressions, all rushed on him. He sought to rise, but barely had he regained his feet than his dizziness returned. Flinging out his arms, he again staggered and fell.

Fasts, vigils, and violent passions had sapped at his strength; and now in the hour of need the ill-used body rose in rebellion against the will that had hitherto held it in subjection. His impotence filled him with terror. Still he would not give in. Struggling to his knees, he sought strength by prayer. But the mystic fire that had burned in his heart, sustaining and strengthening him in dark moments of depression, had cooled. The words were naught without the spirit. A heavy sense of regret swept over him. With all his might he sought to re-kindle the dying flame. The fear of failure added to his torture. Colder and still colder grew his soul, and for all things spiritual he felt only indifference, as of a sluggish heart and a weakened will.

Dejection seized him. Would God never return—never speak with him again? Was this fatal insensibility a prelude to fresh temptation—a sign that he was to be delivered body and soul to the evil one? By a spasmodic mental effort he succeeded in silencing the wild voices of his imagination, in concentrating all his strength upon the determination not to lose courage. But the exertion left him trembling and unnerved.

Bodily weakness attacked him—utter exhaustion and a feeling as though his eyes were two profound cavities penetrating to the centre of his skull. Added to this came a mortal lassitude. Oh, to sleep for ever—to forget all in a blissful state of utter unconsciousness! Closing his heavy eyelids, he began to drift upon a sensuous sea.

All at once a thin note of an owl screeched overhead. Stephanos started violently. With wild affrighted eyes like a hunted thing, he peered around and above, trying vainly to penetrate the darkness. A shudder passed over him. This was the voice of the devil. He felt as certain that the ghostly visitant was the Prince of Darkness as though he quailed before his fiery eyes, or scorched under his poisonous breath. In an agony of fear, he fell to praying aloud, calling upon God to rescue him, to come to his servant out of the waste places of the night. The sharp stones cut into his knees, but he was unconscious of pain.

" God! God! God! " he cried aloud, with passionate insistence. But the cry lost itself in blackness, wailing grievously among the desolate hills.

Then came despair. He was abandoned, doomed to everlasting perdition! With a groan he fell to the ground, his arms outstretched. As he did so, the money-bag at his girdle, striking against a stone, clinked dully.

How long he lay there he knew not. It might have been minutes, or hours. Time ceased to have importance for him. Drowsiness had gone. His brain was now abnormally active. His emancipated thoughts clung to Zetitzka. At first he tried to banish her from his mind, but she returned as persistently as though his brain possessed but one cell, and his memory but one groove, and she claimed both. It was a strange form of retribution. He could no more escape than a man bound with chains can rise and walk. She was within him. No darkness could hide him, no distance separate.

Again he shrank reluctantly from her appealing eyes, again he quailed and thrilled alternately at the sound of her voice, again he shuddered with mingled fear and ecstasy at the touch of her hand. Step by step, hounded forward by the lash of memory, he was forced to re-enact every emotion, to re-visit every scene connected with her presence. The first meeting, the night of the storm in his house, the assignations in the mountains, the parting before he fled to the monastery—all came back vivid as a landscape suddenly illuminated by lightning. At every separate memory he groaned aloud.

Then, with a swift and terrible shock, he remembered that she was now in Barlaam. He longed to disbelieve it, but the explanation of the pedlar, convincing him in spite of himself, left no room for disbelief. It was, moreover, corroborated by his own recollections:—the new lay brother; the chance encounter in the subterranean passage; her faltering speech, till now forgotten, but which returned clearly, word by word, as though it were a photographic negative slowly creeping into life under the action of a developer.

And with hideous inconsistency, in the midst of his horror and fear, he found himself dwelling with guilty and sensuous pleasure upon her bodily attractions, the many charms that had power, even in absence, to stir his imagination and accelerate the beating of his heart.

Suddenly he felt something touch his head. Again and again it came, infinitely soft and caressing, not on his head only, but on his hands, and on his bare neck. With a long sigh he shuddered upwards from the nightmare of his dreams to the blackness of reality. He touched his face with the back of his hand. It was wet. Rain had come. Steadily, persistently it fell from the low drifting clouds, saturating him, trickling over his burning skin, forming tiny rivulets in every fold of his cassock. He lay still and allowed himself to be soaked. As the water penetrated to his body, he shivered slightly. It allayed the fever that consumed him; it acted on his brain, soothing it, and winning it to a calmer mood. His trembling ceased, and, little by little, sinful thoughts lost themselves in the unconscious depths of his soul. With his wounded head pillowed on his arm and his eyes closed, he gave himself up to this gentle presence that fell from heaven like a benediction. He could hear its murmur like a long sigh of relief as it fell and fell in the darkness, on rock and stone, on parched plain and thirsty hill.

All at once he became conscious of a new sound, faint at first, hardly to be distinguished from the soft monotony of the rain, but, as the moments passed, growing louder and louder until it acquired significance. It came from beside him; the small silvery voice of running water, strangely persistent, reiterating something in the night.

Accustomed to associate all natural phenomena with his disordered fancies, Stephanos was suddenly seized with the conviction that this was the Voice of God. An immense awe took possession of him; on his knees, by the side of the unseen rivulet, he abased himself, beseeching guidance in this hour of darkness.

Unwearyingly the small voice spoke to him. With every faculty alert, every nerve strung, Stephanos sought to decipher the message.

Vaguely at first, but more and more clearly as the sound gained in volume, a word suggested itself to his distracted brain—a word that repeated itself persistently, as though the invisible were seeking to impress its wishes upon the listener.

Was it Zetitzka? Who else? God knew how she had imperilled one soul by her fascinations. He knew also that she was seeking to imperil others. What more just than that His wrath should be kindled?

The memory of her winsome face flashed across him, only to be driven sternly from his mind. Her youth and beauty were the devil's wiles. They should avail her naught. A new-born sense of importance came to him, and in the darkness his haggard face shone with a wild light. With the knowledge of Zetitzka's presence in the monastery, this man had passed from a tormented but controlled fanatic to a creature of ungovernable instincts. His every action, nay, his every thought, had become exaggerated beyond all sane possibilities, crudely melodramatic. With the strange hallucination of the insane, he told himself that he, Stephanos, was God's right hand, His scourge to drive this woman from Barlaam. An overweening pride swelled his heart, stifling all pity, overcoming all fear. Suddenly, in the blackness and silence of night, the hills heard an almost inhuman sound—a shrill, crazy voice uplifted in thanksgiving—thanksgiving horrible as a blasphemy.

CHAPTER XLIV

ZETITZKA was waiting for Petros in the cloisters.

The night was dark. A light wind moaned fitfully, causing the semantron to clank at irregular intervals against one of the pillars. Save for this dismal sound and the sighing of the wind, the monastery was plunged in its customary silence.

Before Zetitzka had been there many minutes, steps resounded on the flagstones and Petros stood beside her.

A thrill of joy passed over the girl. The darkness, desolate and full of fear, became beautiful, protective. Instinctively, to assure herself of the tangibility of her happiness, she stretched out her hands, touched the coarse stuff of his cassock with light furtively-caressing fingers; then, confused and trembling, allowed her arms to fall.

" I have somewhat to tell you, Zetitzka," he said.

His voice sounded forced and unnatural. Its tone alarmed her.

" What is it ? " she asked quickly.

There was a silence, broken only by the harsh clanking of the semantron. Then he proposed that they should go into the Catholicon.

Within the building the gloom was combated by the solitary lighted candle that burned continually before the icon of the Virgin. This light, though dim, contrasted forcibly with the groping darkness without. It enabled her to see him. His appearance increased her apprehension. With anxiety, which she never thought of concealing, she waited for him to speak.

He stood at a little distance from her. It was as if he feared to be near. For a moment he gazed at the deep shadows massed behind the Holy Doors, then, drawing a long breath: " Zetitzka you must go away from here."

She stared at him, far as yet from the truth, only be-wildered, troubled.

He continued. "It is not safe for you to remain. At any moment something fearsome might come to pass. Verily, I should have thought of it before. You must go to-morrow night."

Her eyes had contracted. She did not recognise in this young monk who spoke to her with such self-control the boy who, but a few nights ago, had stammered out his love. His very expression had altered. With a sudden sinking of the heart Zetitzka noticed the set mouth. This sign, which only betrayed the effort of his will, seemed to her the expression of an averted heart. The anguish of the thought took away all power of thinking.

Instinctively she pressed her hands to her bosom.

"*You* want me to go?" she asked, trying to control her voice.

"Yes."

She did not see what the word cost him to utter. It was enough for her to know that he was capable of pro-nouncing an affirmative, of dealing her a mortal blow that killed all dreams, all joy, all hope.

Her soul had been on tiptoe to greet him. Borne away on the tide of love, Zetitzka had almost lost sight of the dark and inevitable future. Her every thought had been consecrated to Petros. How·to give him pleasure. For his sake and his alone she had more than once exercised a self-repression that had in it much of the torment and the sweetness of martyrdom. Love was in her: as natural to her as colour to flowers. Love tingled in every vein, shone from her eyes, accelerated the beating of her heart. With the impetuosity of a torrent, long dammed up but now set free, her heart rushed towards Petros; or, rather it fluttered with tremulous wings; for deep and passionate though her feelings were, she would have died rather than acknowledge them. Only under the influence of a passion, impetuous and ardent as her own, would she have confessed to their existence.

Even while waiting for him in the darkness of the cloisters, she had been rehearsing her part, schooling her-self to resist, trembling, yearning, fighting. And all the while, deep down in her heart, she had been conscious of a delicious weakness that whispered to her that at last she had found her master, that she was his to do with as he liked. Ay, but his to keep and cherish, not his to send away.

Suddenly she started, to find that Petros was speaking again.

"All is already arranged," he said. "It were better you left this under cover of night. Dimitri says——"

He was interrupted by a quick gasp.

"*Dimitri!* I see now!"

He gazed at her, speechless. She looked dim as a ghost in the flickering golden light; but the indignation in her eyes was a thing alive—it pierced him like a knife.

"He arranged this?" she demanded fiercely.

At his answer she gave vent to a short angry laugh. "I knew it. You are changed. And in one little hour. You had no thought of this when we parted before sunset. Oh it is monstrous! Base! Do you call this love that changes in an hour? Dimitri! To let him interfere! What right has he? He is no monk."

Taken aback, Petros stammered he scarce knew what.

"Friend!" She repeated his last word angrily. "I need no friend but you. I want no one but you. Do you hear? I want *you!*"

He winced at the cry. Her eyes, devouring his face, saw pain. Hope, that had died so hard, struggled into new life.

"Petros! You *do* care. I see it in your face. God bless you for that, dear. But you have been misled. You are young, unsuspecting; you know not how wicked men are, and he must be a bad man to advise this. I blame him, not you. He deceived me too—with that friendly air of his. I trusted him. But don't listen to him. It would kill me—kill me. I couldn't live without you."

He found no words to answer. Deceived by his silence, Zetitzka continued eagerly:

"Let me stay with you. I will be very careful. Or, if it is too dangerous here, come away with me. We love each other; no one must separate us."

"Hearken, Zetitzka," he cried huskily. "Verily, you do Dimitri wrong. He does not want to part us. He is a noble heart. He offered to help us if—if so be that we went away together. Ah, stop!'' He raised his hand, for the gladness that sprang to her face cut him like a lash. ''It can never be. I am a monk. Holy saints, if only I had to suffer! But you—I have brought misery upon you—I, who would die, and joyfully, to save you even a little pain. I can never forgive myself. My God! Zetitzka, do not look at me like that!''

The hard incredulity in her eyes caused his voice to rise suddenly in a swift uncontrollable note of pain. But her expression did not change.

In a flash all her noble resolutions, all her dreams of self-sacrifice and abnegation vanished, whirled away like withered leaves before a winter storm.

Aboriginal instincts had her in their grip. Her Albanian blood, swift to love and swift to kill, surged to her poor aching heart. The fierce, primitive, and racial passions inherited from lawless ancestors smouldered in her eyes.

The boy was goaded past all endurance. '' You do—nay, you *must* believe me!'' he cried.

She shook her head. The negation was prompted rather by a desire to make him suffer, even as she was suffering, than by unbelief. '' No,'' she said sullenly, '' I do not believe you. If you cared for me you would never drive me away. Oh, you are cruel! You, too, think of your soul. Men do not care what a woman suffers. I might have known. I have suffered enough. But I was mad! Blind! I thought—I thought—I thought I was *so* happy! No, stand back——'' for as her voice broke piteously he had stretched out his hands. '' I do not want your pity. I want your love. I have given you mine—all. I would let you trample me under foot. I would follow you through the world. I would work for you till my fingers were bone. And be proud to do it. But you—Holy Virgin! you cast me off—at a word from another! Ay, 'tis true; you and that man Dimitri, you arrange my future between you. I am not asked. It does not matter what I feel. I am only a woman. But I will not go! I am no child, to be told to stay or go. Ah, it is all this hateful monastery! It is cruel. I hate it—*hate* it—*hate* it!''

All the Southern violence that love had taught her to repress exploded in her voice, blazed in her eyes. She went and came in the narrow space between the stalls and the Holy Doors, breathless, gesticulating, furious, desperate.

"Is this religion?" she cried with fierce scorn. "Is this what it is to be a monk—to break hearts, to ruin lives? Then give me a yataghan. It is more merciful: it kills at once!"

Petros watched her coming and going—watched her, sick with pain.

Suddenly her mood altered. She stopped abruptly. Her hands, now unclenched, were again pressed convulsively to her bosom, as though by the might of her ten straining fingers she could force down the anguish that was choking her. In the dim light Petros noted with renewed misery that her eyes were full of tears. She leant towards him as he stood riveted to the spot.

"Petros," she faltered, "what have I said? In my head everything is confused. I—I forgot myself. You must forgive me. I know you love me. You would not break my heart—would you, dear? You are my own true lover, the sweetest lover ever woman had. You will come with me?—promise it. For the sake of our love, Petros!"

Where was the Fury of a minute ago? Gone! And in her place was this poor woman, this piteous child, her lips trembling, hot tears coursing down her cheeks.

The boy instinctively crossed himself. All vestige of colour fled from his face. All his soul, all his body went out to her in an immense wave of compassion and sympathy and suffering mutely shared.

In the solemn hush of the sanctuary her voice continued, earnest and eager, passionate and imploring by turns. In broken words that were as a cry from her breaking heart, she reasoned with him, struggling to master her distress, to fight down her tears, to tell him of all that he would lose, to paint to him all that he might gain.

And he listened to her as one in a trance, unable to move, seduced by the sweetness and the pathos of that beloved voice that revealed to him a happiness beyond all imagining. To live with her always, always—to make a home for her—to guard and console her—to love her without restraint—to be the father of her children. A terrible longing rushed over him. It communicated itself to every inch of his body. Each separate throb of his heart was like a cry from the night of his loneliness, re-iterating her name.

Under these overpowering influences, his past, his life's training, his vows, all swung back, became faint and for-gotten as dreams at daybreak: nothing in the whole uni-verse was real but Zetitzka, but this dear familiar voice that was as sweetest music to his ears, leading him from darkness into light.

But as he listened and thrilled, moved to profound depths, his heart melted with love and longing, another voice called to him. Like a sleep-walker who awakens aghast upon a precipice brink, Petros awoke suddenly. In a flash he saw reality, and recoiled. He was a monk. For him there could be no such love as he had pictured. He would love her always—that was beyond recall—but his place was here—here till death.

The revulsion of feeling was violent. He felt like one in whose face the gates of all earthly joy are closed for ever. A subdued and profound spiritual responsibility mingled with the anguish that never for one moment ceased to prey upon his mind. Swiftly before his mental vision there passed memories of the solemn rite of initia-tion: the Abbot's voice raised in exhortation, the chanting of the brethren, the immense insurgence of spiritual awe and ardour that—as he had stood before them clad for the first time in the " Lesser habit " of a monk—had swelled his heart and imparted to every detail of the solemn service a holy and mysterious significance.

His material surroundings, which had receded to an immeasurable distance, drew near, claiming him. The shadowy corona with its pendant ostrich eggs; the sombre stalls vanishing into impenetrable gloom; the inner sanctuary behind the Holy Doors, now shrouded in dark-ness—all loomed black and imminent, frowning upon him in mute but eloquent reproach. Only the face of the Virgin, turned towards him, shone with a promise of inter-cession that was humanly tender, yet divine.

Zetitzka, watching, saw his face change. Its expression filled her with dread. She recognised that she had ceased to be all in all to him—that some influence stronger than hers was at work. A dull and burning jealousy seized her —yet, conscious that all effort was now unavailing, she kept silence.

Then, in the dim light, surrounded by the mysterious symbols of the creed that separated them, he spoke to her—spoke with averted eyes that he might not add to her pain.

But Zetitzka paid heed neither to his anguish **nor** to his disjointed speech. His tone was enough for her. In it there was a note of finality that was as a hand of ice laid upon her heart.

The inner light that lent him strength to do his duty was invisible to her. Later it was to dawn upon her that for him there was something higher than human love, and the knowledge was to bring consolation and even thankfulness. But for the moment all was dark.

Her poor distracted heart, racked with suffering, the sport of primitive passions, took note of but one thing— she had lost him for ever.

The blackness of the monastery settled down upon her like a pall. The silence, when Petros had ceased to speak, ate into her bones. Her attitude was one of utter and hopeless abandonment—the helpless acquiescence of one who is crushed. Slowly her head drooped until her forehead came in contact with the hard carven surface of the stalls against which she leaned. Then motionless as one of the sculptured saints overhead, with hands limp and open, with eyelids closed and streaming, she gave herself up to despair.

CHAPTER XLV

In the windy dawn Petros, crossing the court, came unexpectedly upon Dimitri. The muleteer was sheltering under the branches of the fig-tree.

" I could not keep away," he muttered awkwardly, suppressing further explanations as he saw that Petros expected none.

Dimitri looked round the court and at the monastic buildings slowly detaching themselves from the obscurity. Above him, the heavy foliage bent to the blasts. Barlaam, seen in this chill and blustering dawn, had an indescribable air of gloom.

" Where is she ? " he asked.

" In her cell."

" You have told her ? All is arranged ? "

" Yes."

The muleteer looked furtively at his companion. It was plain that he longed, yet feared, to question. Curiosity, however, got the better of him.

" How did she take it ? " he asked awkwardly.

Save with a vague gesture of his hands, Petros did not reply. His surroundings were less real to him than the recollection of Zetitzka, deadly pale, standing out among wavering shadows. Unconsciously he resented Dimitri's presence. He wanted to be alone.

" We must make it easy for her," said the muleteer, gruffly. " We are men, you and I."

The look that Petros turned on him puzzled and even struck him with amazement, for there was a solemnity and an insight in the grave eyes of the boy that made him feel that he had spoken unnecessarily.

" I can do little," he blundered on; " but you, you can do much. See that all is ready before dusk, her belongings and the key to the ladders. No one must see—— But there, you know all about that. As for me, I must

19   289

pass this day somehow. My faith! I am glad I have my business. I go to Meteoron and Kastrati. But at nightfall, you understand? Bah! I talk too much. Holy saints! what a dog's day!"

As he spoke, the high harsh wind swept over the monastery. On its wings came clouds of fine dust whirled upwards from the ravines. It tore at the kilt of the man, the cassock of the boy, buffeting them with irresponsible violence, causing them to clutch at their headgear; then screamed out and away across the ranges to where lay the sunless world.

" This wind, look you," grumbled the muleteer, " 'tis the very devil, the black wind, the worst we have had for years. I met the village priest on the path near Hagios Triada. He prayed aloud as he walked. He said that with this wind comes calamity. One never knows——" He crossed himself. " As a precaution, eh?"

But Petros was not listening. His eyes were fixed on the shadowy dormitories. Dimitri noticed and shook his head. With a curt farewell, he swung off towards the outer court. As he went, he muttered: " Could you not leave them to themselves for one day, and that the last? Beast!"

Even upon the swaying ladders he continued to abuse himself, taking pleasure in doing battle with the gale.

An hour later, several of the brethren were at breakfast.

" I have no appetite," wailed Gerasimos, then cried out lamentably against the wind that made his head go round. His companions likewise complained of bodies glowing with dry heat and skins gritty with dust. Nervous tension and depression weighed upon the spirits; even the gentle Philemon, with flushed face and eyes unnaturally bright, waxed quarrelsome. Superstitious fears added to their physical distress. Muttering low, as though the wind that howled without were capable of taking sudden vengeance, Nicodemus gave it as his opinion that the souls of the damned were abroad, and that it behoved all good monks to watch and pray. The others listened to him with open mouths, wagging their white beards and from time to time casting apprehensive glances towards the door.

The nervous tension deepened as the day dragged towards its close. The change after weeks of clarity and sunlight, was remarkable. A crape veil seemed to be drawn over the face of nature, through which the lurid light penetrated feebly. The outer world, stretching itself away in dim perspective, showed leaden and featureless; while, near at hand, the giant buttresses of Meteora towered grimly. The wind came from the north. It turned the gullies into vent-holes, and stormed about the pinnacle of Barlaam with a hollow and endless plaint that sunk the spirits of its inmates to their lowest ebb. Around the monastery it swept, less in gusts than in a steady besieging uproar; but higher, where the hills piled themselves upon the northern sky-line, its strength was more variable, for there came down at times a far-off canorous wailing, infinitely grievous to hear, and the eye would mark where a sudden column of dust whirled upwards and dispersed instantly like the smoke of an explosion.

Nightfall within the ravines was but the continuation of a darker and more hopeless day.

A little after the sunset hour—for no appearance of sunset had been visible—Stephanos strode rapidly along the path that led to the base of Barlaam. A stranger, meeting him, would have noticed nothing remarkable, save that he talked to himself, for the enveloping gloom hid the monk's features and concealed all signs of discomposure.

But the material darkness found its counterpart within his heart. His unbalanced brain, so long on the verge, had at length leaped into madness—a form of madness rendered doubly dangerous by some show of reason and controlled by a cunning that in itself was an additional cause for alarm.

The wind made walking difficult. It sprang on this lonely wayfarer and contested every foot of the path. As he struggled onwards with bent head and clutching his cassock, he stumbled frequently, and once he fell; but, recovering himself, he again matched his strength against the gale.

His mind was entirely occupied with Zetitzka. When the wind permitted, he rehearsed aloud what he would say when he met her face to face. The effect of this voice haranguing the darkness was uncanny in the extreme. In its tones were to be heard all the evil passions that hounded him on. That which was most noticeable about him was his lack of humanity; for as far as all pitiful and kindly instincts were concerned, he had ceased to be a man. He had become merely an embodiment of evil; obsessed with one idea; a purpose and a peril. His strength had redoubled. He burned with fever. But so intense was the concentration of his thoughts that he was as oblivious of weakness, hunger, and want of sleep as he was of the wind or the stones among which he stumbled.

Arrived at the foot of the ladders, he began the ascent. The clumsy lengths that oscillated to his movements had now no fears for him. He was unconscious of their swaying motion as step by upward step he climbed the face of the cliff; and if the blackness and the danger penetrated to his mind, it was only to thrill it with a sense of exultation.

Having groped his way through the trap-door, he paused irresolute. The darkness that hemmed him in was broken faintly by the square at his feet—a space that told where the topmost ladder hung and the precipice fell sheer. Through this opening the wind forced itself. A fierce spirit seemed to animate it, for unable to prevent the monk's entry it followed him, venting its rage upon the ·crazy hut, every beam of which groaned aloud.

Stephanos was thinking swiftly. Facts detached themselves from the chaos in his mind; so clearly did they stand out that he was able to marshal them into a semblance of order. Yet madness tinged even this show of reason. A pride great as that of Lucifer swelled his breast. The monastery, the pinnacle, all his surroundings, became insignificant, and he himself a giant. This lack of proportion, so common among the insane, persuaded him that he had only to raise a hand and miracles would take place. Was he not the agent of an avenging Deity? In the darkness his eyes dilated and his heart grew big with a sense of illimitable power.

Yet lurking beneath this inflated insanity, there were a doubt and a fear. Swamped by pride and the rush of wild hallucinations, they were existent, nevertheless. The doubt was of himself—the fear of Zetitzka.

All at once it struck him as unusual that the topmost ladder should still be in its place. While recognising this as fortunate, he did not cease to wonder. Was it not the duty of Brother Petros to draw it up at nightfall? The lad had then forgotten. Why?

As he pondered, memory came to his assistance—a comment of one of the brethren uttered in his hearing, till now forgotten. The names of Petros and Angelos had been linked together. Angelos? That meant Zetitzka! Great God! He clasped his hands to his head, for the blood had rushed to his brain. Almost swooning, he leant against the timber wall.

For long he remained without movement. Then, locking the trap-door and concealing the key beneath his cassock, he groped his way towards the courtyard.

CHAPTER XLVI

As he crossed the inner court, Stephanos came unexpectedly upon the Abbot. The old man staggered as the monk stumbled against him.

"Who is it?" he cried, for deafened by the wind and bewildered by the darkness he had heard no approaching footsteps. "Is that you, Brother Philemon?"

"It is I, Stephanos."

"Holy Saints!" The Abbot peered through his spectacles at the tall shadow barely distinguishable in the gloom. "You amaze me, my son. I knew not you had returned. But right glad am I to behold you; 'tis no night for aught human to be abroad. Now, get you to your cell. I will send victuals unto you. God be with you, my son."

"Venerable father——" But, ere he could continue, a hand was laid on his shoulder. "You forget," cried the Abbot's voice from the darkness. "You are under a penalty of silence."

Stephanos stood dumfounded. The fact had entirely slipped his memory. Experience told him that the penalty would be rigorously enforced. The Abbot's word was law. This knowledge, more than the warning hand, held him speechless.

The wind buffeted him in the face and fled screaming. To his mind it was a fiend mocking him.

"Hear me!" he cried in desperation, clutching as he spoke at the old man's cassock. "You must hear me! God sends me. There is deadly sin in the monastery."

"Silence!"

Recovering from his amazement, the Abbot threw into the word a weight of outraged authority. His tone dominated Stephanos as the human eye is said to dominate a wild animal. The Abbot continued:—

"What wild words are these? The black wind has distempered you. You are not yourself to-night. Add not disobedience to disobedience. Do as I command. Go.''

Half an hour later Elias and Gerasimos were dallying over their evening meal. The cheerless interior of the refectory, dimly lighted by the Moorish lamp, was full of wavering lights and shadows. Elias was worn out, for owing to the weather, the long services had been peculiarly exhausting. His grey head leant heavily upon his hand: his elbow propped itself upon a table still covered with the remnants of supper. Opposite him sat Gerasimos listening uneasily to the wind, while endeavouring to extract consolation from a glass of *mastica*.

All at once, the snap of broken glass caused Elias to open drowsy eyes. His companion—the stem of the shattered wineglass still between his fingers—was staring at the window, his whole person eloquent of superstitious terror.

. '' *Kyrie Eleison!* '' cried Elias; but in answer to his questions Gerasimos could do naught but point and gape, while the spilt *mastica* trickled to the floor.

'' A face,'' he whispered, finding breath; '' I saw it there —plainly—as I see you!''

His terror was infectious. Elias also found himself gaping at the stone slit that did duty for a window.

'' What like was it?'' he asked, under his breath.

'' Naught human. Its eyes reminded me of—of——''

He raised his hands, palms outwards, as though to ward off evil; then, in a whisper and bending forward across the table till his lips all but touched his friend's ears— '' You have seen the damned on the wall in the Pronaos.''

Elias crossed himself hastily. For awhile the two old men remained without movement. Outside the wind howled lugubriously. It forced itself under the door, brandished the lights of the smoky lamp, passed shudderingly between the two monks as they sat at table.

'' I shall stay here all night,'' muttered Gerasimos, edging closer.

Elias echoed the resolve; adding with faint hope— '' Peradventure the semantron will frighten it away.''

'' 'Tis not that I am frightened,'' said Gerasimos, his teeth chattering. '' But—my God! what is that!''

The click of the latch and the grating of the door opening slowly were with Gerasimos to his dying day. His boasted courage fled. Elias shared his emotions. But before they could tell who the intruder might be, a gust extinguished the lamp. The refectory was at once plunged in darkness. Nothing was to be heard save the wailing of the wind; a sound dismal at all times, but when accompanied by superstitious fears, sufficient to terrify the boldest. The impression of something standing silent and watchful in the strong draught caused by the open door was unmistakable.

At length a familiar voice was heard, calling upon the brethren by name.

" 'Tis Brother Stephanos! " cried Elias with indescribable relief.

" Let us re-light the lamp," proposed Gerasimos, mopping his brow.

" Nay." The voice of Stephanos rang loud. The two monks heard its peremptory tone with astonishment. It continued:—" I have somewhat to tell you, now, at once."

" But," objected Gerasimos, peering uneasily into the darkness whence the voice proceeded. " But we may not hold converse with you. The venerable father has forbidden it. God forgive us, we have already sinned. But you took us unawares."

" Ay, did he," corroborated Elias warmly.

" You *will* not listen? "

" We may not." The good-natured little monk gesticulated appealingly, as though he could be seen; then with a sudden pang of conscience and addressing himself exclusively to Elias, " May we, brother? "

" By no manner of means. A penance is a penance, and must be obeyed. Come, Brother Gerasimos, it grows late. Let us seek our cells."

" Fools! " The epithet was hurled at them. It caused them to blink with amazement. " O fools, ye that have eyes and see not, ye that close your ears lest ye may hear! But you *shall* hear! There is a woman in the monastery."

But upon neither of the old men did the information take immediate effect. Their senses, dulled by age and grievously harassed by the weather, were simply bewildered. As they gaped into the darkness, the voice of

Stephanos continued to speak. But its warnings were now mingled with wild denunciations, blasphemous pretensions, savage personal rancour, the whole so tinged with the very breath of insanity that the brethren's horror was concentrated upon the monk himself.

Stephanos broke off abruptly. For a moment he lingered; then the protracted silence conveying to his mind only hopeless and inconceivable stupidity, he hurled an imprecation at them and strode away.

Gerasimos sought for and found the arm of Elias.

" Mad! " he quavered. " God forgive us all! "

" Amen," muttered Elias.

CHAPTER XLVII

WITHIN one of the underground passages Petros and Zetitzka kept their last tryst.

A glimmer of light came from the outer world and, dawning through the rude opening cut in the living rock, dimly revealed a section of the passage—a portion of the inner wall pierced by the doorway of a cell—a cave of unmitigated blackness on either hand where the gallery lost itself in gloom—and, finally, the figures of Petros and Zetitzka seated on a log that overlooked the abyss.

Though shorn of its strength by the mass of rock, the wind could be heard raving in the darkness, sweeping over vast, benighted, and desolate spaces; at times with a note of anger; at others, sobbing and wailing piteously.

It wandered, too, into the passage—not with violence, but in fitful draughts, mournful as a sigh.

All around, the monastery brooded. It had the air of one who waits for something inevitable; of one who, intent upon some climax unimagined by others, heeds neither wind nor night.

Never before had this air of sinister expectation been so marked—not even in the dusk of Zetitzka's first ascent. The little old buildings seemed to know all. Since first one stone had been laid upon another no such forbidden companionship had taken place. The deep-rooted and ancient hostility to women that steeped the minds of the monks appeared to have passed to the grey walls that gave them shelter. There was something ominous in their impassivity, in their muteness; something vaguely disquieting in their grim alliance with the night. They darkly threatened, raising themselves with the distortion of things obscure, into the ragged and flying chaos of the sky.

The very wind, a creature of moods, seemed to partake of this emotion. It, too, appeared strangely animate, full of querulous and senile animosity. "A woman!" it seemed to wail. '' A woman ! '' Upon its wings the souls of monks long dead shuddered past—struck with impotent spite of the girlish figure, snatched in angry draughts at her costume; then fleeing back to the monastery, moaned her secret to the cloisters in whispers of inarticulate horror.

For Petros, sitting motionless by Zetitzka's side, neither the night nor the storm existed, except in as far as they had to do with her, with her presence, her departure. A blacker gloom than that which confronted his physical eyes stretched before his mental vision. In one hour, perhaps less, it would have engulfed his life for ever. He was too steeped in the blackness of the present to see, or even to think of any possible light in the future. No inkling of what this experience might ultimately mean to him brought consolation to his mind. He was stunned. '' She is going away—she is going away ! '' He repeated this over and over to himself, repeated it stupidly, mechanically ; but it conveyed nothing definite to his mind. It was all so impossible that he could not believe that it was to him— Petros—that this calamity had come. That the morrow would dawn when he would seek her and find her not—that endless morrows would follow, all empty, all hopeless, was a contingency so appalling as to be unthinkable.

His thoughts slid almost unconsciously into the old familiar groove of prayer, worn deep by training and life-long habit. That God would grant him strength—such was now his passionate, yet inaudible cry—strength to conceal his misery—strength to spare her unnecessary pain. '' Great and Merciful God, for her sake ! ''

And he was answered. Little by little, as during that hour of temptation in the Catholicon, something came to him. With fear, with solemn and unspeakable awe, he was conscious of it taking possession of his soul. Under its influence he grew strong. His fever and restlessness abated. A composure foreign to his nature descended upon him, more spiritual, more saint-like than he had ever before attained. His spirit looked down as from some immense height upon his suffering heart.

And yet never before had all that was human in him desired her more passionately ; never before had his man's heart worshipped her with more complete absorption. That she was going away made her, if possible, more unutterably dear, more inseparable from his very existence.

It was no light-won victory over self that this boy was gaining. Temptation was not dead. It still beset him in a hungering impotent yearning to recall the past.

One memory in particular obsessed him, causing his heart to ache with a wild and barren fervour of regret—one memory, the recollection of one sunset. The pale gleams of the western cliffs had thrown a shadow of light behind her, as though the sun were lingering. From out of this radiance she had come to him. Ah, the grace of her coming!—the gladness that always came with her! Never again would he see that light from the closing of the west without thinking of her. Alas! if it came to that, what hereafter was he to see in earth or heaven without thinking of her?

When the wind moaned along the passage it stirred the white embroideries of her costume. These fluttering draperies, so indissolubly associated with his first recollection of her, reminded him that the moments were fleeting. As never before did he realise the value and terrible evanescence of time; how each little second can be more precious than the heart's blood, yet pass swiftly and lightly, as of no account.

Already something in his soul was deepening, broadening, ripening swiftly to maturity, although he knew it not. Life was dealing with him. Suddenly aroused to the consciousness of her neglect, she was taking him in hand at last. Once, in his ignorance, he had asked for sorrow, and she had given him happiness; now when he longed for happiness, she gave him sorrow. Like a piece of metal full of alloy, yet full also of beautiful possibilities, his soul was tossed into the crucible of suffering. Life waited the result.

The moon struggled through the clouds. Zetitzka's face shone clear. Her eyes hung upon his. Within them Petros read depth beyond depth of passion and sadness, blackness of despair and thoughts too deep for tears.

Since Petros had told her that she must leave the monastery, Zetitzka had been as one crushed; a strange apathy had taken possession of her, a numbness of feeling that enabled her to perform her duties as though another, and not she, were obliged to dust and to sweep.

She had come to this last meeting obeying Petros mechanically, as she would have obeyed him in all things. Her proud free spirit, which even disgrace and Stephanos had been unable to conquer, was at last subdued. She had become gentle and acquiescent, pathetically touching in her resignation; speaking only when forced to do so, concealing her misery beneath a calm exterior. Something in her soul, faintly responsive and unknown to her, already dimly apprehended the spirit that raised and controlled the man she loved.

For long they sat side by side in silence, gazing outwards and downwards, less conscious of the dark world below than of their own sad and profoundly troubled thoughts.

The wind had lulled. Around the monastery it fell strangely silent, as though worn out by its own violence; but it could still be heard sweeping dismally over the benighted plains.

All at once Petros looked round. For a moment he stared into the blackness of the passage, then turning to his companion, asked her if she had heard anything.

" Only the wind," she answered.

" It seemed unto me——" He cast another apprehensive glance over his shoulder. " But, no! none would come here at this hour. And yet—perchance it is Dimitri. He promised to be with us at the tenth hour. Listen——"

They both listened, holding their breath. A distant moaning came from the monastery. It rose and fell fitfully, and again the chill subterranean draughts breathed upon them.

He continued gravely: " The hour is at hand. The brethren are in their cells. The venerable father was aweary to-night; past doubt he, too, sleeps. I marvel much what keeps Dimitri. I must go and see."

She made no attempt to keep him. Something in her attitude pierced his heart.

" I will not be long gone," he faltered. " You do not fear to stay alone? "

Her face was averted, but he saw her shake her head. He said no more. The sound of his retreating footsteps reverberated from the blackness—grew fainter—died away.

Suddenly there fell upon Zetitzka an overwhelming

sense of desolation. It made itself felt even through the dull apathy of despair, striking her with a quivering sense of misery. No longer buoyed up by the presence of Petros, she broke down utterly. Hot tears coursed down her cheeks. Her impotence to do aught but submit roused again her fierce mountain blood. If she could only fight —only tear down this great inhuman monastery with her hands! But, no; Barlaam, stern and impassive opposed her with its old imperturbable silence. Passionately she stretched out her arms to the stars. But they shone down upon her with cold indifference. There was nothing in earth or heaven to lend an ear to her despair.

Little by little she became calmer; her tears ceased to flow. Now and again a laboured sob broke from her. But even that was in time suppressed. Then, with head bowed to her hands, motionless, she sat for long unconscious of her surroundings.

What was that? Zetitzka raised her head. All was still, for the wind had dropped; but the sound behind her had set every nerve ajar.

All at once she felt frightened. She tried to fight down this fear, but failed. Some instinct, stronger than her will, impelled her to turn till she could gaze into the inner darkness.

A black mass half blocked the passage towards which she now looked. She knew it to be firewood, stored against the winter. She told herself so, to shame her fear. But in the very act of reassuring herself, her heart leapt to her mouth. Something moved! Something beyond the margin of moonlight that glimmered a ghostly blue into the gallery. She saw it. There was no mistake. Something was lurking there—in the blackness.

Full of a strange frozen terror, she watched. A moment of suspense, then the darkness appeared to solidify, to come nearer, and in this moving obscurity Zetitzka saw a grey face with eyes fixed on hers—the face of Stephanos.

CHAPTER XLVIII

REACHING the courtyard, Petros paused for a moment where an angle of the Catholicon gave shelter from the wind. Now that he was forced to concentrate his attention upon it, Dimitri's absence distressed him not a little. All had been carefully arranged. He remembered perfectly not only his own suggestion, that they should meet in the underground passage, but also Dimitri's consent thereto. Knowing the muleteer and his feelings toward Zetitzka, Petros recognised that something serious had taken place.

At the extreme end of the cloisters he called aloud, but guardedly, on account of the proximity of the monks. No such precaution, however, was necessary, for the wind, pouncing upon the cry, whirled it exultantly into the night.

The familiar court was a desolate, blustering semi-obscurity hedged about with an impenetrable gloom. Well was it for the boy that he could have traversed it blindfold, for loose and displaced flagstones formed traps for inexperienced feet. As he struggled onwards, buffeted by the gale, a growing anxiety took possession of him. His eyes, smarting from the fine driving dust, sought on all sides for the muleteer's familiar form. In vain. All was deserted.

Entering the dark refectory, he consulted the clock by the aid of a lighted match. It wanted but a quarter of eleven. In three-quarters of an hour the semantron would summon the brethren to the duties of another day. At that a wild hope, scarce formulated, fluttered in his breast —the hope that something might yet happen to prevent Zetitzka's departure. But he drove this weakness sternly from his mind.

With no definite expectation, he bent his steps towards the ladders. In the passage, and in the hut that overhung the ravine, the darkness was opaque. As he groped

his way onward, around him on all sides the ancient woodwork groaned and creaked, the plaintive sounds mingling
ceaselessly with the fierce onslaught of the wind.

Reaching the trap-door, the absence of upward draught
struck Petros with sudden consternation. Swiftly he felt
for the void, but his hands encountered only the massive
lid. The ponderous padlock was in its place. Barely had
he time to recognise all that this meant, when he was
startled by a muffled cry. It rose from the boards at his
feet.

" Dimitri! " he shouted.

Above the elemental clamour came a reply. Only
mutilated fragments reached Petros as he listened, his
ear to the flooring. From them he understood that the
muleteer, having climbed the ladders and finding the entrance barred, was waiting his arrival. A metallic screech
punctuated by dull reiterated thuds, became audible—the
oscillation of the ladder and its violent contact with the
face of the cliff. More than aught else, this spoke of the
danger braved by the man who for the better part of an
hour, had clung to the swaying rungs, shaken to and fro
in the blackness, while below him yawned the invisible terrors of the abyss.

Waiting for a lull, Petros shouted instructions. The
key was unaccountably lost. To seek it now would only
be to court discovery. They must do without it. He,
Petros, would bring Zetitzka to the tower of the windlass, and lower her in the net. Dimitri must wait
below.

In his voice there rang a note of unconscious leadership
that caused the muleteer to wonder. Recognising that
these instructions were the only practical solution of the
dilemma, he contented himself with shouting acquiescence;
then cautiously and with difficulty began the descent.

Petros was already retracing his steps to the court. Impatience burned hot within him, a jealous grudge of each
second that separated him from Zetitzka. This fever of longing was aggravated by a fear lest even now some untoward
accident might prevent him reaching her. These turbulent
emotions were strangely at variance with the spiritual ex-
altation that still was as a lamp to his soul.

As he penetrated the blackness of the underground passage, groping for the wall with extended hands, the sound of a scream, faint yet full of unnameable terror, rang along the gallery.

CHAPTER XLIX

ZETITZKA had started to her feet and now stood facing
Stephanos, her back towards the precipice. The monk
advanced slowly and under compulsion, as it seemed, coming to a standstill within a couple of yards of where she
stood. Rigid in the extremity of her consternation, she
could do nothing but stare. If Barlaam had rocked with
earthquake, she could not have withdrawn her eyes.

The expression of his face had for her a horrible fascination. It almost mesmerised her. Writ unmistakably upon
it were attraction and repulsion. Zetitzka could not dif-
ferentiate between these: she saw only the repellent effect,
and panic seized her.

She was alone, entombed with this man in the heart
of the rock. Until Petros returned, no help could reach
her. So full of brewing danger did he look, as he stood
there, not speaking, only holding her with menacing eyes,
that Zetitzka's brain suggested flight. But what use?
He would overtake her at once. She might have screamed
for assistance, but to do so was foreign to her nature:
and moreover the danger of discovery by others than Petros
was too great to permit of her running the risk.

He recognised her. She felt it. There was that in his
expression that reminded her of their last meeting in the
mountains. It appeared to her now as if this scene were
a continuation of the other, as if all that had taken place
in the interval were a dream.

And yet there was now a more ominous glitter in his
eyes, more fanatical, more unhinged, more hideous in its
warring suggestions of sensuality and abhorrence.

How long they stood thus Zetitzka could not have told.
It was probably to be counted by seconds, though to her
it seemed hours. If only he would move! If only he
would speak! But no—he seemed incapable of doing
anything, save of devouring her with his gaze.

" What do you want? " she cried in desperation.

The inflection of her voice—once so familiar—raced to his brain like wine. It seemed to him to be Zetitzka herself made audible—her very body, with all its appeal to his starved senses, offering itself to him through the medium of sounds. So equally balanced were the contradictory forces that swayed him that it needed but this to give the victory. A tremulous eagerness leapt to his face.

" Speak again! " he entreated.

But Zetitzka stood dumb. His manner filled her with fear, and with loathing stronger than fear. He recalled what she would give her very soul to forget. Then she had been an ignorant girl—wax in his hands—taking the base coin of lust for the pure gold of love. She knew better now. All within her that was noble and womanly, all that had gladdened and thrilled at the innocent worship of Petros, rose in arms. Could this man have seen her eyes, he would have quailed. But her face was hid from him by shadow.

He was gazing hungrily at the dim whiteness of her Albanian costume. Evil thoughts crept from memory like unclean beasts from their lairs. So powerful were they that they even obscured his vision.

Down the passage came the draught, fluttering his cassock; afar off, with a sigh of grievous unrest, raved the wind.

" Zetitzka! " he cried.

The cry sounded a note of unconditional surrender to the flesh. It rendered impotent all stripes, all vigils, all fasts, all penance, all prayer.

He stood before her, speechless, his arms outstretched, his face aflame. So fierce was the repulsion he caused her that she clenched her fists.

As they stood thus, a cloud concealed the moon. Darkness swept across the mouth of the passage. From this obscurity came his voice, low, all but strangled, passionate, incoherent. She was forced to hear him.

He told of his agony of mind, of his nights of torture; of hallucinations, when he had thought to leap into her arms but had dashed himself upon the floor of his cell; of fits of despair, when, thinking himself irredeemably lost, he had torn his flesh with his teeth and rent the air with cries. And through these confessions there rang ever a personal note—his desire for her, for her only, for her face, her hands, her body—for everything that had damned his soul in the past, but which had gnawed at memory ever since.

He returned to this again and again, insisting, imploring, with a spasmodic yet terrible earnestness; gesticulating, now with frenzy, now with fawning, now with a vehement and exalted imperiousness.

At times the madman and at times the devil spoke with his lips. He would turn from incoherent ravings to fiendish triumph. He exulted in her downfall, because he, Stephanos, had been the first to teach her passion. He forgot nothing, repented of nothing, feared nothing. His voice rang loud in crazy elation, while behind him in the blackness, the echoes muttered fearfully.

" What is hell? " he questioned with sombre passion. " Here they would say it was you—to love you. So be it——" He opened wide his arms as though embracing some dark and fearful prospect. " Welcome, hell! We will be there, in flames, but together—you and I, Zetitzka."

She dared not recede. Her position was terrible. She was trapped on that narrow ledge of rock. On either hand rose sheer cliff; behind her, the precipice—a black and windy void descending to appalling depths; before her, this madman, blocking the only exit.

" You do not speak." His voice sank again to low tones of pleading; his face, now but a yard from her own, showed white with glittering eyes. " You do not speak, Zetitzka; but I know what you would say. You love me still. You followed me here. I was a fool to leave you. We were made for each other, as fire is for fuel. Come, Zetitzka, give me peace, in your arms. There only can I find rest and forgetfulness. It has all been a mistake— a woful mistake; but we will begin again."

Then with an eager entreaty which she could not but recognise as sane, he continued: " See! I have the key to the ladders. They will not know till we are gone. Let us fly together, now."

She shot a desperate glance past him into the passage. Would Petros never return!

" Come! " he whispered again.

It seemed to her that he was about to advance. Desperation again came to her aid. Her courage rose.

"Let me pass!" she commanded.

Thwarted desire blazed in his eyes. It reawoke his fanaticism. Remorse, in that he had so nearly succumbed, swept down upon him, causing him to lean against the wall.

His movement left one side of the passage unguarded. Swiftly Zetitzka darted for the opening. But as she thought to speed past him, bending her head to avoid his elbow, his right hand shot out and gripped her by the shoulder.

She struggled violently. The thick stuff of her Albanian tunic was partly dragged from her back, but did not tear. Suddenly she felt his other arm flung around her waist. Doubly a prisoner and resisting desperately, she was drawn towards him, crushed against his chest.

In the draughty semi-blackness of the passage the unequal combat continued. No sound escaped them save their panting breath and the scraping of their feet seeking for purchase.

Naturally strong—her hardy open-air life having trained her to endurance—Zetitzka felt with dismay that her strength was as nothing to his. And that which filled her less with terror than with choking repulsion was that this was to him a moment of ecstasy.

His grip shifted. With a woman's intuition Zetitzka felt that he was straining to join his lips to hers. Her blood boiled. With Petros enshrined in her heart, this was not only an insult, but a sacrilege. Her yataghan was once more in her belt. She struggled to reach it, but in vain. He parried every movement, tightening his arms till she could scarcely breathe.

"No," he muttered, his mouth against her hair. "You shall not escape me. God wills it. We die together."

Gradually she felt herself forced backward, her head held in a vice against his chest. While her body fought, her mind was able to think. Was this her end? Her child flashed to her memory. She would never see him again. The pang of this eternal separation was tempered by dull indifference. Better to get it over now, at once. But even as she welcomed this imminent death, something within her recoiled. She was glad to die; but not thus, not with Stephanos. And again she became conscious of the struggle, and set herself with mute desperation to stay this backward movement that was forcing her towards the verge.

Her woman's strength was failing fast. His, on the contrary, seemed to redouble. She felt his broad chest heave with effort, but the grip of his arms never relaxed. Nearer and nearer they drew to the unprotected edge. Suddenly, as they tottered on the dizzy brink, some release valve opened in Zetitzka's brain. She screamed aloud. The cry rang through the hollow passages, and startled the eagles in the dark and inaccessible crannies of the cliff.

Her impressions of all that followed were so swift in bewildering transition that Zetitzka looked back upon them afterwards with the shuddering aversion with which one recalls a nightmare. She was conscious of a rush of feet—of being clutched—of a short and violent struggle in which she took no part—of a sudden release—of a cry speedily silenced—and, finally, of a blackness that surged over her, and into whose lethal depths she sank with the impassivity of a stone.

CHAPTER L

PANTING from the struggle, his blood aflame, every combative sense roused to its uttermost, Petros stood on the verge.

But silence followed—absolute silence, bringing home more forcibly than any spoken word the reality of the catastrophe. Aghast and overawed, his first thought was Zetitzka; but the girl lay unconscious upon the rocky floor. Filled with a new terror, which in intensity swamped all lesser fears, he fell on his knees beside her. But her hand dropped limply from his fingers. For this there was to his ignorant mind but one solution. Zetitzka was dead.

He still knelt before her in the gloom of the passage, all feeling paralysed, staring stupidly at the beloved figure —lying there so motionless, so quiet—staring with the mute and as yet unrealised despair of a mourner beside a coffin.

And when with returning consciousness, Zetitzka moved, and it was borne in upon him that she really lived, his brain, worn out and still half stunned by violent emotions, accepted the glad tidings calmly; the only audible evidence of feeling being the muttered thanksgiving that broke from his lips.

Zetitzka's memory responded slowly to the efforts of her will. Little by little her surroundings recalled the terrible ordeal through which she had passed—the rough walls glimmering in moonlight, the black passage, the precipice. The flash of time between the struggle for life and the finding herself lying unharmed in this quiet passage was so momentary as to appear non-existent. But neither mind nor body could at once accept the reality. The former was bewildered, stunned; the latter still suffered from the effeet of muscles violently strained.

Her first coherent thought was " Stephanos? " Petros pointed to the abyss.

311

The gale had at last worn itself out.   The contrast between the hubbub and the succeeding silence was trenchant.
The night had donned its mantle of beauty, and the peace,
the ethereal light, the dreamy distance, all gave the lie to
the tragedy.   All seemed so unconscious.   Yet through
that little door, now glimmering in faint moonlight, but
a moment ago a soul had been sent to its account.

Both spectators were overwhelmed by the suddenness
of the catastrophe.   It served as a sombre background to
the tragedy of their own hearts.   To Zetitzka, accustomed
to brood upon a past so poignantly associated with the
dead man, this appalling release gave birth to thoughts as
yet unconscious of their own emancipation.   She could not
realise it.   Gradually, as the power to think returned, the
knowledge came that vengeance had been taken from her
—that the deed she had been unable to perform had been
accomplished by an inexorable decree of Providence—that
God in His inscrutable wisdom had put an end for ever
to the life that had darkened her own.

And to this feeling was joined another, so sad, so hopeless as to be less a thought than a bitter and inaudible cry—
that although this man's death had set her free, both
morally and physically—free to return to her home, free
to link her life with whom she pleased—it yet had brought
her no nearer to the only boon she coveted; that the one
man she loved was still as hopelessly beyond her reach as
though he, and not Stephanos, were lying dead among the
rocks.

It was during these solemn moments that Petros learned
for the first time the relationship between Stephanos and
Zetitzka.   The broken and all but incoherent confession
stirred no violent feelings in his mind.   He listened in
awestruck silence.   Horror was beaten down; personal indignation became a presumption; for uprearing itself like
some dark barrier between the monk and all human censure
th e now loomed the final and completed sentence of
death.

The old monastery had fallen strangely silent.   The uneasy moanings, as of anger with difficulty restrained, had
died away, replaced by a grim voicelessness, an attitude
of sinister satisfaction.   Barlaam had cast forth this err-

ing son, this unworthy monk who had sought to conceal ineradicable vices beneath the holy cloak of monasticism. It had flung him ruthlessly to the abyss, as in olden times men flung traitors. It was as though the stern and mediæval spirit, untamed by centuries and impatient of the light penalty imposed by his fellow-men, had taken punishment into its own hands. Long ago in the dark ages, it had without doubt witnessed bloodshed; and now, outraged, defiled, vindictive and terrible in its wrath as some old heathen deity, it again exacted sacrifice.

But it had not yet found peace. There was still the woman to be expelled.

By day, by night, the monastery had watched her; at dawn, at noon, at dusk; never more awake than when it seemed asleep; with the slow, patient, brooding enmity of one deeply wronged, content to bide his time. That time had now come.

Before they left the passage, Petros approached the verge. Below lay the vast soft-breathing darkness, illimitable space and illimitable profundity shrouded in night. Vague forms loomed through this obscurity, full of the mysterious awe inspired by the faintly-seen, dim outlines, gloomy and chaotic masses, far-off and ghostly uncertainties. Over this weird phantasmagoria brooded an unnatural calm.

Gazing fearfully downwards, Petros noted, thirty feet below, a projecting ridge of rock, jagged and sharply inclined. In all probability this knife-like edge had been the first to strike at the life of Stephanos—terrible as the blow of a guillotine—before his body started upon its last and appalling descent to the rocks below. No thought that life might still exist passed for an instant across the mind of the boy. At this point the precipice fell a thousand feet.

With hearts too big for words, Petros and Zetitzka groped their way back to the court and to the tower of the windlass. The inexorable drew them together, and yet onward to separation; drew them irresistibly and relentlessly, as a river sweeps its waters to the sea. In this current they moved mechanically, crushed beneath the weight of the irrevocable. Each was desperately conscious of something within protesting against fate, clinging to every fleeting moment, rebelling against every onward step, striving piteously but hopelessly to arrest some second of treasured companionship, more vividly, more tenderly realised from the minutes that were hurrying them to their doom.

CHAPTER LI

WITHIN the old wooden structure all was dark and voiceless as a tomb. Seen faintly against the glimmer of the aerial exit, the great barbaric windlass extended its four gaunt, black arms. At this hour the place was full of loneliness and mystery. The gloom of the ravines seemed to have crept upwards, to have enveloped it, for it had something of the ghostliness of that dolorous underworld. Its projection over space lent it an air of intentional precariousness, as though it nursed designs hostile to human life. In its reserve one felt the influence of the monastery. of which, indeed, it was the ante-chamber. All was mute, save the creaking of the worm-eaten boards disturbed by the pressure of unexpected feet.

Petros and Zetitzka stood beside the windlass.

Up to this moment, danger and fear of discovery had swept them along on a stream of excitement—but now one fact alone rose up, not to be denied or postponed—they must say farewell.

They stood together in the gloom, and neither said a word. But what each felt was as visible to the other's heart as though branded upon the darkness in letters of flame. For the moment they had ceased to stand in relation to each other merely as man and woman—they were but two poor human souls united in a frank community of pain. It was like death—worse than death, for the future was not hidden from them in mercy.

All at once something burst in the heart of Zetitzka. The apathy that had enabled her to endure was suddenly dissipated. With uncontrollable sobs she clung with both hands to the breast of the young monk's cassock. He felt her shaking, yet found no consoling word. Her face was raised to his—close. He saw the mouth and the agony in the eyes.

315

"I can't!" she cried, and he sickened at the pain in her voice. "Petros, I can't—I can't!"

Her hands strained him to her. The darkness seemed to bend above them, to hide them from the indifferent world. The old building creaked no longer, but listened to things undreamt of in all its hundreds of years.

"I love you!" she whispered passionately. "I love you!"

Then, as never before, Petros tasted the ultimate bitterness of life. She again broke the silence, speaking through sobs stifled constantly.

"Just now—with Stephanos—I was afraid. But with you—I'm not afraid to die. To fall in your arms. Try me. *Now*, my love! Oh, my love!"

With a sudden cry Petros caught her to himself, crushed her against his breast, as if by that passionate embrace he could knit the fibres of her very existence with his own, so inextricably that neither things temporal nor things eternal could ever tear them apart.

In the sheltering darkness they made one, one body, one soul, one life. The world slid away; the monastery was forgotten. They alone existed. Their natures met and mingled in that fusion of spirit pure and holy wherewith love can bend even sorrow to its uses.

To feel his arms about her, strong as hoops of steel, masterful, translating into fierce pressure all the imperative yearnings of his desolate life, proclaiming his manhood's right to love and possess, filled her with pain that was rapture, and with oblivion that was half 'a swoon. She closed her eyes, holding back the tears. Life seemed suspended—suffering almost ceased.

It lasted but a few seconds, and yet in intensity it was not of moments, nor of hours, nor of years, but of a lifetime.

The silence around them was so profound that it seemed as if all nature was in a state of suspense, wondering what this boy and girl would do. The abyss beckoned—the blackness of the ravine held out soft and dusky arms—the moon lit her pale lamp upon the opposing cliff as though to light their souls to eternity. Only the monastery held aloof, watching and waiting in the darkness with the composure of unshaken confidence.

For Barlaam knew Petros. He belonged to it. Had it not trained him from early youth? Had it not bound his young life to its own with links new-riveted every day? —bound it as indissolubly as though the boy's blood were but a drop of its own, lent to him that it might become renovated by his youth, circulating through his veins only to return to and prolong the existence of its weary monastic heart.

It did not fear this woman, nor what she could do. It treated her as men treat poisonous reptiles—it crushed, then cast her out. It feared to be deprived of Petros by voluntary death, no more than by cowardly flight. It knew his sanity, his loyalty, his allegiance. On these it relied. And as some potent physician might watch by a sick-bed, noting with grave and skilful eyes the crisis of some grievous malady, not without solicitude, yet strong in the assured hope of victory, so Barlaam in this dark hour of trial watched this, its youngest son.

To Petros it was as if his soul were struggling in vast waters. The anguish of severance blinded mental vision. He was but a tool in God's hands, shaping their lives to noble ends.

Later, all his debt to Zetitzka was made plain. She was to reveal to him the hidden meaning, the deep significance of love and sorrow, this girl who had come to him so unexpectedly, like a precious message from the great unknown world. In her and through her he had sounded the depths, soared to the heights; and her last and greatest gift was to be the gift of true inward vision, that came to him afterwards, unawares, the guerdon of mutual self-sacrifice, of solemn and voluntary renunciation.

In the midst of his pain it was brought home to him that he, Petros, held Zetitzka's life and Zetitzka's fate in his hands as absolutely as he held her body within his arms. This discovery seemed to him a tremendous, a wonderful, an awful thing. It imparted a sense of power, of responsibility. It gave him courage, for he saw that all depended on him—that he must think and act at once, and for both.

What it cost him to find words that would reconcile her to this cruel parting, Zetitzka was never to know. It was like cutting out his heart. Pondering upon it afterwards —as he was destined to do, how many times!—pondering upon it with an incredulous wonder, with awe, and with thanksgiving, Petros could recall nothing of what he had said. It seemed that another had spoken, and not he.

And Zetitzka, still in his arms, almost swooning, and all broken with grief, remained dumb. He wondered if she had even heard.

When at last he ceased to speak, she seemed to rouse her·self from some state of profound stupor, then drew one long, sobbing, inward breath.

" Kiss me," she said.

Her voice told him that she had understood; that this meant the end, the supreme farewell.

Their lips met.

They did not speak again. Like a man walking in his sleep, he placed her in the net, looped the meshes above her head, stringing them one by one upon the iron hook attached to the clumsy rope; then, with a half-turn of the great creaking arms, he sent her swaying outwards into mid-air. A moment she oscillated over the abyss; then as he reversed the movement, she slowly disappeared from sight.

Still he laboured, mercifully forced to exert his strength to its utmost, walking round and round, gripping and re-straining the clumsy mechanism that groaned and cried in the darkness like a soul in torment.

At length the relaxation of the strain told him that she had reached earth. Mechanically wiping the sweat from his face, he groped his way to the opening through which he had seen the last of Zetitzka. Beneath him, as he peered downwards, all was indistinguishable. As he stood listen·ing with bated breath, a faint metallic noise tinkled up from the depths—the click of hoofs striking the stones. His hands closed convulsively upon the wooden barrier.

Far within the ravine the moonlight drew a trenchant line across a blackness that was the impenetrable shadow of Barlaam. In this faintly lighted area the rocks and a section of the path were visible. Petros was conscious of something within his brain telling him that Zetitzka· must cross this on her downward way to Kalabaka. Stand-ing motionless, with the strange, unnatural composure that results from entire suspension of thought, he waited.

An interval—then something far below crept into sight

—something dimly distinguishable as a man leading a mule, upon whose back was seated a figure. Slowly yet relentlessly this little group crossed the moonlit space, vanished for a moment behind a rock, reappeared, then gradually neared the final shadow beyond which lay darkness. In another second it would be gone.

Petros, rigid, his hands still gripping the wooden bar, watched it, controlled by some inner force, unconscious even of his pain, his whole soul concentrating itself with a hungry, jealous intensity within his straining eyes. Every movement of those little figures, far below and dwarfed into insignificance, became more momentous, more vitally important than life or death.

Then, as one aroused from a trance to some horror of reality, he suddenly awoke to a comprehension of what was taking place. This mere speck upon the moonlit path was all the happiness and hope going out of his life! Great dumb tears, gathering slowly, obscured his sight. Feverishly dashing them aside, he sought again to see. At first all was blurred, then gradually through a mist he made out the path, silvering in faint moonlight—empty.

CHAPTER LII

" THIS is the Catholicon," said the monk.

The visitor nodded. In spite of his doffed fez it was apparent that he had but little acquaintance with Catholicons. The two men formed a striking contrast— the monk, grave, sedate, slow in movement; the visitor bent with age but still vigorous, his white hair straggling to his shoulders, his bushy and grizzled eyebrows working spasmodically, the one over a sightless cavity, the other above a small, intelligent, and cynically-humorous eye.

The sense of novelty wearing off, the stranger took a keen and apparently professional interest in the vestments.

" You are a pedlar? " questioned the monk, with mild curiosity.

" I am Nik Leka, " said the old man with some astonishment.

But the information conveyed nothing to his black-robed companion.

" How long have you been here? " asked the visitor abruptly, fixing his keen little eye upon his guide.

" Five—nearly six years."

" You did not know—— " He checked himself, adding: " You came after the old Abbot's death? "

The monk replied in the affirmative.

" And your new Abbot—you like him, you others? "

" We love him," said the monk simply.

As though by mutual consent the two men resumed their relation of visitor and guide. Nik Leka, called upon to admire the carving of the pulpit, touched it with the point of an unconsciously appraising forefinger.

" There have been other changes," he blurted, stopping suddenly. His companion looked down into the wrinkled and plebeian face with its raised thatch of eyebrows.

" Deaths? " suggested Nik Leka lightly.

320

"Death is never far away," returned the monk, crossing himself.

The pedlar nodded with the air of one who salutes an old acquaintance.

"And departures," he hazarded, biting his nails.

"Departures?"

"Not lately, perhaps; but before you came."

"I have heard only of one who quitted the monastery of his own will. As you say, it was before I came. But it was no great matter. He had not taken the vows."

"But there was another—Brother Stephanos he was called."

The monk crossed himself.

"Killed?" suggested Nik Leka indifferently.

"Yes—an accident. *Kyrie Eleison!* 'tis strange that you should have heard of that also! The opening is blocked up now. 'Twas a grievous loss to the monastery, so they tell me. He was a saint."

The pedlar made a curious noise in his throat.

"You knew him?" questioned the monk, struck by the old man's expression.

"Yes, I knew him."

"Praise be to God and Saint Barlaam! It is doubtless his holy memory that brings you here?"

"Ay," assented Nik Leka, slowly. "His—and another's."

As he spoke, the doorway was darkened.

"The Abbot," whispered the monk.

Nik Leka waited with a curious feeling of expectation.

The Abbot neared them. In his movements the vigour of manhood was restrained by the calm but unconscious dignity of office. Not till he was come within a few yards of where they were standing did the transverse light from a window enable them to see his face. It awoke in Nik Leka an altogether novel and even disconcerting sense of respect. Something in his cynical old heart tried to scoff at this unexpected emotion, but failed. He continued to stare at the new-comer with a fixity that would have been guilty of rudeness had it not been so unconscious as to appear unavoidable.

The whole aspect of the young priest betrayed the ascetic, living in a world within; yet it told also of a broad-

21

minded humanity, of a ready sympathy with all who rejoiced, of a sense of oneness with all who suffered. For his eyes gave the clue to his character and held a mirror to his heart. Looking into them, one felt assured that their possessor could only have earned the right to that expression by some great victory over self.

"Venerable father," said the monk. He paused as though requesting permission to continue; and Nik Leka, quick to note the incongruity of the title with the youthfulness of the recipient, wondered afresh. The Abbot made a slight gesture with his hand. The monk continned:

"This is he for whom I asked permission to visit the monastery. He knew Brother Stephanos."

A sudden gravity came into the Abbot's face. For a moment he gazed at the pedlar with something more than interest, then turned to his subordinate.

"Leave us," he said quietly.

With a low obeisance the monk left the Catholicon.. The faint shuffle of sandals died away. All was still.

The Abbot was the first to speak.

"You knew Brother Stephanos well, my son?"

"Too well," returned Nik Leka grimly.

The young Abbot gazed straight into the old man's eye. "I know not your name," he said frankly.

The pedlar's answer seemed to strike a familiar chord, for he repeated it twice; then a sudden light of recognition came into his face.

"I have heard of you," he said in a low voice. "You —you befriended——"

"I did nothing," grunted Nik Leka ungraciously.

The two men fell silent. The sunshine, striving to enter, threw the porch into high relief. To and fro in the incense-laden air buzzed a blue-bottle fly. Its little noise made a stir of life and movement that emphasised more than it detracted from the deep and pervading peace.

"You hear of her sometimes?" The questioner was gazing towards the sunlight.

"I saw her last month."

For a moment the Abbot seemed lost in thought; then, looking at the pedlar with the air of one who has nothing to conceal, said:—

"It is long since I heard. News comes seldom over the mountains. But—she is happy."

The last words were not a question, but a statement— something known intuitively, beyond doubt, beyond refutation.

"What is happiness?" asked Nik Leka sceptically, spreading out his coarse palms.

The Abbot looked at him.

His eyes made the pedlar vaguely ashamed; a disconcerting sensation, as though his cynical mask were an unworthy, and, in this case, an inefficient disguise; yet feeling himself pledged to an explanation, he continued:

"She seems content; all the world loves her; her husband works, and is no drunkard—ah, these muleteers; they have the devil's own luck! She has children. One would say that meant happiness! And yet—" he snapped his thick fingers—"women, look you—they are capable of anything, of anything! They even dare to have dreams!"

The young Abbot smiled. This unexpected lighting of his features imparted to them a singularly winning expression. Here was something deeper than, though a reminder of, boyhood's light-heartedness—the optimism of one who, knowing the darkness and seeing the goal, rejoiced also in the sunshine by the way. All at once he laid his hand on the pedlar's shoulder. Nik Leka, consciously honoured, waited with respect.

"We all have dreams," said the young priest in a moved voice; "but only those who love are truly happy."

The pedlar, deeply impressed, kept silent.

"You will see her again," continued the Abbot. "Tell her—tell her of this—" with a slight comprehensive movement he indicated the dreaming Catholicon—"tell her of the peace, of the silence—yes, of the blessed silence." He paused. Nik Leka, watching him with a feeling akin to awe, saw a light come into his face. "Tell her that I rejoice in her happiness—that I see now—I see—the meaning of the old pain. We are all children crying for the little thing, not seeing the greater. Tell her that I bless and thank her every day of my life; and that—that I too am happy."

Silent, out of respect for the hand still on his shoulder, Nik Leka was thinking with unusual seriousness. But it was not till—his visit at an end—he found himself on the path, that he came to any definite conclusion with regard to the message. Looking backward and upward at Barlaam, now peaceful, dreaming, crowned with sunlight, he suddenly shrugged his shoulders.

" I am a fool! " he cried. " But what **matter!** **I can** at least tell her that the Abbot is happy."

[THE END.]

An American Love-Story

MARGARITA'S SOUL

BY

JOSEPHINE DASKAM BACON
[INGRAHAM LOVELL]

Profusely Illustrated. Sixteen full-page half-tone illustrations.
Numerous line cuts, reproduced from drawings by J. Scott
Williams. Also Whistler Butterfly Decorations.

Cloth. 12mo. $1.50

"Filled with imaginative touches, resourceful, intelligent and amusing.   An ingenious plot that keeps the interest suspended until the end, and has a quick and shrewd sense of humor."   —*Boston Transcript.*

"A reviewer would hesitate to say how long it is since a writer gave us so beautiful, so naive, so strangely brought up and introduced, a heroine.   It is to be hoped that the author is already at work on another novel."   —*Toronto Globe.*

"May cause the reader to miss an important engagement or neglect his business.   A love story of sweetness and purity touched with the mythical light of Romance and aglow with poetry and tenderness.   One of the most enchanting creatures in modern fiction."   —*San Francisco Bulletin.*

"It is extremely entertaining from start to finish, and there are most delightful chapters of description and romantic scenes which hold one positively charmed by their beauty and unusualness."   —*Boston Herald.*

"Sentimental, with the wholesome, pleasing sentimentality of the old bachelor who has not turned crusty. . . A Thackerayan touch."   —*New York Tribune.*

"Captures the imagination at the outset by the boldness of the situation. . . We should be hard put to it to name a better American novel of the month."   —*The Outlook.*

WILLIAM J. LOCKE

The Usurper

"Contains the hall-mark of genius itself. The plot is masterly in conception, the descriptions are all vivid flashes from a brilliant pen. It is impossible to read and not marvel at the skilled workmanship and the constant dramatic intensity of the incident, situations and climax."—*The Boston Herald.*

Derelicts

"Mr. Locke tells his story in a very true, a very moving, and a very noble book. If any one can read the last chapter with dry eyes we shall be surprised. 'Derelicts' is an impressive, an important book. Yvonne is a creation that any artist might be proud of."—*The Daily Chronicle.*

Idols

"One of the very few distinguished novels of this present book season."—*The Daily Mail.*

"A brilliantly written and eminently readable book."
—*The London Daily Telegraph.*

A Study in Shadows

"Mr. Locke has achieved a distinct success in this novel. He has struck many emotional chords, and struck them all with a firm, sure hand. In the relations between Katherine and Raine he had a delicate problem to handle, and he has handled it delicately."
—*The Daily Chronicle.*

The White Dove

"It is an interesting story. The characters are strongly conceived and vividly presented, and the dramatic moments are powerfully realized."—*The Morning Post.*

The Demagogue and Lady Phayre

"Think of Locke's clever books. Then think of a book as different from any of these as one can well imagine—that will be Mr. Locke's new book."—*New York World.*

At the Gate of Samaria

"William J. Locke's novels are nothing if not unusual. They are marked by a quaint originality. The habitual novel reader inevitably is grateful for a refreshing sense of escaping the commonplace path of conclusion."—*Chicago Record-Herald.*

EDEN PHILLPOTTS

The Thief of Virtue
Cloth. 12mo. $1.50

"If living characters, perfect plot construction, imaginative breadth of canvas and absolute truth to life are the primary qualities of great realistic fiction, Mr. Phillpotts is one of the greatest novelists of the day. . . . He goes on turning out one brilliant novel after another, steadily accomplishing for Devon what Mr. Hardy did for Wessex. This is another of Mr. Phillpotts' Dartmoor novels, and one that will rank with his best. . . Something of kinship with 'King Lear' and 'Pere Goriot.' " *Chicago Record Herald.*

"The Balzac of Dartmore. It is easy and true to say that Mr. Phillpotts in all his work has done no single piece of portraiture better than this presentation of Philip Ouldsbroom. . . A triumph of the novelist's understanding and keen drawing. . . A Dartmoor background described in terms of an artist's deeply felt appreciation. *—New York World.*

"No other English writer has painted such facinating and colorful word-pictures of Dartmoor's heaths and hills, woods and vales, and billowy plains of pallid yellow and dim green. Few others have attempted such vivid character-portrayal as marks this latest work from beginning to end." *The North American.*

"A strong book, flashing here and there with beautiful gems of poetry. . . Providing endless food for thought. . . An intellectual treat." *—London Evening Standard.*

The Haven
Cloth. 12mo. $1.50

"The foremost English novelist with the one exception of Thomas Hardy. . . His descriptions of the sea and his characterization of the fisher folks are picturesqne, true to life, full of humorous philosophy." —Jeannetie L. Gilder in *The Chicago Tribune.*

"It is no dry bones of a chronicle, but touched by genius to life and vividness. " *—Louisville, Kentucky, Post.*

"A close, thoughtful study of universal human nature." *—The Outlook.*

"One of the best of this author's many works." *—The Bookman.*

MAUD DIVER
A TRILOGY OF ANGLO-INDIAN ARMY LIFE

New York Times: "Above the multitude of novels (erotic and neurotic) hers shine like stars. She has produced a comprehensive and full drama of life, rich in humanity; noble, satisfying—it is not too much to say great."

(New Editions)

CANDLES IN THE WIND
CAPTAIN DESMOND, V. C.
THE GREAT AMULET

Cloth. 12mo. $1.50 each

The Argonaut (San Francisco): "We doubt if any other writer gives us so composite and convincing a picture of that curious mixture of soldier and civilian that makes up Indian society. She shows us the life of the country from many standpoints, giving us the idea of a store-house of experience so well stocked that incidents can be selected with a fastidious and dainty care."

London Morning Post: "Vigor of characterization accompanied by an admirable terseness and simplicity of expression."

Literary World: "Undoubtedly some of the finest novels that Indian life has produced."

London Telegraph: "Some sincere pictures of Indian life which are as real and convincing as any which have entered into the pages of fiction."

The Chicago Tribune: "The characterization is excellent and her presentation of frontier life and of social conditions produces a strong impression of truth."

Boston Evening Transcript: "Knows absolutely the life that she depicts. Her characters are excellently portrayed."

Chicago Record Herald: "Well told; the humanization good and the Indian atmosphere, always dramatic, is effectively depicted. Holds the attention without a break."

Toronto Mail: "Real imagination, force, and power. Rudyard Kipling and imitators have shown us the sordid side of this social life. It remains for Mrs. Diver to depict tender-hearted men and brave, true women. Her work is illuminated by flashes of spiritual insight that one longs to hold in memory."

M. P. WILLCOCKS

The Way Up
Cloth. 12mo. $1.50

This novel is one that touches three burning questions of the hour—capital and labor, the claims of the individual against those of the State, the right of a woman to her own individuality. Besides being a picture of a group of modern men and women, it is also a study of certain social tendencies of to-day and possibly to-morrow.

The Wingless Victory
Cloth. 12mo. $1.50

"A moving drama of passion, of frailty, of long temptation and of ultimate triumph over it." —*Pall Mall Gazette.*

"A most remarkable novel which places the author in the first rank. This is a novel built to last." —*Outlook.*

"A book worth keeping on the shelves, even by the classics, for it is painted in colors which do not fade." —*Times.*

"Fresh and fervent, instinct with genuine passion and emotion and all the fierce primitive joys of existence. It is an excellent thing for any reader to come across this book." —*Standard.*

"A splendid book." —*Tribune.*

A Man of Genius
Ornamental Cloth. 12mo. $1.50

"Far above the general level of contemporary fiction. . . A work of unusual power." —PROFESSOR WILLIAM LYON PHELPS.

Widdicombe: A Romance of the Devonshire Moors
12mo. $1.50

MRS. JOHN LANE

According to Maria
Cloth. 12mo. $1.50

"Mrs. Lane's touch is light, yet not flippant. She is shrewd and humorous, and a miracle of tactful good temper; but she hits hard and straight at many really vital social weaknesses. Future social historians will find here ample material. Present-day social delinquents and social critics alike may read with pleasure and profit."
—*London Morning Leader.*

The Champagne Standard
Cloth. 12mo. $1.50 net. Postage 12 cents.

"Mrs. John Lane having been brought up in this country, and having married in England, is in a position to view British society as an American, and American society as a Londoner. The result is this very entertaining book." —*New York Evening Sun.*

DOLF WYLLARDE

12mo. $1.50 each

"Dolf Wyllarde sees life with clear eyes and puts down what she sees with a fearless pen. . . . More than a little of the flavor of Kipling in the good old days of Plain Tales from the Hills."
—*New York Globe.*

Mafoota

A Romance of Jamaica

"The plot has a resemblance to that of Wilkie Collins' 'The New Magdalen,' but the heroine is a Puritan of the strictest type; the subject matter is like 'The Helpmate.'"—*Springfield Republican.*

As Ye Have Sown

"A brilliant story dealing with the world of fashion."

Captain Amyas

"Masterly."—*San Francisco Examiner.*
"Startlingly plain-spoken."—*Louisville Courier-Journal.*

The Rat Trap

"The literary sensation of the year."—*Philadelphia Item.*

The Story of Eden

"Bold and outspoken, a startling book."—*Chicago Record-Herald.*
"A real feeling of brilliant sunshine and exhilarating air."
—*Spectator.*

Rose-White Youth

** The love-story of a young girl.

The Pathway of the Pioneer

** The story of seven girls who have banded themselves together for mutual help and cheer under the name of "Nous Autres." They represent, collectively, the professions open to women of no deliberate training, though well-educated. They are introduced to the reader at one of their weekly gatherings and then the author proceeds to depict the home and business life of each one individually.

Tropical Tales

** A collection of short stories dealing with "all sorts and conditions" of men and women in all classes of life; some of the tales sounding the note of joy and happiness; others portraying the pathetic, and even the shady side of life; all written in the interesting manner characteristic of the author.

CHARLES MARRIOTT

The Intruding Angel
Cloth. 12mo. $1.50.

The story of a mistaken marriage, and the final solution of the problem for the happiness of all parties concerned.

When a Woman Woos
Cloth. 12mo. $1.50.

"Unique. The book is on the whole a study of the relations of men and women in the particular institution of marriage. It is an attempt to define what a real marriage is, and it shows very decidedly what it is not. Full of the material of life."
—New York Times Book Review.

A Spanish Holiday
Illustrated. Cloth. 8vo. $2.50 net. Postage 20 cents.

"The spirit of Spain has been caught to a very great degree by the author of this book, and held fast between its covers."
—Book News.

NETTA SYRETT

Olivia L. Carew
Cloth. 12mo. $1.50

An interesting character study of a passionless, self-absorbed woman humanized by the influence of a man's love and loyal devotion.

Anne Page. A Love-story of To-day
Cloth. 12mo. $1.50

"Readers must judge for themselves. Women may read it for warning as well as entertainment, and they will find both. Men may read it for reproach that any of their kind can treat such women so. And moralists of either sex will find instructions for their homilies, as well as a warning that there may be more than one straight and narrow way." *—New York Times.*

Six Fairy Plays for Children
Sq. 12mo. $1.00 net. Postage 8 cents.

9 780483 517615